CLEOPATRA'S DAGGER

ALSO BY CAROLE LAWRENCE

Ian Hamilton Mysteries

Edinburgh Twilight

Edinburgh Dusk

Edinburgh Midnight

CLEOPATRA'S DAGGER

CAROLE LAWRENCE

This is a work of fiction. Names, characters, organizations, places, events, and incidents are either products of the author's imagination or are used fictitiously. Any resemblance to actual persons, living or dead, or actual events is purely coincidental.

Published by Thomas & Mercer, Seattle

www.apub.com

ISBN-13: 9781542014304
ISBN-10: 1542014301

Cover design by Micaela Alcaino

Printed in the United States of America

For Kylie Isaack, a most awesome niece—a witty and wondrously gifted young woman

You have waited, you always wait, you dumb, beautiful ministers

—*Walt Whitman, "Crossing Brooklyn Ferry"*

PROLOGUE

New York City, 1880

Oh, they were soft, so soft . . . and so beautiful—pliable as raindrops, their limbs round and white as bone china.

But he knew they were evil—Jezebels, Salomes, Delilahs, all of them. They lured men with sweet siren songs, entrapping them with their wicked ways—either by withholding their favors or by letting them taste the splendors of heaven, lulling their victims into a senseless stupor until it was too late. They were spiders, and men were but hapless insects struggling vainly to escape their sweet, sticky webs. Their beauty was the most treacherous weapon in an arsenal of snares, designed to entrap and control their all-too-willing prey.

His hand absently stroked the pure white fur of Cleo, his prized Persian, as he gazed out the window at the hazy late-summer afternoon. She purred and stretched under his touch, her supple spine shivering with pleasure.

"Ah, Cleo," he said. "You'll never betray me, will you?"

She gazed up at him with wide blue eyes, the tip of her tail twitching.

Outside, the sky darkened as a thick gray cloud passed over the landscape of the city. A gust of wind tickled the leaves on the tree outside his window; they fluttered and then became still. They reminded him of a fly in a web, struggling weakly before giving in to their inevitable fate. He drew a deep breath, feeling the air course into his lungs, energizing his body. He vowed to never be one of those flies—he would be neither victim nor hunted.

Instead, he would be the hunter.

CHAPTER ONE

Elizabeth van den Broek hurried from her apartment building on East Eighteenth Street, in such a rush she was halfway down the block before the heavy front door closed behind her. It was nearly eight o'clock, and she had overslept—again. It had been less than a week since she had taken up residence in the Stuyvesant, and she was up most nights unpacking and arranging her things. She felt lucky having managed to secure a suite of rooms in the building, the first of its kind in New York. Built just a decade ago, in 1870, it was the first example of "French flats" in a city that previously had consisted of only tenements and town houses. The Stuyvesant had a certain cachet, and Elizabeth's status-conscious mother had pulled some strings to get her an apartment there.

A gust of wind caught Elizabeth's hat and nearly swept it from her head. She clamped it back on with her free hand, the other clutching her precious briefcase. Her mother always chided her for not using enough hairpins to secure her auburn hair. Thick and coarse, with stubborn curls, it was difficult to manage at the best of times. This time, she reflected ruefully, her mother was right. Holding the hat onto her head, she scurried awkwardly down Irving Place toward the entrance to the Third Avenue "El," the elevated train that would take her to her job at the *New York Herald*.

As the newspaper's only female reporter, Elizabeth wanted desperately to make a good impression. Approaching the entrance to the El, she thought briefly about hailing a cab but reasoned that, at this hour, traffic would likely slow down even the fleetest of horses. And streetcars were notoriously prone to congestion. No, she thought, the train might be noisy and dirty and smelly, but she was better off aboveground during the city's infamous rush hour.

Ahead of her, Fourteenth Street swarmed with activity. At this hour, the city was a symphony of movement. Pedestrians competed with cabs, carts, carriages, and horse-drawn trams running along east–west trolley lines. Small boys darted in front of oncoming vehicles with breathless daring as their mothers shouted unheeded words of caution to their reckless offspring. Dogs barked; horses trotted; parents yelled at their children; well-heeled businessmen called for cabs; cart merchants hawked their wares with a variety of colorful phrases. City officials frowned upon street vendors, due to the city's already excessive noise level, so they tended to cluster near certain train stations and ferry ports. The Fourteenth Street El station was a vendor gold mine, with thousands of potential customers passing through during rush hour. Oyster sellers competed with ragmen, corn vendors, and other merchants for the public's attention.

"Oyy-sters! Get cher fresh oyy-sters here!"

"Rags, rags, any old rags! Ol' cloth! Old clo'! A-a-any old cloth!"

A thin female voice piped up over the deeper male ones: "Hot corn, hot corn, all hot! Just came out of the boiling pot!"

The smudge-faced girl selling corn was young—too young, Elizabeth reckoned. She could not have been more than ten. In spite of being late, Elizabeth pressed a nickel into the girl's grimy hand. Brushing aside a strand of matted hair, the child stared at her, confused. "It's two fer a penny, miss."

"I'll take one."

"But, miss—"

"Keep the change."

The girl's eyes widened in alarm as she handed Elizabeth an ear of roasted corn in its shaggy green husk.

"Thank you," Elizabeth said. She knew better than to give the girl more—any excess money would likely end up in the pockets of her "handler," anyway. The hot-corn girls differed from prostitutes only in that they were usually younger and (hopefully) not sexually available. Otherwise, their lives were similar—in the thrall of a husband or pimp of some kind, too desperate and poor to hope for a better life.

Stepping carefully over a pile of horse manure, Elizabeth shouldered her way through the crowd toward the Third Avenue station. Several cabs lined up in front of the entrance, the drivers in long dark coats and top hats. Driving a hack—named after the high-stepping Hackney horse bred for such work—was hard, cold work, especially in bad weather. Hansoms, by far the most popular type of cab, required the operator to perch above the carriage, exposed to the elements, while his passengers enjoyed the comfort of the cozy—if somewhat cramped—interior. Elizabeth glanced at the sky, the sun already obscured by threatening clouds. It was a warm day, but the cabbies would soon need their long coats if the glowering thunderclouds delivered the downpour they portended.

As she passed, the hack drivers advertised their services in hoarse voices coarsened by weather and drink: "Cab, cab, cab!"

One of them caught Elizabeth's eye and tipped his hat, smiling broadly. His teeth were the color of overcooked liver, stained gray, probably from years of cheap cigarettes. He wore tattered cloth gloves with the fingers cut off, making it easier for him to produce change when his customers paid him.

"Keb, miss?" he said, bowing slightly. His pronunciation of the word left no doubt about his working-class origins. New York liked to advertise itself as the city of opportunity, but one had only to spend a day there to know that was a lie.

"Not today, thank you," she said, looking away. Her mother was forever cautioning her to "behave like a lady," and ladies did not return glances from strange men, even if they were trying to sell her something. She certainly did not stare at them—though Elizabeth, possessed of an insatiable curiosity, often ignored this rule, especially when her mother was not around to correct her. Now, as a journalist, Elizabeth considered it her job to follow her curiosity wherever it led her—and if that involved staring at strange men, so be it.

As she climbed the stairs to the train platform, tightly bundled among the crowd surging up the steps with her, Elizabeth smiled to think how her mother would much prefer she take a cab—another reason she enjoyed using public transportation. Stepping onto the platform amid her fellow citizens, she could hear her mother's protests: "It's ridiculous. Your father can afford it, you know. You're just being stubborn."

Stuffed into the third car of the El, sandwiched between law clerks, office boys, and retail workers, Elizabeth momentarily regretted resisting her mother's will so doggedly. She held her breath as a whiff of garlic sausage assailed her nostrils, no doubt coming from the bulky fellow to her left. The nicks and cuts on his fingers revealed his profession of butcher as surely as the aroma of beef tallow and lamb fat emanating from his rumpled jacket. On her other side, a thin, pinch-faced woman of middle years squirmed to avoid touching the stocky, leering lad next to her. Clad in coarse wool trousers and a worn jacket, his face and hands browned by the sun, he could be a bootblack or an errand boy for one of the many shops lining Lower Broadway. He tried to catch Elizabeth's eye, but she looked away, aware of his gaze on the back of her neck. Her mother would be horrified that she was crammed in among such unsavory types, but Elizabeth had full confidence in her ability to look after herself.

The train lurched and swayed along its narrow trestle, belching black soot and smoke into the air, a great gray beast chugging its way past tenement buildings and shops, churches and brothels. The train afforded a view into the third floor of the buildings it passed, which must have shocked the occupants when it was first opened two years earlier. Suddenly their privacy was shattered—the only way to maintain some semblance of discretion was to cover their windows, shutting out light and air, precious commodities in an overcrowded city.

Yet Elizabeth was always amazed at how many people seemed indifferent to the passengers' curious gazes. It was as if they refused to accept the new reality of their situation, ignoring the thousands of strangers staring into their living space. Perhaps they believed the glimpse afforded by the rapidly moving train was hardly worth bothering about—and some, she was convinced, derived a thrill from being observed by strangers. Anna Brodigen, her first roommate at Vassar, was like that, flaunting her body in public, feeding on the attention of men. Elizabeth was just the opposite, modest and shy about such things, and viewed Anna's shenanigans with a combination of aversion and fascination.

As the train passed the Cooper Union, the northernmost point of the Bowery before it split into Third and Fourth Avenues, Elizabeth spied a pair of drunks loitering outside McSorley's Ale House. It was not an unusual sight, even at this hour, she reflected as the train continued its southern journey on the Bowery, the street most associated with all that was wicked, degraded, and vile. The avenue possessed a dizzying number of saloons, taverns (licensed and unlicensed), flophouses, brothels, and gambling establishments, and was the entertainment center for New York's more impoverished citizens.

As they slowed to pass an oncoming northbound train near the intersection of Rivington Street, Elizabeth glanced out the window at a crumbling tenement building. On the first floor was a butcher shop. But it was the third-floor apartment that drew her eye. The sheer curtains, once white but now soiled from soot, were parted slightly, so that she could make out two figures—a man and a woman. She was

CHAPTER TWO

"You already have a column," Karl Schuster said. "And lucky to have it, I might add."

She followed her editor into his cluttered second-floor office, closing the door behind them as he lowered himself heavily into his desk chair. He was a large, strongly built man, and the chair creaked beneath his weight.

"But I'm certain I saw—"

"We can't afford to go chasing after every *Streit* between husbands and wives," he said, shuffling through the papers on his desk. His nearly unaccented English was perfect, but he still sprinkled his sentences with German words and phrases.

"He might have been an intruder! And what decent husband attempts to strangle his wife? Are you not concerned over the fate of the poor young woman?"

"Das macht nichts," he said, rubbing his forehead. "Our best copy editor is home looking after his pregnant wife about to give birth, two reporters are out with dysentery—"

"No doubt the effect of gobbling several dozen oysters at a dubious tavern yesterday—"

"And I am obliged to cover the local news page today while Mr. Atwood buries his mother."

"But that is perfect!" Elizabeth cried. "This story is local news—"

"*Genug!* Do not press me further on this matter," he said, bringing a fist down on the desk with a thump, his square face reddening. Tall and broad shouldered, his blond hair always in need of a comb, Karl Schuster had thick fingers and extremely pale blue eyes. He looked more like a dockworker or a farmer than a newspaper editor. He had left a position as senior editor at the *New Yorker Staats-Zeitung*, the venerable German-language weekly newspaper, to work at the *Herald*. It was rumored that he had resigned over a disagreement with the paper's renowned editor in chief, Oswald Ottendorfer.

Elizabeth drew herself up with as much dignity as she could muster. "I see I shall have to explore the darker deeds of my fellow citizens on my own time."

Schuster leaned forward, resting his elbows on the solid oak desk, which was remarkably messy. Elizabeth's mother always praised Germans for being extremely orderly, but Karl Schuster seemed to have taken it upon himself to destroy that reputation. His office was a masterpiece of untidiness. Old copies of the *Herald* and other New York dailies sat in dusty stacks in corners. Towers of tomes teetered in precarious piles; there were more books on the floor than in the bookshelves. Mounds of paper littered his desk, protruding from drawers, stuffed into crannies, and scattered on the carpet like fallen leaves. Instead of an air of chaos, however, all the jumble created a curious aura of calm. The room was rather cozy, the excess of objects creating the feeling of being cradled in a warm cocoon.

Karl shook his shaggy blond head. He appeared almost rueful. "Miss Van den Broek, as much as I commend your single-minded determination, may I remind you that as the only female reporter at the *Herald*—"

"All the more reason to concern myself with the oppression of women!"

Schuster peered at his pocket watch. "You have exactly two hours to get to the Astors' brownstone on Fifth Avenue."

"Why?"

"You are covering Mrs. Astor's garden party. Everyone in high society will be there. You hardly have time to change, so I suppose you'll have to go dressed as you are."

"And what is wrong with how I am dressed?"

"Nothing—for a newsroom. But for a society garden party . . ."

"I'll borrow something from my mother on the way."

"How is your mother?"

"Fretting over every decision I make. But she enjoys suffering, as it improves her complexion."

"*Eine feine Dame.* Fine woman. *Ganz würdig.*"

Elizabeth frowned. The German for "worthy" was close enough to the Dutch word that she understood him. But she did not care to be reminded that her job at the *Herald* was in part the result of her parents' connections. She liked to believe that her academic record at Vassar had contributed somewhat, but suspected she was only fooling herself. The Van den Broek family could trace its roots to the city's original Dutch settlers, who had named the area New Amsterdam before the English rechristened it.

And now many people flocked to the shores of Manhattan, as the potato famine drove poor Irish families to seek refuge in the city's ever-expanding slums. They were soon followed, in fewer numbers, by the Chinese. Germans such as Karl Schuster tended to be better educated and more prosperous; the city had even elected a German mayor in 1863.

"Well?" he demanded. "For what are you waiting?"

"Very well," she said. "But you have not heard the last of this." She turned in one smooth movement, crossed the room in three strides, and yanked the door open so forcefully she nearly pulled it from its frame. She was a tall, strong girl, taking after her father rather than her more delicate, extremely beautiful mother.

Hurrying down the white marble staircase from the second-floor editorial offices, Elizabeth nodded at a couple of fellow reporters on their way up. They smiled warmly at her, though she could imagine what might pass between them once they were alone. Most of her colleagues made no secret of their belief that women belonged nowhere near a newsroom, except to fetch coffee or clean the floors.

On the second-floor landing, she saw Simon Sneed climbing the stairs toward her. He was a sleek, slippery sort of person who seemed to leave a trail of slime in his wake, like a slug. He had recently been promoted from reporter to assistant editor, and it was rumored he had links to the corrupt politicians at Tammany Hall.

Stopping in front of her, he smiled, a toothpick dangling from one side of his mouth. "Well, if it isn't the famous Miss Van den Broek," he said, looking her up and down as if she were a horse for sale. Tall and slim, he had the sinuous movements of a panther, and always seemed poised to strike. Ever since her first day at the *Herald*, Elizabeth had felt Sneed's eyes upon her. It was not so much what he said as how she felt in his presence: confused, flustered, and unsure of herself.

"Good morning, Mr. Sneed," she said, avoiding eye contact.

She moved to pass him, but he caught her by the elbow. "Why the hurry? Are you on your way to a fire?"

"Excuse me; I have an assignment—"

"Which surely can wait another minute or two," he said, gripping her arm firmly. "It won't do to be impolite to your colleagues, will it? I should think you need all the friends you can get."

His impudent tone irritated her. "I have quite enough friends," she said, pulling away to brush past him. But before she could make it to the first step, he grabbed her wrist and drew her toward him.

"Oh, I don't think one can ever have too many friends," he said, his face so close to hers she could smell his lime aftershave. "You never know when they'll come in handy." Eyes hooded, he leaned in closer, as if to kiss her. At that moment, Elizabeth heard footsteps and voices coming from below them. Someone was approaching from the lobby—two men, by the sound of it. Elizabeth seized the moment to pull away, but he held fast to her wrist and leaned forward to whisper in her ear. "Remember what I said—you never know when you'll need a friend." Releasing her, he laughed and tripped lightly up the stairs, whistling softly.

Feeling heat rise to her cheeks, Elizabeth rubbed her wrist and shook herself before continuing down to the lobby. The two men she had heard earlier tipped their hats as they passed; she nodded curtly in return, unable to force a smile. Her forehead burned—not from shame but anger. She vowed to keep an eye on Simon Sneed, even as she turned his words over in her mind, examining the invitation within the implied threat. He certainly was not one to have as an enemy, but she could sense that he might be useful as a "friend," if only she could play him as he had tried to play her.

Once outside, she took a deep breath. While New York's atmosphere in August was hardly the cleanest, it felt sweet in comparison to sharing the air with the likes of Simon Sneed. Across the street, at the western corner of Ann and Broadway, people were filing in and out of St. Paul's Chapel, as they did all day long. She turned to glance up at the five-story Herald Building behind her, with its soaring mansard roof and white marble exterior. Built in the French Second Empire style, it was the brainchild of James Gordon Bennett Jr., son of the *Herald*'s famed founder. He had purchased the site of the former Barnum's American Museum to create the elegant cast-iron building with elaborate dormer windows and ornate ironwork.

Normally Elizabeth found the sight thrilling, but she was in a bad mood, frustrated at the limitations imposed by her sex. She was keenly aware that if she were a man, she would not be stuck covering a garden party instead of a potential murder. Walking rapidly north along Park Row, known as Newspaper Row (or Printing House Square, after the London location of the same name), she passed the grand *Times* building, the *Tribune* with its clock tower, the much smaller *Staats-Zeitung*, and at the northern corner, the *World*, with its rounded dome echoing that of City Hall across the street.

Elizabeth thought of hailing a cab but decided to take the El back uptown, hoping to catch a glimpse into the room where she had seen the woman being assaulted. She thought she might be able to identify it, but as the train rumbled along the avenue, she couldn't even be sure which building it was. The tenements on that part of the Bowery were similar, and peering across the street, the downtown track between her and the west side of the street, she looked in vain for a glimpse of the butcher shop on the first floor. Curtains were drawn in many of the third-floor windows. Then, as a final insult, a downtown train barreled past, obscuring her view entirely.

CHAPTER THREE

Elizabeth took the train as far as Twenty-Eighth Street, walking the two blocks north to her parents' house. The French château–style town house was just four blocks south of the Astors', and though its interior was not as lavish as the much-photographed Astor brownstone, it was nonetheless grand enough that Elizabeth felt her moral values compromised whenever she stepped inside.

As she entered the marble foyer, with its gleaming chandeliers and glassed cabinets filled with antique Chinese pottery, Elizabeth heard the familiar sound of a grand piano coming from the parlor. Her mother was playing Beethoven. Elizabeth recognized the devilishly difficult "Presto" of the *Pathetique Sonata*, having struggled through it herself more than once. But her mother rattled it off with her usual brilliance, every note a jewel of precision and beauty, gleaming droplets in a flowing fountain of perfection.

Catharina van den Broek had the kind of gift that filled musicians of more ordinary talent with envy. Being one of the latter, Elizabeth had long ago given up feeling anything but wonder for her mother's ability, not to mention her discipline and dedication. It was perhaps the one aspect of her mother's character for which she could feel pure, unabashed admiration. And then, of course, there was her beauty: undeniable, breathtaking, ethereal. It never failed to impress Elizabeth, as it did everyone who met her—an impression magnified by her apparent indifference to her looks, though Elizabeth knew quite well that was only a studied pose. Her mother was very aware of her appearance, and quite adept at using it to her advantage.

The piano playing stopped abruptly. The sound of heels clicking lightly across the polished parquet floor was followed by the appearance of her mother's slim figure in the open doorway. Unadorned by makeup, framed by wisps of golden hair, her face was so perfectly lovely that Elizabeth's breath caught in her throat. The intensity of her mother's beauty was always a little shocking. Clad in a honey-colored dress that brought out the gold in her pale-brown eyes, creamy French lace lining her décolletage, Catharina van den Broek looked at least a decade younger than her forty-two years.

"Elizabeth, darling—what a pleasant surprise!" she cried, hurtling toward Elizabeth with her customary energy, kissing her on both cheeks. She pronounced her daughter's name "Ay-lees-a-bet," even though it was the English spelling rather than the Dutch "Elisabeth." It had been Elizabeth's father's idea to give his daughters names that could pass as English, as he said, "in keeping with the city's future, rather than its past." The Dutch colonists had displayed a similar practicality when they simply handed Manhattan over to the British, avoiding what surely would have been a bloody war.

Catharina stepped back to observe her daughter. "You're thinner," she said, frowning. "You're not eating."

Elizabeth smiled. It had been her mother's constant complaint ever since Elizabeth went away to Vassar. Though by no means fat, she had always been plumper than her sylphlike mother, and yet Catharina always fretted that Elizabeth was too thin, even after she experienced the customary weight gain her first year at school.

"I am eating quite well," Elizabeth replied. "The Beethoven sounded wonderful," she added, quickly changing the subject.

Her mother dismissed the compliment with a wave. "I'm still struggling with the arpeggios in the left hand."

"I thought it was magnificent."

"You sound like your father. He's no musician, but you should know better."

"Very well, then. It sounded terrible."

"There is no need to be sarcastic. I was just about to have tea in the north parlor—come join me." Her parents' house contained not only north and south parlors but a splendid dining room that could seat up to fifty, as well as a grand ballroom.

"I'm afraid I cannot—"

"Nora was just about to set it out. I'll just tell her to bring an extra cup."

Nora O'Donnell was their Irish maid—a sullen, resentful girl her mother was unaccountably fond of, declaring her to be invaluable. Elizabeth knew that Nora was stealing from her parents, but knowing the plight of so many of the city's Irish immigrants, Elizabeth said nothing.

"I regret to say I cannot stay. Please do not bother Nora on my account."

Catharina sighed. "I do wish you would procure a maid. Your father would gladly pay for one."

"The Stuyvesant offers a cleaning woman once a week at very reasonable rates."

"Well, at least it is a respectable residence. Though I must say, I do not care for some of the riffraff in that neighborhood."

"I am quite safe there, Mother."

"If you say so," Catharina replied dubiously. "But if you cannot stay for tea, why have you come?"

I have just stopped by to borrow a dress."

"Whatever for?"

"The *Herald* has sent me to cover the Astors' garden party—"

"The Astors, did you say?"

"Yes."

"Today? At their Fifth Avenue mansion?"

"It begins in less than an hour."

Her mother gave a bitter little laugh. "No doubt it will be a grand affair." A look of bereavement passed across her features. "I cannot understand why *the* Mrs. Astor—as she insists on calling herself—doesn't consider the Van den Broek family to be one of the Four Hundred. It is a pity your father does not care about such things. I'm certain if he did, we would be on the guest list."

Elizabeth was both irritated and touched by her mother's attempt to save face. "The Four Hundred" was supposedly a list of people who mattered in fashionable society, a collection of New York's elite. It was rumored that the list was apocryphal—that there was no such document—and that the number four hundred merely reflected the guest capacity of Mrs. Astor's ballroom.

"But why come here?" Catharina asked.

"As you can see, I lack the proper attire," she said, pointing to her rather unadorned green frock and matching tailored jacket. "I have a few dresses at my apartment, but nothing elegant enough for this assignment."

Her mother nodded. "You will certainly stand out like a sore thumb at the Astors dressed like that. Your column is the Society Page, after all."

Elizabeth sighed. "I cannot imagine who reads such a column."

"Presumably other women."

"Foolish, shallow ones, perhaps, with too much time on their hands."

Her mother crossed her arms. "You are a fine one to talk—you owe your job to your family's prominence, as you well know."

"I am not proud of it. Indeed, I—"

"You were not too proud to accept our influence."

"It was necessary, if I am to do any good in the world."

"What matters right now is that you dress properly for this assignment." Her mother allowed a superior smile to cross her face.

"Everyone knows you have the most beautiful frocks in the city," Elizabeth said, substituting flattery for the truth, which was that she did not have time to stop by the Stuyvesant to change.

"I don't know about that," Catharina replied. "But I'll see what I can do."

She turned and glided gracefully from the room, just as Nora entered from the door leading to the kitchen, carrying a gleaming silver tea service. When she saw Elizabeth, she struggled to contort her face into the shape of a smile. It was like watching lava trying to flow backward, but the girl finally managed a sickly, simpering smirk.

"Mornin', miss," she said, curtseying. "I didn't know you were comin'."

"Neither did I, Nora, yet here I am. How are you?"

"Can't complain, miss," she replied, setting the tray on the sideboard. "I'll just fetch another cup—"

"I'm not staying," Elizabeth said, enjoying the girl's attempt to cover her relief with yet another unconvincing facial expression. Nora O'Donnell was not a gifted actress, but she was a clever thief, purloining small trinkets from Catharina's considerable jewelry collection, always carefully choosing cheaper items her mistress rarely wore. Her antipathy toward Elizabeth was no doubt fueled by her knowledge that Elizabeth knew her secret, having seen Nora stuff stolen items into her pockets on more than one occasion. She pretended to be unaware of the girl's stealing, and Nora pretended not to know Elizabeth was onto her. It was a little game they played, one in which Elizabeth had the upper hand, which infuriated Nora—hence her barely contained anger. Elizabeth had considered confronting the girl, but she rather admired the maid's audacity. She was also irritated by her mother's blindness to the thefts taking place right under her nose—but even more dismayed that she would hire such an ill-tempered girl.

"Kin I get you anythin' a'tall, miss?"

"No, thank you, Nora—I'm fine."

Brushing a strand of dark hair from her forehead, Nora curtsied once again, holding it just a tad longer than necessary to signify her defiance before leaving the room. Elizabeth was relieved to have her go. She did, however, find the girl quite pretty, with shiny black curls and clear white skin—even if her mother had declared more than once that Nora's rather thick ankles were the "legs of a peasant." Catharina van den Broek had a knack for putting people in their place with insults posing as observations, thus ensuring her own superiority. Elizabeth believed her mother was unaware that her behavior was condescending. She was equally certain that if she pointed it out, Catharina would deny it, utterly mortified by the suggestion that she was capable of anything less than courteous politesse.

This paragon of social graces entered the parlor with a yellow silk gown Elizabeth recognized from many balls and soirees. It was one of her mother's favorites, just a few shades lighter than her golden hair, with a gathered train and black-lace flounces around the shoulders.

"This has always been a bit loose on me," Catharina said, laying it on the divan. "And you are quite thin now, so I believe it may fit."

"Are you certain you want to lend me this one?" Elizabeth asked, running her hand over the glossy fabric. "It's one of your favorites."

"Pish tosh—I have too many gowns. Your father delights in buying them for me, no matter how much I scold him for his extravagance."

Elizabeth smiled. The first statement was true: Hendrik van den Broek doted on his beautiful wife and took great pleasure in showing her off dressed in finery befitting the wife of a prominent judge. As to her mother's protesting the acquisition of new frocks, Elizabeth had seen no evidence of it. She had yet to meet a woman who disdained the gift of pretty clothes.

"It is very generous of you," she said, and went to try on the dress.

It did fit, even if it was a bit snug, and complete with matching gloves and a silk purse her mother provided, Elizabeth felt quite elegant indeed.

"Take my best parasol," her mother said, fetching a handsome gold one with black-lace trim from the front hall. "It's real whalebone—not metal, like some of the cheaper ones these days."

"I don't need—"

A frown darkened Catharina's lovely face. "Do not even think of appearing at Mrs. Astor's sans parasol. Too bad we don't have time to do your hair properly. Hold still," she added, threading a yellow ribbon through Elizabeth's auburn curls. "That will have to do," she said, stepping back to admire her work. "Unfortunately, you are rather taller than is considered polite for a woman, but that can't be helped. Never mind—you have naturally thick hair, and Lady Astor's is notoriously sparse. She often wears wigs—very expensive ones, of course. She will be envious of you, and in high society, envy often masquerades as admiration."

"I have no interest in being envied or admired—"

"Ah, that is where you are mistaken. Flattery is the currency of society, and envy its greedy cousin. When people envy you, they pretend to admire you to save face—which gives you power over them."

"I do not wish to have power over other people."

Catharina van den Broek stroked her daughter's face. "Oh, my dear, you are too young to know what you want."

Elizabeth backed away, angered by her mother's condescension. "I know one thing that I want."

"And what is that?"

"For my sister to be cured."

Her mother's face lost its color, and her lips compressed tightly. "That is in the hands of God," she said quietly.

"Why do you never talk of Laura?"

"Your father finds it too painful a topic."

"Do you ever visit her?"

"What time does your party begin?" her mother asked, flitting across the room to fuss with the tea service. "Are you sure you wouldn't like some tea?"

"No, thank you."

"Nora can bring an extra cup. It's no trouble," she said, avoiding looking at Elizabeth.

Seeing her mother's discomfort, Elizabeth regretted bringing up the topic of her sister's illness. Growing up, the two had been nearly inseparable. Just two years older, Laura had mothered Elizabeth, protecting her from Catharina's sharp edges, and Elizabeth had coaxed her quieter sister out of the house to join her in the many adventures two young girls could have on horseback in Central Park, or riding ponies in the pine woods near their summer house in Kinderhook.

Laura first began hearing voices when Elizabeth was away at college. Paranoid imaginings soon followed. She believed people were sprinkling glass on the floor of her bedroom while she slept. She refused to eat food unless she could watch it being prepared, convinced someone was trying to poison her. When Elizabeth returned for the Christmas holidays during her second year at school, her mother tried to hide her sister's affliction and, when she failed, minimized and finally denied it altogether.

Catharina—whose arsenal included icy glares, stony silence, and when all else failed, fleeing the room in tears—firmly rebuffed Elizabeth's father's attempts to bring up the subject. Hendrik was helpless in the face of his wife's emotional volatility. He had an old-fashioned view of women as fragile creatures who should be protected and indulged—an opinion that amazed Elizabeth, since Catharina was so obviously iron-willed and domineering. But her father adored his beautiful, clever wife with a desperate passion that reminded Elizabeth of Charles Bovary, Emma's tragic, lovesick husband in *Madame Bovary*. The book had been a staple of her French literature class at college, and though Elizabeth had struggled with the French, the story had captivated her.

After observing her sister's distressing symptoms, Elizabeth returned to Vassar troubled and puzzled, but somehow managed to lose herself in her studies. When she came home after finishing her sophomore year, there was no denying the change in her sister. Thin and pale, Laura was at the mercy of voices only she could hear. Sometimes they made her laugh, but more often they terrified her, and Elizabeth could only watch as her beloved sister retreated deeper into a world where no one could reach her. There had been talk of art school once, but that ceased as Laura's illness worsened.

By the end of Elizabeth's junior year, their parents had placed Laura in the recently completed pavilion for the insane at Bellevue Hospital. When Elizabeth returned to the city after graduation, she visited once a week, but frequently returned home in a state of nervous exhaustion at seeing her sister receding from reality.

"I saw her two days ago," Elizabeth told her mother, who was still fidgeting with the tea.

"Did she recognize you?" Catharina asked without turning around.

"Yes," Elizabeth declared, though in truth she could not be sure. "They moved her to a private room."

"Your father arranged that," her mother said. "He's on the hospital board."

"We might visit together sometime," she said, just as her mother dropped her teacup, which shattered, sending shards of bone china scattering across the parquet floor.

Catharina stared down at the mess for a moment, then her face crumpled like a Chinese fan. "I really am so clumsy. Whatever will become of me?" Bursting into sobs, she ran from the room.

A daughter in a normal family might have gone to comfort her, but Elizabeth was only too aware they were not normal. Catharina van den Broek hated to be seen crying, even by her own daughter. Fleeing the room was the equivalent of a Roman centurion drawing his cloak across his face to hide his suffering. Elizabeth knew better than to follow after her mother.

She picked up the parasol, silk purse, and gloves Catharina had lent her, tucked them under her arm, and slipped quietly out of the house.

CHAPTER FOUR

A light rain was falling when Elizabeth stepped out onto Fifth Avenue. Not wishing to soil her fancy shoes, she took a hansom cab to the soiree, arriving to see a line of carriages stretching four blocks in both directions. Most of the guests at a party given by Caroline Astor owned their own carriage, and were intent on showing it.

Compared to the French château–style building across the street, the Astors' brownstone was surprisingly unimposing from the outside. After paying the driver, Elizabeth alighted from the cab and climbed the heavy stone staircase to enter the four-story building. The butler was a husk of a man with skin the texture of dried field corn. After studying her at some length through his bifocals, he reluctantly accepted her calling card, raising one frosty eyebrow when he saw the heading *New York Herald* over her name.

"You are a *journalist*, then?" he said, pronouncing "journalist" in the same tone of voice one might use to describe an unsavory bodily function.

Weary of his attitude, Elizabeth nodded curtly and was silently escorted into a lavish ballroom, located in its own wing of the house. Plush Oriental rugs coated nearly every inch of the gleaming parquet floor; the walls were covered with massive paintings, mostly landscapes, so closely hung that many of the heavy frames touched each other. Marble statues, potted plants, and elaborate light fixtures graced the corners of the room; settees, armchairs, and hassocks lined the walls. Elizabeth even spotted Mrs. Astor's famous divan, a plump little armchair with a colorful striped armrest, suitable for a Turkish prince.

Having seen only rather idealized portraits of Caroline Astor as a young woman, Elizabeth was not prepared for the heavily built middle-aged woman with thick facial features perched on a red circular ottoman in the center of the ballroom. She presided majestically over a roomful of guests, all expensively and elaborately dressed. The hostess herself wore a rich purple velvet gown, so dark it was nearly black, with creamy French lace at the neck and elbows. The abundance of dark hair piled atop her head made Elizabeth suspect it was a wig, if what her mother said was true.

The room glowed softly in the light from the dozens of candles on the enormous chandelier hanging over the ottoman. The chandelier itself was another ostentatious display of wealth—apart from the exquisite cut crystal, it required the use of dozens of candles, so much messier and more time consuming than the room's multiple gaslight sconces. Only someone of great wealth could afford the staff necessary to clean the chandelier and replace the scores of spent candles.

As Elizabeth stepped somewhat hesitantly into the room, the hubbub died abruptly, and Mrs. Astor swung her rather large head in her direction. Eyes narrowed, her lips compressed, she tilted her head to the side, as if appraising Elizabeth, then her face broke into a wide smile.

"Come here, child," the great lady said, beckoning her over.

Elizabeth took a step in her direction.

Mrs. Astor stretched out a bejeweled hand. "Do not worry—I shan't bite, in spite of what you may have heard."

A few of the ladies tittered, the gentlemen smiled, and Elizabeth realized at that moment that her mother was right: Mrs. Caroline Astor was indeed queen of all she surveyed.

Mrs. Astor regarded Elizabeth with her pince-nez. "Why do I not know you? Who are your parents?"

"My father is Hendrik van den Broek, and my mother is—"

"Catharina van den Broek, née van Dooren. Her father was a man of some distinction." She smiled at Elizabeth's puzzled expression. "And your father is a well-respected judge, a member of the Knickerbocker Club, I believe." The Knickerbocker was New York's oldest and most exclusive men's club, accepting members only from wealthy, long-established families.

Elizabeth felt herself blush. "You are indeed correct."

Mrs. Astor smiled. "No doubt I know a deal more than is good for me. But my position requires that I keep track of everyone who matters—or who might matter—in New York society."

Elizabeth was amused to think that Mrs. Astor considered her mother someone who "might matter."

"And your name, my child?"

"Elizabeth van den Broek."

"Where do you reside?"

"The Stuyvesant, on East Eighteenth Street."

"A very respectable address," she said, with a glance at her acolytes, who nodded, the ladies fluttering their fans as they inspected Elizabeth over the French-lace rims. She felt like a lone gazelle being studied by a group of hungry lionesses. Mrs. Astor turned back to her. "Calvert Vaux resides at the Stuyvesant, and General Custer's widow lives on the first floor."

"You astonish me, madame," Elizabeth replied. "It is said you know everyone, but your reputation does not do you justice."

"*Tu es très agréable, ma petite*," said Mrs. Astor, peering at Elizabeth through her pince-nez. "*Très belle.*"

"*Merci, madame*," Elizabeth replied, noting her use of the informal "tu," a subtle reminder of the older woman's superior social standing. "*J'espère que vous aurez quelque chose à dire pour le* Herald."

"*Ah, tu es journaliste. Admirable.*"

Elizabeth was surprised to feel a shiver of pleasure at Mrs. Astor's words. She had long believed that social status was essentially trivial nonsense. And yet standing here now, in the inner sanctum of the most powerful figure in New York society, surrounded by the soft glow of a hundred candles, her skin tingled. Stroked by the feather of affluence and approval, she felt that, somehow, she had arrived.

At Mrs. Astor's insistence, Elizabeth helped herself to tea from one of the flowered china pots on the sideboard. Having rid herself of the extra weight she had gained while at college, she refused the lady's offers of sweets except for a small slice of lemon chiffon cake, which looked too good to refuse.

"Come meet some of my guests," Mrs. Astor said, escorting Elizabeth to a pair of expensively dressed ladies standing next to a cut-crystal punch bowl. "Allow me to introduce Mrs. Lillian Abernathy," she said, indicating the older of the two, "and her niece, Miss Eloise Pratt."

"How do you do?" said Miss Pratt, offering her hand. She wore creamy yellow kid gloves that matched the lace on her dress. She was young and comely, with lustrous black hair and lively dark eyes.

"Pleased to make your acquaintance," Elizabeth said, shaking her hand.

Her aunt was scarcely less attractive than her niece—tall and slim, with a long white neck and small, well-formed head. She seemed somewhat less pleased to meet Elizabeth than her niece did, but was civil enough, inquiring politely about Elizabeth's life.

"My word," she said, upon learning Elizabeth was a journalist. "That is very enterprising of you."

"Are you not afraid?" asked her niece, her large brown eyes wide with anticipation.

"Of what?" said Elizabeth.

"Why, of wicked people, of course."

"I do not meet a great many of them, as I write for the society column."

"Oh," said Miss Pratt, who could not help sounding disappointed. She pursed her pretty lips and fluttered her fan as her aunt leaned in toward Elizabeth.

"There *are* so many unsavory types about these days," Mrs. Abernathy remarked, her tone conspiratorial. "Especially downtown, it would seem, wickedness abounds."

Elizabeth frowned. "If that is true, no doubt it is the product of poverty and disease."

"Lack of character, I rather think," said Mrs. Abernathy.

"And breeding," her niece added. "Papa always says breeding will out."

"I should think bad behavior exists even among the upper classes," Elizabeth remarked drily.

"Surely not in the same degree," said Mrs. Abernathy. "I mean, *those people*—some of them live like animals."

"If so, it is because they are forced to," Elizabeth replied tightly, not bothering to hide her irritation.

Mrs. Abernathy's eyes widened, and Miss Pratt fluttered her fan furiously.

"Well!" said the older woman. "I *never*—"

"No, madame," Elizabeth replied coolly. "You never did, and that is precisely the problem."

"And who is this enchanting creature?" said a male voice behind her.

Elizabeth turned to see a tall, distinguished-looking gentleman with swept-back silver hair, a broad forehead, and intense, deep-set gray eyes.

At his side was Mrs. Astor, her arm linked around his. "Allow me to introduce Mr. Charles Abernathy, renowned Egyptologist."

"Pleased to make your acquaintance," said Elizabeth.

"The pleasure is mine, I assure you," he said, bowing and kissing her hand, his lips lingering a shade longer than necessary.

She pulled away with a nervous little jerk, looking apprehensively at Mrs. Abernathy. His wife's dour but stoic expression indicated she had seen this behavior a hundred times, and had long since given up trying to change it.

"Mr. Abernathy is on the staff of the Metropolitan Museum," Mrs. Astor said.

"That must be very gratifying work," Elizabeth remarked, and thought she saw Mrs. Abernathy roll her eyes behind her fan.

"I have endeavored rather unsuccessfully to convince them to establish an Egyptian wing," he said with a modest shrug.

"Have you heard of the ancient obelisk known as Cleopatra's Needle?" asked the excitable Miss Pratt. It was hard to dislike her, even with her unenlightened views; she was like a young spaniel, all wriggles and curls. Elizabeth felt there was hope for her yet.

"It is in London, I believe," said Mrs. Astor. "Please excuse me for a moment—I must greet my guests," she added, indicating a middle-aged couple entering the room.

"There is also one in Paris—and we are about to get our own, in New York!" Miss Pratt said. She seemed very enthusiastic about it.

"Yes," said Elizabeth. "The *Herald* did a story about it earlier this year. It is Egyptian, but has no actual connection to Cleopatra."

"I see you are as well informed as you are attractive," Mr. Abernathy remarked.

His wife pursed her lips and frowned. Turning to the punch bowl, she helped herself to a large glass. Fanning herself, she moved to join a group of people across the room. It was impolite, to say the least, but Elizabeth could not blame her. Her husband ignored her behavior, and her niece hardly seemed to notice. She gazed rapturously at her uncle as he spoke of his involvement in procuring the obelisk. Elizabeth waited patiently for him to finish before excusing herself. There was something unsavory about the man, and she did not like Miss Pratt's obvious reverence, which, she feared, hinted at something darker.

Using thirst as an excuse, Elizabeth crossed the room toward the tea service. As she passed Mrs. Astor, who was seated on her ottoman, the lady beckoned to her.

"Alas, I fear the rain drove our party indoors," she said, setting down her teacup. Elizabeth calculated that the ruby ring on her right hand could fund several years of decent lodging for a family of four. "But if it is not raining too hard, perhaps you would like to see my garden?"

"I do not wish to monopolize your attention," Elizabeth said, putting down her own cup on an intricately carved, marble-topped table, as her hostess rose from the plush velvet ottoman. Several elegantly dressed ladies poked their male companions, who leaned forward to offer their assistance.

"I am perfectly capable of maneuvering myself, thank you," Mrs. Astor said. "I hope I am not yet that decrepit. Come along, child." The faint aroma of orchid blossoms wafted from her as she took Elizabeth's arm. "Let us promenade the garden, where we may converse in private. Stokes," she called to the cadaverous butler, who had positioned himself near the entrance to the ballroom.

"Yes, madame?" he said, stepping forward.

"Has the rain stopped?"

"It has, madame, though the ground is still quite damp."

"Thank you, Stokes."

"Would madame like me to—"

"I shall inform you should I require further assistance, thank you."

Mrs. Astor led Elizabeth through a narrow corridor to a long, bountiful garden bordered by azaleas on two sides and a copse of willow trees in the rear. The damp air was heavy with the scent of blossoms and the sweet aroma of loamy soil. They walked down a stone path, past rows of lilies, chrysanthemums, and carnations, until they reached the centerpiece of the garden, a large bed of roses. Drooping in the late-August light, well past their peak, the blossoms cast off a heady, overripe fragrance.

"*Rosa gallica officinals*," Mrs. Astor said, surveying her roses. "My favorite variety—old and sturdy, rather like me."

"Surely you are not old."

"Do not flatter me, my dear. It does not become you."

"They are lovely roses," Elizabeth replied, reddening.

"Indeed they are, though admittedly past their prime. So, my dear, what did you hope to learn about New York society?"

Caught off guard by her frankness, Elizabeth stammered her reply. "W-why, I'm not really sure."

"One must always convey certainty," her hostess said, plucking the reddest rose from its stem, carefully avoiding the thorns. "Even if it is merely a pose." She sniffed the flower, then tossed it on the ground and continued onward. Looking down at the crumpled blossom, Elizabeth thought that such a woman might well discard people as easily as she did flowers.

CHAPTER FIVE

"It is abundantly clear you are here against your will," Mrs. Astor remarked, strolling to the back of the garden, where a stone goldfish pond lay beneath the willow trees. "But that is precisely why you interest me."

"I don't know what gave you the impression I—"

Her hostess laughed, showing large, uneven teeth, strong looking, like the rest of her. "I have a certain ability to read people, which has stood me in good stead, as everyone in society presents a front. I have made a habit of seeing past what people want me to see, and I can plainly perceive you are not delighted to be here."

"I beg to disagree—"

"It is not an accusation, my dear—merely an observation," she said, watching the fish swimming lazily in their stone enclosure. The afternoon sun was peeking through the cloud cover, and their golden scales shimmered in its pale beams. "Look at them, swimming in circles," she remarked. "I wonder if they ever get bored."

"Mrs. Astor, I wish to protest that I—" Elizabeth began, but knew her tone was unconvincing.

"To be quite honest, I admire your independence of thought. Most people would sell their grandmother to be invited to one of my parties. And yet you are restless and unhappy here. One has to respect that."

Elizabeth could not tell if her wry tone of voice was a cover for anger and disapproval, or if Mrs. Astor really meant what she said. Her manner was so impeccably formal that it was difficult to perceive her true feelings.

"I suppose I should tell you to give a favorable account of my little soiree, but of course you must write what you think."

Elizabeth was about to reply when a young man of about seventeen entered the garden. Tall and lanky, he had a high forehead over a clean, well-formed brow, and light-brown hair. His generous mustache emphasized his cleft chin, which gave his face a certain masculinity it otherwise might have lacked. His eyes were his best feature—large, light colored, and deep set, they lent a modicum of gravitas to his youthful visage.

"What treasures have you been hiding out here?" he asked Mrs. Astor.

"Allow me to introduce Miss Elizabeth van den Broek," she replied, turning to Elizabeth. "This is my son, John Jacob Astor IV."

"Call me Jack," he said, bounding toward them with an awkward, loping gait. He was clad in a striped frock coat and matching trousers, obviously of the finest fabric, but they appeared too large on his gawky form. He broke into a wide smile, displaying the same broad, uneven teeth as his mother. "Awfully pleased to meet you."

"Miss Van den Broek is a journalist," Mrs. Astor said.

"Indeed? She is frightfully pretty."

"Pay no attention to him," she told Elizabeth. "He is a young man, and young men are given to ridiculous behavior."

"My mother has never taken me seriously," he said. "She considers me an afterthought."

"I'm sure that's not—"

"Did you know I have four older sisters?"

"Do stop prattling, Jack," his mother said. "I must return to my guests." She gathered the train of her gown to avoid it sweeping over a sodden bed of pansies.

"I'll accompany you," Elizabeth said quickly.

"Then I shall join you," Jack declared.

"You abhor tea parties," his mother replied.

"I am turning over a new leaf," he said, offering Elizabeth his arm.

Elizabeth spent the rest of the party trying to do her job while Jack followed her around like a lovesick puppy. By the time she was ready to leave, she had spurned the attentions of an elderly viscount, spilled tea on a duchess, and been snubbed by a plump society hostess who, Jack told her, was "a poseur with grand ambitions." Several times Mrs. Astor introduced her as Elizabeth van den Broek, "younger daughter of the Kinderhook Van den Broeks," though how she knew of Elizabeth's sister, let alone the family's presence in Columbia County, Elizabeth had no idea. She made no mention of the fact that Elizabeth was a journalist.

By the end of the soiree, Elizabeth had come to the conclusion that, for all their money and influence, the members of high society were very much like everyone else—petty, self-interested, and foolish. When she presented this view to young Jack, he threw back his head and laughed, his prominent Adam's apple bobbing energetically above his starched white collar.

"I shouldn't put that in print if I were you," he said as he stood in the foyer watching Elizabeth pull on her gloves.

"I have no intention of doing so. Indeed, I am not sure why I told you."

"Never fear—your secret is safe with me," he said, handing her the parasol her mother had lent her.

As she turned to leave, Mrs. Astor entered the foyer. "My dear Miss Van den Broek, are you leaving us so early?"

"I do regret it, but I have a story to file."

"You do not regret it a bit, but it is a pretty lie nonetheless." Mrs. Astor took her hand and pressed it between her own. "It was a pleasure meeting you. Please give my regards to Mr. Bennett. I knew his father—such a lovely man."

"I shall, thank you," Elizabeth said. She had not yet set eyes on the *Herald*'s wealthy and eccentric publisher, James Gordon Bennett Jr., let alone spoken to him, though she was hardly surprised Mrs. Astor knew him.

"Tell him I have a splendid crystal owl paperweight I found in Paris."

"If I see him, I will be sure to tell him." Mr. Bennett's obsession with owls was well-known. He wore owl cuff links and tiepins, and it was rumored he even kept live birds as pets.

"Oh, and pray tell your mother I will call on her sometime soon."

"Thank you—I shall," Elizabeth said, with a glance at Jack, who winked at her. They were all aware of the significance of this statement. The rules of etiquette in "polite society" were rigid and immutable. For example, Mrs. Astor had famously never "called on" the wealthy Vanderbilt family, considering them nouveau riche, and therefore beneath notice by "old money" families such as the Astors. Consequently, the Vanderbilts were not considered part of polite society. To be called on by Caroline Astor was to be given the imprimatur of approval by the self-appointed queen of New York society.

"I'll walk you to your carriage," Jack told Elizabeth.

"I did not arrive in a carriage," she replied. The truth was, her parents did not own one. They could well afford it, but her father considered it a frivolous expense, preferring to invest his money with the advice of his cousin, who worked on Wall Street.

"I'll call you a cab, then," said Jack.

"I prefer to walk."

"Then I shall—"

"Forgive me," said Elizabeth, "but how old are you?"

"I'll be seventeen next July."

"As it is August, you have only recently turned sixteen."

He frowned and tugged at the knot on his lavender silk cravat. "A gentleman never asks a lady her age, you know."

"Then I shall freely tell you. I am twenty-two, which makes me six years older than you."

"It is not such a great number."

"It is when the boy is as young as you are."

Jack sighed. "Girls my age are tedious. They care only for pretty dresses and cotillions. Why must I wait until I am older?"

"Because that is the way of things."

"I do not like it at all."

"There are a great many things I do not like, but the world cares very little for our preferences."

"Now you sound like my mother."

Elizabeth smiled. "Good day, Mr. Jack Astor," she said, offering her hand.

He grabbed it and kissed it, then looked at her with a searching expression. "Perhaps in a few years, you may feel differently."

"I cannot say, but I am quite certain *you* will feel differently."

"I tell you I will not."

"Goodbye," Elizabeth said, and set off down the wide expanse of Fifth Avenue.

"I hope to see you again!" he called after her.

She waved without turning around. She told herself that his eagerness was simply a case of puppy love, yet even so, she felt there was something unsettling about young Jack Astor.

CHAPTER SIX

He stood in his front parlor window, gazing at the city, stretched out before him like a compliant lover. His fellow citizens scurried to and fro, under the impression that their lives were important, that they *meant* something. Wiping the sweat from their brows, parcels tucked under their arms, snotty-faced children in tow, they were slaves to habit, to convention, to the assumption that they had agency over their fate. They toiled and sweated and slept and quarreled in dirty, overcrowded streets because they believed they could better their lot if only they worked hard enough. They had crossed foaming, storm-ridden oceans and harsh, hostile deserts to land on this shore, full of hope for a future they'd hardly dared dream about in their homeland. They came in droves, in flocks, in herds, in hordes—fleeing plague, famine, persecution, and poverty and landing, panting and exhausted, in the bustling port of New York.

The promise of a fresh start was built into the city's very name: *New York*. They thought they had arrived to procure a brighter future. He knew better.

Pouring himself a cup of chamomile tea, he sipped from the delicate china cup with tiny pink flowers as Cleo rubbed against his leg. He reached down to scratch her ears, and she licked his fingers with her sandpaper tongue.

The city they believed embraced them would in fact chew them up and spit them out like so many undigested pebbles. No amount of labor, energy, ambition, or goodwill could succeed in a city that embraced so much evil and corruption.

He understood all this, and this knowledge gave him power over the meek sheep who inhabited the crowded and heartless streets and alleyways. They believed hellholes like Five Points, Rogues' Alley, and Water Street were anomalies in an otherwise kind and forgiving city. But he knew they were the very heart of the beast, and the activities that went on there—whoring, gambling, thievery, fighting, butchery—defined life in New York. It was vast, it was impersonal, and it would suck the life out of you if you were not careful. Or lucky or smart or rich. Most of the wretched souls who stepped out of overcrowded steamer ships onto its shores were none of those things, and no one was all of them.

Finishing his tea, he wiped his mouth with a starched white-linen napkin. The wretches outside his window hurried to their beer gardens and taverns or the corner "groceries" selling cheap liquor, anxious to wash off the filth of the day with a mug of ale, a shot of whiskey, or a tumbler of gin.

But he did not drink or smoke or visit the opium dens hidden down dimly lit basement stairs on Mott Street. No, he kept his own body unsullied, his mind sharpened by years of fastidious living, so as to rise above the stink of the masses, the stench of the streets. With a sigh, he turned from the window and sauntered into the kitchen, the ever-faithful Cleo following at his heels.

New York was dark and dirty and dangerous. And it was his playground.

CHAPTER SEVEN

"She said *what*?" Elizabeth's mother asked breathlessly, pacing in front of the bay window overlooking Fifth Avenue. Elizabeth had stopped by to change clothes, and her report of her encounter with Mrs. Astor had set Catharina all atwitter. Now her mother was doing what she always did when excited or anxious: pacing back and forth, wringing her hands. "Tell me precisely what she said! Omit nothing."

"That she would call on you soon."

"Are you quite certain she used that phrase—that she would *call* on me?"

"Oh, Mother, do you suppose I am ignorant of its meaning?"

"No," Catharina said. "But are you *quite* certain—"

"Do not ask me that again."

"What was she *like*?"

"Pretending to be sterner than she is. And infinitely more intelligent than people give her credit for."

"Yes, yes," Catharina said, wringing her hands. "But what of her attire, her manner? Are her jewels as fine as they say? Is her house as grand as everyone claims?"

"I must get back to the *Herald* offices," Elizabeth said, pulling on her gloves.

Seeing them, her mother frowned. "Elizabeth, are those *cotton*?"

"A cotton-and-silk blend, I believe."

"Why don't you wear finer ones? Surely you can afford a pair of kid gloves. Why, I gave you some last Christmas."

"Because it is summer, and I dislike sweltering clothing."

Catharina shook her head. "People will judge your social class to be inferior—"

"Then *let* them," Elizabeth said, exasperated. "Perhaps people will talk to me more readily if they believe I am closer to them in social status."

"I trust you are showing some discretion as to whom you associate with," her mother said with a superior little sniffle.

Elizabeth threw her arms up in frustration. "I am a *journalist*, Mother! I do not intend to spend the rest of my life in the drawing rooms of hoity-toity society ladies—"

"I fail to see why that would be so terrible."

"Because the world outside is large and wide and full of adventure," Elizabeth said, her voice trembling with emotion. "And I mean to have as many as I can."

"You should take more care for your safety, my dear," Catharina said, patting her arm. "The world is far more dangerous than you seem to understand."

"That sort of attitude is exactly what keeps women from seeking more fulfilling, exciting lives!" Elizabeth cried out impatiently.

"Excitement is not everything you think it is, Elizabeth. You think because you have gone to college, you know everything. I am sorry to be the one to tell you that you do not."

"I do not claim to know everything, Mother; I only wish to be allowed to live my life my own way, without the weight of old values holding me back."

Her mother was silent, and Elizabeth feared she had wounded her pride. Catharina was touchy on the subject of her age, and had just been reminded that they were of different generations. She seemed taken aback, staring wordlessly at the floor.

"Don't be cross with me," Elizabeth said softly, impulsively kissing her on the cheek. "And thank you for the dress. It was perfect—even Mrs. Astor said so." This last remark was a lie, of course, and Elizabeth was a little shocked to hear herself utter it.

Catharina's face brightened, but before she could respond, Elizabeth was out the door. Angry at herself for inventing a silly falsehood to soothe her mother's feelings, she sighed as she left the building. Waiting in front of the town house for the Fifth Avenue express coach, Elizabeth could hear the strains of a Chopin étude coming from the parlor. She recognized it as opus 10, no. 4, and her mother's mastery of the difficult piece was breathtaking. Elizabeth listened as she navigated the prestissimo runs and pounding bass octaves—even with her delicate frame and small hands, Catharina played the piano with the power and energy of any male virtuoso. Once again, Elizabeth wondered how anyone could be so gifted and yet so traditional.

Elizabeth reached the *Herald* shortly after most everyone had left for their midday meal, which could last for hours on a slow news day, as the men headed for the nearest oyster bar, preferably one with plenty of cheap ale on tap. Relieved to find the offices quieter than usual, Elizabeth settled into her corner desk on the third floor overlooking William Street. The trees along the side street had the tired look of late summer, the leaves dry and dusty, as if they could hardly wait to surrender to the pull of autumn winds.

She had been given this spot in the reporters' pool, tucked behind a column, next to a small, rather grimy window, because it was not deemed desirable, but she liked her far edge of the busy newsroom. She cherished the relative solitude, just as she loved her battered secondhand desk, with its squeaky drawers and scarred surface. It might be ancient, but it was made of good heavy oak, as solid and reassuring as an old friend. Being an independent professional woman was thrilling. She did not care to emulate her mother's comfortable, aimless life, with its parties and teas and endless ambles around fashionable museums and fancy shops. Gifted and beautiful as she was, Catharina van den Broek was an appendage to her husband—a pretty, talented one, no doubt, but an appendage nonetheless.

Elizabeth suspected the lack of purpose in her mother's life had made her volatile and high strung, so desperately mindful of social status.

Closing the blinds to obscure the sun on what had turned into a blindingly bright afternoon, Elizabeth settled down to compose her article. When she was writing, if her concentration was good, the world around her ceased to exist, and she was unaware of the passage of time. Other times, the words wouldn't come, and she struggled with restlessness and the feeling she would rather be doing anything else.

Today was one of the good days—her pencil flew across the page, barely keeping up with her rapidly spinning thoughts. At its best, writing was a series of revelations and realizations. The very act of putting her impressions down on paper helped her understand what she thought and felt, as if the writing itself were not only pulling truths and observations from her brain but creating them in the process.

She was still hunched over her work an hour later, when her colleagues staggered in from their afternoon repast, bleary-eyed, bellies full of beer and oysters. Freddy Evans ambled into the room and plopped down at his desk, which was next to hers.

"Hello, miss. Haven't seen you all day." A staff photographer at the *Herald*, Freddy was short and muscular, with a thick clump of sandy hair. His face hosted a convention of freckles so numerous that they nearly blotted out the rest of his skin. Today his face was pinker than usual, no doubt the result of lunch at McCallister's Ale House, the favorite haunt of many who worked on Newspaper Row. Freddy was all right—he liked to play the rascal, but was good natured and well-meaning, with none of the malice some of her coworkers displayed toward her. He hailed originally from London's East End and had a cocky, casual way about him that belied the fact that he was a very good photographer.

"I've been at a garden party," she said.

"All right fer some," he said, brushing a lock of hair from his forehead. Bleached from months of summer sun, his hair had turned the color and consistency of straw. "Where 'bouts?"

"The Astors'."

"Ooo, ain't you the swell, then?" he said, leaning back in his chair so far that it nearly tipped over.

"No, mate, she's more of a nob," came a voice from behind them. Elizabeth looked up to see Freddy's pal Tom Bannister. Tall and stringy, Tom had the face of a basset hound, with bags under his eyes, even though he was only twenty-seven. Originally from Yorkshire, he had come over from London with Freddy, after a few years working at the *Guardian*, the country's most liberal paper. The *Herald* was hardly a progressive newspaper, but it did have a certain prestige. Apart from possibly imbibing too much ale at his midday meal, Tom was one of the paper's hardest-working photographers. He and Freddy had a friendly competition and, when not out on assignment, were seldom apart.

"Tom's got a point," Freddy said, smiling at Elizabeth. "Yer more of a nob, ain't ya?" It was no secret at the *Herald* that she came from a distinguished old family of means, "nob" being the slang word for such a person. A "swell" was a member of the nouveau riche, and as their wealth was more recently acquired, it was not highly regarded by New York's elite, as epitomized by the Astors and their ilk.

"A nob? Her? I doubt it." The three of them turned to see Simon Sneed slink into the room. "In order to be a nob, one must have class," he said, arms crossed, his thin lips curled in a sneer.

"What'd you know 'bout class, Sneed?" said Tom, his pale face flushing a deep scarlet. "I heard yer ma were a scullery maid."

Sneed took a step toward him. "I'd apologize for that remark if I were you. That is, assuming you wish the arrangement of your face to remain as it is. Though if you ask me, it could do with some improvement."

Tom didn't flinch, though Elizabeth could see his fingers twitching, and his Adam's apple bounced up and down as if it were on a spring.

Freddy slipped in between Tom and Simon Sneed, fists clenched. "You'll 'ave t'go through me first, Sneed," he said calmly. Though several inches shorter than Sneed, Freddy was built like a bullmastiff, with muscular shoulders that left little room for his neck.

"Gladly, if you care to step outside," Sneed replied smoothly.

"What is going on here?" Karl Schuster demanded, entering the room. He strode toward them, his large feet heavy on the bare wood floor.

"We were just having a little discussion," said Sneed.

"Is that right?" the editor said, turning to Freddy.

"Yeah, boss," Freddy replied. "A conversation, it were."

"Well, have it on your own time," Schuster replied, scowling. "Have you finished your story yet?" he asked Elizabeth. "We need to get it into tomorrow's edition or the *Sun* will scoop us."

"The *Sun* was at the Astors'? I didn't see—"

"Just get it to me by four, all right?" he said, leaving the room without looking back.

"I'll see *you* later," Sneed told Freddy before sauntering away.

"Not if I see you first," Freddy muttered. After Sneed had gone, he turned to Elizabeth with a lopsided smile. "Don' you worry 'bout the likes a 'im, long as I'm around."

Elizabeth smiled. She thought Freddy was sweet, with his combination of East End bluster and boyish charm. From the moment she'd arrived at the *Herald*, he had taken on the role of protector, with equal parts pride and swagger. In spite of her determination to project confidence, Elizabeth found his presence reassuring.

Returning to her writing, she concentrated on finishing her story, turning it in fifteen minutes before the deadline. Her thoughts were elsewhere—she could not wait to leave the *Herald* to go back to the third-story apartment on the Bowery. Putting on her hat and gloves, she skipped lightly down the marble stairs to the first floor, stepping out into the late-afternoon sun. The rain had dried up, but a lingering mist rose from the street, reflecting the golden light back onto the damp cobblestones as Elizabeth walked rapidly to the Park Row Elevated Station.

CHAPTER EIGHT

It was not yet rush hour, so the train was less crowded, and Elizabeth took a seat by the window. Staring out the window at the smoke puffing from the locomotive as the train chugged its way uptown, the air thick with soot and ash, she could see her mother shaking her head in bemusement at her choice of transportation. "So dirty—and smelly! Why on *earth* would anyone who could afford better want to—"

Her reverie was interrupted by the sight of the storefront with the wrought-iron railing and old-fashioned lettering.

HERMANN WEBER—METZGER
FEINES FLEISCH

Her German was decent enough: *Hermann Weber—Butcher. Fine Meat.* She stood up quickly, and was nearly thrown to the floor when the engineer braked abruptly for the next stop.

Alighting from the train, she walked back toward the shop. This part of the Bowery was on the southern outskirts of the neighborhood known as Little Germany, or *Kleindeutschland*, home to a large population of the city's German immigrants. The more prosperous lived north of Houston; the farther downtown you went, the more poverty held residents in its grip. Laundry flapped on lines strung across alleys and balconies; children with unwashed faces darted in and out of doorways, unattended by mothers who struggled under the yoke of daily deprivation. The sound of crying babies and barking dogs competed with the rumble of the uptown El as it roared by, spewing smoke and soot into the already polluted air. Such was the life of the working poor in New York, and Elizabeth longed to write about them instead of the pampered peacocks of Fifth Avenue.

A tall man in a canvas apron and bowler hat stood in front of the butcher shop, smoking an intricately carved pipe. He had a mustache like a shoe brush—dark, thick, and bushy—and his shirtsleeves were rolled up to his elbows, displaying muscular forearms. As he was middle-aged, with an authoritative air, Elizabeth took him to be Mr. Weber himself. An orange cat wound its sinuous body around his shin, its tail straight in the air, eyes half-closed, the picture of feline serenity. Many shops in the city had store cats, and Elizabeth could hardly imagine a better life for a cat than residence in a butcher shop. She envied the animal's easy contentment.

Social etiquette prohibited a respectable young lady from approaching a strange man on the street. Looking up at the dark third-floor window, she was pondering what to do when the butcher tapped his pipe on the iron rail, emptying its remains, and stepped back into his shop.

Elizabeth gazed up at the third-floor apartment but saw no movement behind the dingy windows—the apartment was quiet, with no sign of life. She was about to enter the butcher shop when she heard a hissing behind her.

"Psst, miss! You there—miss!"

Turning, she saw a woman of indeterminate age with pockmarked skin and keen, dark eyes. She could have been forty or eighty, drink and dissipation having already taken their toll on her body, dulling her skin and thinning her bones. She was standing in front of the Thirsty Crow, the saloon two doors down. Such establishments were plentiful on the Bowery, with often three or more to a block.

Dressed all in black, with a prominent, thin nose and sharp cheekbones, the woman reminded Elizabeth of a crow. Indeed, she displayed a birdlike watchfulness as she approached, looking side to side with a curious, quick twist of her neck, as if checking for danger. Her wariness seemed unnecessary; everyone on the street appeared caught up in their own affairs, with the usual hurried attitude of the typical New Yorker. It was said that people from other places had to live in the city for only a month before they were walking faster, talking faster, even eating and drinking faster.

She peered at Elizabeth. "You lookin' fer th'young lady, ain't ya?"

Elizabeth smelled alcohol on her breath—cheap grain whiskey, the kind that would scour your insides and rot your teeth. "What young lady do you mean?"

"Th'one who lived on the third floor there, in th'apartment you were lookin' at."

"Do you know her?"

"Knew 'er. She's not there no more," the woman said, burping loudly. The sour smell of sausage and onions emanated from her ill-kempt mouth.

"Where did she go?"

The woman put her face so close to Elizabeth's that she could see each pockmark clearly. Her skin resembled the cratered surface of the moon. "S-s-she jes dish-appeared," the woman said, slurring her words. "Here this mornin', an' now the rooms is empty. All 'er things are gone. Didn' even say g'bye."

"How do you know this?"

"The landlord hires me t'clean sometimes. Tol' me t'tidy up fer a new tenant, someone movin' in tomorrow."

"What happened?"

"Somethin' bad."

"Like what?"

"I dunno, but you won' get any answers from anyone 'round here."

"Why not?"

The woman looked at the butcher shop. "Someone paid 'em off, is wot I think."

"Who?"

"Don' know, but I seen ol' Mr. Weber with a fair wad o' cash earlier today. So much he closed up shop midday t'go to the bank."

"Might he have just sold a lot of meat this morning?"

The woman laughed, which set off a spasm of coughing.

"Perhaps you need a drink of water?" Elizabeth suggested.

"*Water?* That stuff'll kill ya," she said, laughing harder, which made her cough more. Finally she pounded her chest, then hawked and spit an enormous wad of phlegm into the already filthy gutter.

Fighting an impulse to gag, Elizabeth took a deep breath. "Have you any idea who gave him this money?"

"I might do," the woman said with a sly smile. "If it were worth my while, like."

Elizabeth dug in her purse and found fifty cents. She barely had it out when the woman grabbed it greedily.

"That's right, love. Grammy Nagle needs to eat."

"You should eat well tonight, if you don't spend it on whiskey."

The woman tucked the coins into the pocket of her shabby coat. "Don' you worry 'bout Grammy, love. She kin take care a' herself."

"Is that your name—Grammy?"

"Me real name's Mathilde, but everyone calls me Grammy."

"Well, then, Grammy, who gave Mr. Weber money?"

"I didn' get a look at 'is face, mind you, but I can tell ya he was tall an' robust lookin'."

"What about his clothes?"

"They were nice enough. His hat were brushed, and he wore a maroon frock coat an' gray-striped trousers. What struck me mos' was that 'is shoes were clean, like he never walked on these here streets," she added, gesturing at the cobblestones spattered with horse manure, orange peels, cigar butts, and all other manner of trash. Even the famously tidy Germans weren't able to keep their streets clean in New York, it seemed.

Grammy's mention of the maroon frock coat caught Elizabeth's attention. "You saw him give Mr. Weber money?"

"Not exactly . . . but he went into the shop and came out without a package. Mos' people go into a butcher shop t'buy somethin', don' they?"

"Perhaps he had other business there."

Grammy shrugged. "Alls I know is later Mr. Weber closes the shop t'go to the bank, an' he seemed in a great hurry."

"Thank you, Mrs.—"

"Jes call me Grammy. Is there anythin' else ya need t'know?" she asked, licking her lips.

"No, thank you," Elizabeth said, giving her another fifty cents.

"Thank *you*!" she declared, pocketing the money. "If ya need me again, y'know where t'find me."

Elizabeth watched as Grammy slipped back in through the side door, or "ladies' entrance," of the Thirsty Crow. She wondered where the poor woman slept at night, if indeed she slept at all. Pulling her jacket around her shoulders, Elizabeth headed into Hermann Weber's butcher shop in search of more answers. Perched on the crossbeam of a gas lamp, a lone crow peered down at her with its beady black eyes.

The butcher's memory proved to be distressingly bad—either that or, as Elizabeth suspected, he was hiding something.

"*Nein, Ich habe keinen solchen Mann gesehen*," he said when she asked him about the well-dressed man Grammy had described. "No such man came in today."

"Perhaps your assistant met with him?"

"I have no assistant," he said, wiping his broad pink hands with a bloodstained towel.

Throughout their conversation, he remained steadfastly amiable, which Elizabeth saw not as friendliness so much as a façade designed to allay her suspicions. She left with the distinct impression she had been lied to. What she didn't yet know was why.

CHAPTER NINE

A yellow August moon was rising by the time Elizabeth wended her way home, as the sun sank slowly over the North River. She decided to walk, heading uptown along the Bowery until it bifurcated into Third and Fourth Avenues at Cooper Square. Like every other "square" in New York except Tompkins Square Park, it was far from the geometrical shape its name suggested. It was actually a lopsided trapezoid, at the top of which stood the majestic Cooper Union, where Abraham Lincoln had delivered the stirring speech that later helped him gain the presidency. She could not pass the building without thinking of that night; though she'd been only two years old at the time, her father had attended, and his eyes still lit up when he spoke of it.

Walking up Fourth Avenue, she approached Union Square, where the statue of Lincoln gleamed, stern and tall in the twilight. Though only seven years old when Lincoln fell to an assassin's bullet, Elizabeth still remembered her father's despair. He'd sat staring out the window for days afterward, shaking his head whenever her mother importuned him to eat. Catharina was volatile and given to emotional outbursts, but Elizabeth always saw her father as the tender one, and sometimes wondered whether he had passed some of his vulnerability on to her sister.

She thought about visiting Laura before going home, but a wave of exhaustion convinced her otherwise. With a pang of guilt, she continued north to the Stuyvesant on East Eighteenth Street. Trudging up to her third-floor apartment, she passed a compact young woman coming down. A small black-and-white terrier trotted behind her.

"Why, hello!" she said in a voice as smooth and cool as water.

"Good evening," Elizabeth replied politely, continuing on up the stairs.

"I've not seen you before," the woman said. She was dressed like a bohemian, in a long, colorful skirt and loose, full-sleeved white blouse with elaborate hand embroidery. Thick gold bracelets encircled her thin wrists, and gold hoops dangled from her ears. Her dark hair was long and loose, and her lips and cheeks shone artificially pink in the dim lighting of the stairwell. "Do you live here?" she asked, brushing a strand of hair from her face.

"I'm on the third floor," Elizabeth answered.

"How jolly—my studio is on the fifth floor."

"Oh, you're a painter?" The fifth floor was reserved for artists' studios, but Elizabeth had yet to meet any of them.

"A sculptor, actually. I paint a bit, but I like the feel of clay between my fingers. And you? I'll wager you're a writer."

"I am a journalist for the *Herald*."

"I knew it! With a novel in your drawer, no doubt?"

"Hardly. I dabble in poetry, but—"

"You have always wanted to write a novel, a roman à clef, but are afraid it might offend your family."

Elizabeth laughed. "I fear only offending my readers, due to my poor skill."

"So you *are* working on a novel—capital!"

Coming from anyone else, the young woman's insistence on such sudden intimacy might be impertinent, but her liveliness and intelligence were so attractive that Elizabeth found it impossible to take offense.

"I'm Carlotta," she said. "Carlotta Ackerman."

"Elizabeth van den Broek."

"Very pleased to meet you," she said, seizing Elizabeth's hand. Hers was warm and strong, the skin somewhat rough. "Did you know General Custer's widow lives on the first floor?"

"So I've been told."

"And Calvert Vaux himself, the designer of Central Park! Do you know him?"

"I am afraid I do not. I have not been here long."

"I think it's simply divine—can you *imagine*?"

It was an open-ended question that seemed to require no response, so Elizabeth just nodded.

"Well, I shan't keep you any longer. Come along, Toby!" Miss Ackerman said to the terrier, who had been sitting patiently at her feet. "Good meeting you, Elizabeth van den Broek."

"And you," said Elizabeth, continuing on her way.

"Until tomorrow morning, then—seven o'clock sharp on the steps of the Metropolitan Museum. Don't be late!"

Elizabeth stopped, her hand on the railing. "I beg your pardon?"

"I like to walk Toby in the park. The Metropolitan makes a good meeting place."

"I didn't—"

"Everyone needs a daily constitutional. It does wonders for your complexion."

"But I—"

"I'll bring beigels."

"What is that?"

"You'll see—you will love them! See you tomorrow!" she said, skipping lightly down the stairs, her little dog trotting briskly after her.

Elizabeth stood for a moment, listening to her departing footsteps, before climbing the final story to her flat. She was aware she had just met a singular individual, but had little intention of pursuing a friendship with her, let alone rising at dawn to do so.

And yet when the first rays of sunlight poked through the gap in her rose-damask curtains early the next morning, she found herself wide awake, staring at the ceiling. Rolling onto her side, she pulled the bedclothes over her head, but it was no use. Irritated, she swung her legs over the edge of the bed and slipped her feet into fur-lined slippers, a gift from her mother her freshman year at Vassar.

After a quick ablution, Elizabeth dressed and was out the door in thirty minutes. This time she indulged in a hansom cab—it was early enough that the streets would not yet be clotted with carriages, milk carts, horse-drawn trams, and pedestrians. The sleek chestnut gelding trotted smartly up Park Avenue, and it was just past seven o'clock as they turned west onto Seventy-Second Street. Minutes later they pulled up in front of the museum's entrance on Fifth Avenue.

"It won't open for another two hours, miss," the cabbie said as Elizabeth paid him.

"I am meeting someone."

"Would you like me t'wait, miss?"

"No, thank you," she said, spying the lone figure with the dog in front of the bulky Gothic-revival building. The cabbie tipped his hat and drove away as Elizabeth hurried toward Carlotta.

Toby barked, strained at his leash, and wagged his stump of a tail as Elizabeth approached. Carlotta waved at her. "I was beginning to fear you wouldn't show up."

"I almost didn't."

"You would have missed this," Carlotta said, handing her a small package wrapped in waxed paper, still warm.

"What is it?"

"A beigel, of course! With poppy seeds and butter," she added as Elizabeth unwrapped it, inhaling the soft, yeasty aroma.

"It looks like a giant dough-nut."

"But it's not sweet. Try it."

"Mmm," she said, taking a bite. "Where do these come from?"

"Poland, originally—but these are from my family's bakery on Orchard Street. It's a staple of Jewish cuisine. You are not bothered that I am Jewish, I hope?" she asked in her frank way.

"Certainly not. I would never—"

"Come along, then," Carlotta interrupted, shoving her beigel into a satchel, which she slung over her back. "At this hour we'll have the park to ourselves."

Chewing on the beigel, Elizabeth followed her along the south side of the museum and into the park. The dew on the grass sparkled like tiny diamonds in the morning sun, and birdsong filled the air. Her dark thoughts of the night before evaporated with the mist rising from the meadows as they wandered deeper into the park.

"Toby loves it here," Carlotta said as the dog dashed about, poking his nose into bushes, hedges, and burrows. "What's that?" she asked as they approached a construction area behind the museum, mountains of excavated dirt stacked in neat piles. "Are they expanding the museum?"

"Oh, this must be the site for the obelisk," Elizabeth said.

"Obelisk?"

"Have you not heard of Cleopatra's Needle?"

"I might have read something about it," Carlotta said airily as Toby charged off to investigate the tempting mounds of dirt.

"It's an ancient Egyptian obelisk. There is one in Paris, and London got one three years ago, and now *we* are getting one."

"Why?"

"From what I have read, it is a gesture of gratitude from Cairo."

"I wonder if it's cursed," Carlotta said. "That's going to be a massive hole," she added as they approached. The area was cordoned off by a simple fence made from red rope wound around wooden stakes pushed into the ground.

"I doubt that rope really deters anyone," Elizabeth mused as they surveyed the construction site. The hole was still rather shallow, perhaps six feet deep, but the bottom lay in deep shadow, invisible from the slanted rays of the morning sun. As they walked around to the other side, Toby began barking furiously from behind a mound of dirt.

"Toby!" Carlotta called out, but he ignored her. His barking grew louder and more insistent, interspersed with growls. "Toby, what on earth—" she said, following him.

As she stepped behind a pile of dirt, the dog suddenly went silent. Elizabeth heard a squeal of surprise from Carlotta, then what sounded like a body falling to the ground.

"Carlotta? Carlotta!" Elizabeth yelled, but there was no reply. Panicked, she dashed to the other side of the dirt pile, and saw Carlotta on the ground in what appeared to be a dead faint. Toby stood over her, licking her face frantically.

As Elizabeth knelt beside her, something at the bottom of the hole caught her eye. Shielding her eyes from the sun, she peered down at the object, now visible from this angle. Her breath caught in her throat when she saw what it was. Her first reaction was that she must be hallucinating, but she realized that Carlotta and Toby had seen it, too.

Lying at the bottom of the newly dug hole, wrapped in clean white cloth, was what appeared to be a perfectly pristine Egyptian mummy.

CHAPTER TEN

"So you see it, too," Carlotta said, sitting up and brushing the grass from her hair. "It's not a mirage."

"Not unless we are both hallucinating," Elizabeth said, helping her to her feet. "Are you quite all right?"

"I just fainted. It's nothing."

"You should take care."

"I'm perfectly fine, I tell you."

"You may have some underlying condition—"

"Please refrain from continuing this inquiry. We have something much more pressing to contend with," she said, peering down at the mummy. Toby looked at her expectantly, wagging his stump of a tail eagerly. "It looks like a woman. Do you suppose it's real?"

"It's probably a practical joke," Elizabeth said, dropping to her knees beside the hole. "But there's only one way to find out. Give me a hand, would you?"

"You're not . . . No, you can't!"

"I can and I will."

"But surely we should inform the police."

"And so we shall. But first I'd like to take a closer look."

"You don't really believe there's . . . a *body* in there, do you?"

"If there is, it is a story my editor cannot afford to refuse. Hand, please."

Carlotta helped lower her down into the hole, which was surprisingly cold and damp. *Like the grave.* Elizabeth shivered as she stepped toward the still figure in white. Her conviction that it was a practical joke faded as she approached—the closer she got, the more it looked like an actual body.

"Be careful!" Carlotta called down to her. "It might carry any manner of diseases." Elizabeth looked back up at them as Toby started barking again. Carlotta grabbed hold of his collar. "Be quiet, Toby!" The terrier obeyed, perching at her side obediently, but his body strained forward eagerly.

Elizabeth swallowed hard and leaned over the motionless figure. She half expected it to abruptly come to life, and thought that if it did, she, too, would faint. Bending over, she hesitantly touched its shoulder. It was stone cold—no warmth of life coursed through the still limbs, but she realized at once something she had not allowed herself to believe. She was in the presence of a recently deceased person. It was also clear the body was that of a woman.

She knelt beside it and laid her entire hand on its arm. It was not pliable, the flesh still under the influence of rigor mortis, but the stiffness was already beginning to fade. The faintly sour smell with a hint of sweetness emanating from beneath the cloth wrappings left little doubt. As the realization sank in, she recoiled, her stomach contracting in an involuntary impulse to retch.

"Well?" said Carlotta. "What is it?"

Elizabeth swallowed, the acid rising in her throat. "We must notify the police—now."

An hour later, the two women stood beneath an umbrella held by a patrolman while a small phalanx of policemen carefully removed a stretcher containing the body. The weather had deteriorated, the sunny skies of early morning giving way to a drizzling rain. Shivering, Elizabeth watched as the white-clad figure on the stretcher was laid on the back of a police wagon. Even the horse seemed uneasy with its cargo, fidgeting as the men secured the stretcher before covering it with an oilcloth to protect it from the rain.

Overseeing the process was Detective Sergeant (DS) William O'Grady, who, after listening carefully to the women's account, had requested they remain until the body could be removed. Elizabeth had reluctantly agreed but was increasingly anxious to leave. She did not want to be late to work but was even more worried that a reporter from a rival paper might get wind of the story and scoop the *Herald*. Carlotta had said little, her natural ebullience dimmed by the disturbing discovery. Even Toby seemed chastened. He sat quietly next to Carlotta, his little body pressed up against her shins.

After supervising the wagon loading, DS O'Grady walked over to them. Of medium height, with curly black hair and gray-green eyes, he was the epitome of a New York policeman. The hills of the Emerald Isle rolled through his speech, as was true of so many of his colleagues on the force, where Ireland was heavily represented. The rain was coming down harder now, bouncing off the shoulders of his oilcloth duster and dripping from the bill of his cap onto the tip of his nose. Flicking away the droplets, he rubbed his hands together for warmth.

"Is there anythin' else you ladies can remember? You didn't happen to catch sight of any unsavory characters loiterin' about, did you?"

"I'm afraid not," said Elizabeth. "The park was quite empty. By the look of it, the body was put there sometime in the night."

"How can you tell?"

"It appears to have been rained on, but the ground beneath it was dry."

"Well spotted, Miss . . . Sorry, what was your name again?"

"Elizabeth van den Broek."

He looked at Carlotta, who was shivering. "And you, Miss . . ."

"C-Carlotta A-A-Ackerman," she replied through chattering teeth.

"Did you notice anythin' at all, then, Miss Ackerman? Anythin' out o' the usual?"

"N-n-no."

"We need to get her to a warm place," Elizabeth said. "Before she catches her death."

"Do you live nearby, then?" he asked Carlotta.

"N-n-no. I live downtown."

"I can take you to the station house and give you a nice hot cuppa. Get you some blankets."

"W-what about Toby?"

"The lads will take good care of him. Prob'ly feed him more than they should, like as not. What about you, miss?" he asked Elizabeth.

"I must go. I'm already late for work."

"An' where would that be, miss?"

"The *New York Herald*."

He frowned. "The newspaper?" The police were wary of the press, and the feeling was mutual, even though many reporters relied on police informants and weren't above paying them handsomely. It was strictly against the rules, of course, but it was a mutually beneficial arrangement.

"Yes. I'm a reporter," she said.

"I'd offer you a lift, but we're goin' in diff'rent directions."

"I can find my own way, thank you."

DS O'Grady tipped his hat and looked over at the police wagon. Having secured the body, his men were looking rather miserable in what had now become a light but steady downpour.

"Come along, then, miss," he said to Carlotta. "You can ride up front."

She turned to Elizabeth and hugged her impulsively. "Do take care. I shall call on you tonight."

"Oh, you needn't—"

"Don't be silly. Of course I will," Carlotta said firmly. She appeared to be somewhat recovered from her shock, and resolutely followed DS O'Grady to the wagon. Elizabeth watched them drive away before she crossed the short distance to Fifth Avenue to hail a cab. She looked over her shoulder a few times as she walked, and couldn't escape the feeling that her shivering was from more than just the rain.

CHAPTER ELEVEN

Elizabeth sat silently as the cab rattled through rain-drenched streets, staring out at the droplets bouncing off the cobblestones like tiny, crazed dancers. The rain drained the color from the city, softening the sharp edges, dulling the constant hum and hubbub to a low thrum.

Carlotta's impulsive display of emotion had been touching, but Elizabeth was uncomfortable with such an intimate gesture from someone she had just met. Still, she told herself, the circumstances were exceptional, and Carlotta was understandably upset. Elizabeth was rattled herself, but sensed she had a steadier emotional gyroscope than Carlotta, who seemed to have a more erratic personality.

By the time Elizabeth arrived at the *Herald*, the downpour was increasing, and she entered the building just as a thunderclap shook the streets of lower Manhattan. Jagged shards of yellow lightning streaked across the sky as she climbed the marble staircase to the second floor. She imagined the poor woman they'd found in Central Park, battered by the elements as she lay alone in her makeshift grave, and was glad she and Carlotta had discovered her before the storm hit.

"Of course, it was really Toby who found her," she murmured as she approached the second-floor landing.

"What did you say?" said a voice, and she looked up to see Simon Sneed staring at her, a smirk on his sleek, smooth-shaven face. Even his lack of facial hair, unremarkable on anyone else, made him seem more threatening. Lacking the softening effect of a beard, the sharp lines of his chin and cheekbones were more pronounced, giving him the look of a large, predatory bird.

"Nothing. I was just, uh, muttering to myself," she replied, making to step around him, but he blocked her way as a loud thunderclap shook the skies. She jumped a little, and he moved even closer. She could see the pores on his long, pointed nose.

"You'd best be careful—some people might take that as a sign of a disordered mind. I understand it runs in the family."

Rage coursed through Elizabeth's body. How did he know about Laura? And for that matter, who else at the *Herald* knew? She fought an impulse to punch him in the face, scratch his eyes out, push him down the stairs. She did not trust herself to speak or even move, so she remained silent. Her eyes narrowed as she stared him down, arms crossed, as if daring him to speak again. She could feel sweat gathering under her collar and on the palms of her hands.

After what felt like an eternity but was probably only a moment or two, there was the sound of a heavy tread behind her, and she turned to see her editor, Karl Schuster, lumbering up the stairs. A large man, he moved like one, but his footsteps were quicker than usual—not a good sign.

"There you are!" he said, frowning. "Where have you been?"

"I will explain, but not here, sir," she replied firmly, a little surprised at her own self-assurance. "We can talk in your office."

Schuster appeared taken aback, his blue eyes widening in surprise. "Very well," he said, continuing up the stairs. But after a few steps, he stopped and glared at Sneed. "What the devil are you staring at?"

"Nothing. I was just—"

"If you've nothing to occupy your time, I'm sure I can find something for you."

"Y-yes, sir," Sneed sniveled. "I was just going—"

"Not fast enough!" Schuster bellowed. "Be on your way, man!"

Elizabeth smirked at Sneed as he hurried down the stairs, catching his eye as he passed. The glare he returned would have been enough to shoot terror down a more timid spine, but Elizabeth was feeling her oats after asserting herself in front of her editor. It was only after she'd followed Karl Schuster into his office that she wondered whether she might regret her boldness.

"Now then," Schuster said, plopping into his chair, "I need to speak with you about your story on the Astors."

"Sir, I need to speak to you about another matter—" she said, standing in front of his desk.

"For one thing, it's too literary. All the details about Mrs. Astor's personality and the like."

"You see, the fact is—"

"Nobody cares about that. They just want to know what people wore, what they ate, and how much it cost."

She brought her fist down on the desk. "Sir!"

He swung his head up to look at her, no doubt stunned at her impertinence. "Now see here, Miss Van den Broek—"

"The Astors be damned!" she declared. "I have an *important* story. If we act quickly, you can scoop all the other papers."

"What could you possibly have—"

"If you will just *listen*, I'll tell you. But first I want an assurance."

"What kind of assurance?"

"That you will let me cover this."

"What sort of story is it?"

"It involves a murder—lurid, exotic. A front-page, banner-headline kind of murder." She was breathless, excited, and surprised at her ability to think of a poor dead woman as a springboard to her own career success.

"A banner headline?" he said dubiously.

"Well, front page, certainly."

"Tell me about it."

"I need your promise first."

"Who discovered the body?"

"I did. But before I tell you anything more, your promise, please."

"There are no female crime reporters at the *Herald*—or any other paper I know of, for that matter."

"Then I shall be the first."

"I'll have to get approval from Mr. Bennett."

"There isn't time. As we speak, the *Times* or the *Sun* could be onto the story. Or maybe the *Staats-Zeitung*," she added with a little smile.

He frowned at the mention of his former place of employment. "*Guter Gott.* How can I justify this to Mr. Bennett?"

"Sure it takes but a drop of courage, Herr Schuster. *Haben Sie keinen Mut?*"

He sighed deeply and ran a hand through his untidy thicket of blond hair. "Follow me," he said, launching his bulky body from his chair with surprising speed.

Heart pounding, Elizabeth followed him down the hall to the crime editor's desk. Fast-talking and brusque, Kenneth Ferguson had the kind of hard-bitten accent she associated with the City of Brooklyn, mixed with a hint of his Glasgow roots. He had been at the paper since the reign of Gordon Bennett Jr. began, and was a famously energetic and eccentric editor. Rather short in stature, with a keen, sharply lined face, he had a long beak of a nose with an edge like a razor, and dark, deep-set eyes. He wore his thick brown hair long, parted in the middle, and kept an unlit, half-chewed cigar between his teeth at all times. He was in constant motion, an extreme of kineticism that had left his compact body shorn of any excess fat, like a long-distance runner.

"Schuster!" he exclaimed when he saw Karl and Elizabeth. "What brings you t'our little den of thieves?" His remark bore more than a little truth—some of the reporters who worked for him were not that far removed from the criminals they wrote about. One of them was rumored to have murdered a man in Kentucky.

Schuster patiently repeated everything Elizabeth had told him. When he finished, Ferguson removed the cigar from his mouth and looked her up and down. "Well, I'll be. You have some gall, young lady. Is high society not exciting enough for you, then?"

Elizabeth returned his gaze. "'The blood more stirs to rouse a lion than to start a hare.'"

"Ha! Quote Shakespeare at me, will you? Capital! I like her," he told Schuster, who nodded glumly. Shoving the cigar back in his mouth, Ferguson turned to Elizabeth. "Well, since you seem to be fond of the Bard, let me say it's a valiant flea that dares eat his breakfast on the lip of a lion. Is that what you're after, then? Danger, excitement?"

"Justice," she said. "I am after justice. If that involves daring the lion to eat me, so be it."

"Ha! She's a firebrand, so she is," he told Schuster.

"Do we have a deal, then?" she asked.

He grinned, the cigar dangling precariously between his teeth. "It would be churlish to deny such a stalwart and determined young woman as yourself. Assuming, of course, the story turns out to be as newsworthy as you claim."

"I believe I did not mislead you on that account," she said, and told them everything she and Carlotta had seen.

Karl Schuster's eyes grew wider with each twist of the story, but Ferguson displayed little reaction. Arms folded, head cocked to the side, he listened carefully to every word. When she had finished, the two men exchanged a look.

"That is indeed quite a story," said Ferguson. "What was the name of this detective sergeant?"

"William O'Grady, Twenty-Third Ward. The station house is on East Eighty-Sixth Street and Fourth Avenue."

Karl Schuster shifted his weight onto his back foot. "If you will excuse me, I have work to attend to."

"By all means," Ferguson said. "Good day, Schuster."

"Good day to you. And good luck," he added, with a glance at Elizabeth.

"Are you going to run my article on the Astors?" she asked him.

"With some rewrites, we should be able to run it in tomorrow's edition."

"Do you require me to—"

"I shall do my best to amend it appropriately."

When Schuster had gone, Kenneth Ferguson rubbed his hands together vigorously. "Now then, I shall have to cable Mr. Bennett, but if he agrees, we will run this on tomorrow's front page."

James Gordon Bennett Jr. spent much of his time in Paris, where he was establishing an international branch of the *Herald*, but it was widely believed he had fled to Europe because of a scandal involving his fiancée, socialite Caroline May, in 1877. Apparently he had arrived late and drunk at a party at her family's mansion, and proceeded to relieve himself in the fireplace. (Some claimed it was a grand piano.) But whatever the location of his makeshift latrine, the engagement was off, and Bennett left for Europe shortly afterward.

"Before we proceed," Ferguson said, "I must remind you that it is not too late to change your mind."

"Why should I want to do that?"

He removed the cigar stub and perched on the front of his desk, arms folded. "The notion of being a crime reporter may sound very exciting, but I feel it is my duty to warn you that you may find it more than you bargained for. And perhaps not a profession ideally suited to young ladies such as yourself."

"Mr. Ferguson," she said slowly, "I have no doubt you mean well. And by 'young ladies such as yourself,' I assume you refer to my privileged and rather sheltered background."

"Well, you are—"

"It is true that I have had little strife in my twenty-two years. But I have witnessed firsthand New York's stunning inequalities—as would anyone who bothers to open their eyes and look at what life in this city is really like. As a judge's daughter, I grew up with the notion that it is imperative to oppose injustice. If I may be even a small part of making the city a safer place for the oppressed, then I consider that *my* duty."

"I take your point, and I expected no less than such a response. But I felt compelled to warn you."

"Now that you have fulfilled *your* duty, may we proceed?"

"Very well. You may begin writing your story. Be sure to include your own role in the affair—readers will find a first-person account most interesting."

"How shall I—"

"Just tell them what happened. Try to make them feel they are there with you." He pulled a pocket watch from his vest. "And now I must get over to Ah Ken's before he closes for lunch."

Ah Ken was a Chinese man who ran a very popular smoke store on Park Row. Elizabeth had passed it by many times, and Mr. Ken never lacked for customers, partially because of his large and varied inventory. But his jovial personality and unfailing good humor played a part as well. Many Chinese immigrants viewed white New Yorkers with well-founded suspicion, but Ah Ken's friendly manner and witty observations had made him something of a celebrity to locals and tourists alike.

Without further comment, Ferguson charged out of the office. Elizabeth retreated to her own desk in the reporters' pool, pencil in hand, a sheet of clean white paper staring blankly at her. Outside the window, the rain had slowed to a drizzle, but the wind still whipped at the boats on the East River. She watched a sleek schooner battle its way southward, headed for New York Harbor, the wind pushing heavily against its sails. The Brooklyn ferry chugged its way eastward, dark wings of smoke hovering over its long black chimney, charcoal against the gray sky. She thought of Walt Whitman, and of the many souls aboard that vessel—her countrymen, fellow citizens all.

The thought of being responsible for this front-page headline made her light-headed. She was keenly aware of the ticking of the elaborately carved wall clock with roman numerals just above her desk. *Tick-TOCK, tick-TOCK.* She could feel the minutes slipping away and, along with them, her chance at the one thing she wanted more than anything else in the world. She looked down at the blank paper. *Try to make them feel they are there with you.* She took a deep breath and bent over her desk.

> The Mummy Behind the Museum
>
> Were it not for the curiosity of a small spotted terrier, the body of a woman in Central Park might have suffered the additional indignity of being soaked in a rainstorm. As it was, someone saw fit to wrap her in white cloth before depositing her in the large hole being dug for the Egyptian obelisk known as Cleopatra's Needle. Whether or not this personage is responsible for her untimely demise has yet to be determined, but the ghoulish treatment of her body can leave little doubt that a monster is at large in our city. Perhaps this is his idea of a joke, but if so, it is a hideously twisted one.

She was aware that her prose was more than a little purple but also knew that highlighting the story's macabre elements would help sell papers. She was still scribbling furiously half an hour later when Kenneth Ferguson returned.

Striding over to her, he leaned one hand on her desk and gave a triumphant smile. "I had a bit of a time convincing Mr. Bennett, but when he learned you discovered the body . . . well, he's a good enough newsman to know a good thing when he sees it."

That he could speak of their mutual employer with such condescension spoke of his own supreme self-confidence. She had yet to meet a man with such an unshakable opinion of himself.

"Now then," he said, "what have you written?"

"I am not finished, sir."

"Let us see what you have so far."

"But—"

"You have completed at least a page, have you not?"

"I have."

"Come along, then—we've no time to waste."

She handed him what she had written, sweat prickling the fine hairs on the back of her neck, watching as he read, the cigar stub still inexplicably in place between his teeth. She wondered whether he used the same one day after day, keeping it in a box on his desk.

"Hmm, not without merit," he said after what seemed like several hours, though it was probably less than a minute. "You are not entirely without talent, Miss Van den Broek. Oh, I believe Mr. Bennett knows your father?"

"Yes, indeed, sir."

"That did not hurt your cause, I'll wager. Well, then," he said, snapping his fingers, "you'd best be off."

"Beg pardon, sir? Where am I to go?"

"To report the rest of the story. Who is the victim, are there any suspects, and so on. This Sergeant O'Grady—he knows you now, does he not?"

"Detective Sergeant O'Grady—yes, sir, he does."

"Tell him our readers deserve to know if there is a madman at large, that it is a matter of public safety—et cetera, et cetera."

"And if he does not care?"

"Work your wiles on him. Use your feminine charm. No man is impervious to the entreaties of a beautiful woman—at least not for long."

He said this in such a matter-of-fact, impersonal way that Elizabeth did not feel he had any designs on her; it was merely a practical assessment. In spite of his keen intelligence and energy, there was something bloodless about Kenneth Ferguson. He was like a bird dog on a scent, all business, with nothing to distract him from his goal. She feared—and hoped—that she was a bit like that herself.

"Take young Freddy with you. He's not our most experienced photographer, but he's eager, and has shown some ability."

"Freddy Evans?"

"You know him, then?"

"I do."

"And you get on well enough?"

"Yes, sir."

"Then what are you waiting for?"

"What of my article, sir?"

"I shall finish it myself."

"But—"

"Tut-tut—you've done the hardest part. I'll only clean it up a bit and put in any missing bits of information. And do not be concerned—your name will appear first on the byline."

"That is very generous of you, sir."

"Nonsense. It's simply good business practice. It does not do to mistreat people—it will only turn on you in the end."

"Well spoken, sir," Elizabeth said, but he had already turned his attention elsewhere. Stuffing her notebook into her satchel, she left the office to find Freddy. Aware of eyes on her as she hurried down the hallway, she turned to see Simon Sneed glaring at her with such malice that she was overtaken by a wave of dizziness. Pulling air deep into her lungs, she returned his gaze with as steely a stare as she could manage before continuing on her way. In spite of her confident stride, she knew that if looks could actually kill, she would be dead.

CHAPTER TWELVE

It was perhaps a measure of Elizabeth's sheltered life that she had never before set foot in a police station. When she entered the sturdy stone building on East Eighty-Sixth Street, she was unprepared for the level of activity she encountered. Patrolmen scurried in and out, charged with purpose, full of their own self-importance. The constant shuffle of leather soles on the polished floor reminded her of her trips through Grand Central Depot when taking the train to and from Vassar.

Everywhere there were buttons—in single or double rows down the fronts of navy-blue uniforms, decorating the back panels of knee-length tunics, along collars or cuffs, shiny brass buttons that matched the polished badges worn over the policemen's hearts. And on everyone, the same mustache, or so it seemed—thick and bushy, trimmed just over the upper lip, adding to the impression of uniformity.

As Elizabeth stood amid the hustle and bustle, DS O'Grady approached her. Unlike his colleagues, he sported no facial hair, and the sight of his clean-shaven face was comforting.

"Good afternoon, Miss Van den Broek," he said, tipping his hat, with its broad, flat top and stiff leather brim. Some of the beat patrol officers wore bulkier helmets, decorated with a brass insignia.

"Is it always so chaotic here?" she asked, pleased that he remembered her name.

"You've arrived durin' a shift change, I'm 'fraid. It should calm down presently."

Elizabeth looked around for Freddy Evans. He had been right behind her when she entered the station but seemed to have disappeared.

"That's funny," she murmured. "Where did he—" But at that moment, the front door was flung open and Freddy entered, out of breath, clutching his camera in one hand, a bulky tripod under the other arm.

"There you are," she said. "What happened to you?"

"Sorry, miss," he said, panting. "I saw an amazin' shot jes as we were goin' in. I called after you, mind, but you didn' hear me."

O'Grady frowned at the sight of the stocky photographer, with his freckled face and Cockney accent. "And who might this be, then?"

"This is Freddy Evans, staff photographer at the *Herald*."

"And exactly why have you brought along Mr. Freddy Evans, staff photographer? For that matter, to what do I owe your presence here?"

"I should think it was obvious," she said, coloring. "I was the one who discovered—"

"Not here," he said, looking around nervously. "Come with me."

Elizabeth and Freddy followed O'Grady into a corner room at the back of the station, which was being used as a storage area. Boxes of paper and printed forms were stacked along one wall; in front of them were a few broken chairs and a desk missing a leg. A cracked truncheon lay in the corner. She shuddered, imagining the crunch of bone under heavy blows, broken skulls, and other gruesome injuries. She had seen enough of police behavior to know that her fantasies were not altogether unreasonable.

Apart from an unlit gas wall sconce, a small window was the room's only source of light. Hazy summer sunlight filtered in through the grimy glass, bathing the room in a gray gloom. O'Grady seemed glad for the relative darkness as he closed the door behind them.

"He knows about the . . . body, then?" O'Grady asked, indicating Freddy.

"I explained it to him on the way over. Why do you ask?"

"How much do you know?"

"Only what I saw in the park."

O'Grady bit his lip and looked from Elizabeth to Freddy. "The thing is . . . it's a very strange case, so it is. Unlike any I've seen."

"That's not surprising."

"This is a very disturbed criminal."

"I should think that anyone who would wrap a dead woman up like a mummy—"

"No, there's more."

"More?" she asked, suddenly aware of how stuffy the room was, the air dusty and stale. "What do you mean?" she croaked, her throat suddenly dry.

O'Grady looked at Freddy. "Can he be trusted?"

"Detective Sergeant O'Grady, I am here as a representative of the *Herald*, and so is Freddy. So anything you have to say . . ."

O'Grady removed his cap and ran a hand through his wavy black hair. Elizabeth could not suppress a shiver of pleasure at the sight of his abundant locks. "Y'see, the report just came in from the coroner's office."

"Was the cause of death determined?"

"There was evidence of strangulation, but that wasn't what killed her."

"Then . . . what did she die of?" Freddy asked, his voice barely audible.

O'Grady crossed his arms, as if protecting himself from their reaction. "Exsanguination."

Freddy's already pale face went a shade whiter. He swallowed hard, his Adam's apple bobbing up and down like a cork. "Is that—"

O'Grady fixed his gaze on the young man. "Someone drained her of all her blood."

Freddy gasped.

Elizabeth took a deep breath and let it out slowly. "Is it logical to assume the same person who did that also wrapped her up and left her body where we found it?"

She uttered these words with such a lack of emotion that O'Grady stared at her, as if startled by her coldness. The truth was, the situation affected her deeply, but as a reporter—and a woman, to boot—she wanted to project an air of professionalism she hoped would garner his respect.

"Aye," O'Grady said slowly, "unless he had an accomplice."

"Have you identified the woman?"

"No. Underneath the wrappings, she was . . . unclothed, I'm afraid. Beggin' pardon, miss," he said, a flush creeping up his cheeks.

"Do any of them know this yet?" she asked, with a nod toward the closed door, on the other side of which were the policemen of the Twenty-Third Ward.

"No one knows except myself and the captain. But he's out at the moment."

"I would like to see the body."

"I don' have the authority—"

"You just told me your captain was not available."

"Yes, but—"

"You are the lead investigator, are you not?"

O'Grady chewed on his thumbnail and stared at the floor. "I don't know if—"

"It's like this, Detective," Elizabeth said. "In order to solve the crime, you need to identify your victim. What better way than to put her picture on the front page of the *Herald*?"

"But—"

"I'd like to remind you it was I who discovered the body and brought it to your attention promptly. I could have contacted my editor first, but I came to you straightaway." She declared this boldly, though aware of her specious reasoning. By the time she alerted the *Herald*, someone else might have stumbled upon the body, but she hoped this would not occur to DS O'Grady.

"So you did," he said. "But as to viewing the body, per'aps I'd best wait for the captain—"

"We have no time to waste. The *Herald* will go to press in less than two hours. I promise you, Freddy will be tasteful in his photographs . . . won't you, Freddy?"

He nodded eagerly. "So 'elp me God."

"You must protect the public from this monster," Elizabeth continued. "Let us help you, please. The *Herald* has always cooperated closely with the police department." This was a bald-faced lie and could not be said of any newspaper in the city. But she hoped its very boldness would help it slip by.

There was a knock on the door. "What is it?" the detective barked. The door opened a crack to admit the smooth, pink face of a tall, very young policeman. "Yes, Jenkins?" O'Grady said impatiently.

"Beggin' pardon, sir, but I was just wonderin' if you wanted your tea."

Elizabeth had heard from her father often enough that the preferred beverages of men on the force were whiskey, beer, tea, and coffee, in that order. They would drink gin, rum, or cider in a pinch—they would even drink grain alcohol, if it came to that. But most policemen earned enough to stay away from the stuff served in blind tigers or flophouses that would rot your gut or actually cause blindness.

"I'll be out presently, Jenkins," O'Grady said. "Close the door behind you."

Elizabeth seized the opportunity to press her point. "Well, Detective?" she said, taking a step closer to him. "What do you say? Will you let us help you bring a murderer to justice?"

The detective ran his hand through his hair again and sighed. "I s'pose it couldn't hurt."

"That's the spirit!" Elizabeth said. "You won't regret it."

"I hope you're right, miss," he said dubiously. He handed her a business card.

Detective Sergeant William O'Grady
23rd Ward, East 86th Street
New-York City

The old-fashioned spelling of the city caught her eye as she slipped the card into the pocket of her fitted jacket.

"Ask to see Vic Novak—short for Viktor. He's Polish, but he's all right. If you're lucky, he'll be the morgue attendant on duty. Give him this an' tell him I sent you."

"Much obliged, Detective," Elizabeth said. She hurried from the police station, followed by Freddy Evans, lugging his cumbersome equipment. She did not look back, as if doing so might turn her to stone.

CHAPTER THIRTEEN

The city morgue was located on the grounds of Bellevue Hospital, which Elizabeth was familiar with from her visits to her sister. That did not make her any more eager to visit the rather gruesome place. The rain had stopped, but the streets were sodden. As Freddy was towing his photography equipment, she hailed a cab, promising the cabbie a large tip if he reached Bellevue quickly. He took the challenge, splashing through Second Avenue traffic, skittering through intersections, past streetcars, ragpickers, and trade carts, intimidating pedestrians with a loud whistle. He seemed pleased enough with Elizabeth's payment, tipping his hat before tapping his long whip, sending his bay gelding into a smart trot up First Avenue.

As Elizabeth stood in front of the main building, with its handsome brick, gabled mansard roofs, and fanciful turrets, it occurred to her, not for the first time, that it resembled a fairy castle more than a hospital. Her eyes strayed to the north wing, where her sister was a resident in the newly established "pavilion for the insane." She hadn't visited Laura for a few days, and her sense of duty was even stronger than her affection for her beleaguered sister. But she had not been lying when she told DS O'Grady that the paper would go to press within hours, and she wanted to include a picture of the mysterious mummy in her story.

"Y'know where the morgue is, do you?" Freddy asked as he followed her into the building, tripod on one shoulder, carrying the camera in the other hand.

"I do not, but such information is easily procured."

A stern-looking matron, whose face appeared to have been starched along with her uniform, regarded them dubiously when Elizabeth made her inquiry. The woman directed them toward a dim, narrow corridor leading to the back of the building. They passed the ambulance bay, where they saw two horse-drawn wagons, similar to the ones the police used to cart away suspects and criminals. "Bellevue Hospital" was stenciled on the side of each vehicle. While visiting her sister, Elizabeth had learned that Bellevue had pioneered the use of hospital ambulances. It was the brainchild of a Civil War staff surgeon who, in 1869, adapted methods of transporting wounded from the battlefield to use in a crowded metropolis.

The morgue, though not large, was well ventilated and lit by a wall of tall windows along one side. Gas wall sconces added to the illumination. Half a dozen metal tables were lined up against one wall, each containing a recently deceased person. A metal water pipe hung over each table, suspended from the ceiling, emitting a constant spray of cold water on the cadavers. Though naked, each one was draped in a long white sheet, for the sake of propriety. What Elizabeth assumed was the deceased's clothing hung on wall pegs behind them.

Viktor Novak was indeed on duty, but he was not alone. A group of well-dressed people hovered over the pale form of a young woman. A handsome middle-aged woman Elizabeth took to be the deceased's mother wept inconsolably, wringing her hands, while a young boy stood awkwardly next to a prosperous-looking man with a top hat and muttonchops. His aristocratic face was fixed in an attitude of stoic suffering; it was clear he was the family patriarch. There was something unseemly about witnessing their grief. Elizabeth felt profoundly uncomfortable, and judging by the way he shifted from one foot to the other, so did Freddy.

Viktor Novak seemed to have no such compunctions, however. Though his round face wore an expression of compassion and patience, Elizabeth couldn't help but notice that he was tapping his left foot while stroking his wispy blond beard. The mourning family lingered for some time, finally turning from their vigil to leave their loved one to Mr. Novak's ministrations.

The patriarch pressed some coins into the morgue attendant's hand as he left, and Novak bowed respectfully. Elizabeth dug some money from her purse, thinking it might behoove her to tip before requesting his help.

"Death comes to all, alas," Mr. Novak said rather cheerfully after the family had gone, pocketing the coins he had just received. "Still, it's a pity—so young, and so comely. Now then, miss," he said, turning his attention to Elizabeth, "how may I be of service?" Though he had a hint of a Polish accent, his English was perfect. Of medium height, he was slight of build, with a cheerful, round moon face, unusually pale eyes, and dusty blond hair with matching beard and eyebrows. He was neatly dressed in a mustard-colored sack suit with a matching vest and cravat; a bowler hat perched rakishly on his head.

"I'm Elizabeth van den Broek, and this is Freddy Evans."

"How d'you do?" Freddy said, tipping his cap.

"Viktor Novak. Good to know you. Welcome to my little kingdom."

"Kin I ask a question?" said Freddy. "What's wif the water?" he asked, indicating the spray coming from the suspended ceiling pipes.

"Oh, that's to keep the bodies as fresh as possible while they're in here. Most of them are on ice in that room," Novak said, indicating an entrance to another chamber. "This is where people come to view their recently deceased loved ones, and bodies tend not to do too well once they start to warm up. Hence the cold water—though after a day or two, it does tend to give them a rather bloated appearance. I try not to keep them in here for long. Speaking of which, will you excuse me for a moment?" he said, stepping out into the hallway.

Moments later he returned with another man dressed in a white coat similar to the ones worn by the hospital physicians.

"This is Mr. Benjamin Higgins, hospital orderly and ambulance driver extraordinaire. And, when he has the time, my trusty assistant. This is Miss Van den Broek and Mr. Evans."

Higgins tipped his hat. Rather taller than average and fair skinned, he was powerfully built, with a broad-shouldered, stocky body. His eyes seemed too small for such a massive head; otherwise his face was pleasant and unremarkable beneath thinning light-brown hair.

"Pleasure t'meet you both."

"How d'ya do?" said Freddy.

"Have you come to photograph the dead folks?" His voice was higher than Elizabeth would have expected from such a large, strong-looking man. His accent was working class, though with an edge that suggested some education. His face radiated intelligence.

"Not exactly," Freddy said. "We're—"

"Pardon me," Novak interrupted. "But Mr. Higgins' time is quite valuable."

Freddy's freckled face reddened. "S'all right—I understand."

The morgue attendant turned to his colleague. "Mr. Higgins, if you would be so kind as to remove Miss Wells to the next room, I would be very grateful. I don't think she is very *well* at the moment," he added, almost under his breath. "I know," he said in response to Elizabeth's surprised look. "It's terrible, but I can't seem to stop myself."

He sighed as Mr. Higgins gently lifted the dead woman from the table, wrapping the sheet around her so as not to reveal anything unseemly. "Death is a very grave matter—there I go again, you see?" He stepped aside as Higgins passed with Miss Wells in his arms. Now then," he said, turning to Elizabeth, "how may I help?"

She handed him the card DS O'Grady had given her.

"So Detective O'G sent you, did he?"

"He sent his regards."

"Did he, then? Well, well. Be sure to return the greeting, won't you?"

"I shall."

"Fine fellow. A bit on the serious side, perhaps—but a *dobry człowiek*. A good man. How do you know him?"

"We are collaborating on a case together."

"You work for the police?"

"I am a reporter for the *New York Herald*."

"A lady reporter—well, strike me dead! No offense," he said to the bodies on the slabs behind him.

Elizabeth exchanged a glance with Freddy. Viktor Novak was an odd duck, but they needed him. She slipped the money into his hand, which was curiously soft and smooth, like a woman's. "I would greatly appreciate your assistance."

"Your wish is my command," he replied with a wink. "Right this way."

He led them into the second, larger chamber just as Higgins emerged from it. "Thank you kindly," Novak said with a tip of his hat.

"My pleasure," Higgins responded. "Good meetin' you both, an' good luck with whatever yer lookin' for."

"Thank you," Elizabeth said, following Novak down the steps into the room. It was lined floor to shoulder height with wooden cabinets with metal hinges that appeared to be oversized iceboxes. Each door bore a slot for a label card; some were empty, but most contained a white index card with a name written in neat cursive letters. While waiting for Mr. Novak to find the right drawer, Elizabeth read several of the notecards.

Mr. Theodore Hines
Miss Wynneth Greggs
Infant Boy, Unknown

Though she wondered how Mr. Hines and Miss Greggs had met their demise, it was the unknown infant who tugged at her heart. Had he been abandoned by his mother to die? Or had his mother met the same sad fate, her identity gobbled up by a vast, uncaring metropolis that allowed women and children to starve in the streets? Even Freddy seemed chastened by the dozens of names lining the walls. He leaned against a granite pillar at one end of the room, his heavy camera slung over his shoulder, while Mr. Novak perused the rows of names.

"Ah, here she is!" he exclaimed, examining one of the cards. Seizing the handle of the drawer, he gave it a yank, and it slid smoothly forward on metal rollers.

Elizabeth wasn't sure what she had expected, but at the sight of the pale white face, her breath caught in her throat. Even in death, it was easy to see the young woman's beauty—her heart-shaped face and small, pointed chin making her appear even younger than she probably had been in life. But what struck Elizabeth most of all was the curious shade of white-blond hair—the same color as on the woman she had seen from the train. The sight of her lying cold and still removed any doubt. Elizabeth had been a witness—perhaps the only one except her killer—to her death. She said nothing; for now, at least, she thought it was best kept to herself.

A simple white sheet covered the slim form, which appeared even paler than the bodies in the other room. A purple bruise encircled her porcelain throat, but her face was unmarred. Elizabeth turned to see Freddy preparing his photography equipment, setting the camera on the sturdy wooden tripod.

"I understand she has not yet been identified," Elizabeth said as Viktor Novak gently brushed the long pale locks from her face.

"No, poor thing," he said, his face expressing sorrow for the first time since they had arrived. "Though, sadly, that's not so unusual here. You'd be surprised at how many people who turn up here leave unclaimed by relatives or loved ones."

"'Scuse me," said Freddy from behind his camera. "I'm ready t'go now, so if you don' mind steppin' away for a moment, I'll get on wiffit."

"By all means," Novak said, as he and Elizabeth removed themselves to the side of the room. Novak withdrew a pipe from his jacket pocket. Filling the pipe, he lit and drew on it thoughtfully while Freddy worked, moving the camera to get various angles of the dead girl's face.

"There is clearly evidence of strangulation, but I understand the coroner has ruled the cause of death to be exsanguination," Elizabeth remarked.

"It's most extraordinary," Novak replied. "There are no obvious gaping wounds, as one might expect—no gunshots or deep knife slashes, but I did find one curious thing."

"Oh? What's that?" Elizabeth asked as Freddy waved to them.

"All right, I'm finished," he said, moving from behind his camera. "I think I got enough shots that at least one of 'em should turn out."

"Allow me to show you," Mr. Novak said as they approached the girl on the metal slab. Turning her head gently to one side, he pointed to the left side of her neck. "Here."

Elizabeth bent over the body, inhaling the faint, slightly sweet aroma of decay. An unusual design had been carved into the side of her neck: three intersecting circles, comprised of swirling lines forming increasingly tight concentric circles.

"What is it?" she asked.

"It seems to be a symbol of some kind."

Freddy gulped hard. "Was it . . ."

"It appears to be the wound through which her blood was drained. It is positioned right over the jugular vein."

"Can you take a clear picture of it, Freddy?" Elizabeth asked.

"Yes, miss," he said, positioning his camera.

"You seem very knowledgeable on medical matters," Elizabeth remarked to Novak.

"I studied medicine in hopes of becoming a coroner, but my family's financial situation . . . Luckily, I found good employment here."

Elizabeth nodded. "How long would it have taken for her . . . ?"

"It would not take long to die of blood loss. And she may have been unconscious when he . . . well. The really curious thing, though, is that her body was drained of virtually all its blood."

"What kinda fiend would do somethin' like that?" asked Freddy.

"A vampire," said Novak.

Elizabeth looked at him, thinking he was making a dark joke, but he was not smiling.

"Vampires don't exist," she said. "They're just folklore." But even as she said it, her words sounded as hollow and empty as the poor shell of humanity lying on the cold metal slab in front of her.

CHAPTER FOURTEEN

"That fella was awful cheery, weren't he?" said Freddy as they bounced along a bad stretch of road in the back of a hansom. Elizabeth had sprung for another cab, though she hoped Kenneth Ferguson would reimburse her after he saw Freddy's pictures and heard her report.

"Perhaps that's what allows him to do his job day after day."

"Kinda odd, though, bein' so jaunty wif all those dead folk 'round."

"It's better than succumbing to melancholia."

"I s'pose," he said, hugging the tripod closer to his body. There was barely room for the two of them and all his equipment in the vehicle's cramped interior. With every bump, the tripod's wooden legs rapped against his shins.

"Melancholia" was the original diagnosis the doctors at Bellevue had given Laura, a term Elizabeth viewed as woefully inadequate to describe her sister's torments. They'd soon amended their opinion, after observing her engaged in heated conversations with invisible people, imagining her room was filled with mythical creatures, and believing that the nurses were intent on killing her—although, having met some of the flintier members of the senior nursing staff, Elizabeth could understand her sister's concern.

"D'you think it's a vampire what killed 'er?" asked Freddy as the cab jostled over a pothole.

"There is no such thing."

"What about Ludwig the Bloodsucker?"

"He's just a myth."

Ludwig the Bloodsucker was allegedly a short, hirsute German who prowled lower Broadway, preying on the drunks and barroom brawlers who frequented dubious establishments such as Bismark Hall and the House of Commons. He supposedly had "hair growing from every orifice," according to one supposed eyewitness; according to another, he "quaffed human blood as if it were wine." Elizabeth had always thought the stories harmless nonsense, the sorts of rumors common in large, dangerous cities such as New York.

Freddy adjusted the camera on his lap. She didn't envy him, dragging heavy equipment around all day. "If that isn't the work of a vampire, then what was it made those marks on 'er neck? And why drain all 'er blood?"

"That wasn't the work of a vampire," she said as the cab pulled up in front of the *Herald*. "It was someone seeking to create an authentic Egyptian mummy. The question is, why?"

The air was still damp from the storm, and an uneasy haze settled over lower Manhattan as the sun dipped around the southern tip of the island on its journey from the East River to the mighty North River.

Elizabeth was about to enter the building with Freddy when she heard a voice behind her.

"Miss Van den Broek?"

She turned to see John Jacob Astor IV, dressed in a gray-striped frock coat and matching trousers. Even though the clothes were expensive and well-tailored, they seemed ill suited to his angular form. He didn't seem to know what to do with his hands, and his elbows looked as if they wanted to burst from the prison of his coat sleeves.

"Why, Mr. Astor," Elizabeth said, surprised.

"Please, call me Jack," he said, nervously removing his top hat.

"What are you doing here?"

"I came to see you, of course," he replied, his fingers twitching upon the brim of the hat.

"You gave me no warning of it."

"I rather thought I might surprise you."

"You certainly have accomplished that."

Astor nodded at Freddy. "Hello there—I'm Jack Astor."

"Forgive me," said Elizabeth. "This is Freddy Evans, my colleague. Freddy, this is John Jacob Astor IV."

"Please, call me Jack."

"Hello, then, Jack," Freddy said with a frown, looking him up and down.

"You're a photographer, I see—how jolly."

"Yeah. Luggin' this stuff around all day is real jolly. If you'll excuse me, I'd best be getting on. We have a deadline," he added, with a meaningful glance at Elizabeth.

"I quite understand," Jack said amiably. "Very nice meeting you."

"Well, Mr. Astor," Elizabeth said when Freddy had gone, "what did you want to say to me?"

"Jack, please," he said, with the pleading eyes of a puppy. "I suppose I just . . . Well, I just wanted to see you."

"Well, now you have seen me."

"The thing is . . . I know you think I'm just a child, but chaps like me, you see, we only get to meet girls in our own circle, so to speak, and, well, they're . . ."

"What?"

"Boring." He heaved a deep sigh and stared at his immaculately polished maroon shoes, of the finest Italian leather. They gleamed like ripe apples in the August sun.

"I doubt that."

"But it's true! They have no verve, no drive, no . . . *juice*."

"I see," Elizabeth said, suppressing a smile. She had always hated being talked down to when she was a child, and did not want to simply dismiss young Jack's opinions.

"They may be young, but they're already as dry as little wisps of winter wheat."

"You're quite the poet, Mr.—uh, Jack."

"And they're silly and shallow and care only for pretty things. Knowing that you'll never have to make your way in the world . . . it *does* something to a person, you know."

"I should imagine it does," she said, crossing her arms. "Of course, you could do something about that—find a vocation of some kind."

"You think I'm just a boy," he said, scuffing the toe of his shoe on the sidewalk.

"You are only sixteen."

"Yet I'm a man all the same. At least, I feel like one."

"I am delighted to hear it," Elizabeth replied, glancing wistfully at the people coming and going from the Herald Building. "And now if you'll excuse me, I must go inside."

He sighed again, so loudly that several people passing by looked at him. "I envy you. You have a *purpose*, an aim in life, whereas I . . . It seems I am only an idle, lovesick boy."

He leaned in toward her, and she took a step backward. "You will be a man soon enough, Mr. Jack Astor. In the meantime, I suggest you cast about for something to give your life purpose and focus."

"Perhaps you can help me."

"I am extremely busy at the moment. I have—"

"Yes, yes—you have a career. Oh, Miss Elizabeth—may I call you that? You are so . . . *admirable*."

She couldn't help but smile. He was annoying, but there was something touching in his fervor that inspired her protective instinct.

"I don't know about that, but I must be going. Thank you for taking the time to stop by."

"May I see you again?" He had the open, trusting face of a child, an innocence possessed only by those who have never suffered from a broken heart.

She raised her hands in surrender. "I don't suppose I can stop you."

"Perhaps when you are not quite so occupied—"

"Good day, Mr. Jack Astor," she said, and went inside the building.

Kenneth Ferguson was in his office with Freddy when she arrived. She did not mention Jack Astor's unexpected appearance, but from the look he gave her, she guessed Freddy had said something. She decided to let sleeping dogs lie.

When she told Ferguson of their expedition to the morgue, he rubbed his hands together vigorously. "Well done, both of you!" He turned and patted Freddy heartily on the back. "Now, get down to the darkroom and develop those prints right away! You can leave your tripod here—I'll look after it."

When he had gone, Ferguson scooped some papers from his desk and thrust them at Elizabeth. He attacked the simplest action with great vigor, as if by injecting every moment with his own considerable energy, he could bend the outcome of events to his will.

"Here is your article, with a few emendations—no, *suggestions*—from myself." He glanced at the ever-present wall clock, its thick black hands churning off the minutes until the next deadline. Newspapers ran on deadlines much as Bowery drunks ran on cheap liquor—both were inescapable, ever present, and immutable. "Now finish it yourself. You have two hours. Feel free to use my desk."

Elizabeth could not suppress her astonishment at this—it was unthinkable that an editor would offer a lowly reporter the use of his own desk. She took it as an indication of his eagerness to publish the story. Granted, it had all the elements to guarantee a spike in sales—to "move papers," in newspaper parlance—sex, violence, and mystery. The thought of her first real story being featured prominently in the *Herald* made her giddy.

"Thank you, sir," she said firmly. "But I think I'd sooner use my own."

"Fine, fine. Off ye go, then—good luck! Let's see what you can do."

Clutching the papers, Elizabeth made a rapid retreat from the office, heading back to her desk. As she rounded the corner to the main corridor, she saw Karl Schuster in a side passageway, having an intense discussion with another person. Schuster's bulky body blocked her from seeing who it was until she was nearly past them. Turning her head at the last moment, she caught a glimpse of his companion, which immediately caused a sinking feeling in the pit of her stomach. Karl Schuster was deeply engaged in conversation with Simon Sneed.

Elizabeth increased her stride, looking away before Sneed could catch her eye. She had no intention of giving him the satisfaction of sneering at her. Still, she could not help wondering what poison he was filling Schuster's head with. Sneed was a potentially dangerous enemy, but everyone had their weakness—or so she believed. She just had to find out what his was.

The reporter pool was thinning out; her colleagues were either on assignment or filing their stories with their respective editors. The large, airy room was half-empty, and at this late hour in the day, the only sounds were the scratch of pencil lead over paper, mixing with the usual street noises so ubiquitous in New York. As she settled at her desk near the window, Elizabeth could make out the faint clip-clop of horses' hooves, and the cries of street vendors competing with the caws of seagulls swooping in from the harbor, scavenging for food.

"Fresh eels, get your fresh eels here!"

"Bi-caaaw! Bi-caawww!"

"Chess-nuts! Hot roasted chesss-nuts!"

"Bi-caaawww!"

Elizabeth fished half a dozen pencils from her desk drawer and laid them out in front of her. She always sharpened them first thing in the morning so they were ready when she needed them. Fountain pens were elegant, but she did not like pausing to refill them and found pencils more efficient. Bending over her work, she engaged in the kind of intense concentration made possible by the presence of a looming deadline. Blocking out all external distractions, she immersed herself in the strange events of the past two days.

> The body was wrapped all in white, laid out carefully, like an offer to the gods. Strangely, it did not seem out of place at first, as though it somehow belonged in this sacred little corner of the enormous green park.

An hour later, she raised her head, stretched, and put down the last of her pencils, having worn each of them down to the wood. Looking up at the clock, she saw she had half an hour left, but she had already written and rewritten the article, erasing and scratching out words, and scribbling so furiously in the margins that she hoped her editor could read it. Standing up decisively, she swept up her papers and headed toward the exit. It was only as she wove her way through the sea of desks that she realized the room was now nearly empty.

Kenneth Ferguson was in his shirtsleeves, his coat jacket hanging on a wall peg behind him. His feet were up on his desk, a fresh unlit cigar dangling from the corner of his mouth. Elizabeth was relieved to see his trip to Ah Ken's store had provided him with a less disreputable-looking prop. The door was open, but she didn't think it was appropriate to march straight into his office, so she knocked on the doorframe.

"Ah, Miss Van den Broek!" he said, swinging his feet down. "Come in, come in! Now then, what have you got for me?"

Elizabeth's hand trembled slightly as she handed him the article, but Ferguson didn't seem to notice. He snatched it eagerly and placed it on the desk, bending over the pages, his lips moving from time to time as he read. She stood in the middle of the room, watching, painfully aware of the ticking of the wall clock behind him. There was something odd about the mechanism; it had an extra beat, so that instead of *ticktock*, it said *tick-aTOCK, tick-aTOCK*. She knew it was just a machine, but it seemed to be mocking her efforts to rise above the expectations of her sex and do something important with her life.

"Well, well," Ferguson said at last, brushing cigar ash from his sleeve. "I do believe you have something here, young lady. It's quite a story, with all its macabre elements. The coroner's report is indeed quite shocking. Perhaps the headline should read 'Vampire Loose in the City?'"

Elizabeth frowned.

"What? You don't agree?"

"Well, sir . . ."

"Speak up! We haven't got all day, you know."

"For one thing, vampires don't exist."

Ferguson let out a bark of a laugh. "Of course they don't! But the great unwashed don't know that, do they? They believe in all sorts of nonsense."

"But surely we shouldn't encourage such ignorance."

"Blah! Our job is to sell papers, not educate the public."

"Why shouldn't we seek to educate them?"

Ferguson gaze her a puzzled look, then burst into a fit of laughter. "By Jove, you are a precocious lass, I'll give you that! But educate the public—in this city? Why, we might as well try to teach pigs how to fly!"

"I don't see why we shouldn't try."

"I'll tell you what I'll do. If you come up with a suitable headline, I'll consider using it instead."

Elizabeth gazed out the window. She could see the glint of sunlight on the East River, the low evening rays snaking across the island as the sun sank over New Jersey to the west. Seagulls swooped and cawed and swiped any bit of food they could find. Even the birds in New York were rapacious—pigeons pilfered scraps on every street corner;

robins, sparrows, and jays prowled Central Park, along with predators like hawks and owls, always in search of their next meal.

She turned back to Ferguson. "How about 'Murderous Fiend Preys on Defenseless Woman'?"

He stared at her, then blinked twice. "Good God. You're—you're just—"

"What?"

"Well, a woman, for Christ's sake."

"Mr. Ferguson, I just viewed the naked body of a dead murder victim in the city morgue. Do you suppose that because I am a woman, I am faint of heart?"

"Obviously not. 'Murderous Fiend' it is, then. It's good. What's more, it will sell papers."

"There's something else."

"Yes?"

"I believe I witnessed her murder."

Ferguson's eyes opened so wide she could see the tiny blood vessels on his lids. "And when were ye plannin' on telling me *that*?" he asked, his Glaswegian accent thickening.

"I did not want to until I was fairly certain."

"And are ye?"

She told him everything she had witnessed from the train, including the location of the building. He was silent for a few moments, chewing on the insides of his mouth, in lieu of the cigar stub.

"I see," he said finally.

"Should we include it in the article?"

"For the time being, no."

"Why not?"

"For one thing, I don't want to put you in any danger."

"But we could just say 'a witness'—"

"Do you not think the killer might very well surmise it was you?"

"Then how do we proceed?"

"Investigative reporting."

"How so?"

"We follow the same leads the police might to identify the suspect."

"But do you not think we should tell the police what we know?"

Ferguson peered at her. "Forgive me for saying so, lassie, but you have a lot to learn about the way things work in this town."

There was a knock on the door. Elizabeth opened it to find a breathless Freddy, clutching photographic prints in both hands. A thin sheen of moisture still lay on the surface as he held them up, waving them back and forth to hasten the drying process.

"Ah, Evans—come in, come in!" Ferguson said. "And close the door behind you, eh? We don't want anyone getting wind of this story before we go to press."

"Yes, sir," said Freddy, giving the door a shove with his foot.

"Now then, laddie, what have you got for me?"

Freddy held up the prints so they could all see. Elizabeth could not suppress a sharp intake of air when she saw the stark image of the dead woman lying on the metal table, covered in only a white sheet. Even though she had been there in person not three hours ago, the camera had captured something beyond what she had seen with her naked eye. Perhaps she had been distracted by Mr. Novak's personality or the novelty of her first trip to the morgue. Only now, seeing it in black and white, stripped of any nuance of color, did she fully appreciate the utter desolation, the sheer tragedy, of such a young woman coming to such a violent end.

Willing herself not to cry, she looked at Kenneth Ferguson, noting with some surprise that his eyes appeared to be damp.

"Will it do, sir?" asked Freddy.

"Yes," said Ferguson, his voice thick. "It will do."

CHAPTER FIFTEEN

He stood outside the Water Street bawdy house, rain dripping from his chin and nose, inhaling the familiar, sickening odor. He knew it well, from early childhood. It was the smell of sin. The sickly, sticky smell of lust and longing, of lasciviousness and desperation. He could not remember a time when he did not shiver with disgust at the aroma that permeated the damp, rat-infested tenement where he lived with his mother. He was no different from the other children who played in the streets surrounding the hellhole known as Five Points, that dreaded nexus of crime and poverty and vice. They were all ragged and hungry; they all ran wild, if they were lucky enough to escape the sweatshops, factories, and mills.

He could not, however, escape the brothels. His mother's chief source of income was the men who staggered, swaggered, and stumbled into the various establishments that catered to the slews of sailors, soldiers, and souses seeking solace in the arms of women who were carriers of any number of venereal diseases. Sometimes his mother entertained her "clients" at home. Lying in bed at night, he was forced to listen to the grunts and groans of men who were, to him, no better than animals—coarse, sweaty sailors who stank of fish blood and seawater, drunken merchants and businessmen who often didn't bother to remove their clothes, dropping their pants to their knees before plunging into his mother with a fierce, primal lust.

He hated them all. He wanted to kill them, to grind them into dust beneath his shoe, to obliterate them from the face of the earth. He dreamed of whisking his mother off to another life, one in which she would never have to submit to the lewd embraces of strangers. He imagined a mansion on the water, upstate somewhere, with a long, sloping lawn like the ones he had seen in magazines—the kind of yard rich people had, one that served no purpose except to display the owner's wealth.

But seeing her more and more dependent upon the bottles she brought home from saloons, gin mills, or the corner grocery—downtown, liquor was available nearly everywhere—he despaired that their life would ever change. Inevitably, her looks began to fade. Her skin coarsened, her eyes were perpetually bloodshot, and fluid gathered in her once-slim ankles. Her patrons changed, too—they became older or much younger, poorer, and even less refined. Sometimes they were rough with her. He lay in the tiny alcove that served as his bedroom, separated from the main room by only a thin, worn curtain, holding his breath as he listened for heavy footsteps on the dimly lit staircase as yet another stranger invaded their dingy tenement. Afterward, he covered his ears to block out the sound of his mother whimpering. He despised the men who hurt her, and he despised her even more for letting them.

The sound of braying, hollow laughter floated from the Water Street brothel. He was familiar with that, too—it was the wail of lost souls, people covering their misery with the cacophony of false enjoyment. Shaking himself from his reverie, he forced his feet to move forward, as seagulls swarmed along the quay, their beady yellow eyes scanning the skies, before diving down to scavenge for scraps. He felt as if he'd spent his entire life scavenging for scraps, grateful for leftovers, the pickings of other people's pleasure.

But no longer. Now he felt powerful, strong, dangerous. He was Osiris the Reborn, God of the Underworld, Judge of the Dead. It had come to him in a dream, and he knew when he awoke that it was no simple dream—it was prophecy. He flexed his arms, feeling the hard, taut muscles beneath the layers of fabric. The girl had been given to him to explore his power, and he had bestowed upon her the honor of becoming a goddess. She was the first, but she would not be the last.

He looked at his watch. It was time to go home—Cleo would be waiting for her dinner.

CHAPTER SIXTEEN

After leaving the *Herald*, Elizabeth returned to Bellevue. The last feeble rays of the sun crept across the building's façade as she stepped into the main foyer for the second time that day. Visiting hours had technically ended, but the staff knew her and might let her spend a few minutes with her sister. The nurses told her that Laura was in the patients' common room, a large, airy space filled with wicker chaises and board games.

The hospital was emptier at this hour, as evening descended over the city. Her footsteps echoed through the tiled corridors as she walked through the ward. There were a handful of other patients in the room. An old man in a red checkered bathrobe hovered over a chessboard, talking loudly to an imaginary opponent. A young man in blue-striped pajamas and slippers paced back and forth at the far end of the room, laughing and uttering outbursts that sounded like gibberish to Elizabeth, but each vocalization made him laugh even harder.

Laura was sitting in a wicker chair, legs tucked under her, staring out the window. An unopened book lay in her lap. She had always loved to read, and since her illness, Elizabeth had noticed that the mere presence of a book seemed to cheer her up. Clad in a simple white frock, hair loose around her shoulders, her pale face illuminated by the dying light of dusk, she looked like a Renaissance painting by a Flemish master. The gas lamps had been lit, and the room was suffused with a rich golden glow.

Gazing at her sister's profile, Elizabeth could see the map of their Dutch ancestry—the prominent mouth and full lips, delicate nose, wide forehead, and slightly recessive chin. Laura turned toward her, and the emptiness in her gaze sucked the breath from Elizabeth's body. She had an urge to flee this sad place, and for a moment she sympathized with her mother, who hated visiting Laura. Forcing a smile, she took a step forward.

"Hello, Lolo." It was their childhood nickname, the way Elizabeth had said her older sister's name when she was too young to pronounce it properly.

Laura smiled at her vaguely, as if trying to remember who she was. Scratching her nose, she stretched and yawned. "Did Ewoud send you?"

"Who's Ewoud?" Elizabeth recognized it as an archaic Dutch name.

"He's the little man who lives under my bed. I think he may be a kabouter." Kabouters were the Dutch equivalents of Irish leprechauns—shy gnomelike creatures who lived underground in hills or caves.

"No," Elizabeth said. "Ewoud didn't send me."

She was used to Laura's odd behavior, though it was hard to tell whether it was the illness or a side effect of the pills she took. Her medication consisted mostly of sedatives—bromides, valerian, laudanum, and morphine. Elizabeth had once come upon the staff using ether to subdue her sister. When she threatened to report them to her father, who had donated significant amounts to the hospital, they vowed never to do it again. But she did not trust them and did her best to monitor Laura's treatment.

Elizabeth approached slowly. She knew from experience that Laura could be frightened by abrupt movement. "I brought you something," she said, holding out a copy of *Little Women*, which included both Alcott's original tome by that title and its sequel, *Good Wives*, recently published together in one volume. "Remember how you used to read it to me?"

Laura examined the volume as if she had never seen a book before. "You always reminded me of Jo," she said dreamily. "I am more like Beth. I shall die young, just like her."

"Do not say that," Elizabeth said. "You will live a long life." Removing her bonnet, she took Laura's hands in her own. "I went to a garden party at Mrs. Astor's this week."

"Mother must have been very jealous," Laura said with a little smile. "What is Mrs. Astor like?"

"Very intelligent and forceful. It is little wonder that she is such a commanding presence."

But Laura's gaze was focused on a point behind her. Elizabeth turned to see a young man in an olive-green tweed suit with a matching tie and scarlet waistcoat. The stethoscope protruding from his coat pocket identified him as a doctor.

"Hello there," he said, smiling. Of medium height, he had a broad forehead, curly dark hair, and a long, rectangular face with symmetrical features that would be considered handsome on any man. His lips were full and sensual, his nose thin and straight, but it was his eyes that made his face memorable. Large and deep set, they were the most extraordinary shade of green. Even in the subdued lighting of the dayroom, they shone like polished jade.

Laura's affect brightened in his presence. Energy flowed through her limbs, and a shy smile flitted across her face. "Dr. Jamison. You didn't forget me."

"How could anyone forget you, Laura?" he said softly.

Her shy smile was replaced by a sly one. "I wish Nurse Stark would," she said, referring to the head matron, an implacable and humorless monolith in a starched white uniform.

Dr. Jamison laughed, showing slightly uneven but perfectly white teeth, unusual in a city where smoking and heavy consumption of coffee were common. He turned to Elizabeth. "Forgive my breach of etiquette. I'm Hiram Jamison, the new resident. And you must be Laura's sister, Elizabeth."

"Indeed I am," she replied, drawing herself up a bit grandly. She wasn't sure why she wanted to impress this young doctor and was embarrassed to realize she was sucking in her stomach.

"I knew it the moment I saw you. You have the same well-defined zygomatic bones."

"Zygo—"

"Sorry—cheekbones."

"Ezekiel in the valley of dry bones," Laura murmured, twirling a strand of hair around her finger.

"Your sister seems to have an encyclopedic knowledge of the Bible," Dr. Jamison said.

Elizabeth frowned. "That's odd. She's not really religious."

Laura began to rock. "Jerusalem will fall. The time to atone is now."

Dr. Jamison approached her and laid a hand on her shoulder. At first she flinched, but then she grabbed it and pressed it to her cheek. "Jerusalem . . . will fall," she muttered, holding on to it tightly.

"You're safe here," he said, pulling his hand gently away to check her pulse. He took out his stethoscope and listened to her heart and checked her eyes, though what he was looking for, Elizabeth did not know. Laura submitted meekly to the exam; she actually seemed to enjoy it. Returning the stethoscope to his pocket, he turned to Elizabeth. "She wasn't this bad yesterday."

"Her fits come and go," she answered, pulling up a chair to sit next to her sister. "They always have, ever since she became ill."

"And when was that?"

"Is it not in her medical record?" Elizabeth asked, stroking Laura's hair. The physical contact seemed to calm her; her eyelids grew heavier, and she seemed to doze off.

"Alas, the case histories here leave much to be desired. I am working to change that, but it is difficult. I regret to say many of the staff here—"

"Do not consider lunatics to be quite human."

"I dislike that word. But yes, you are right."

"What word do you prefer? 'Insane'? 'Maniac'? 'Hysteric'?"

"I prefer thinking of them as patients, just as we might regard someone with a broken leg or a case of typhus."

"That is very enlightened of you," Elizabeth said, not without some bitterness.

"I consider the current attitude toward mental patients to be woefully antiquated—barbaric, even. But I am just one man."

"You are an alienist, then?"

"I prefer 'psychiatrist.' It is actually a much older term, and it means one who treats the soul."

"What is wrong with 'alienist'?"

"It emphasizes the notion that mental patients are separated, or alienated, from themselves and others."

"Is that not true?"

"But not very hopeful. And in truth, I am at present a general practitioner, though my chief interest is psychiatry." He cocked his head to the side. "You are an inquisitive young lady, Miss Van den Broek."

"My mother says I am contrary."

He laughed. "Does she indeed?"

"I have always been contrary. My mother says it is most unladylike."

"Perhaps, but also most intriguing."

Elizabeth was annoyed to feel a blush creep into her cheeks. She gave a little cough and looked away. She drew a small boar-bristle hairbrush from her purse and began working through the tangles in her sister's hair. Laura snuggled up against her like a puppy. Her breathing became more regular as her eyes gradually closed.

"Have they increased her medication?" Elizabeth asked. "She seems very lethargic."

"The sun is setting. Some people experience drowsiness at this hour."

"My sister is a natural night owl. Whereas I prefer mornings, she was always most alert in the evening."

"I have only just begun my residency at Bellevue, but I will find an answer to your question."

"I am most grateful."

"Where can I reach you?"

This struck Elizabeth as inappropriately forward, and she frowned.

"I beg your pardon," he said quickly. "I did not mean to be overly bold."

"Indeed," she replied. "I shall return for another visit soon enough, and you may tell me then."

"I look forward to it," he said with a little bow, and turned to leave.

"What do you make of my sister's condition?" she asked, realizing she did not want him to go.

"She obviously suffers from a serious mental condition."

"Do you believe she can be cured?"

A loud noise came from the other side of the room—it sounded like a piece of furniture falling. Elizabeth turned to see the chessboard table lying on its side, the pieces scattered all over the floor. The young man in the blue pajamas stood over it, a triumphant smile on his face. Even in the dim light, Elizabeth could see the deep pits and scars on his face, likely remnants of a bad case of smallpox.

The old man stared at him in disbelief, then launched himself straight at the lad, arms flailing, screaming with rage. "I'll kill you! So help me God, I'll eat your liver!"

Unprepared for the attack, the younger man fell backward, hitting the floor hard, as the elderly fellow threw himself on top of the lad, pummeling him with his fists. Elizabeth and Dr. Jamison rushed to pull him off, and she was surprised at the strength in the old gentleman's wiry arms. Writhing and wriggling to free himself from their grasp, he nearly succeeded.

"You dirty dog! You cur! I'll tear you apart! Unhand me!" he shouted. "Let me go, I say!"

The commotion attracted the attention of two burly orderlies, who rushed into the room. One of them seized the elderly gentleman and restrained him; the other plucked the young man from the floor by the scruff of the neck, hauling him to his feet with one hand.

"What have you two been up to now?" said the larger of the orderlies, a bald giant with a shiny, shaved head. With his heavily tattooed forearms and single gold earring, he looked like a pirate. He even sounded like one. "Well?" he demanded. "What's been goin' on, then? Or do I need t'pound it outta you?"

"There will be no need for that," Dr. Jamison said, stepping forward.

"I ain't seen you on the ward yet," the orderly replied, squinting at him.

"Dr. Hiram Jamison. I'm the new resident."

"Well, Dr. Hiram Jamison, you ain't been here long enough to know how things work. Hey there!" he said as the elderly man attempted to free himself. "Where do you think yer goin'? One more move outta you and it's a padded room fer the night!" he added, wrenching the patient's arms behind his back.

"He's an old man!" Elizabeth cried. "There is no need to be so rough with him."

"He may be old, but he's cagey—ain't ya, Sam?" the orderly asked the elderly gent, who gnashed his teeth and twisted in his captor's grip.

"Cur! Dirty dog," he muttered, glaring at the young man in the blue pajamas, who, though being restrained by the other orderly, offered no resistance, a meek expression on his pockmarked face.

"Ezekiel in a river of bones," Laura murmured from behind them. "Jerusalem will fall."

Elizabeth turned to see her walking unsteadily toward them. Hurrying to her side, Elizabeth clasped Laura in her arms and guided her back to her chair. "It's all right," she cooed. "Everything will be all right." Even as she said the words, she felt like a liar. More than anything in the world, she feared that, for her sister, things would never be all right again.

CHAPTER SEVENTEEN

By the time the orderlies had departed with the two patients, Laura was calm and seemed to be getting sleepy, so Elizabeth and Dr. Jamison escorted her to her room. The private room their father had secured for her had a magnificent view of the East River. It was filled with personal effects and objects: a stuffed giraffe from their father, a carved mahogany jewelry box, a watercolor of a daffodil Laura had painted in school.

Dr. Jamison went to check on other patients while Elizabeth helped her sister get ready for bed. After she changed into her nightgown, Elizabeth tucked her into bed, just as Laura had done for her when they were children.

"Would you like me to read to you, Lolo?"

Laura stretched and yawned, snuggling deeper under the covers. "You should go home—no doubt you are very tired." She reached for Elizabeth's hand, squeezed it, and closed her eyes. Her palm was cool, the skin smooth and dry.

It was a curious aspect of her disease that at times she appeared utterly normal. It was as if a curtain were lifted to reveal the gentle, loving sister Elizabeth had always known. For a long time she'd been seized by hope at these glimpses of Laura at the onset of her illness, believing for a moment that the delusions and terrors had fallen away like autumn leaves in October. But these periods never lasted. All too soon the voices reappeared, and her sister's odd behavior would return—the muttering and inappropriate laughter, the strange fantasies and delusions. The dark cloud of her illness, it seemed, was never far away. When Elizabeth finally realized this bitter truth, she no longer clung to her illusion that Laura would suddenly "snap out of it" and be her old self once more. But she did not lose hope that a cure was someday possible.

"Go home," Laura murmured. "Ewoud will keep me company."

Elizabeth gazed at her sister, looking so serene, her yellow hair spread over the pillow like a scattered sheath of summer wheat. It was hard not to imagine they were in their childhood bedroom on an ordinary summer night, with their parents downstairs. Their father would be smoking his pipe, going over legal briefs, and their mother would be at the piano. Elizabeth could almost hear the soothing strains of Brahms' *Lullaby*—sometimes their mother would play them to sleep, and that was their favorite. For years Laura and Elizabeth slept in the same room—they had their own bedrooms but found comfort in each other's presence.

A soft knock on the door jolted her back to reality. She turned to see Dr. Jamison standing just outside the room. "Is she asleep?"

"I believe so," Elizabeth said, and tiptoed from the room. Laura did not stir as she turned down the gas lamp and pulled the door closed behind her.

"She calmed down quite a bit," Dr. Jamison said. "Did you administer laudanum?"

"I do not approve of excessive use of sedatives."

"I agree. Too often they are used to make patients more pliable, with little thought to their effect on their general health. Has she mentioned Ewoud to you?"

"Ah, yes—the little elf who lives under her bed." Elizabeth sighed. "This is a new fantasy, I take it?"

"Yes. At least she seems to take some comfort from him. Some of her other imaginings are much more disturbing."

As she walked down the hallway toward the exit, Dr. Jamison followed. She was not altogether displeased by his presence but, like any well-bred young woman, took little heed of it, striding briskly down the dimly lit corridor, illuminated by gas wall sconces on either side.

"Would it be too bold to offer to accompany you to your door?" he asked as they approached the lobby.

"Thank you, but I am quite capable of seeing myself home," she said, donning her bonnet before stepping outside. She had removed it during her visit, as it was too hot to wear indoors. But of course no fashionable woman would think of venturing out in public without a proper head covering. Though she often found societal rules wearying, she dutifully tied the ribbons under her chin.

"The city is not safe at night," Dr. Jamison said as they descended the front steps onto First Avenue. She was surprised at how balmy it was outside; the warmth of the day had not yet dissipated, and the storm had cleared the air. Moths fluttered around the gas lamps above them, their frail wings reflecting white in the glowing light. Behind them, the East River was calm, a few boats gliding beneath a pale gibbous moon.

She stood for a moment, admiring the beauty of the night. "How could there possibly be any danger abroad on a night like this?"

"Evil does not cease to exist merely because of fine weather."

"You sound like my mother. She is constantly warning me of the perils of New York."

"She is right. Please allow me to escort you home."

"Very well," she said, feigning resignation, though she felt a quite different emotion.

Placing two fingers between his teeth, he produced the loudest whistle she had ever heard. A passing hansom cab swerved abruptly toward them, nearly colliding with a carriage in the cabbie's haste to procure a fare.

"Where did you learn to whistle like that?" she asked as the cab slid to a stop in front of them.

"From my grandfather," he said, holding the door open for her.

The cabbie looked down from his perch, waiting for instructions.

"The Stuyvesant, please," she said. "East Eighteenth—"

"Very good, ma'am," he said, tipping his hat. "I know where it is."

"Was your grandfather a physician, too?" she asked Jamison as they rattled down First Avenue.

"Uh, no," he replied, adjusting his cravat. "How do you like the Stuyvesant? I hear it is quite commodious, not to mention fashionable."

The change of topic was not lost on her. "Fashion does not concern me, as my mother is constantly harping upon it," she replied. "But yes, it is very well appointed."

"I understand from your sister that your father is Judge Van den Broek," he said as the cab turned east on Twenty-Third Street.

"You have heard of him?"

"I know he has a reputation for integrity in a city where such a thing is rare."

Elizabeth gazed out the window at a young couple strolling arm in arm. The man's head was inclined toward the woman, as if he were listening intently to what she was saying. Elizabeth imagined her parents as that young couple, in the early days of their courting. Something in the young man's attitude reminded her of her father; he was so obviously enamored with his companion. Even after many years of marriage, her father remained dazzled by his glamorous and talented wife. In fact, Catharina's ability to inspire the love of such a good man was one of the things Elizabeth most admired about her.

The young couple passed beneath a streetlamp, the light falling on them like a protective golden beam, and Elizabeth silently wished them well. Happiness was such a fleeting thing, and it touched her to see the flush of young love, even if it lasted no longer than this late-summer evening.

She turned to Dr. Jamison, feeling the heat of his body next to hers. "What do you make of Laura's condition? Do you believe she can be cured?"

"I am only in my second year of residency, so I am hardly an expert."

Elizabeth sighed deeply.

"What is it?" he asked.

"Though I chide myself for it, I sometimes feel angry at my sister. I know her condition is not her fault, and yet . . . sometimes I wish she would just pull herself together."

"That strikes me as perfectly natural."

"Am I wicked for having such thoughts?"

"You are human. You must not punish yourself for thoughts you cannot control."

A silence passed between them, as the cab rattled on, and then Elizabeth said, "You mentioned you only just arrived at Bellevue."

"I spent my first year at Bloomingdale."

"My parents wish to send her there as soon as a bed becomes available. The grounds are very lovely, are they not?"

"They are indeed."

"Yet you left after a year," she said. "Did you not like it there?"

"I wanted to be at a proper hospital, where there was a spirit of innovation, medical research, and advances in patient treatment."

"And Bellevue is such a place?"

"It is. Do you know of Dr. Stephen Smith?"

"Was he not one of the health reformers responsible for taking on Tammany Hall?"

"He accused them of being behind much of the poverty in the city. It is said he helped take down Boss Tweed." Jamison became animated as he warmed to his subject. His eyes glittered, and his body tensed with excitement. "He is the most singular man, a true pioneer. As city health commissioner, he established a national vaccination campaign, was a founder of the medical college, and has done much for the plight of the poor. It is men like him that make Bellevue such an extraordinary place. Did you know—"

"I beg your pardon," she said, "but I believe we have arrived."

The cab pulled up in front of the building, and Jamison leapt out, holding the door for Elizabeth.

"How much do I owe you?" he asked the cabbie.

"That'll be twenty-five cents, sir."

As Jamison was digging the money from his pocket, Elizabeth stepped forward and gave the man thirty cents. "Please, keep the change," she said, closing her purse.

"Thank you, miss," the cabbie said. Turning his horse around, he flicked his whip lightly and trotted off into the night.

Dr. Jamison frowned. "I must protest. We agreed—"

"I consented to your escorting me home, not to paying my fare. Where do you reside?"

"I have rooms near the hospital."

"This is over a mile out of your way."

"It is a fine night. I shall enjoy the walk back."

"I should think you have better things to do with your time."

"I must dispute that. I can think of no better use of my time."

"Good night, then," she said, digging her key from her purse and opening the front door.

"Good night."

"Thank you for seeing me home," she said, turning to him with a smile. "And now you know where to find me."

Before he could respond, she stepped inside, closing the door behind her. But she stood peering out the lobby window at his retreating form, as he passed in and out of the pools of light beneath the gas lamps on East Eighteenth Street. Sighing, she turned and climbed the staircase leading to her third-floor apartment. She did not waste much time getting into bed, but tossed and turned restlessly, unable to sleep, her bedroom bathed in the pale light of the waxing moon. Finally, she got out of bed and closed the damask curtains to block out the light.

She lay in bed for some time, hands behind her head, staring up at the ceiling, sleep still evading her. Something had changed—the air felt different, fuller somehow, as if charged with a vague but exhilarating sense of possibility. When sleep finally claimed her, she dreamed of wandering dimly lit hallways, looking for her sister, only to find her wrapped like a mummy at the bottom of a deep and freshly dug grave.

CHAPTER EIGHTEEN

Elizabeth was awakened by a pounding on her apartment door. Alarm flooded her body as she staggered from her bed and reached for her dressing gown; she had barely pulled it on when there came another loud knock on the door.

"Who is it?" she called out, still groggy as she stumbled through the apartment.

"It's me—Carlotta!"

Elizabeth glanced at the grandfather clock in the parlor, a present from her mother. It was not yet six thirty. The pale predawn light from her window indicated that the sun had not yet crept over the horizon.

She flung the door open. Carlotta stood in the hallway, a bakery bag in one hand and a leash in the other. At the end of the leash was a very chipper-looking Toby. He peered into the apartment, sniffing the air and wagging his tail, his bright little eyes full of happy anticipation.

"Good morning," Carlotta said cheerily.

Elizabeth yawned and fastened her robe. "Why are you always up and about so early?"

"I'm an artist. We have to seize the light. May I come in?"

"I suppose you must," she replied, opening the door wider.

Carlotta looked even more bohemian than the day before—she wore a full, multicolored skirt over tightly laced leather boots, and a frilly white blouse under a scarlet bodice with gold trim. A matching red-and-gold scarf encircled her head. She did not appear to be wearing a corset.

"I brought beigels. Have you any coffee?"

"I can make some."

Elizabeth padded through to the kitchen, hoping she did not get a splinter, as she had neglected to put on her slippers. Carlotta and Toby followed close behind, with the dog straining on his leash to investigate each room as they passed through. The kitchens in the Stuyvesant flats were located in the back, as it was considered lower class to have the smell of cooking permeate one's home.

"Where are your servants?" Carlotta asked, sitting at the kitchen table.

Elizabeth opened the cupboard to get the coffee. "I have none."

"Yet you live in such a grand apartment."

"I do not care to have servants. I do not believe people should live to wait on others."

"Then you will get along capitally with my brother. He is an anarchist."

Preparing the coffee, Elizabeth stopped midscoop. "I don't believe I've ever met a real anarchist."

"I should probably say he fancies himself an anarchist. I sometimes think it's a pose to annoy our parents."

"I look forward to meeting him," Elizabeth said, continuing her coffee preparation. "This should be ready soon."

"Excellent. Beigels taste so much better with it." As Elizabeth filled the coffeepot from the sink, Carlotta said, "You have running water."

"Your family does not?"

"We live on Orchard Street."

Elizabeth was aware of the squalid conditions in downtown tenements but had never actually been inside one.

"We draw our water from a pump in a courtyard shared by other tenants. I like it strong," Carlotta said as Elizabeth filled the pot with fresh grounds. "That is, if it suits you."

"I prefer it strong, too," she replied, turning on the gas burner. The thought of Carlotta and her family pumping water in a cold, dark courtyard filled her with shame at her own good fortune. "If you don't mind my asking, how can you afford to rent an art studio in this building?"

"I have . . . a benefactor."

"How mysterious."

"And my parents' bakery is doing well. They are saving money and hope to move to more commodious lodgings soon."

"I am very glad to hear it. Do you reside with them, then?"

"Yes. Though I do have a daybed in my studio, and I occasionally spend the night there."

"Perhaps someday you will tell me more about this very generous benefactor."

Carlotta gave a little cough and turned away, avoiding her gaze. "Would you mind if I let Toby off his leash?" she asked, leaning down to scratch his ears.

"I have no objection, as long as he is well behaved."

"Be good now, Toby," Carlotta said as the little dog took off across the room, nose to the ground, sniffing frantically. Elizabeth had to admit he was appealing, with his scruffy little terrier beard and energetic manner.

"Have you any butter or jam for the beigels?" Carlotta asked as Elizabeth set out plates and cups on the kitchen table.

"In the icebox," Elizabeth said, pointing.

"We do have one of those," Carlotta said, as if reading her mind. "So no need to feel sorry for us."

"I wasn't feeling—"

"Of course you weren't. Now sit down and tell me everything," Carlotta said, as if she were the hostess instead of Elizabeth. "I don't suppose you have any cream?" she added as Elizabeth poured them each a mug of the hot black brew.

"It's in the—"

"I'll get it," Carlotta said quickly, rising from the table, jewelry jangling as she crossed the room and opened the small icebox in the far corner. The morning sun peeked in through the pale-gold curtains, casting a warm glow over the room. Elizabeth's mother had insisted on helping her decorate the kitchen, and as Catharina adored yellow, the motif was various shades and hues of that color. The walls were covered with a light wash of pale lemon, and the floor tiles were black and gold; even the towels and napkins matched the general decor.

"Now then," Carlotta said, pouring a generous amount of cream into her coffee, "what transpired yesterday after we parted? I am awash in curiosity."

Elizabeth told her everything, between bites of beigel and gulps of coffee. To her surprise, she was ravenous, and when Carlotta offered a second beigel, she did not refuse. She chose one coated with plump sesame seeds, smearing it liberally with butter. "These are quite singular. Like bread, and yet chewier. How do they get the seeds to stick to it?"

"I shall have to ask my mother. Her brother was a baker in Krakow," Carlotta replied, feeding a small piece of her beigel to Toby, who waited patiently at her feet. He swallowed it in one gulp, wagging his tail for more. "That's all for now," she told him, and Elizabeth was surprised to see him trot obediently to the other side of the room, sniffing at a small hole in the baseboards.

"My father always told us never feed a dog at the table. He claimed it would teach bad habits."

"No doubt your father was right about most dogs, but Toby is an unusual animal. He was exceedingly easy to train."

Hearing his name, the dog pricked his sharp little ears, glanced at the two women, then returned to his business of investigating the kitchen's many intriguing smells.

"You must be so gratified that your story will appear in today's paper," Carlotta said.

"I must admit, I did not think they would agree to my terms. I just hope they will not make me return to writing about high society and fashion. I cannot bear it."

There was another knock at the front door.

"Good heavens," said Carlotta. "Who else are you expecting at this hour?"

Elizabeth was about to reply that she had not expected Carlotta, either, when the rapping intensified to a pounding.

"Whoever it is, they are in quite a hurry," she remarked as she headed back through the apartment, Carlotta trailing after her, clutching the remainder of her unfinished beigel.

"Who is it?" she called.

"It's me, Jonah!"

"That's my brother," Carlotta said.

"How does he know you are here?"

"I told him I was visiting you on the way to my studio."

Elizabeth pulled her dressing gown closer to her body. "I am not properly dressed to receive a young man."

"It's only my brother. He's practically a child."

Elizabeth reached for her cloak on the bentwood coatrack and threw it over her shoulders. "Very well—let him in."

Carlotta unlatched the dead bolt and opened the door. Standing in the hallway was a comely youth whose resemblance to his sister was unmistakable. Like her, he was on the short side, with the same olive complexion and curly black hair. But unlike her, he was conservatively dressed, in a short beige jacket, cream-colored waistcoat, matching gloves, and neatly tied cravat. His boots were polished to a sheen. He did not look like an anarchist—in fact, he looked a bit like a dandy. The one touch marking him as an immigrant was the wide-brimmed homburg upon his head.

"May I come in?" he said, removing his hat. His manner was agitated, his voice urgent.

"Of course," Elizabeth replied.

Wiping his boots carefully on the mat, he entered the apartment and stood in the foyer.

"May I present my brother, Jonah Ackerman," said Carlotta. "And this is Miss Elizabeth van den Broek."

"Pleased to make your acquaintance, Miss Van den Broek," Jonah said with a little bow. "Please forgive me for disturbing you so early, but I am here on an errand of some urgency."

"I sensed as much," said Elizabeth. "Please do not let me disturb any communication with your sister."

"I am much obliged to you," he said as Carlotta laid a hand on his arm.

"What is it, Jonah? What's the matter?"

He placed a hand upon hers, his affection evident in this small gesture. "It's Mother—she is unwell."

"What is it? What is wrong?"

"This morning she was violently ill. I fear it may be cholera."

She clutched his hand tighter. "Oh, no—it cannot be! Please say you are mistaken."

"I hope indeed that I am."

"What of Father? Is he with her?"

"He has taken her to Bellevue. I am on my way to join them."

"Forgive me," Carlotta told Elizabeth. "I must go with my brother."

"Allow me to accompany you," said Elizabeth. "Please."

"No!" Carlotta exclaimed. "We cannot allow you to expose yourself to a terrible disease. Apart from that, your job awaits—today of all days, you must not be absent."

Carlotta was right, yet Elizabeth felt an urge to join her, even though they had not known each other long.

"Come," said Jonah. "We've no time to waste."

As Carlotta gulped down the rest of her now cold coffee, Elizabeth fetched Toby's leash and handed it to her. "I know someone at Bellevue. You must ask for him."

"Who is it?" asked Carlotta, fastening Toby's leash.

"His name is Dr. Hiram Jamison. He is only a second-year resident, but he is a talented doctor." The last remark just slipped out. She did not know whether or not he was gifted, but he was clearly intelligent and caring, and she imagined he must be an excellent doctor.

"Thank you," Carlotta said as they rushed out the door.

It was nearly eight by the time Elizabeth had finished dressing to leave for work. Warring emotions battled in her breast—she was concerned about Carlotta's mother but could not deny her excitement at the prospect of seeing her article in the *Herald*. Gulping down the last of her beigel and coffee, now gone quite cold, she hurried from the apartment to catch the Second Avenue El.

Across the street, a lone figure in a dark overcoat stood beside a lamppost, smoking a cigarette. The smoke curled around his face, which was mostly obscured by the wide-brimmed hat he wore low over his eyes. No one took much notice of him as he ground the cigarette beneath his shoe, pulling his hat lower as he strode off in the direction of the Second Avenue train station.

CHAPTER NINETEEN

When she arrived downtown some forty minutes later, Lower Manhattan was bustling with energy. Street vendors were doing a brisk trade—Germans sold sausages on bread rolls with mustard and sauerkraut; the ubiquitous oystermen plied their trade from rickety carts filled with clams and oysters over a bed of ice. Pretzels were everywhere, stacked on wooden posts protruding from the carts of vendors also hawking fruit and nuts. She found her favorite newsboy at his spot near the train station, a stack of newspapers in his arms.

"Read all about it—Egyptian mummy found in Central Park! Git your exclusive here! Only in the *Herald*!"

"Hello, Billy," she said, fishing in her purse for money.

"Paper, miss? Big story today, y'know."

"Yes, please," she replied, giving him a dime.

"Thank you, miss," he said, fishing in his pocket for change.

"Keep it, Billy," she said, tucking the paper under her arm.

"Thanks, miss!" he called after her, as she hurried away, her heart in her throat, his words ringing in her head. *Egyptian mummy found in Central Park. It was the lead story!* Of course the boy misrepresented the actual facts, but she had to admit it was a clever ruse. People were mad for all things Egyptian, and the idea of a real mummy might be more intriguing than a dead woman dressed as one.

She entered the five-story Herald Building, pausing momentarily to drink in the magnificence of the marble lobby with its polished, winding staircase, the sun streaming in through the tall first-floor windows. It was only once she was safely inside the building that she dared to look at the front page. She stepped behind a column, and her hands shook as she opened the paper to read the headline on the left side of the front page.

HORROR IN CENTRAL PARK

Murderous Fiend Preys on Defenseless Woman!

So they had used her headline, but underneath the main one, which, she had to admit, was eye-catching. Her eye fell on the byline: Elizabeth van den Broek and Kenneth Ferguson. She released her breath, and only then did she realize she had been holding it. With it, she let out a tirade of emotions so torrential she couldn't separate them—fear, excitement, sadness, relief, pride.

Freddy's picture of the dead girl stared out at her from the page. He had caught something about her in death, a serene innocence in her heart-shaped face, and a universality of humanity, as if she represented every guileless young woman who had left this earth too early. She appeared to be peacefully sleeping, her face a blank canvas; she could be anyone's daughter. Beneath the photo was another headline: ***Do You Know This Woman?***

This was followed by instructions urging anyone who might be able to identify her to contact the *Herald*. There was also mention of a reward. As Elizabeth looked at the girl's face, her elation at seeing her writing in print was followed by another, more unsettling emotion: shame. A woman had died—had been *murdered*, no less—and yet Elizabeth's first thought in seeing the headline was of her career.

Heat flared on her face, as she let it sink in. Her ambition was not evil or wrong in itself, but it did not compare to the death of an innocent young woman. The morning sun ducked behind a cloud, leaving the lobby in shadow, and Elizabeth shivered. Did she want to bring a murderer to justice, or was the poor girl simply a tool to advance her career? But then, she reasoned, why must it be one or the other? Why could it not be both?

Her skin tingled with anticipation as she climbed the staircase to the second floor. She wondered what Kenneth Ferguson would have to say. As she rounded the corner to the hallway leading to the editorial offices, she was aware of footsteps behind her. Someone was approaching quickly. Before she could turn to see who it was, she felt a hand on her neck, as another grasped her upper arm.

Her assailant forced her forward, pushing her into a small supply closet with such speed and efficiency she had no time to react. She was shoved against a metal shelf containing reams of office paper, and as she opened her mouth to scream, a cloth was shoved into it. Her attacker yanked both her hands behind her back, tying them with something smooth and soft—it felt like a cravat, but she couldn't be sure. Whatever it was, the thought occurred to her that it probably wouldn't leave marks.

Fear surged through her body, leaving her knees weak. She struggled to free herself, but he held her with an iron grip, one hand around her neck, as the other fumbled with her clothing. Realizing what he was after, she instinctively closed her eyes tightly. Her stomach heaved, threatening to rebel, but she fought it back, afraid with the cloth in her mouth she would choke.

She felt his breath, hot and wet on the back of her neck, as he lifted her skirts. When he released the grip on her neck, she tried to twist around, to see his face, but he pressed his body hard against hers, pinning her to the spot. The metal of the shelf was cold against her cheek, and she could feel him growing hard as he panted and groaned behind her.

Though she had never told anyone, Elizabeth was not a virgin. She knew exactly what was happening. She could feel him, hard and urgent against the cloth of her undergarments, as he pleasured himself with his right hand, while holding her down with his left. She struggled and writhed, but to no avail; he only pushed her harder against the metal cabinet. His grunts became louder, his breathing coarse and uneven, as the tempo of his self-gratification increased. Finally, he climaxed in a spasm of panting and groaning.

And then the strangest thing of all: he laughed. A soft giggle, almost like a woman's, a laugh of relief rather than mirth. His body went limp for a moment, and then he drew air into his lungs and laughed again, a more sinister sound this time, a triumphant snicker. Untying the cloth around her wrists, he yanked the gag from her mouth, opened the closet door, and slipped out, slamming the door after him, still without revealing his identity.

She twisted around and pulled at the doorknob, but it was locked from the other side. She pounded and yelled, and after a couple of minutes, the door opened to reveal a maintenance man, clad in overalls and work boots, a puzzled look on his face. In his right hand he carried a wrench; in his left was a length of rope.

"What happened to you, miss?" He was big and young and ruddy-faced, with the smooth, plump cheeks of a cherub. His hazel eyes were earnest and kind, and she nearly cried at the sight of him.

Her first instinct was to tell him everything, but another impulse triumphed. She saw clearly the outcome of such an admission, how it would affect her career, what it would look like to her colleagues, and who would be blamed. She could hear the voices of condemnation. *She should not have inserted herself into a male profession. She deserved what she got. Served her right, putting herself in that position. She should have known better. When it came right down to it, really, she was little better than a common whore.*

Fighting back the tears threatening to spring to her eyes, she shocked herself by doing what, just minutes ago, she would have thought impossible: she looked him in the eyes and smiled.

"It's quite stupid of me—I managed to lock myself in," she said, doing her best to steady her voice.

He cocked his head to one side. "How'd you manage that?"

"When I closed the door, I heard the bolt slide into place," she said, acutely aware of how absurd it sounded. "It was silly of me," she added with a false little laugh, chiding herself for not being a better actress.

Her pathetic lie seemed to satisfy him, though—he smiled indulgently. She thought he was about to say something about women in the workplace, but he just chuckled. "Never mind, miss—once got locked in my own basement, so I did. Had to saw my way out. Ruined a perfectly good door."

"Thank you for rescuing me," she said, sincerely grateful.

"Think nothin' of it. This lock wants a bit of oil so it don't happen again—I'll see it gets done."

"Thank you so much. You are very kind."

"Jes doin' my job, miss," he said, tipping his cap politely before continuing down the hall.

As she watched him retreat, Elizabeth was glad she had said nothing. She would not be stigmatized as a "fallen woman." She knew enough of how things worked to know that her word would never stand up against that of her assailant, whoever he was. She stood in the empty hallway for several moments, wanting to scream, to cry, to howl like a wounded animal. There was no way to prove who had done this to her, but she thought she had a pretty good idea.

Elizabeth possessed an unusual gift—if it could be called that—of putting difficult or inconvenient feelings aside until such time as she could address them. As she stood in the hallway of the Herald Building, she realized she needed this ability now more than ever. This was the most important day of her career—she had triumphed, with her byline on a front-page article. She needed to march up to Kenneth Ferguson's office, claim her victory, and make it clear she intended to follow the story wherever it might lead.

Yet she felt anything but victorious. She felt small, dirty, and to her disgust, ashamed. She had been used and discarded. She knew intellectually that what had happened wasn't her fault, but she was unable to rid herself of the feeling of utter humiliation. She felt soiled and unclean. She started down the hall, but her knees suddenly seemed to be made not of bone but of some viscous substance that would not support her weight. Grasping at the nearest doorknob to steady herself, she saw that her hands were trembling. It was not fear that gripped her, but rage and repulsion. Drawing in a deep breath, she walked unsteadily down the hall to the ladies' lavatory. Instinct told her she needed to purge what had happened to her before she could go forward.

The lavatory was empty. Grateful for this bit of good luck, she walked through to the rear stall, aware of the echo of her hard leather heels on the porcelain tiles. Her brain felt foggy, her reasoning impaired, yet her senses were preternaturally heightened. She was mesmerized by the pale-yellow sunlight diffused through the glass bricks in the tall window. Every sound was magnified, from the creaking of the hinges on the wooden door of the stall to the click of the metal latch as she locked it. When she closed the heavy stall door, it sounded like a gunshot.

After locking herself into the stall, she vomited profusely. When she was finished, she went to the sink and washed her mouth out vigorously. If she had expected to feel better, she was disappointed. Her head was clearer, but her hands still shook. She felt hollowed out, as though someone had scraped away everything inside her, leaving only an empty shell, like the dead horseshoe crabs she and Laura used to find on the beaches on Long Island.

The face gazing back at her in the mirror was not one she recognized. It looked older, tired, and infinitely sadder than the one she had seen that morning. She wondered whether she was losing her mind. She had an image of herself as one of the tattered, addled women roaming the Bowery, talking to themselves, lugging their few belongings in a ragged sack tied up with a bit of frayed rope.

Elizabeth leaned on the sink, gripping the sides until her knuckles turned white.

"You won't win," she muttered through clenched teeth. "I won't let you."

Looking at her own reflection, she realized the parallel between her and the girl lying lifeless in the morgue at Bellevue. Now she understood, not as a reporter but as a woman, and felt the weight of their common lot. They had both been silenced—violently, viciously, and at the hands (so she assumed) of men—simply because they were women. Weaker in every respect: physically, socially, financially—in short, in every way that mattered.

The Bellevue victim had been silenced forever, but Elizabeth still possessed a voice. And if she could not use it to speak for herself, she would use it on behalf of the young woman with the white-blond hair who lay cold and still in the darkness of the city morgue.

She took a deep breath and let it out slowly, as her father had taught her to do when she was little and given to temper tantrums. Her world had changed forever, and she would never be the same. Somehow, she would find a way to turn that bleak knowledge to her advantage. Loss could cripple a person for life, but it could also be used to construct an armor of strength.

She might be privileged, affluent, and pampered, but she could not ignore the unbreakable bond between her and the girl on the metal slab. They were not reporter and subject—they were sisters. She vowed that realization would drive her forward relentlessly, no matter what lay ahead. Straightening her dress and smoothing her hair, she left the room, the door clanging shut behind her with a hollow sound.

CHAPTER TWENTY

He stood on Forsyth Street, gazing up at the squalid tenement where he had spent too many years of his childhood, its windows grimy and dusty as ever, thinking about the poor souls now living within its unwelcoming walls. Did the children huddle around the woodstove in the kitchen, the only source of heat in the winter? Did they run rampant on the streets, as he had, or slave away in a factory, slaughterhouse, or sweatshop? Were they disregarded and unloved, as he had been, with no father and a poor excuse for a mother?

He sighed and kicked at a stone, sending it scuttering into the gutter, as a tired-looking woman hung laundry from a line that stretched from a second-story window. Clad in a blue-and-white plaid pinafore over a worn cotton frock, she wiped her sleeve across her damp brow. A small boy clung to her skirts, wailing. She bent to say something to him, to comfort him perhaps, wiping the tears from his chubby cheeks. He stopped crying and, after a few hiccoughs, plunged a grubby thumb into his mouth, the other hand still clutching his mother's skirts.

At least she comforted the child, he thought as he turned away to wander down the street, which smelled of manure, rotting vegetables, and desperation. In spite of her circumstances, she did what she could to be a decent mother. Treading the familiar route as the August sun rounded the bottom of the island on its westward journey, he let his mind wander back to a day many years ago, on such a summer afternoon as this, shortly after his thirteenth birthday. His mother was having "tea" with a couple of her girlfriends (though the liquid she served in chipped flowered teacups was cheap whiskey, bought for a few pennies a bottle at the corner grocery). He'd been seated in the corner of the room mending one of his mother's dresses—it was a task she regularly assigned him, and by the time he was ten, he was quite adept with a needle and thread.

The three women sat at the kitchen table, eating oranges and fanning themselves as they swilled liquor, laughing and gossiping about their johns—their "tricky boys," as they called them. They loved sharing stories about these men, depicting them in the most derogatory way. In fact, listening to them, he got the impression they hated all men.

"A judge, he was," said Long Sadie, a lanky redhead with a horsey face and a wandering eye. None of his mother's friends were beauties, which to him confirmed their general opinion of men as desperate dopes who would stoop to anything to "tickle their gizzard," as Sadie called it. "And he would only do it if he was wearin' his judge's robe!" she went on. "Wanted t'know if that was all right, an' I told 'im, 'Sugar, long as you're payin' me, you kin bang your gavel all night far as I'm concerned!"

The other two cackled as his mother refilled their glasses. Her other friend, a plump girl nicknamed Brassy Betty, yawned and stretched. "I surely wish it would cool down a bit," she said, adjusting her blond wig, which she wore to cover her thinning hair. "This heat makes my head spin, so it does." She was Irish, and sometimes sang him Celtic folk songs in a sweet, warbling soprano.

As he watched her guzzle the liquid in her cup, it occurred to him that it wasn't the heat making her dizzy. But he said nothing—he had learned that, with his mother's friends, it was better to keep a low profile, especially after they had been drinking. He bent over his mending, biting the thread to cut it rather than get up and get scissors, which he feared would attract their attention. But it was to no avail—Long Sadie's wandering eye swiveled in his direction, and her lips curled in a smile.

"You've been awfully quiet, laddie," she said sucking on an orange slice. "How about a wee dram?" Sadie claimed to have been born in Scotland, and every once in a while, she trotted out Scottish terms such as "wee" and "laddie."

"No, thank you," he said, concentrating on his work.

"Aw, c'mon," said Sadie, licking her lips. "Have you never had a drink before?"

"He has not," said his mother.

"I've had beer," he said. "Lots of times." It was a lie. His friends all liked to boast of their drinking, exaggerating how much they'd actually did, but he did not like it and knew too well the effect it had on his mother.

"What about whiskey?" asked Sadie.

"Won't touch the stuff," said his mother.

"Why not, then?" asked Betty.

His mother shrugged. "Claims he don't like the taste."

Sadie laughed. Even her laugh sounded equine, like a horse neighing. "It's not *about* the taste, luv! It's about the *effect*."

"How old is he?" Betty asked his mother.

"Just turned thirteen last week."

"He's practically a man!" Sadie whinnied. "It's high time he started actin' like one."

Her statement was confusing. From the stories the women told, acting like a man was nothing to be proud of. Bending over his mending, he tried to quiet his spinning head. He did not like where things were heading.

"Yes," Betty said. "We should celebrate yer birthday properly now!" Refilling her cup, she held it out to him. "Here—have some."

"Go on, then," Sadie said when he hesitated. "Show us what yer made of."

He looked at his mother, his eyes pleading, but she just shrugged. Her face was blurry, her eyes dim from drink. When she was like this, he was on his own. Setting down his mending, he reached out and took the cup. The yellowish liquid inside reminded him of piss.

"What're you waitin' fer, then?" Betty said, leaning forward, so that he could see her fleshy breasts pressed together like two eager puppies. Her broad grin displayed a chipped front tooth, bits of unchewed orange clinging to it.

He raised the cup to his lips and took a tentative swallow, but the harsh liquid burned his throat, making him choke and sputter. Tears spurted from his eyes. It was like drinking flames. The women laughed.

"C'mon, boyo, you can do better than that!" Sadie said, slapping her bony knee with her palm.

"If he don't want to, he shouldn't—" Betty said, but Sadie interrupted her.

"He wants to prove his manhood, don't he?"

He glanced at his mother, but she appeared to have dozed off, chin resting on her collarbone, fingers still wrapped around her teacup. He dutifully raised the cup and took another sip. This time he was prepared, and most of the whiskey slid down his throat before he gagged and choked.

"There ye go," Sadie said, slapping him on the back. "That's better now, ain't it?"

He nodded, forcing a smile.

"Drink up, then," she said. "Finish your glass."

He did, and before long a curious tingling enveloped his limbs. It was pleasant enough, though he was unprepared for the foggy sensation in his head, as if it were swathed in cotton.

"There now," Sadie said, crossing her long, thin arms. He could see the blue veins in her hands, roughened and red from years of toil.

"How do you feel?" asked Betty.

"All right," he said.

"Want some more?" asked Sadie.

"No, thank you."

"Leave him be," said Betty. "He's just a wee tyke."

The women poured themselves more whiskey, drinking in silence as the light dimmed outside the grimy kitchen windows. While their flat was small and dark, like most tenements, at least it was in the front of the building. Rear tenements were even unhealthier, being darker and more airless than those in front. And they were fortunate to have a window in the kitchen, let alone two. No matter how wretched the lives of some New Yorkers were, it seemed there was always someone even worse off, as his mother never tired of reminding him.

Now, however, she was snoring gently, head to one side, a bit of drool hanging from the side of her mouth.

"So," Sadie said, looking at him with her good eye, "you've just turned thirteen."

He nodded, his head fuzzier by the minute.

"Y'know what would *really* make you a man," she said. It was more of a statement than a question.

Betty looked at her. "Oh, you're not—"

"And why not?" she demanded. "He has to sooner or later—why not now?"

"He's only thirteen."

"I reckon if he's old enough for whiskey, he's old enough for that."

A thin trickle of terror threaded through his gut as he realized what they were talking about. He froze. His mother was still asleep in her chair, snoring loudly now, legs akimbo. When she slept like this, there was little point in trying to wake her—she rarely responded, even to being shaken.

"No," Betty told Sadie firmly. "I'll not have anythin' to do with that; neither will you."

"But—"

"I said no, and that's final!"

Sadie shrugged and lit a cigarette. "Fine, have it your way."

Relief flooded his body, and he took a deep breath, but as he did, his stomach heaved, and without warning, vomit shot from his mouth. It was yellow, with specks of green from the watercress he had gobbled down with a crust of bread for lunch.

The two women looked at it with surprise, and then, to his horror, they exploded with laughter.

"Don' quite have yer sea legs yet, do ye?" Sadie asked, her long body shaking with mirth.

"Never you mind, dearie," said Betty, wiping away tears of laughter. "It happens to the best of us, so it does."

He did not answer. His face burned with shame and disgust. Leaving the two women, he went to his alcove in the wall. Lifting the curtain, he crawled under the covers and buried his head beneath a pillow to drown out the terrible mocking sound of their laughter.

CHAPTER TWENTY-ONE

Elizabeth strode down the hall, trying to project a confidence she did not feel. As she approached the editorial department, she saw a line of people gathered outside Kenneth Ferguson's office. They seemed to come from all walks of life. There were shopgirls and sailors, blacksmiths in leather aprons, clerks and accountants with green eyeshades, longshoremen in boots and overalls.

She stood staring at them when she saw Freddy Evans hurrying toward her.

"What is all this?" she asked. "What's going on?"

"It's the announcement in this mornin's paper. Folks are showin' up in droves t'help us identify the poor young girl."

"I expect they want the reward money," Elizabeth said as they walked past the line of people.

"I don't know about anyone else," said a tall, stringy woman. A pince-nez was perched on the bridge of her nose, and she carried a small carpetbag that appeared to be full of books. Elizabeth took her to be a librarian. The woman wrinkled her long, thin nose. "But *I* have come to do my civic duty."

Elizabeth followed Freddy into Kenneth Ferguson's office, feeling curiously numb.

"Amazing, isn't it? So many people taking time off work to help out the Fourth Estate," the editor said as they entered. "Close the door behind you."

"How much is the reward?" asked Freddy.

"That has yet to be determined. And it's contingent upon whether their 'lead' proves useful. Congratulations, by the way," he told Elizabeth. "The paper is selling like hotcakes."

She opened her mouth to respond, but her throat closed and she gagged. Ferguson peered at her, the ubiquitous cigar stub clenched between his teeth. "Are you all right?"

She nodded. "Yes." Her voice sounded rusty, like a hinge in need of oil. She took a deep breath to quell the ringing in her ears.

"Good. Because those people out there need to be interviewed."

"All of them, sir?" asked Freddy.

"Each and every one. Are you up to it?" he asked Elizabeth.

"Me, sir?"

"It's your story, isn't it?"

"Certainly, sir. Thank you, sir." Her voice sounded far away, like it was coming from somewhere other than her own body.

"Off you go, then," Ferguson said. "Let me know what you find out."

"And me, sir?" said Freddy.

"You can help Miss Van den Broek. She'll need an assistant."

"But I'm—"

"A photographer, I know. You've been promoted. Now get on with the both of you."

"Where shall we—" Elizabeth began.

"Use my office."

"But where will you—"

"Where is your desk?" he asked Elizabeth.

"It's in the back of the reporter pool, near the window."

"I'll find it."

"But—"

"Come get me when you're finished. And don't forget to take notes."

"Yes, sir," she said as he gathered papers from his desk into a folder. Even arranging papers, his wiry body brimmed with energy. His self-confidence and sense of purpose were oddly comforting.

"Right, then," he said, striding briskly from the room, the folder tucked underneath one arm, a handful of sharpened pencils in the other.

She and Freddy stood without moving for a few moments. It was rather like being in the aftermath of a tornado, as if all the air in the room had been sucked out in the wake of his leaving.

"Well," she said finally. "Shall we begin?"

The interviews provided a welcome distraction. For a while Elizabeth was able to put aside what had happened to her and turn her attention elsewhere. Most of the people seemed eager to help. More than a few of them brought up the reward money, to which Elizabeth repeated what Ferguson had said—that it was contingent upon the usefulness of their information. Some seemed disappointed by this, a few were angry, but most took it in stride. Living in New York, you quickly learned that nothing was as good as it first appeared. There was always a price to pay, and the sooner you cultivated patience, the better.

She and Freddy sat talking to people and scribbling notes for more than an hour, which turned into two, until there were only a few people still in line. Most of the tips they had received were sufficiently vague as to be useless; remarks like "I seen a girl lookin' like her on Broadway last week" were common. No one seemed to know her name or even what neighborhood she lived in; some people hadn't seen her picture or even read that morning's *Herald*. They were there as the result of a tip from a friend or colleague, who claimed the paper would pay for information, somehow oblivious to the fact that they did not possess such information. The thin woman with the pince-nez turned out to be a self-proclaimed "clairvoyant"; she claimed the dead girl had shown up in a dream and revealed her killer to be none other than the ghost of Boss Tweed.

"Sit right here, miss," Freddy said as a wan-looking girl stepped hesitantly into the room. She was neatly but plainly dressed, with a becoming air of modesty. Her clean-scrubbed face was pretty without being beautiful; there was something nun-like about her. Her light-brown hair was pulled into a tidy and unobtrusive chignon at the back of her neck, wound around with a simple black ribbon. Her hazel eyes were large and guileless, her skin so pale it almost appeared sickly. Though they were about the same age, she inspired in Elizabeth a protective maternal instinct.

Sitting in the chair Freddy offered, the girl quietly folded her hands in her lap and gazed at him and Elizabeth, waiting for one of them to speak. Her demeanor got Elizabeth's attention—most of the other people were hardly able to contain themselves, bursting to blurt out what they had to say.

Elizabeth pulled her chair nearer to the girl so that their knees almost touched.

"I'm Elizabeth van den Broek," she said gently. "And this is Freddy Evans."

"I'm Maddy—short for Madeline. Maddy Tierney."

"Thank you for taking the time to come in, Miss Tierney. You have some information for us?"

"Well, miss, I work at the Bowery Mission, you see."

"Very commendable, I'm sure," said Elizabeth. Established in 1879, the Bowery Mission was the second rescue mission in New York. Started by a reverend and his wife, it welcomed needy people of all faiths and backgrounds.

"So, Miss Tierney, did this young woman work with you?" Elizabeth asked, holding up the front page of the *Herald*.

"No, miss—she was a, um, client. Reverend Ruliffson tells us to call them that, you see," she added shyly. "He says it shows respect."

"Quite rightly," said Elizabeth. "When did she come to you?"

"She showed up about a week ago."

"What was the reason she gave for needing your assistance? Had she taken to drink?"

"I don't believe so. I didn't take her for a lush."

"Did she say why she was there?" asked Freddy.

"She was a bit vague about it, to say truthfully. But we don't turn anyone away, no matter their reason."

"Did she give her name?" said Elizabeth.

"Only her first name—Sally. That's what she said, anyhow."

"I shouldn't imagine everyone gives their real name, do they?"

The girl shook her head. "Some do, some don't. But she looked like a Sally, so I took her at her word."

"Did y'learn anythin' else about her, then?" asked Freddy.

"She said she used to work at Harry Hill's Concert Saloon, but that she was tired of the life."

Elizabeth and Freddy exchanged a look. Harry Hill's was the most notorious example of a popular type of establishment generally considered disreputable even by the people who frequented them. "Concert saloons" offered diversions—music, variety acts, boxing matches—all aimed at getting people to drink more. Not that there was any challenge in that—comely "waiter girls" served up booze along with the promise of sex, and anyone found at a concert saloon wasn't there for the quality of the entertainment.

"Were she a waiter girl at Harry's?" asked Freddy.

Miss Tierney twisted her fingers around a bit of black ribbon on the front of her frock, clearly uncomfortable discussing such wickedness. "Apparently so. She didn't care for it, or so she said."

"And you believed her?" said Elizabeth.

"I had no reason to doubt her. She came to us, after all."

"This was a week ago?"

"Yes. Reverend Ruliffson said she could work at the Mission, at least temporarily, until she managed to get on her feet. Meals were included."

"And did she accept his offer?"

"She arrived early the next morning, and the day after that. Worked hard, too, so she did."

"And then?"

Maddy Tierney heaved a mournful sigh. "She just disappeared. Didn't show up the next day or afterward."

"And you took that to mean she had lost her interest in reforming her life?"

"Didn't know what to think, to be honest. She seemed so set on following the path of virtue. It was disappointing—to me and Reverend and Mrs. Ruliffson. We all liked her."

"She gave you no address?"

"We never asked for one. We respect people's privacy."

"Did she have enemies you knew of?"

"Not really, no."

"Did she mention bein' afraid of anyone?" Freddy asked.

Maddy shook her head. "She didn't really share personal things much."

"Did you ever notice anyone hanging about, maybe loitering on the street, who looked dangerous?" Elizabeth said.

Maddy smiled. "Beg pardon, miss, but our mission is on the Bowery. I see people like that every day."

"Did she seem to know any of them?"

"No, miss. She mostly kept to herself."

"Thank you so much for coming in," Elizabeth said, rising. "If we should need to speak with you further—"

"I can be found most days at the Bowery Mission."

"Thank you again," Elizabeth said, shaking her hand. Miss Tierney nodded shyly and slipped out of the room, hurrying down the hall, avoiding eye contact with any of the people still waiting in line.

In the end, Miss Tierney proved to be the only promising lead, and it was not long before Elizabeth went to fetch Kenneth Ferguson from the reporters' pool. She found him in the hall outside, talking with

Karl Schuster. When the two men saw Elizabeth, they broke off their conversation. Ferguson walked toward her, smiling, and Elizabeth felt a flush of pride at the thought that the *Herald*'s respected crime editor found her worthy.

Her happiness did not last long. Rounding the corner behind Ferguson, his face fixed in its usual smirk, was Simon Sneed. Elizabeth's heart shot into her throat at the sight of him, her vision darkened, and she felt her legs give way. The last thing she was aware of was a roaring in her ears, before blackness overtook her.

CHAPTER TWENTY-TWO

"Water—fetch her some water!"

She was aware of a man's voice, urgent but very far away. It was familiar . . . someone older, someone she was fond of and trusted . . . her father? Her eyes fluttered open, and Elizabeth saw the worried face of Karl Schuster peering down at her, his blue eyes wide with alarm, beads of sweat gathering on his broad forehead. She tried to speak, but it felt like too much effort. He patted her cheek, which was annoying, and she raised a hand to make him stop, but he seized it and squeezed it fervently. Were there tears in his eyes?

She heard footsteps clattering down the hall. "Here you are, sir!" Freddy appeared with a glass of water, the liquid sloshing over the sides as he handed it to Karl Schuster.

"Careful!" Schuster commanded. "You've spilled half of it."

"I . . . I'm all right," Elizabeth said, raising herself onto her elbows. "What happened?"

"You fainted." The voice belonged to Kenneth Ferguson, who stood next to Schuster, shifting his weight back and forth. Ferguson was simply too kinetic to stand still for long. Elizabeth's stomach clenched as she remembered where she was and what had happened. To her relief, Simon Sneed was nowhere in sight.

She sat up, and Karl held out the glass of water. "You must drink this."

Her hand shook as she took it from him. The moment her lips touched the glass, she realized she had a searing, scorching thirst. She gulped it down and handed the glass back to Karl. "Thank you. Now I'd like to stand up."

Kenneth Ferguson frowned. "Are you sure you're all right?"

"Yes. Help me up, please." Half a dozen hands reached out and pulled her gently to her feet. Much fuss was made over her, and though she begged to stay, Ferguson insisted she go straight home. She knew full well why she had fainted, but also knew she could not reveal it to anyone. Over her protests, Ferguson insisted on escorting her downstairs himself to fetch her a cab.

"If you are not well enough tomorrow, please take the day off," he said as he bundled her into the back of a hansom. "The Stuyvesant, East Eighteenth Street, quick as you can," he told the driver.

"I'm sure I shall be fine," she replied, but he rapped on the roof of the cab, the driver flicked his whip, and the horse set off at a trot. She waited until they had gone several blocks before she knocked on the roof again to stop.

The driver's face appeared upside down in the window. "Yes, miss?"

"I'd like to change the address, please—can you take me to Hermann Weber's butcher shop on the Bowery?"

"Yes, miss—I know the place."

Mr. Weber was doing a brisk lunchtime trade when she arrived. Elizabeth stood on the curb watching people leave his shop with tidily wrapped brown paper packages. She saw an equally busy scene at the Thirsty Crow; she could hear the shouts and laughter of the patrons inside the two-story, ramshackle wooden building.

A young man strutted out of the bar, well lubricated but not yet stumbling. Even under the influence of drink, he had an open, kind face, sunburned and freckled, beneath a swatch of orange hair. He was dressed in typical working-class garb—a woolen cap, a short jacket with broad lapels, a fitted vest over heavy trousers, and work boots. The white cotton stock tied around his neck was the only suggestion of his pretension to a higher social status. Though it was highly unseemly—indeed, unheard of—for a lady of social standing to address a strange man, Elizabeth stepped forward boldly. "Pardon me, sir."

The young man stopped, a look of surprise on his face. "Yes, miss?" he said politely, tipping his cap.

"I wonder if you visit this establishment often?" she asked, indicating the Thirsty Crow.

He grinned. "I s'pose you could say I'm there more than I am at me own home."

"Do you happen to know a lady who calls herself Grammy?"

His face widened into a smile. "Oh, sure—Grammy Nagle, is it?"

"Yes. Her name is Mathilde, but—"

"Everyone calls her Grammy. Aye, she's a good sort, so she is. Taken by drink somethin' terrible, but a good sort nonetheless."

"Have you seen her recently?"

Removing his top hat, he scratched his head. "Come t'think on it, it's been a few days."

"When did you last see her?"

"Monday, I think it were."

"You wouldn't happen to know where she lives?"

He smiled. "Nix. I kinda figured she slept hangin' upside down from a tree branch, like a bat."

"Thank you very much. I appreciate your time."

"You a friend o' hers, then?"

"In a manner of speaking."

"Well, good luck findin' her," he said with a little bow, and was on his way.

Elizabeth turned around to see Hermann Weber step outside his butcher shop to smoke a cigarette. As he raised the lighted match to his face, she caught his eye and waved. He took a step backward, but she crossed the ground between them in a thrice.

"*Guten Tag*, Herr Weber," she said, hoping that speaking German might create a bond between them.

But he was having none of it. "Good afternoon," he said in his heavy Bavarian accent. She knew it was Bavarian because one of her teachers at Vassar had been from Munich. "Vat vould you like today—some bratwurst, perhaps, or a nice Sunday roast?"

"Actually, I was hoping for a few minutes of your time, if you can spare them. But yes," she agreed, thinking it would soften him up, "a nice bit of beef would be lovely—after you finish your cigarette, of course."

He squinted at her warily. "Vat did you need to ask me?"

"The young lady who lived on the third floor—"

"I tell you, there is no such person! *Wer ist sie*, zat you vould be so curious about her?"

For a moment she considered telling him she was a relative of the missing girl, but opted for the truth. "I am Elizabeth van den Broek, crime reporter with the *New York Herald*."

"*Aber Sie sind nur ein Fräulein*," he said, frowning.

"I may be just a woman, but I can assure you I am a reporter as well. *Ich bin eine echte Reporterin.*"

He shrugged. "*Ihr Deutsch ist nicht so schlecht.*"

"Thank you. I wish it were better."

"Can you promise I remain anonymous?"

"You have my word."

Looking around to see that no one was listening, he took one last drag of his cigarette before grinding it out beneath the heel of his shoe. "*Komm herein*," he said, beckoning her inside.

Elizabeth followed him into the shop, but when he closed and locked the door behind them, her heart thumped in her chest. For the first time in her life, she was afraid of being alone with a man. The sight of his orange cat perched on the windowsill calmed her somewhat. The animal gazed at her languidly through half-closed eyes, which her sister always said was the feline equivalent of a smile.

Herr Weber was clearly nervous himself, which also put her more at ease. Turning the sign around to indicate that the store was closed, he pulled down the window shades. The shop was immaculate, the glass case holding the meat polished to a sheen, but there was something ominous about the aroma of butchered flesh pervading the air.

"*Jetzt*," Weber said, loosening his collar. "You must never tell anyone I haf told you zis." Though the interior of the shop was cool, he was sweating.

"I will never mention your name to anyone."

"Zere vas a young woman upstairs. I do not know her name. And suddenly she vas gone—disappeared."

"Who paid you to keep quiet?"

Surprise registered on his face. "How do you—"

"You were seen going to the bank with a large amount of cash after being visited by a well-dressed man."

"I cannot reveal his identity."

"You knew him, then?"

"I know who sent him."

"And you cannot tell me?"

"If I do, my life vill not be worth zat pile of bones," he said, pointing to a bowl of soup-bones behind the counter.

"What can you tell me, then?"

"The police vill not help you."

His words hung in the air, echoing in her head. *The police will not help you.*

CHAPTER TWENTY-THREE

After meeting with Herr Weber, Elizabeth was seized with a fatigue so profound she could barely summon the energy to board a streetcar home. Once safely inside her apartment, she undressed and stumbled to the bathroom, where she ran a deep, hot bath in the lion-paw tub. The bathtub was one of the amenities that had drawn her to the Stuyvesant when she was searching for a place to live after college. Much to her mother's disappointment, returning to her family's town house on Fifth Avenue was out of the question. Though her father had understood, Elizabeth's mother had felt slighted. But Catharina van den Broek enjoyed drama, and this allowed her to play the long-suffering, unappreciated mother.

Lying in the tub, steam rising around her, Elizabeth slid down until the water was up to her neck. The water siphoned the physical pain from her limbs but could not relieve the ache that had closed itself on her like a vise. Closing her eyes, she tried not to think of anything except the soothing soak. But that only made it worse. She was back in the supply closet, inhaling the aroma of paper and cardboard, of lead pencils and musty metal shelves. There was another odor, though—something familiar, but she couldn't place it. Her eyes shot open. She recognized the smell.

Pulling herself from the steaming tub, she reached for a towel—Egyptian cotton, courtesy of her mother—and wrapped it around her body. As she did, she saw an image of Sally, swathed all in white, at the bottom of the pit in Central Park. She stared at the water vapor condensing on the bathroom window, forming droplets that slid down the panes, much as the rain had slid down the policemen's faces as they pulled Sally from her untimely grave.

Unwilling to think of it any longer, Elizabeth turned away as a yawn shuddered through her. Though it was only midafternoon, her body was heavy with fatigue, and after pulling on a flannel nightgown, she dropped onto her bed without turning down the coverlet and succumbed to the pull of sleep.

She awoke to the sound of pigeons cooing outside her window. Most people either ignored pigeons or complained about them, but she had always been fond of the sturdy, resourceful birds. Rolling onto her back, she stared at the ceiling, with its graceful circular molding. Apprehension gathered in her stomach as she remembered what had happened earlier. To her relief, she'd had no dreams that she could recall. Yawning, she sat up, slid her feet into a pair of bedroom slippers, and pulled open the top drawer of her dresser. In the back, wrapped in a soft cloth, was her grandfather's Stormdolk, or assault dagger, a family heirloom her father had given her years ago. Taking it out, she ran her fingers over the leather scabbard, with its nail-studded sheath. It was beautiful, and it was deadly. Closing her hand over the sturdy handle, she pulled out the blade, thin and sharp, with delicate beveling. Holding it, she felt her fear drain away. She felt powerful and dangerous.

As she admired it, there was a loud knocking on her front door. Panic gripped her—annoyed, she shook it off. Clenching her teeth, she resolved to take hold of her emotions. Clutching the dagger, she strode through the parlor to the foyer as the knocking continued. Lifting the peephole cover, she peered out to see Carlotta. Relief swept over her like a wave. There was no sign of Toby.

Elizabeth unlocked the door and let her friend in, bolting it securely once Carlotta was inside. "What time is it?" she asked, yawning. She felt as though she had slept for decades, like Rip van Winkle.

"Seven o'clock in the evening," Carlotta replied, wiping her feet on the mat. "Have you taken to sleeping during the day now?"

"I just awoke from a nap."

Carlotta wore her usual outré clothing—a long flowered frock with a loose, flowing skirt, a scarlet scarf wrapped around her head. A silver-and-turquoise necklace hung around her throat; matching bracelets encircled her wrists. "I would kill for some tea. I brought beigels," she said, handing Elizabeth a brown paper bag.

"How is your mother?" Elizabeth asked as they went through to the parlor.

"Better, thank you—my brother found the Bellevue doctor you recommended."

"Dr. Jamison?"

"Yes," Carlotta said, sitting on the yellow-silk settee by the fireplace. "He administered an herbal tincture that he said was an old family remedy, and it relieved her symptoms greatly."

"Did he believe it to be cholera?"

"He seemed to think she may have ingested a poison of some kind."

"Poison?"

"That's not the word he used . . . what was it? Oh, yes—toxin! That's what he called it. He said it could have been from infected meat or spoiled vegetables, and that it would probably run its course. He said she is not yet out of the woods, but is much improved."

"I am so glad to hear it. Now I'd better fetch that tea."

When she returned to the parlor with the tea tray, Carlotta was standing in front of the french windows, gazing onto the street.

"I am always amazed at the variety of the human animal," she said.

"How so?" Elizabeth asked, setting the tray on the marble coffee table.

"There is the most delightfully plump family walking down the street, and behind them, pushing a stroller, is a woman so thin she appears to be made of sticks."

"The city is a wonderful canvas," Elizabeth said, pouring the tea. "As a painter you must appreciate that," she added, handing her a cup.

"Indeed. And you must feel the same as a writer."

"I do," Elizabeth said, taking a sip of tea.

Carlotta helped herself to a beigel smeared with fresh butter. "You know, we eat these with cream cheese. You must try it sometime."

"I shall."

"You should write a book someday that I can illustrate. Wouldn't that be jolly?"

"Very jolly," Elizabeth replied absently. Setting her teacup on the mantel, she fidgeted with the tie on her dressing gown.

Putting down her own cup, Carlotta studied her. "Are you quite all right? You seem preoccupied."

Elizabeth related the events of the day, omitting the incident in the supply closet. She intended to tell no one, fearing that if she let it slip to Carlotta, it would eventually reach her parents—or worse, her employer. Moreover, she found herself unable to talk about it. The very thought of it nauseated her.

Carlotta listened carefully and, when Elizabeth had finished, jumped up from her chair. "So in order to discover the identity of the dead girl in the park, we need only go to Harry Hill's concert saloon!"

"That was my intent."

"Of course I shall accompany you."

"I don't think—"

"Nonsense. It is settled. But first, do you not think we ought to go to the police?"

Elizabeth ran a finger along the rim of her teacup. "Presumably they are doing their own investigation."

"Yes, but—"

"I do not entirely trust them."

"Why on earth not?"

"You are aware that even after the death of Boss Tweed, Tammany Hall is corrupt?"

"So my brother tells me ad nauseam."

"And that the police extort payoffs from merchants as 'protection' money."

"Do you not remember that my parents own a bakery?"

"Then you are familiar with the extent of their venality."

"But what about that nice Detective Sergeant O'Grady? Do we not owe him—"

"We know little of him, only that he is polite and presents a good front."

"But did he not make it possible to view the body at the morgue? You told me he gave you his card as an introduction."

"That is true."

"It seems to me he has gone out of his way to help you."

"He is not the one who concerns me. It is his superior officers who are most likely to be corrupt."

Carlotta peered at Elizabeth, a little smile on her face. "Has your editor instructed you to keep the information exclusive to your newspaper?"

"Not at all," she answered truthfully, though she knew it would not hurt her career if she were to reveal the girl's identity in the *Herald* before the police discovered it. "But I strongly believe there is a link between the mummy and the girl I saw through the window."

"But murders are committed every day in this city. And people disappear. Sometimes they turn up alive, sometimes dead."

"And I tell you, I believe this is the same girl I saw being strangled. They both had the same striking hair color."

"But how will you possibly prove it?"

"I will find a way."

"You had better not challenge those in power—especially the police."

"I will if necessary."

"Take care. The determining factor in human affairs is power—getting it and keeping it," Carlotta said, twirling her spoon in her teacup.

"I thought your brother was the nihilist."

"He is an anarchist, not a nihilist."

"Then you are the nihilist."

"Far from it. Nihilists believe that life is meaningless; I find it full of meaning."

"But to believe that all human relations come down to power—that strikes me as dangerously close to nihilism. Surely love also comes into play?"

Carlotta added more sugar to her tea and stirred it. "I think its importance is highly exaggerated."

"What a sad place your mind must be."

Carlotta smiled. "Consider the age-old struggle between men and women. Surely you agree that men have the vast majority of power in our society. And," she continued, "we have but one card to play in a high-stakes game."

"What is that?"

"We have something they want. That is our sole source of power over them."

Elizabeth looked down at her hands, tightly clenched in her lap. "Which they can take whenever they choose," she muttered, her eyes hard.

Carlotta peered at her, then gave an uncertain little laugh. "Well, yes, but unless they are utterly depraved, they need our cooperation."

"Do not underestimate the number of those who are, as you say, 'utterly depraved,'" Elizabeth said with an edge of bitterness. Rising abruptly, she gathered the tea things and took them to the kitchen.

"What is wrong?" Carlotta asked, following after her.

Instead of answering, Elizabeth set about tidying the kitchen counter. Her hands shook as she washed out the teapot.

"I sensed earlier something was the matter. Please tell me what it is."

Elizabeth plunged a fistful of silverware into hot water, nearly scalding her hand. "I would prefer to move on to another topic, if you don't mind."

"How shall we grow closer as friends if you insist on keeping from me something that is obviously troubling you?"

Leaning over the kitchen counter, Elizabeth clenched her teeth. "Who said that we must grow closer?"

"Well, I thought—"

She wheeled around to face Carlotta, her face hot. "You inserted yourself into my life, based upon the fact that you occupy a studio upstairs. You knew nothing of me or my background, or whether we had anything in common."

"Forgive me, but I thought—"

"There is but one person I share a close friendship with, and she languishes in the mental ward at Bellevue Hospital."

Carlotta stood up. "I believed we shared a mutual regard," she said coldly, but her lower lip trembled. "You have made it quite obvious that I was mistaken. I shall trouble you no further." Snatching up her gloves and satchel, she turned and strode from the room.

Moments later, Elizabeth heard the click of the front door closing behind her. She stood perfectly still for some time, the only sound in the room the ticking of the wall clock over the sink. Then her legs crumpled beneath her, and she sank to the floor, her body shaking with deep, shuddering sobs.

CHAPTER TWENTY-FOUR

New York City in 1880 was a place where it was possible to indulge practically any human desire, holy or unholy. Entertainment of every kind abounded—there were beer halls, dime museums, tattoo parlors and circuses, Punch-and-Judy puppet shows, and theaters offering everything from Shakespeare to burlesque. Vices of every kind were available and plentiful. You could sate your appetite for gambling, drinking, fighting, or whoring in any of the thousands of establishments catering to such pursuits. On the Bowery, it was not uncommon to see half a dozen saloons per block; betting opportunities abounded, from keno and faro parlors to street hustles like three-card monte.

A decade earlier, at Kit Burns' Sportsman's Hall, terriers were pitted against rats in a brutal death match. (The most prolific of these dogs, a fox terrier by the name of Jack Underhill, reputedly dispatched a hundred rats in less than twelve minutes in Secaucus, New Jersey.) Burns was shut down in 1870 by the ASPCA, formed only four years earlier, but that did not dampen people's appetite for illicit forms of entertainment.

The more unsavory establishments were located downtown, many on the notorious Bowery, while others were scattered along Broadway. Some of these dens of iniquity enjoyed enviable longevity—John

Morrissey's gaming house at 818 Broadway lasted for more than thirty years. Most of the public gambling "hells" were sordid establishments catering to drunks, sailors, and rubes, as well as unsuspecting tourists. The most infamous were little more than brawling dens along the East River waterfront. Anyone who stepped inside such a place risked being robbed, drugged, mugged, or murdered.

Gambling was also available to the well-heeled in the genteel mansions of Park Row. The gaming came with elaborate dinners, crystal chandeliers, and fine wines to soften the victims' willingness to part with their cash. The surroundings might be lavish, but the result was the same: the house always won.

One of the most famous—or infamous—of these dens of iniquity was Harry Hill's Concert Saloon, at the corner of Houston and Crosby Streets, where any woman who entered was presumed to be for sale. The "concert" part of the saloon usually consisted of several soused gentlemen on various instruments. The dancing, if it could be called that, was required of the men, and expected of the women. In reality, it was an extended form of foreplay, which might or might not lead to sex. Although not permitted on the premises, it was generally understood that if a gentleman left with a lady he had encountered at Harry Hill's, it was to engage in some form of sexual congress. In any case, the gentleman was expected to buy drinks for the lady, as well as himself. Anyone not complying with these rules would be asked to leave, and if he had any sense at all, he would do so at once, as the second request might come with a more insistent physical component.

Apart from the usual gamblers, gangsters, and gawkers, Hill's clientele included politicians, writers, policemen, and other members of "respectable" society. These gentlemen—and indeed, anyone favored by Harry—were permitted to drink without being required to engage a lady in dancing. It was not uncommon to see a judge, police captain, or well-known author lingering at the bar, although when the young Mark Twain accompanied some friends to Harry Hill's in 1867, he left shortly after rejecting the advances of a rather persistent young lady, after realizing her true intent.

It was to this esteemed locale that Elizabeth repaired, armed perhaps with less knowledge than might be deemed advisable for a young lady unaccustomed to such places. But such young ladies did not often carry weapons in their purses, Elizabeth thought as she felt the reassuring hardness of her grandfather's Stormdolk. She paused for a moment outside the establishment, recognizable by the singular red-and-blue lantern hanging over the entrance. The night was warm, and raucous laughter, shouting, and singing crested over the strains of an out-of-tune piano and a tinny violin cranking out "Buffalo Gals." Drunken voices in various stages of tunefulness bleated out the lyrics.

Buffalo gals, won't you come out tonight
Come out tonight,
Come out tonight?
Buffalo gals, won't you come out tonight
And dance by the light of the moon?

It occurred to her that this was a terrible idea, an utterly foolish notion. It was suddenly obvious that, even with a dagger in her purse, she would be better off turning around and going straight home. Sweat bloomed on her palms, her breath quickened, and she felt dizzy. Elizabeth was not the same person she had been the day before; she would never be that person again. A part of her had been sliced away. The easy confidence she'd once worn like a protective cloak was gone forever. Why had she not waited a day, until she could ask Freddy to join her? He would have agreed, and his presence would have made all the difference. Inside the saloon, there was the sound of glass breaking, followed by bellows of laughter.

"How would your mother react if she knew what you were up to?" said a voice behind her. She turned to see Carlotta, a half smile on her face.

"I expect she would throw a fit." Elizabeth looked back at the saloon, its windows blazing with light. "I must apologize for the way I treated you earlier. You did not deserve it."

"I quite agree."

"Yet you came here to meet me."

"You told me at your flat you were going here."

"But why did you—"

"Because I know you did not mean what you said. Something is troubling you, and—"

"Please do not inquire further."

"I was about to say that, therefore, I forgive you. And you do not have to go in there—you can still back out. There is no need to prove yourself to me or to anyone."

"You can leave if you wish, but I intend to follow through," Elizabeth said firmly, in an attempt to inspire herself with confidence. In spite of her bravado, her stomach felt hollow and her legs weak.

"I'll not desert you," said Carlotta. "Lead on, Spirit."

Elizabeth recognized the quote from *A Christmas Carol.* "I thought you were Jewish."

Carlotta rolled her eyes. "Yes, but I *read.*"

Taking a deep breath, Elizabeth squeezed through the narrow side door next to the main entrance. A handwritten sign over it read "Women Only"—men were expected to come in through the front door, where they were charged twenty-five cents for the privilege. The side entrance led the women up a short, rickety staircase. After climbing the uneven steps, which seemed hardly fit to bear their weight, they emerged onto the main floor of the saloon.

The scene they encountered was like something out of Dante's *Inferno*. Several of the Seven Deadly Sins were on bold display, most prominently lust, closely followed by gluttony, in the guise of reckless consumption of alcohol. The room was plainly furnished. Apart from the boxing posters plastered on the walls, the decor consisted of little more than simple wooden tables and empty beer barrels, with a few chairs scattered along the edges of the hall. It was packed with members of both sexes. The men were somewhat older than the women, who were festively dressed, some quite expensively. The men had the hungry look of underfed dogs, while the women displayed a false gaiety covering a watchful wariness. The more intoxicated ones looked more vulnerable, their inhibitions dulled by drink.

The room was clotted with bodies and cigar smoke; a long bar stretched along one wall, while a stage took up the one opposite. Upon it were seated a handful of unenthusiastic-looking musicians. The violinist, a cadaverous man in a mangy toupee, sawed away at his instrument stoically, while a pudgy pianist pounded the keyboard with fingers as thick as sausages, a bowler hat perched rakishly upon his head. A third man stroked a bass violin with a languid look on his long, clean-shaven face.

The patrons were either dancing, drinking, or singing, some engaged in all three at once. A few muscular men roamed the room watchfully—Elizabeth took them to be Harry Hill's famed bouncers, charged with enforcing the rules posted on the large sign tacked to the wall: "People Who Are Drunk Must Leave the Premises."

Looking at the hooting, hollering clientele gallivanting around the dance floor, Elizabeth concluded that Harry Hill had a very lenient definition of being drunk. Waiter girls circulated the room. She imagined the fresh-faced girls ten years from now, the bloom of youth gone, struggling to make their way in a city that neither knew nor cared they existed. Now they were dressed in finery, swirling on the dance floor in the arms of some would-be swell in his cheap suit and cheaper shoes, feeling like the belle of the ball, but most of the men were there for only one thing. Down deep, the girls no doubt knew this, but they kept up a brave front, as if each of the young and not-so-young swains they danced with was a potential husband.

"What do we do now?" Carlotta asked as a couple of men approached the two women, grinning widely.

"How now, lovelies?" said the shorter of the two, a balding, bullet-headed man with a diamond tiepin and a swagger to match. "Never seen you two here before."

The taller one was good-looking in a country-rube sort of way. His homespun suit was too small, gawky arms protruding from the sleeves, his bony wrists exposed. He stood by shyly as his companion strutted and chatted up the women.

"Live around here, do you?" the balding one said, licking his lips.

The women exchanged a glance when a third man approached, shouldering his way through the crowd so confidently that Elizabeth knew at once who he was.

Harry Hill was a squarely built, muscular man of middle years with short graying hair and a lined, expressive face. His burly build bespoke the boxer he used to be—his saloon was noted as much for its displays of pugilism as its prostitution.

"Well, now!" he crowed. "What have we here, eh? Two young lovelies, come ta spend the evening with ol' Harry." His accent was a strange mixture of New York working class and British—it was well-known that he'd been born in Surrey.

"I'm Elizabeth van den Broek," Elizabeth said, offering her hand.

Hill seized her hand and shook it warmly. "Ah, yes, indeed—of the Fifth Avenue Van den Broeks. I know yer father—a fine gentleman, indeed! Welcome, welcome!" He turned to Carlotta, bestowing upon her a toothy smile. "And who might this be?"

Carlotta did not return his smile. "'This' is Carlotta Ackerman," she replied tartly. "Of the Orchard Street Ackermans."

"Allow me t'welcome you properly," he said, completely missing her sarcasm. Wrapping an arm around each of their shoulders, he bellowed, "Come have a drink on ol' Harry!" He escorted them away, much to the disappointment of their would-be suitors, who watched dejectedly as Hill whisked them through the haze of cigarette and cigar smoke toward the bar. Elizabeth felt many eyes upon them as they wove past groups of patrons, who momentarily interrupted their carousing to check out Harry's latest favorites. He was known for taking a shine to certain guests, treating them with deference and respect. Of course, the fact that they tended to be members of society's upper strata was no coincidence.

Hill's words echoed in her ears. *I know yer father.* How, exactly, she wondered, had a man such as Harry Hill crossed paths with a man who was not only a respected judge but a paragon of integrity? She could not imagine her father setting foot in such an establishment, but the past twenty-four hours had shattered enough of her beliefs that she no longer trusted her own judgment.

"Come along, luv," Hill said, pulling her toward a bar stool. "What'll it be, then? Drinks are on ol' Harry tonight!"

CHAPTER TWENTY-FIVE

"A drink on ol' Harry" turned out to be a watery affair, a much-diluted glass of whiskey. Carlotta opted for gin, and Elizabeth doubted she had fared any better.

"Now then, what brings you to my humble establishment?" he asked Elizabeth. "I mean, bein' as how you're a judge's daughter an' all?"

Elizabeth set her glass of watered-down whiskey on the bar. The surface was sticky to the touch, tacky from years of beer steins and whiskey glasses. She resisted the urge to wipe her hands on one of the bar rags wielded by the tattooed bartender. Tall and ruddy faced, he had a tattoo of an anchor on one sunburned forearm and a mermaid on the other, so she took him to be a sailor. A long, thin scar snaked across his sinewy neck. She imagined how he might have received such a wound. For all she knew, after leaving Harry's, he would venture down to Water Street to help shanghai some unlucky drunk into forced servitude aboard one of the many vessels docked there. He grinned at her, displaying a gold front tooth, but she avoided eye contact. Not to be discouraged, he turned his attentions on Carlotta, but was rewarded with such a withering stare that he nearly dropped the beer stein he was filling.

Elizabeth turned to Harry Hill. "How is it you know my father?"

Hill cleared his throat nervously. "Well, I mean, *everyone* knows yer father, yeah? He's quite a respected judge, ain't he?"

Before she could reply, there was a loud commotion on the dance floor. People stopped what they were doing to watch—a fight was considered good entertainment. Even the musicians stopped playing to observe the action, no doubt glad for the break.

The short pug-faced man who had been Elizabeth and Carlotta's would-be suitor had squared off with another man, a middle-aged working-class fellow with a solid build and a bristle of blond hair.

"Git away or I'll brain ya!" said the blond fellow. Elizabeth took him to be a farmer; his face and neck were sunburned, and he had the look of a hayseed, with powerful arms and strong, weathered hands.

"Oh, you will, eh?" said the bullet-headed fellow. "I'd like ta see you try!"

The farmer tore off his jacket and tossed it into the crowd. "I'll make mincemeat out a' ya!"

"Go on, then—take yer best shot!"

A circle had formed around the two combatants, with people shouting and cheering them on. A couple of men were hastily taking bets on the outcome. Even the women's eyes were shining, as they slapped their legs and hollered as vigorously as the men. Clearly this was all good fun to anyone who attended Harry Hill's.

"Get 'im, William! He's just a country bumpkin!"

"Go on, then, Caleb—show the city boy who's boss!"

"My money's on you, Will!"

"Pound 'im to a pulp!"

Before they could engage in combat, Harry Hill launched himself across the dance floor, accompanied by two of his bouncers. Seizing the stocky fellow by the back of his collar, Hill lifted him as if he were a child. The man struggled to free himself, but Hill dragged him to the front door, tossing him into the street as if he were made of papier-mâché. Meanwhile, his two henchmen closed in on the farmer, escorting him somewhat less roughly to the end of the bar, where they allowed him to cool off a bit before ejecting him into the street.

There was a collective sigh of disappointment from the crowd as they saw their source of entertainment so quickly dispatched. The impromptu bookies sullenly returned people's money, and everyone returned to their previous activities with somewhat dampened enthusiasm.

"Sorry 'bout that," Hill said, rejoining the women at the bar. He had the same pleased-with-himself look Elizabeth remembered seeing on her border collie when he had successfully fetched a ball. "Now then, what was I sayin'?"

"You were telling Elizabeth how you knew her father," Carlotta remarked drily.

"Never mind about that," Elizabeth said, pulling the photograph of Sally from her purse. "Do you know this girl?" she asked Hill. He studied it a little too long, and she knew, whatever his reply, it would be a lie.

"Nope, can't say she looks familiar," he said, scratching his head. "But I get a lot a' folks in here every night."

"I was told she used to work here."

His expression of bemusement deepened, and Elizabeth braced herself for the next lie.

"I don't handle the hirin' of our waiter girls. That job falls to Martin."

"Can I speak with him?"

"He ain't here tonight."

"When will he be in?"

"Well, he's here most nights, but he's took to his bed a coupla days past—a touch of the lumbago, don' cha know."

Carlotta frowned. "Lumbago?"

"Yeah, torments him somethin' awful. Gets worse in damp weather. Say," he said brightly, "you wouldn't be lookin' fer employment now, would ya?"

"Certainly not," said Elizabeth.

"She has a job," said Carlotta.

"That's too bad. I could use a coupla new waiter girls right now."

"She's a reporter," Carlotta added.

Harry Hill frowned and scratched his head. "Fer a newspaper?"

"The *New York Herald*."

He managed a smile. "How about another drink, then? On the house."

"Thank you, but we must be going," Elizabeth answered.

"What's the rush? Stay awhile—have some fun! Things are jes warmin' up."

"Mr. Hill, I don't think—"

"I'll look after yer. Let no one say Harry Hill don' take care a' his friends!"

"Perhaps another time," Elizabeth replied. "Good night, Mr. Hill."

"It was a pleasure meeting you," Carlotta said, shaking his hand, but her eyes were cold.

A few men whistled as they headed toward the exit, and one or two tried out some rude remarks as they passed.

"Hey, Red! Does the carpet match the drapes?"

"Heya, honey, how 'bout a dance?"

Elizabeth and Carlotta pushed through the weathered wooden door, which was dented and scarred from years of pounding by fists, boots, and beer steins. There were some deep cuts that looked like knife marks, and even a couple of bullet holes.

"He's lying," Carlotta said once they were outside.

"I wonder what he's hiding," Elizabeth mused.

The two women headed east on Houston Street. They had not gone far when a carriage pulled up in front of the building.

"That's odd," said Carlotta as a cadre of well-heeled young men spilled out of the vehicle, whooping and laughing. Most of them were dressed in evening clothes, sporting top hats and fancy canes.

"Indeed it is," Elizabeth agreed, as a sudden wind whipped in from the west. Carlotta grabbed her hat to prevent it flying from her head. Elizabeth did the same and was about to fasten hers with a pin when one of the young swells caught her eye. Tall and gangly, he did not seem to fit his expensive clothing. She could not be sure in the dim gaslight, but he looked very much like Jack Astor.

"What is it?" said Carlotta as the young men piled into the building, braying and bellowing with the high spirits of clueless youth.

"I thought I recognized one of them," Elizabeth said. She considered going back, but thought better of it. She'd had quite enough of Harry Hill for one evening.

The two women resumed walking and had not gone far when Elizabeth heard quick footsteps behind them. Alarmed, she wheeled around to see the tattooed bartender running after them. Seized by terror, Elizabeth felt her legs falter, and had Carlotta not grabbed her to steady her, she might have fallen.

"Sorry—didn' mean to startle you. I'm Zeke—Zeke Donlevy. I heard you askin' 'bout Sally."

"Do you have information about her?"

"She did use ta work at Harry's."

"Do you know her last name?"

"Mos' girls don' give their real names. A lot of 'em use a bunch a' diff'rent ones. Why are you lookin' fer her?"

"Because she was murdered."

He looked genuinely surprised. "Sally? *Murdered?*"

"Her picture was on the front page of the *Herald* this morning."

He gave a little cough. "I, uh, don' always get 'round ta readin' the paper."

Elizabeth suspected he didn't know how to read, but wasn't about to embarrass him by calling him on his lie. "What about Harry Hill?"

"Oh, he reads it ev'ry day."

The two women exchanged a look.

"Really?" said Carlotta. "So he would have seen her picture already, then?"

"Well, he don' always read *your* paper, miss. Sometimes he reads the *Sun*. Poor Sally," he said sadly. "Who kilt her?"

"That's what we're trying to find out."

"What 'bout the police? Isn't dat their job, like?"

Elizabeth adjusted her hat as another gust of wind threatened to remove it from her head. "Mr. Donlevy—"

"Call me Zeke."

"Uh, Zeke, how much does Harry Hill pay the police every month for 'protection'?"

Zeke scratched his chin. "Around five hunnert dollars."

"You can see why we don't entirely trust them to solve the murder of a former employee."

"I take yer point."

"So you don't know Sally's last name?"

"No, but I kin tell yer where she lived."

"How would you know that?"

"I walked 'er home one night. It was late and she were nervous—thought someone might be followin' her."

"Did she say who?"

"Nix. I didn' really believe her—sometimes the girls, they take things, y'know, an' it makes 'em see things wot aren't der."

"Where did she live?" asked Carlotta.

"On the Bowery. I kin take you der."

"Do you remember what number?" said Elizabeth.

"No, but der was a butcher shop downstairs, an' a saloon on the corner."

"Was it the Thirsty Crow?"

"Yeah, that's it. How'd you know?"

"Thank you, Zeke," Elizabeth said, shaking his hand. "You have been very helpful."

"I'm glad," he said. "Sally were awright, y'know? Didn' deserve t'be kilt." Elizabeth thought she saw a tear slide down his cheek, glinting damply in the gaslight. He sighed. "Well, I'd best git back before Harry has a conniption."

"Thank you again," Elizabeth said as he loped back toward the saloon.

"What now?" asked Carlotta.

Elizabeth was silent. She was too busy thinking about how a young woman from the Bowery had ended up wrapped as a mummy in Central Park.

CHAPTER TWENTY-SIX

After Elizabeth promised to be in touch, Carlotta headed downtown to her family's tenement on Orchard Street. Familiar with the crowded, often squalid, conditions among immigrants on the Lower East Side, Elizabeth wondered how her new friend's family was faring. She was comforted by the fact that they owned a bakery, which Carlotta had assured her was doing well.

It was not yet eleven, but in spite of her nap, Elizabeth was tired. She decided to take a cab for the short ride home, the Stuyvesant being a scant mile uptown. She also did not care to be alone on the street at this hour. Her formerly insouciant attitude had been replaced with an edgy wariness. Everyone seemed vaguely threatening—the street vendor selling roasted potatoes on the corner, the one-armed beggar riffling through the trash in the back of an alley. There was even something sinister about the couples strolling arm in arm along Houston Street; she sensed a hardness in the men's eyes, the women glancing at her before tightening their grips on their partners' arms.

Elizabeth thought about the frenzied, sexually charged scene at Harry Hill's concert saloon. She supposed that every once in a while, love was met in crowded, sweaty saloons, but that it was rare. In spite of Harry Hill's insistence on decorous behavior, everyone knew down deep the mad, frenzied dancing and copious alcohol was a prelude not to love and marriage but to something much more brutish.

Not that she blamed the girls, or even the men. Anonymity came easily in New York. The city was filled with people looking to escape their pasts or find futures they dared not dream of in the vast hinterlands of America, or whatever country they had managed to flee. But dreams could evaporate overnight and, in a place like Harry Hill's, alcohol could soften life's harsh realities for only so long.

Back at the Stuyvesant, she locked and double-bolted her door. Her mother's insistence on extra security had seemed overwrought when Elizabeth first moved in, but now she was grateful for that caution. She propped up the forged iron cane bolt, comforted by the heavy clang as it locked into place. Until now she had rarely used it, and even though her rational mind told her the chances of an intruder were minuscule, that part of her mind was not in charge now.

Finally satisfied she was safely barricaded inside, Elizabeth undressed for bed. Slipping between the cool, clean sheets, she fell asleep almost immediately. But she would not rest easy. Dark thoughts invaded her dreams. She found herself in a crowded saloon, amid strangers carousing, drinking, and dancing. She looked around for Carlotta but saw only unfamiliar faces. Searching for the exit, she made her way through the crowd. Aware that people were staring at her, she attempted to hide behind a Punch-and-Judy stage at the end of the room, but the mob closed in, forming a circle around her, much as they had with the two fighters at Harry Hill's.

Elizabeth suddenly realized that she was utterly naked. In the dim world of dream logic, she did not question why this was so; her only thought was to escape as quickly as possible. Panicked, she attempted to break through the press of bodies, but hands reached out to grope her as she twisted to avoid their grasp. The sound of mocking laughter flooded her ears as she tried unsuccessfully to evade the unwelcome touch of strangers.

Elizabeth awoke shivering, the blankets flung off around her feet. Pulling them back up to her chin, she lay awake in the darkness for some time, trying to vanquish the thoughts running through her head. Would she find her attacker, and if so, what, then? She thought she knew who it was but could not be certain. What if she was wrong? Why was she unable to tell Carlotta? The only person she would have confided in lay in a mental ward at Bellevue Hospital, her wits slipping away as fast as the night.

An owl hooted softly outside her window. The sound was comforting. Staring at the bedroom ceiling, illuminated only by a faint glow of gaslight from outside the window, Elizabeth imagined the bird's soft feathers and large round eyes, but also its hard, sharp beak and long talons. Closing her eyes, she vowed to be like the owl—she would make an ally of the night, transforming herself into one of its creatures. She heard the soft flapping of wings outside, the sound receding into the darkness. Elizabeth turned over onto her side, breathing easier now. She resolved to visit the Thirsty Crow to look for Grammy and perhaps have another chat with Herr Weber. Yawning, she stretched and dug deeper into the covers.

And for the third time that day, sleep claimed her.

CHAPTER TWENTY-SEVEN

Patrolman Seamus Spencer—"Spence" to his friends—strolled sleepily through the darkened paths of Madison Square Park. Inhaling the park's nighttime fragrances, he stifled a yawn as he passed a row of wooden benches. He gazed at them longingly. How he would love to have a quick lie-down, just long enough to close his eyes for a few minutes.

Working the night shift usually agreed with him—he liked the relative peace and quiet—but tonight he was tired. His wife had been up with their son, Brendan, the previous night, as he was suffering from catarrh. Spence had curtailed his own sleep schedule that day so she could get some rest. Each time the boy coughed, Spencer felt a sharp pain in his own chest, as if a knife were being plunged into his heart. When Brendan finally fell asleep, it was time to report for duty. Spence had dressed in the dark as usual, and set out around eleven thirty to clock in for his midnight-to-eight-a.m. shift.

Now it was barely three—the witching hour, according to his superstitious mother-in-law—and he was knackered. The moon was bright in the cloudless sky, casting its pallid glow over the trees bending gently over the all-but-deserted park. He passed a vagrant stretched out on one of the benches, fast asleep, snoring softly. Spencer didn't have the heart to roust him—even his wife said he was too kindhearted to be a cop—but he didn't see how the sleeping man was harming anyone.

Ahead of him, the disembodied hand from the Statue of Liberty glinted darkly in the moonlight. Jutting skyward from its concrete base, its fingers clutching an unlit torch, it was taller than most of the trees in the park. He peered at the plaque embedded in the massive square built to display the sculpture—the base alone was the height of two carriages stacked on top of each other. On the plaque, a painting of the completed statue was accompanied by a few lines of text relating how it was a gift of friendship from France, along with a plea for contributions.

By now everyone in town was aware that the hand had been placed in the park to raise funds for its erection in New York Harbor, and it had become one of the city's tourist attractions. But Spence found the sight of a gigantic disembodied hand disconcerting. In fact, it was downright creepy. He shuddered as he passed beneath the massive metal fingers, thinking about how nice his sardine-and-cheese sandwiches would taste when he took his break shortly. His wife had made him an extra one, grateful to him for sacrificing his own rest so she could sleep.

An object in the bushes behind the statue caught his eye, and he took a step closer to get a better look. He had a bad feeling as he approached—his wife often claimed he had "the gift" of foresight. Whether or not that was true, as he drew near, he suddenly stopped. He did not want to get any closer. Though he could not see the object clearly, his first impression was that it was something dark and twisted and evil. Taking a deep breath, he forced himself forward. He had been a policeman for more than a decade, but Patrolman Seamus R. Spencer was not prepared for what lay in the bushes of Madison Square Park.

Tucked behind the statue, partially obscured by foliage, were the charred remains of a human body.

Patrolman Spencer's own limbs stiffened, his body as rigid as the twisted, blackened flesh before him. He wanted to run, to flee into the night, to leave this terrible sight behind him. He looked around, but the only person nearby was the drifter asleep on the park bench. Tiptoeing forward as if he might wake the corpse in the bushes, he examined it more closely. The long, frayed strands of human hair told him the body was likely that of a woman, which was confirmed by the red dress draped over her. Curiously, the dress appeared undamaged, as if it had been put there after the fire had burned itself out. Peering at it more closely, he saw something white reflecting the pale moonlight.

Draped carefully around the victim's neck was a necklace, which appeared to be strung from the teeth of a large animal. Sharp and white, they gleamed in the moonlight like a talisman of evil things to come.

CHAPTER TWENTY-EIGHT

The next morning dawned gray and unpromising, and for the first time since being hired at the *Herald*, Elizabeth dreaded going to work. Her resolve of the previous night faded in the dull morning light. She knew if she asked Ferguson for the day off, he would agree, but she feared that he would take her off the story. Dragging herself out of bed, she washed her face and put on a plain gray frock she rarely wore because she did not think it flattered her figure or her complexion. Now she chose it for that very reason. Gulping down a cup of cold leftover coffee, she tied on a bonnet, grabbed her purse and briefcase, and left the flat, carefully double-locking the door behind her.

When she arrived at the *Herald*, it was after nine. She was glad to see Freddy Evans in the lobby.

"How are you, miss?" he asked. His skin looked pink and sunburned, the freckles on his forehead more pronounced.

"I should think you can call me Elizabeth by now, Freddy."

"Yes, miss. Are y'all right, then?"

"I'm quite well, thank you," she said briskly.

"Everyone was worried yesterday."

Not everyone, she thought. "I'm just on my way to see Mr. Ferguson."

"Me too. He seemed very excited earlier this mornin'."

"You've seen him already?" she asked as they climbed the marble staircase, the morning light streaming in through the tall side windows.

"I got here a bit early t'day—he was sayin' we've sold a lot a' papers in the past two days. Seems t'think your story's the reason why," Freddy said, scampering up the stairs ahead of her.

Elizabeth followed, and as they neared the second-floor landing, she saw someone just ahead of them. She recognized Karl Schuster's shambling, awkward gait even before he turned to see her.

"Well, if it isn't the woman of the hour. Looks like you've become a bit of a star. Congratulations."

"Thank you," she answered. "But what—"

"You'll see," Schuster said, walking down the hall toward his office. Trailing after him was the same scent Elizabeth had noticed in the supply closet, a combination of lime and mint. A bolt of fear shot through her body. Surely Karl Schuster could not be her attacker. Perhaps he and the man who assaulted her shared the same barber. Or maybe the aroma had already been in the closet prior to her attack—she could not be certain. Lime-scented aftershave was popular; even her father sometimes wore it.

"Miss?" said Freddy. "Y'all right, miss?"

"Uh, yes, I'm fine."

"It's true wha' I said, miss. Mr. Ferguson's all thrilled t'bits 'bout your story."

Freddy wasn't exaggerating. When she entered the editor's office, Ferguson greeted her with a broad grin, which he wore like a badly fitted suit. On a face not naturally given to such expressions, it was strangely out of place, like a cravat on a goat.

He seized her hand and shook it warmly. "They said I was making a mistake, letting a woman write a story like that, but we showed them, didn't we, Lizzie?"

"Yes, sir," she said, taken aback by his sudden display of warmth and his use of a nickname she didn't allow anyone except her father to utter.

"Now then," he said, shoving the ubiquitous cigar stub into his mouth, "what have you got for me today? I understand you were out following up leads until all hours last night."

Elizabeth wondered where he had procured this intelligence. "Yes, sir. I have some clues as to the girl's identity."

"Out with it, then!" he said eagerly, rubbing his hands together.

She conveyed everything that had transpired at Harry Hill's, including the conversation with Zeke. Perched on the edge of his desk, arms crossed, Ferguson listened carefully.

"So," he said when she had finished, "you have her address, but no last name?"

"I cannot even be certain of her first name. I only know she went by the name of Sally."

"These girls often use an alias in their line of work, as a safety measure."

"It didn't work very well for her, did it?"

Ferguson removed the cigar stub and rested it on an ashtray. "It is a dangerous trade, to be sure—a fact many people are not adequately aware of, I fear."

"Perhaps this story will help them understand."

"I would not hold my breath if I were you."

"I have another suggestion as to how we might procure her identity."

"Yes?"

"Do you recall the photograph of the strange symbol on her neck?"

"I do, now that you mention it. I should have a copy of it somewhere," Ferguson said, shuffling through the tornado of papers on his desk. Elizabeth wondered if it was a requirement that editors at the *Herald* keep a horrendously chaotic desk. "I do admire your progressive spirit," Ferguson said, seizing a stray sheet of paper and peering at it before dropping it back into the pile. "But people read stories like this for the prurient thrill of it. If they want to examine society's moral failings, they will attend a lecture."

"I refuse to believe that people are as heartless as you make them out to be."

The editor shrugged as he continued the excavation on his desk. "You are a good deal younger than I am. Perhaps when you are my age—"

"I will share your jaded view of human nature?"

"The newspaper trade does nothing to improve one's opinion of humanity. Ah!" he cried, holding aloft a photograph. "Here it is! Yes, indeed," he said, studying it. "Quite a strange sort of symbol. And you believe it is linked to her death?"

"It was etched into her neck. And it was the only wound on her body."

Ferguson paced the floor and stroked his beard, which was as dark as his eyebrows. "We need to find out what it signifies."

There was a knock at the door. The editor flung it open to reveal Detective Sergeant O'Grady, a determined expression on his face.

"Mr. Kenneth Ferguson?"

"The same. What can I do for you?"

"Detective Sergeant William O'Grady, Metropolitan Police, Twenty-Third Ward."

"Why, good morning, Officer," Ferguson said courteously. "Won't you come in? Allow me to introduce—"

"The lady and I are already acquainted. Hello, Miss Van den Broek."

"Good morning, DS O'Grady. How kind of you to spare me a trip to your station house."

"Have I really?" he said, cocking his head to one side. "Spared you a trip?"

"Yes, indeed. I was about to come see you."

"Were you, then?"

Ferguson removed the cigar stub from his mouth and gave an unconvincing smile. "We at the *Herald* are always anxious to cooperate with the police, naturally."

"Well, now, I am gratified to hear it," O'Grady replied. "What have you to tell me?"

Elizabeth told him what she had learned about Sally's identity. "But I assume you have your own ongoing investigation, do you not?"

O'Grady cleared his throat. "We've not yet discovered anything of real substance."

"Too busy collecting graft money," Ferguson muttered under his breath.

O'Grady peered at him. "What was that, then?" he said sharply.

"I was reflecting that we're daft and funny. You know, newspaper people."

The sergeant turned to Elizabeth. "Need I remind you that I gave you an introduction to Mr. Novak, enabling you to procure the picture you splashed across the front page of your paper?"

"Is that true?" Ferguson asked her.

"Well, yes, but . . ." Elizabeth was about to say that she would have managed to get the photographs anyway, but thought better of it. No sense in annoying a policeman who believed he had done her a great service.

"Your newspaper is the most widely circulated of any New York daily," O'Grady said. "I would appreciate it—the captain would appreciate it—if henceforth you would encourage your informants to convey anything they know directly to us."

"Are you offering a reward for such information?" Ferguson asked.

"It is not the policy of the Metropolitan Police—"

"Then what incentive do you imagine people have to report to you rather than to us?"

"The satisfaction of doing one's civic duty."

"Satisfaction does not pay the gas bill, nor does it feed a hungry brood of children."

O'Grady's fair skin reddened. "See here, Mr. Ferguson—"

"What if we take it upon ourselves to report anything we find to you?" Elizabeth suggested.

"Of course," Ferguson added hastily. "We will gladly keep you abreast of anything we uncover."

"See that you do," O'Grady replied.

"We would consider it *our* civic duty."

"Would you, indeed?" His tone indicated he was unconvinced.

Ferguson tilted his head to the side. "County Cork, is it?"

"Well, yes—"

"My father was Glaswegian, but my mother's Derry Cross, born and bred."

O'Grady's face softened. "Oh? Y'ever been back, then?"

"No, but it is my fondest dream."

"Aye, it's a fine green place."

"I would welcome any suggestions about what to do and see there."

O'Grady gave a little nod and sighed wistfully. "Well, I'd best be on my way," he said after a moment, and turned to leave. Hand on the doorknob, he paused and looked back at Ferguson. "Derry Cross, then, your mum?"

"I think she sometimes wishes she was there still."

"That reminds me," O'Grady said, with a glance at Elizabeth. "I stopped by to see our friend Viktor Novak this morning on an unrelated case, and he told me that late last night one of our patrolmen discovered a most unusual murder victim."

"Oh?" Elizabeth said. "Do you believe it relates to our mummy in some way?"

"I couldn't say, but as it happened in the middle of the night, none of the other papers are onto the story yet. I thought you might like to have a chance to—what's the term—scoop them?"

"I am grateful, Detective," Ferguson said. "Did Mr. Novak give you any details?"

"Only that she was hideously burned—and she was found in Madison Square Park."

Elizabeth and Ferguson exchanged a glance. "That does not sound at all like our other victim," the editor said. "But thank you for the tip."

"It didn't come from me."

Ferguson smiled. "Understood. I'll send someone right over. Thank you again—I am in your debt. And you may rely upon me not to forget it."

O'Grady smiled. "Good day, Mr. Ferguson—Miss Van den Broek."

"Good day, Detective Sergeant."

After he had gone, Ferguson closed his office door. "This is very intriguing information. But now we owe Detective O'Grady two favors."

"That is not entirely—"

"Did Detective O'Grady really give you access to Sally's body?"

"Yes, but it's no secret that dead bodies go to the morgue, and I am certain I could have persuaded Mr. Novak to let us photograph her, in the interest of justice."

"Detective O'Grady may indeed be well meaning, but he is operating within a corrupt system. The police are all in bed with Tammany Hall. Therefore, he cannot be trusted."

"I agree about the police in general, but O'Grady seems—"

"'Seems' is the operative word."

"I was about to say he seems to want justice."

"Perhaps. But the interests of the press rarely coincide with those of the Metropolitan Police."

Elizabeth was silent. She liked DS O'Grady, and he had just volunteered some useful information.

"Surely you are not too young to remember the Tompkins Square Park riots? It was but six years ago."

"Of course I remember," she said hotly. "My father's friend City Alderman Kehr was forced to leap from a streetcar to avoid an angry mob."

"There would have been no angry mob if it were not for the unconscionable actions of the police."

The 1874 Tompkins Square Park riots had begun as a peaceful protest by workers unemployed as a result of the Panic of 1873. Unbeknownst to them, the police department had persuaded the Parks Department to revoke their permit the night before. Police, some of them on horseback, descended on the crowd, beating men, women, and children with clubs to disperse them.

"You see how well justice was served in the aftermath of that debacle," Ferguson said bitterly. "No one from the Police Board was fired, and police surveillance is stronger than ever."

"I did not realize you harbored such progressive ideas."

He sighed. "I've often thought I'd be better off at the *New-York Tribune*, but here I am."

The *Tribune*, the creation of famed reformer Horace Greeley, was noted for its progressive journalism, including early opposition to slavery.

"I read some of the essays Karl Marx wrote for them," she said. "Very enlightening."

Ferguson grunted. "Our readers will be expecting the next article about the fate of poor Sally. What of this mysterious sign on her neck?"

"I have an idea."

"Oh?"

"I met a gentleman at Mrs. Astor's who may be of some service."

"Indeed?"

"He is connected to the Metropolitan Museum."

"So your little garden-party assignment was not a complete waste of time, after all."

"That remains to be seen."

"By all means, then—off you go. Here," he said, fishing some money from his pocket. "Take a cab. And don't forget this," he added, giving her the photograph.

"I will report back to you when I know anything."

"Quick as you can—I should like to have another story in tomorrow's paper, if possible."

"Shall I pay a visit to Mr. Novak as well? It could be related to our other victim."

"Very well, but mind how you go. I don't want to wear out our welcome."

Tucking the photograph safely into her purse, Elizabeth hurried from the office, eager and full of purpose. She had been charged with an important task, and she had no intention of failing. She had no way of knowing what fate had in mind for her.

CHAPTER TWENTY-NINE

He stood staring at the stacks of books lined up in front of him, intoxicated by the familiar smell of leather bindings, yellowing paper, and dust. The discovery of the Astor Library on Lafayette Place had transformed his boyhood. He had managed to pick up enough schooling to learn how to read; his teachers always remarked on what a quick study he was. The head librarian took pity on the young ragamuffin who wanted only a warm place to sit and immerse himself in tales of adventure, heroic exploits, and lives so unlike his own.

There were books on science and nature, which he found interesting, but what he really enjoyed were the books about crime, especially stories from real life. The best were the memoirs of detectives, who wrote about their cases, the ones they solved and the ones they didn't. He followed each case with interest, hoping they would prevail, especially over the stupid or artless hooligans. But he also enjoyed the exploits of the more daring and successful criminals, exulting in their victory when they triumphed over the luckless detective.

But when, quite by chance, he discovered ancient Egypt, everything changed. A book had been left open on one of the tables in the corner of the main reading room, with its vast ceilings and sepulchered silence.

He was not put off by the room's tomb-like atmosphere; it was a refuge from the noisy squalor of his daily life.

His face felt hot as he turned the pages of *Gods and Goddesses of Ancient Egypt*. They seemed so much more lifelike than biblical deities, in the smattering of Christianity he had acquired. Here were flesh-and-blood gods—ambitious, lustful, vengeful, and spirited, full of the same desires that animated humans. The book seemed to radiate energy; as he read, he felt enveloped by an unknown force. He read for hours, pausing only to go to the privy, which was indoors, an almost unimaginable luxury.

He was smitten; he swooned, his mind swirling with images of a land of sun and sand, so unlike his city of sweat and soot. When he went home that night, he dreamed deeply and well for the first time he could remember.

When he awoke, he knew with an unshakable certainty why the book had spoken to him so vividly. He was the reincarnation of Osiris, Lord of the Underworld, Judge of the Dead, important and powerful, eternal as the sky. It was a secret as delicious as it was unknowable—to ordinary mortals, that is. He alone knew it, and it would change the course of his life forever.

CHAPTER THIRTY

Elizabeth was beginning to regard Kenneth Ferguson in a more favorable light. He was not just the fast-talking, ambitious editor she at first had thought him to be; he genuinely appeared to care for the plight of the common man. She gazed out the window as the cab approached the Metropolitan Museum. Though at first glance the building appeared rather chunky and plain, as the cab drew nearer, she could see the warm redbrick façade and high windows with their striking white-and-gray stone arches. After paying the driver, she climbed the steeply raked stairs leading to the entrance and stepped inside, her heels clicking on the black-and-white marble floor.

The young woman seated at the desk in the foyer greeted her in hushed tones, as if they were in church. She wore a stark white blouse with a high, ruffled neck over a maroon skirt belted with a wide black ribbon, her dark-brown hair upswept into a simple but elegant bun.

"May I help you?"

"Is Dr. Abernathy available, by any chance?"

A flicker of displeasure crossed her face. "May I say who is calling?"

"Elizabeth van den Broek."

"Just a moment, please." Rising from her swivel chair, she walked quickly and quietly from the room, disappearing down a long corridor.

Elizabeth watched her go, wondering how she managed to muffle her footsteps so effectively, when every sound seemed to echo in the entrance hall, with its vaulted ceilings and marble floors.

She returned shortly, her face carefully composed into a smile. "Dr. Abernathy will see you now. His is the last office on the left," she said, indicating the hallway from which she had just returned.

"Thank you," Elizabeth said. Heading toward the corridor, she could feel the girl's eyes on her back. She read the words stenciled upon the glass panel of the last door.

Dr. Wm. Abernathy
Egyptology

As Elizabeth raised a hand to knock, she remembered the way Dr. Abernathy had looked at her during Mrs. Astor's party, and his wife's sullen exasperation. But surely nothing untoward could happen in a museum office, where anyone could knock on his door at any time? She lifted her hand once again, but before her knuckles touched the door, it was opened from within.

In front of her stood Dr. Abernathy. He was even taller than she remembered. With his thick silver hair, elegant build, and finely molded features, he cut a handsome figure. He was dressed in a dove-gray frock coat with matching cravat, his Italian leather boots polished to a sheen. His gray eyes widened when he saw Elizabeth, and his face broke into a smile.

"Well, well, Miss Van den Broek—what a pleasant surprise!" he said, opening the door wider.

"I hope I am not inconveniencing you," she said politely.

"Not at all—please, come in."

When she hesitated, he took a step backward to make room for her. Ignoring the small voice in her head, Elizabeth stepped inside.

"Do have a seat," he said, indicating a pair of matching hickory Chippendale chairs. Tutored tirelessly by her status-conscious mother, Elizabeth knew a good deal about valuable furnishings. As she perched upon one of the Regency-era chairs, upholstered in yellow and burgundy silk, she reflected that Dr. Abernathy was obviously a man of means, to have such furniture in his office. She supposed that was to be expected of someone on Mrs. Astor's guest list. Paintings by Old World masters covered the walls; the carpet was a deep, plush Persian, a floral design with burgundy accents to match the chairs.

"To what do I owe the pleasure of your company?" he asked as he sat behind his desk. Intricately carved of gleaming mahogany, it also looked to be a Chippendale, though she was uncertain of which period.

"I hope you do not think it forward of me to ask for your help."

He laughed—a hearty, self-assured rumble—and leaned back in his chair. "No man in his right mind would begrudge a visit from such a charming young lady. Now then, what can I do for you?"

Elizabeth extracted the photograph from her purse and put it on his desk. "Do you recognize this symbol?"

He studied it for a moment. "Why did you think to come to me about it?"

"I thought that perhaps the symbol bore a connection to Egypt."

"Why?"

"Did you know that a woman was found murdered near the museum recently?"

"My dear girl, the story was spread across the front page of your newspaper. Anyone who doesn't know of it by now must be living in a cave."

"This symbol was found on the young woman. She was dressed as a mummy," she said, omitting the detail about exsanguination. "And she was found—"

"In the hole being dug for Cleopatra's Needle. In fact, I am involved in making preparations for its transport."

"I do not believe these details to be accidental."

"Lovely young ladies like yourself should not concern themselves with such gruesome matters." His tone was fatherly, kind, and perfectly condescending.

"But since I *am* concerning myself with it, are you able to help me?"

He slid the photograph back across the polished surface of the desk toward her. For a moment she thought he was not going to help her, but as she tucked the photograph into her bag, he cleared his throat and leaned his elbows on the desk.

"Your instinct was correct. It is an ancient Egyptian symbol."

"You know it, then?"

"It is an old symbol for the earth. Here's a tome you may find useful," he said, perusing a tall built-in bookshelf behind his desk. Pulling a book from the shelf, he handed it to her. The leather binding was cracked and worn; on the front, embossed in gold, was the title: *Ancient Egypt: Myths, Gods, and Goddesses.*

Elizabeth ran her finger over the raised gold lettering. "May I—"

"Take it with you. I have others."

Her forehead tingled at his words, an oddly pleasant sensation, and she shivered a little.

"Are you cold?" he asked.

"No," she answered, but he was already on his feet, halfway to her when she rose from her chair.

"Are you quite all right? You do not look well."

"I am perfectly well, thank you. I am much obliged for your assistance," she said, backing away.

"What is your hurry?" he said, stepping between her and the door.

"I must—I n-need to—" she stammered. Her tongue suddenly felt thick, her legs heavy, as panic threatened to hijack her will.

Looming over her, he raised a hand to touch her cheek. She could smell the faint odor of gin on his breath and see the bloodshot rims of his eyelids. Without willing it consciously, she slapped his hand away. Surprised, he stepped back, and that was all she needed. Lurching for the door, she grabbed the handle and yanked it open.

"I'm sorry—I must go," she blurted out, and fled. She was all the way down the hall before she dared look back, but the corridor was empty. Striding past the young woman at the front desk, she realized why the girl was displeased at her presence—Elizabeth represented competition.

Pushing open the heavy front door, she stood for a moment in the welcome glare of the August sun, until sweat prickled her brow and she felt an uncomfortable dampness gathering under her jacket collar. Still tightly clutched in her hand was the book Dr. Abernathy had given her. Shoving it into her briefcase, she drew a deep breath and descended the front steps, continuing onto Fifth Avenue to join the roiling mass of humanity that was New York City.

CHAPTER THIRTY-ONE

Elizabeth did not stop walking until she reached Seventy-Second Street. Stopping to catch her breath, she realized she had no memory of the past ten blocks. The August air was balmy, the park fragrant with the blossoms of late summer; birds glided overhead as squirrels darted over logs and burrowed for nuts in the soft earth. In the park, a field of goldenrod nodded in the late-morning sun. But she had seen none of it, nor had she noticed the couples strolling along the sidewalk, or the carriages, cabs, and carts rolling down the avenue.

Sinking onto one of the wooden benches along the low stone wall bordering Central Park, Elizabeth took stock of what had just happened. She had seen the signs at Mrs. Astor's party, of course, so she could hardly be surprised by Abernathy's behavior. But of course she could not tell anyone. She would be condemned for attempting to besmirch the reputation of the respected historian, a man in Mrs. Astor's inner circle. All she could do was avoid him henceforth, which she hoped would not prove a challenge; she certainly had no plans to return to Mrs. Astor's in the near future.

But Abernathy *had* helped her, even though he'd obviously hoped to trade the information for her honor. *What honor?* she thought with some bitterness. As far as polite society was concerned, Elizabeth had given that up long ago. She had never breathed a word of her college escapades to her mother, and she certainly had no intention of relating anything of recent events.

A wind gust blew a haze of goldenrod pollen in her direction; she sneezed as she brushed the yellow dust from her skirt. This time of year her nasal passages were likely to swell; proximity to so much pollen was already making her eyes water. She looked up to see the Fifth Avenue Express Omnibus approaching the Seventy-Second Street stop, pulled by two high-strutting white geldings. She rose from her bench just as the coach driver pulled up to the curb to discharge passengers. Elizabeth paid her fare and took a seat next to a large woman in an extravagantly feathered hat. She feared her sneezing would start up again, but luckily the woman got off at the next stop.

Disembarking at Thirtieth Street, Elizabeth walked across town to First Avenue. She found Viktor Novak in a small office to the side of the morgue's main rooms. He was seated at his desk, eating a midday meal of sausages, black bread, and beer. The city's water supply was still regarded with suspicion by some; in 1832 a cholera outbreak had killed thousands. Even though the construction of the Croton Aqueduct brought clean water to New York in 1842, some people still refused to drink it. Elizabeth personally thought this was simply an excuse to resort to alcohol instead.

But she said none of this to Novak, who greeted her cheerfully.

"Miss Van den Broek—what a pleasant surprise!"

How he could maintain such high spirits surrounded by dead people was a mystery to her, but Elizabeth found his presence comforting for all that.

"I did not mean to disturb your meal; I can return at a more commodious time."

"Nonsense! I was nearly finished, anyway. My wife always packs me too much food, bless her soul. She wants to stuff me like one of these fine sausages! Now then," he said, rising from his chair and wiping his mouth, "let me guess why you have come."

"I was hoping—"

"You are interested in the mysterious corpse discovered last night in Madison Square Park."

"Yes. Well, that is, I—"

"I do not blame you. I am afraid the body is still awaiting examination in the medical examiner's office, so I cannot show it to you. Perhaps it is just as well. I do not think it is a very pleasant sight, even for such a stalwart young lady as yourself."

Elizabeth was about to protest that she was quite capable of viewing the body, but the truth was she was relieved. She'd had quite enough horror of late.

"There is not much to see, in any case. I am afraid the poor thing was burned quite beyond recognition."

"Could you tell whether it was a man or a woman?"

"The strands of long hair indicated it was most likely a woman. According to the medical examiner, there were other more, uh, biological indicators as well. Oh, and this," he added, plucking a garment from a pile of clothing on the row of shelves lining the far wall. Unfolding it carefully, he held it up so she could see it. It was a crimson dress, rather well made, with a matching sash and decorative buttons. Though it reeked of smoke, it did not seem to be burned in any way.

"Was she wearing that?" Elizabeth asked.

"Not exactly. According to the policeman who found her, it was draped over the body."

"How curious. Is there anything else you can tell me?"

"The young patrolman who found it was terribly upset, poor fellow. I was just coming on duty when they arrived with the body."

"Did he mention anything of interest, such as how he found it?"

"Let me see . . . Oh, yes, that's right—he kept saying he nearly missed it, as it was hidden behind the hand."

"The hand?"

"Yes. I thought perhaps he was delusional, he seemed so distraught."

"Perhaps he was referring to the hand of the Statue of Liberty?"

"Goodness me—of course, that's it! I nearly forgot it's been there these past four years. Zofia keeps saying she wants to go see it, and yet I find something rather unsettling about an enormous disembodied hand . . . I suppose I shall relent and go, in any case. I find that giving in to my wife's wishes is a wonderful way to ensure marital harmony."

Elizabeth found it odd that a man who seemed quite at home around dead bodies was queasy about a statue, but said nothing.

"Is there anything else you can tell me?"

"Oh, there is one thing—there was a curious necklace left on the body. Quite deliberately, I should think—it was not damaged in the fire, which means it was left postmortem."

"What kind of necklace?"

"I think we still have it, unless it was sent up to the medical examiner's office. Just a moment," he said, poking his head out his office door. "Mr. Higgins—are you in there?"

The orderly appeared a moment later, wiping his broad hands with a towel. "What kin I do fer ya, Mr. Novak? How do, miss?" he said to Elizabeth with a little nod.

She returned his nod. "Good afternoon, Mr. Higgins."

"I was wondering if we still have that necklace from the victim who came in earlier this morning?" Novak asked.

Higgins frowned. "That poor burned girl? Terrible thing, that."

"Yes, that's the one."

"I think it's in the possessions box, yeah."

"Would you mind fetching it?"

"I think I can lay my hands on it—be right back," Higgins said, withdrawing from the office.

Novak smiled. "Good man, always there when you need him."

"What's the possessions box?" Elizabeth asked.

"It's a collection of items we find on people—hatpins, keys, notecards, bits of string. You'd be surprised what people carry around. I once found a live rabbit inside a dead man's coat pocket. Turns out the poor fellow was a magician."

Higgins returned moments later holding a necklace comprised of what looked to be animal teeth strung on a strap of thin leather.

"That's it," Novak said, handing it to Elizabeth.

"How odd," she said, examining it. The teeth were large and sharp and very white. "I wonder what animal these come from."

"You can buy necklaces like these in Chinatown," Higgins remarked. "They might be tiger teeth."

New York's Chinese population had exploded in the 1870s, partly as a result of anti-Chinese violence in the western states. The same underpaid immigrants who had worked for a pittance to build the railroad now fled east to Manhattan, congregating in an area of downtown around Pell, Mott, and Doyers Streets.

"What do you think it means?" asked Novak.

"You don' think this is related to yer other dead lady, do ya?" asked Higgins.

"I confess, I do not know what to think," she replied, but as she gazed at the necklace in her hands, the back of her neck tingled.

CHAPTER THIRTY-TWO

There was a tram stop right in front of Bellevue, and after leaving the morgue, Elizabeth hopped aboard a downtown-bound car. Lulled by the clop of horses' hooves and the swaying of the vehicle, she buried her nose in *Ancient Egypt: Myths, Gods, and Goddesses*. Engrossed in the lurid escapades of Isis, Osiris, and Horus, she was struck by some of the similarities to other cultures, including Christianity. She was fascinated to discover that Osiris, like Abel, was killed by his brother—yet he bore a resemblance to Jesus in that he was resurrected from death, at least partially.

She arrived at the *Herald* to find most people out to lunch, which suited her perfectly. She went straight to the telegram office on the first floor. Plucking a blank form from the pile, she scribbled a message to Detective O'Grady at the Twenty-Third Ward station house.

> SYMBOL ON VICTIMS NECK ANCIENT EGYPTIAN SIGN FOR EARTH. CONTACT ME AT HERALD FOR DETAILS —E. VAN DEN BROEK

After handing it to the telegram operator, Elizabeth climbed to the second floor and settled in at her desk by the window to write her next article. Bending over her work, she lost track of time, until the rumble of distant thunder broke her concentration. She looked out the window to see a storm brewing over the East River. Purple clouds hovered low over the water as a brisk wind gathered momentum, swirling trash and dead leaves in the streets below. The rumbling grew louder, until a sudden crash of thunder made her jump from her seat. Darts of lightning forked and twisted across the sky as fat raindrops pelted the sidewalks. The downpour was so sudden and violent that she felt for her colleagues, who would have to navigate their way back to the office through such a deluge. Most of them would no doubt see it as an excuse to gulp down another dozen oysters along with a stein or two of beer.

Elizabeth settled back in to continue her work, raindrops hurling against the windowpanes to the accompaniment of thunder and lightning, as the gale continued its assault of lower Manhattan. She felt sheltered by the storm, as though the violent weather were a perimeter of protection, keeping her from harm. She leaned over her work, her pencil flying over the pages. Free of distraction or intrusion from the outer world, she finished the story in just over an hour.

Putting it aside, she opened the book Abernathy had given her. As she leafed through it, her attention was caught by an entry on Sekhmet, the goddess of fire: "A fierce warrior goddess, she is depicted as a lioness dressed in red, the color of blood. Protector of the pharaohs, she led them in warfare, and continued to protect them after death, bearing them safely to the afterlife."

A lioness dressed in red. The dress on the burned corpse had been red—and what if the teeth on the necklace were from not a tiger but a lion? Her heart thumped with such abandon that she feared it might leap from her chest. The placement of the body suddenly became clear as day: it was not the hand of the statue that mattered, but the torch! The poor unidentified woman was, in the killer's twisted mind, none other than Sekhmet, the ancient Egyptian goddess of fire. Was Sally, then, meant to be an earth goddess? That would explain so much—the symbol on her neck, the fact that she was found in a hole in the earth, dressed as a mummy. Elizabeth searched the book for mention of an earth goddess but could find none. Strangely, the Egyptian earth god—Geb—was male, and the pharaohs claimed to be descended from him.

As she pondered this puzzle, reporters began to straggle in from the rain-soaked streets. Tom Bannister loped in, laughing at something one of the other fellows—a slight, quick lad with a small, finely boned face and sharp eyes—had said. His name was Archibald Swinburne, but everyone called him Archie. Word had it that he had risen from newsboy to copyboy to cub reporter in the space of a couple of years. He was known to be very ambitious.

"Afternoon, Miss Elizabeth," Tom said, his long hound-dog face breaking into a bleary smile. "Yer luckeh to have missed that downpour, you are," he said, brushing water from the sleeves of his green tweed sack jacket. "It were like the wrath of heaven barrelin' down on us."

"Good afternoon, Tom, Archie," she said. "I trust you had a good lunch."

"I reckon we 'ad a bit more than were good fer us," Tom said, plopping down in a chair. "Eh, Archie?"

Archie gave a tight little smile and perched on his desk chair, prim as a cat.

Elizabeth gathered up her papers and the rest of her things and started out of the room.

Tom swiveled around in his chair. "Oiy, where you goin'?"

"To turn in my story."

He chuckled. "See that, Archie? That's a *real* reporter fer ye. Never mind 'bout oysters an' beer—she jes gets the job done, eh?"

Archie's reply consisted of one raised eyebrow. Elizabeth was fascinated with his economy of expression.

"See ya later, then," Tom said, lolling back in his chair to study some prints.

When Elizabeth entered his office, Kenneth Ferguson was seated with his feet up on his desk, eating an apple while proofreading an article. To say that his informality was unorthodox was an understatement. Elizabeth imagined that if Gordon Bennett Jr. were to see his editor like this, Ferguson would be summarily fired.

"Ah, come in, come in!" he said, removing his feet from the desk. "How is your article going?"

"It is finished," she said, putting it on his desk.

He straightened up in his chair. "Already?"

"But I have new information—"

"Hang on—let me have a look first." Snatching it up, he took another bite of apple.

"I believe there is a second victim."

"What?" He spit the chunk of apple into the trash bin. "Did I just hear you correctly?"

"Yes, sir." She proceeded to tell him of her visit to the morgue, and her conclusions based upon her reading.

"Well," he said when she had finished, "assuming you are correct, that puts us in an odd position."

Before he could continue, there was a knock on the door.

"Come in!" Ferguson barked.

The door swung open to admit a figure familiar to any New Yorker who had seen a newspaper, tabloid, or broadsheet in the past two years. Tall, though otherwise rather unprepossessing of appearance, with a soft body, a round, globular face, and a drooping handlebar mustache, Thomas Byrnes was nonetheless the most renowned figure in the Metropolitan Police. Newly appointed inspector and chief of detectives, he was known as an innovative and dogged policeman who was not averse to beating a confession out of a suspect.

"Good afternoon, Inspector," Ferguson said warily.

"Good afternoon, Mr. Ferguson. I see I am known to you," Byrnes replied, his voice betraying a slight hint of his Dublin roots. He removed the bowler hat from his rounded head to reveal closely cropped, thinning hair. Turning to her, he gave Elizabeth a slight bow. "Thomas Byrnes, Metropolitan Police."

"Allow me to introduce Elizabeth van den Broek, one of my best reporters," Ferguson said. Elizabeth smiled, realizing this was his attempt to impress Byrnes, rather than a frank assessment of her ability.

"Van den Broek?" Byrnes said. "Are you related to Judge Hendrik van den Broek, by any chance?"

"He is my father."

"A fine man, of impeccable reputation," Byrnes said, fingering his mustache. "Please convey my regards."

"I shall be certain to do so."

Ferguson took a box of cigars from his desk and offered it to the detective.

"Thank you, no," he replied. "My wife complains of tobacco odor on my clothing."

Ferguson smiled. "Mine is none too fond of it herself."

Elizabeth thought this explained the ubiquitous unlighted cigar.

"Would you care to sit?" Ferguson asked.

"What I have to say will not take long."

"Well, then, Inspector, what can we do for you?"

"I would very much appreciate it if you would decline to publish this image," he said, holding out a drawing of the Egyptian symbol from Sally's neck.

Frowning, Ferguson crossed his arms. "And why might that be?"

"I find it useful to withhold certain information from the public—things known only to the perpetrator."

"But surely in this case, informing the public—"

Byrnes' doughy face assumed a poor imitation of a smile. "As I said, I would very much appreciate your cooperation in this matter."

The implication was clear. It was not a request; it was a threat, and Byrnes made no attempt to conceal the fact. Refusing to cooperate would bring the wrath of the Metropolitan Police down upon the *Herald*. The consequences varied from inconvenience to deadly peril for anyone who dared to cross them.

Ferguson dropped his hands at his side. "Very well, Inspector, if that is your demand."

"I did not say it was a demand—"

"Let us drop the pretense, Inspector Byrnes. I have acceded to your 'request.' Shall we leave it at that?"

"And I would further request that before revealing any other information to the public, you run it by my office first."

"May I be so bold as to ask what you have uncovered in your investigation?" said Ferguson.

"At such time that we deem it advisable, we will schedule a press conference."

"What of Detective Sergeant O'Grady?" Elizabeth asked. "Is he still on the case?"

"I have decided to oversee the investigation myself."

"But—"

"Good day, Mr. Ferguson," Byrnes said, donning his bowler hat. "Good day, Miss Van den Broek."

With a tip of his hat, Thomas Byrnes departed as briskly as he had arrived.

"Well," Ferguson said when he was gone, "I regret to say you shall have to entirely rewrite your article."

"I see you did not mention any of what I just told you."

The editor gave a brusque laugh. "I felt no compulsion to do so. After all," he said with a sly smile, "at this point it's just a theory."

Elizabeth had already come to that conclusion, and another as well: she did not like Chief Detective Inspector Thomas Byrnes.

CHAPTER THIRTY-THREE

As the day was late, and he had other matters awaiting his attention, Ferguson gave Elizabeth permission to go home and turn in her work the following day. She was greatly relieved, as fatigue was taking its toll, and she would have to entirely rethink her article. They agreed not to mention the theory that there might be a link to the burn victim, treating it as an unrelated story, at least for the moment.

The brief thunderstorm had refreshed the air of lower Manhattan, and Elizabeth stepped over several puddles as she crossed City Hall Park, passing a row of young bootblacks in front of the graceful government building. They were dressed in overalls and cloth caps, their fingers stained dark from the polish they slathered on shoes and boots all day long. A couple of the boys appeared to be no older than nine or ten. City Hall was a popular place to ply their trade, as they could serve politicians as well as the newspaper men from Printer's Row. As she passed, the youngest, a pale lad with a flop of yellow hair, caught her eye and smiled. The tallest boy, in overalls too small for his gangly body, stuck out his tongue at her. Normally such a gesture might amuse her, but now it struck her as lewd.

Halfway across the park, Elizabeth had a sudden urge to see her father. His chambers were in the nearby Tweed Courthouse, so she put aside her hunger and walked north to the rear of City Hall. Its façade faced downtown, having been built at a time when most of New York's population lived on the southern tip of Manhattan.

The Tweed Courthouse was an imposing neo-Romanesque structure at 52 Chambers Street, on the northern end of City Hall Park. The rear of the courthouse faced the back of City Hall, a thin strip of greenery separating the two buildings. Commissioned by Boss Tweed himself, its construction ironically helped lead to the politician's downfall, after the *New York Times* exposed his embezzlement of large sums from building funds.

Elizabeth climbed the long staircase up to the front entrance, past the four massive stone columns supporting the classical portico, passing through the middle of the three tall arches leading into the building. She did not care for Greek and Roman building façades, with their pedantic, oppressively symmetrical lines, but the rotunda of the courthouse was another matter. The brickwork was spectacular in shades of carmine, forest green, and soft yellow; a series of decorative arches and balconies rose to a stunning stained-glass skylight. Sunlight splashed into the room from the tall arched windows as well as from the skylight. The effect was both stimulating and soothing—an odd legacy for a corrupt politician obsessed with his own glorification.

She walked across the elaborately tiled floor, the echo of her footsteps softened in the massive space. It was like being in a Persian palace. Her father's chambers were located on the second floor, and she climbed the heavy wooden staircase, admiring the golden chandeliers hanging from the balcony ceilings, illuminating their corners with soft, diffused light.

She entered the office to find her father seated at his desk—a heavy maple affair, rather grandly carved, the surface inlaid with green leather and gold trim. Her mother had ordered it from London after seeing it in a catalog.

Hendrik van den Broek was a tall man with shoulders stooped from a lifetime of bending over to converse with people of smaller stature. A pile of curly ginger hair covered a large head that seemed to be in danger of toppling his long, spindly body. He had the same deep-blue eyes as his younger daughter, the same pale skin and high cheekbones. His lips were rather too full for a man, and his nose was on the long side, lending him a slight resemblance to the French philosopher Denis Diderot. Perhaps it was not a handsome face, but it was a striking one—which happened to be Elizabeth's opinion of her own looks. She took after her father; her sister, Laura, was the one who had inherited Catharina van den Broek's delicate, ethereal beauty.

When he saw her, her father's face widened into a smile. "Lizzie! What a pleasant surprise."

For a moment she was afraid he would sense what had happened to her, and begin asking questions. She felt different following the attack, and feared that this change would be visible to someone who knew her so well. He came around the side of his desk and hugged her, his embrace lasting longer than usual. She was not certain what to make of it—he was glad to see her, he missed her . . . or did he indeed realize something was amiss?

But she need not have worried. "I do hope this is not an incommodious visit," she said, straightening her dress.

He laughed—a hearty, unaffected chortle, like running water tumbling over stones. "'Incommodious'? Ha! Since when has seeing my favorite daughter ever been anything other than a complete delight?"

Elizabeth squirmed a bit at his label of "favorite," though she knew it to be true. She felt she should protest on Laura's account, but under the circumstances, she feared it might seem disingenuous.

Her father was an important man, a judge in the criminal courts with a reputation for incorruptibility at a time when nearly everyone and everything in the city could be bought, for the right price. Boss Tweed might be dead, but Tammany Hall still exerted a fearful influence throughout town. But Hendrik van den Broek radiated integrity; no one in the city had a more unblemished reputation. Yet for all his prominence, Hendrik was a kind, mild-mannered man who preferred tending his tulips to passing judgment on his fellow citizens.

"I do not want to interrupt your work," she said.

"As it happens, I have a little time before my next court case. Now then, sit down and tell me everything that has been going on in your young life."

He indicated a pair of delicate French antique armchairs, another of her mother's conquests, plucked from an estate sale "for a song," she claimed, though she never revealed exactly what that meant. Elizabeth lowered herself carefully onto the creamy silk upholstery, her skirts rustling as she sat.

Her father perched on the opposite chair, leaning forward eagerly. "Congratulations on your article—people have been talking of little else."

"I did not expect it to make such an impression upon members of the legal profession."

"On the contrary—we are great consumers of scandal. Truthfully, though, it is quite a dreadful murder. Are you certain crime reporting is a proper occupation—"

"For a young lady such as myself?"

He gave a rueful smile. "It does sound odd when you say it."

"I am not certain it is a proper occupation for anyone. But since you ask, I am determined it will not be closed to women."

"But are you not the only—"

"Oh, there will be others after me, no doubt some of them more talented and successful than I could ever hope to be. I shouldn't wonder if some achieve great renown."

"But you are content to be the vanguard."

"Nothing of merit is ever built without breaking ground first."

"That's my Lizzie! You always did have a mind of your own. You take after your mother in that respect. Are you making progress on finding that poor girl's identity?"

"We are, yes."

"I do hope you aren't putting yourself in danger."

She had no intention of relating her trip to Harry Hill's, though she longed to ask her father just how well Hill *did*, in fact, know him.

"Is something wrong?" he asked.

"No, nothing," she replied.

"I know that troubled look. What's on your mind?"

"I saw Laura this week," she said finally. It was the truth, and would distract them both from what she actually had been thinking.

Her father gave a little cough and pulled at his cravat. "Did she recognize you?"

"She did."

"How was she?"

"I've no doubt she would improve more quickly if she saw her family more often."

His face assumed a pained expression. "I do encourage your mother to go, but . . . it upsets her."

"Are you suggesting her state of mind is more important than Laura's recovery?"

Closing his eyes, he squeezed the bridge of his nose with his thumb and forefinger. She recognized the gesture. He did it when suffering from a headache.

"Lizzie," he said softly, "I think you have to face the possibility that your sister may not get better."

Elizabeth pressed her lips together and stared at the floor. The pattern of the lush Persian carpet swam before her eyes. "She *must*."

"Her condition—"

"Do not speak of her like that—I will not allow it!"

"But—"

"We must keep hoping! If we do not, she will sense it and lose hope herself."

He sighed and looked away.

Elizabeth studied her father. "What is it you are not telling me?"

He stood and gazed out the long window by his desk. New York was splayed out before them—Lafayette Place shot uptown to the east of the park, while Broadway rose to the west. The old city lay behind them; to the north was the future. As he stood there, the sun broke from behind a bulky gray cloud cover. Shining in through the tall window, it outlined her father in a halo of light.

He turned back to her and hung his head, like a guilty man headed to the gallows. "It should be your mother telling you this, but as she has not yet, I fear she never will."

Her heart went cold. "Tell me what? What has she hidden from me?"

"Your mother had . . . a brother."

"I have an uncle?"

He looked down, avoiding her gaze. "I said she *had* a brother."

"He is no longer alive, then?"

"He committed suicide at the age of twenty-five."

"One year older than Laura. Was he—"

"The same symptoms, emerging at exactly the same age. He and your mother were very close, like you and your sister."

"So Mother did not tell me because she—"

"Oh, Lizzie, she feels so desperately guilty. She is convinced the flaw lies within her bloodline—that she is responsible for . . ."

"For Laura's illness."

"Yes."

His voice was a whisper, barely audible, but in that moment Elizabeth saw her mother in a new light. Her restlessness, her brittle cheerfulness and obsession with status—all a desperate attempt to hold at bay what must be the great sorrow of her life. Elizabeth looked at her father's face, for the first time realizing the depth of pain and love that bound them as a family.

"Why did she never tell me of this?"

"She did not want to burden you with her loss."

"*Burden* me?"

"She wanted to shield you from her suffering."

Elizabeth snorted, and immediately heard her mother's voice in her head. *Such an unladylike sound, Elizabeth!*

Well, so be it, she thought, reflecting on how well being ladylike had served her mother. "Her secret only served to distance her from me," she said bitterly.

"I feel I have betrayed her in telling you this," her father remarked, sinking into his desk chair.

"You have betrayed no one. But if you like, I will not reveal what you told me."

"I would be grateful if you did not," he said as the ship's clock on the mantel chimed three times. "Forgive me, but I have a court session."

"You must go, then. It will not do for the judge to be late."

"I daresay most of the lawyers in this town have made me wait on more than one occasion," he said, pulling on his black robe.

"Then they deserve a taste of their own medicine."

"It was good to see you, Lizzie," he said, brushing his lips across her cheek. "Please come by anytime. You are free to stay," he added, opening the office door. "Just close the door behind you when you leave. See you on Sunday."

Sunday dinner was a ritual in her family. Since her return from college, they had clung to it especially tightly, though Elizabeth could not say she was looking forward to it this week. She stood gazing out her father's window for some time. Secrets were a slow poison, doing their damage in the dark, she reflected as she watched the ebb and flow of life on the streets below. The city, too, had secrets nestled within its breast—dark, dangerous ones, she thought as she stepped at last out into the late-afternoon haze.

CHAPTER THIRTY-FOUR

After leaving her father's chambers, Elizabeth spied Marco, her favorite oyster vendor, on the other side of City Hall Park. Having eaten nothing since early breakfast, she was feeling quite faint with hunger.

"Afternoon, miss!" he said as she approached, tipping his moth-eaten cap. He was short and broad, with a beard stubble so rough it looked as if it could cut diamonds. His rheumy brown eyes were bloodshot and cheerful. Perhaps it was a result of his prodigious diet of whiskey and red wine, but she had never seen Marco in a bad mood.

"Hello, Marco. I'd like a dozen of your freshest, please."

"Nothin' butta the best for you, miss," he replied, scooping them from the layer of ice on his flatbed cart, shucking them as fast as she could eat them. His gnarled hands resembled the shells of the oysters he sold. Rough and thick, they were nicked and scarred from decades of cuts from oyster knives and shells. Even the most skilled shellfish vendors had hands like his—it came with the trade, just as bent backs and bad knees were endemic to construction workers and longshoremen.

Tilting her head back, Elizabeth slurped them down one after another, savoring the sweet, tender flesh tasting of brine and seawater. She polished off the first dozen so quickly she considered ordering a second, but a line was forming behind her, and she felt the urge to be on her way. As always, she paid him a little extra—partly out of generosity, but also to ensure that she got the freshest oysters. She had eaten a bad oyster once, some years ago, and it was not an experience she cared to repeat.

Wandering up Broadway, she bought a hot potato and an ear of corn, followed by a Viennese waffle, a recent craze, from another cart. By the time she reached Worth Street, she felt as stuffed as the roast partridges her father loved for Sunday dinner. She was about to board a streetcar when she had an impulse to return to the Thirsty Crow and see what she could find out. She decided to walk for the exercise, and to clear her head.

Walking east, she could see the Tombs two blocks to the north, looming over the crisscross of streetcar tracks bordering it on two sides. Thick and imposing, with chunky masonry columns, the Egyptian Revival building housed the city's jail. Its official name was the Halls of Justice, but everyone called it the Tombs. The design was rumored to be modeled after an Egyptian tomb, meant to inspire dread and awe in criminals unlucky enough to be housed within its dank walls.

Elizabeth continued east, toward the notorious neighborhood known as Five Points. She had been warned since childhood of the dangers and diseases lurking within its ramshackle wood buildings—degradation and drunken depravity, murder and mayhem, all congregated roughly in the area bordered by Chatham Square to the southeast and the intersection of Canal and Center Streets to the northwest. This was the infamous Sixth Ward, said to be the epicenter of all that was malignant and menacing. Named after the intersection of Baxter, Worth, and Park Streets, the neighborhood was poor, crowded, and neglected—small wonder the murder rate was higher than anywhere else in the country, and a majority of children born there died in infancy.

Since her attack, she had experienced constant anxiety, even in relatively safe locations. Now, she thought—perhaps foolishly—if she could tread the narrow streets and closely packed buildings of Five

Points, perhaps she could rid herself of fear's unwelcome presence. She could anticipate the arguments against it—she could make them herself—but even greater was her desire to rid herself of the dread chipping away at her.

Continuing east on Worth Street, she passed dilapidated tenements, with laundry strung up between buildings, hanging across damp alleyways, flapping in the gentle August breeze. Children played in puddles, poked at piles of trash with sticks, or played at hoops, seemingly oblivious to the saloons and brothels lining the streets. Women in various stages of undress skulked in doorways, in hopes of luring men inside. The lucky ones might escape with their wallets intact; more often, they would fall prey to "panel thieves," confederates of the prostitutes who would sneak into the room through sliding wall panels and relieve the customer of his valuables while he was otherwise engaged.

Passing through the intersection from which the neighborhood drew its name, Elizabeth turned up Park Street, approaching the notorious Mulberry Bend, where the street hooked to the northeast. With its warren of dank, menacing back alleys, boasting names such as Bandit's Roost, Bottle Alley, and Ragpickers Row, "the Bend" was widely considered to be the dark core of Five Points.

A sad-eyed young prostitute stood in a dilapidated doorway scanning the street, one side of her crimson dress pulled down to expose a thin white shoulder. A burst of cackling laughter erupted from the second story of one ramshackle building as a besotted middle-aged man staggered from the first floor of another. A couple of young toughs in bowler hats leaning against a lamppost whistled as Elizabeth passed. One of them bore a striking resemblance to the oldest bootblack in front of City Hall.

The tinny sound of a banjo floated out of the entrance to a saloon by the name of Lucky Jacks. A crudely painted sign of a pair of aces indicated that there was gambling to be had inside the establishment. A handful of voices, ragged with alcohol, stumbled along with the banjo as best they could. Elizabeth recognized the tune as a popular sailing song. When they reached the chorus, the saloon patrons bellowed out the lyrics lustily.

Sailing, sailing, over the bounding main;
For many a stormy wind shall blow, ere Jack comes home again!
Sailing, sailing, over the bounding main;
For many a stormy wind shall blow ere Jack comes home again.

The stink of the streets caused Elizabeth to hold her breath between shallow gulps of air. It was a fetid combination of ash, rotting garbage, human waste, and despair.

Through one of the alleys, Elizabeth spied a young woman about her age bending over a bucket of grimy laundry. Seeing the girl in her rough gray frock, stained and tattered from years of wear, Elizabeth felt a flush of shame creep to her cheeks. She was embarrassed by her own finery, her green silk dress made in London, with its velvet trim and pristine matching parasol, and her soft Italian leather boots.

But what stopped Elizabeth in her tracks was the close resemblance between them. They had the same light-auburn hair, the same build, and a similar facial structure. The girl wiped her forehead wearily as she bent over her work. She looked up at Elizabeth, a greasy lock of hair falling over one eye, a shock of recognition on her face. Her blue eyes widened as she stared boldly, long enough to be considered rude—except that Elizabeth was staring back at her.

Looking into the girl's eyes, Elizabeth felt as if a bolt of electricity had shot through her body. It was suddenly blindingly clear that her own relative wealth and comfort were merely a trick of fate that had rewarded her, but left this girl destitute, doing laundry in an old bucket in a wretched alleyway.

These thoughts rushed through her head like a speeding freight train, all in the few seconds before she and the girl broke their gaze. The girl gave an insolent smile, which seemed almost a dare, before returning to her work. Elizabeth stood for a moment before willing her legs to carry her forward. It was not far to Rivington Street, and Elizabeth reached her destination just as the sun dipped around the southern corner of Manhattan, to continue its journey along the North River before sinking over the Watchung Mountains.

Herr Weber's butcher shop was closed, but the Thirsty Crow was doing a brisk trade, judging from the shouts and hoots coming from within. As Elizabeth drew nearer, she could smell fumes of cheap tobacco, sweat, and stale beer. As she was debating whether to risk entering, a patron sauntered from the building. Leaning against the iron railing that had steadied many an intoxicated gent, he fanned his face with his hat and lit a cigarette.

He was dressed in the manner of a Bowery B'hoy—brushed silk top hat and trademark red shirt, his black pants rolled up over heavy boots. His heavily oiled hair was plastered close to his face, and he carried a black frock coat over one arm. Though the heyday of the "B'hoys" was past, you could still see people affecting the look of the once-notorious gang, strolling along the avenue with their signature swagger. The term "B'hoy" was a representation of a typical Irish pronunciation of "boy," though the working-class B'hoys were violently anti-Irish and anti-Catholic. The B'hoys' most violent days were behind them, their famous skirmishes with their rival gang, the Dead Rabbits, having culminated decades earlier.

Seeing her staring at him, the B'hoy smiled and held out his pack of cigarettes. "Care fer a smoke, miss?"

"Thank you, no—but I would like a minute of your time, if you would indulge me."

"Well now, I 'spect I kin manage that, fer such a fetchin' young lady." He pulled deeply on his cigarette and flicked a tobacco flake from his lips. "So what's on yer mind, missy?"

"Do you know a woman named Grammy? That's the name she goes by."

"'Course I do. Everyone 'round these parts knows Grammy—or knew her, I should say."

"Knew her?"

"I'm 'fraid she's dead, miss."

"Oh, no," Elizabeth said, fear curdling in her throat.

"Sorry 'bout that. She were a friend of yours?"

"What happened? I mean, how did she—"

"She were found yesterday, I think it was. Looked like she'd been strangled."

"Are you sure?"

"That's what everyone's sayin'."

"What about the police? Are they investigating?"

He snorted contemptuously. "Sure they are. 'Cause they really care 'bout the death of a poor old crone who was a known boozer." He shook his head as he stubbed out his cigarette, grinding it beneath his heel. "Poor ol' Grammy. Never met a drink she didn't like, but she was a good pal, so she was."

Elizabeth glanced at the dark third-floor apartment above the saloon. Whatever Grammy had known about the dark events that had transpired there, someone evidently thought it was too much.

CHAPTER THIRTY-FIVE

People were strangely difficult to kill. Or so he'd thought at first. But as his skill grew, he was surprised at how quickly and easily life ebbed from the eyes of his victims. He never tired of watching as fear turned to astonishment, then anger, followed finally by resignation. It was always the same—the process never seemed to vary from person to person. At first there was pure animal terror, as the body mounted its instinctive survival response; then, as the victim realized there was no way out, there was the incredulity that this was it—that her life was indeed going to end like this. The anger came from the realization that there was nothing she could do to stop it. Finally, there was the surrender to her fate, as her body relaxed and her eyes assumed that faraway gaze that told him death was near.

The process, which at first seemed chaotic and jerky, had become smooth and almost graceful, like a ballet, a pas de deux, as intimate and personal as the sexual act. At times it was positively ethereal. As he became more familiar with the process, he was able to relax and enjoy it more, to savor each precious stage. He had concluded that murder was like anything else: practice made perfect. In a few short weeks, he had gone from novice to master, all by dint of hard work and preparation.

His friends sometimes commented slyly that he must have a mistress—and in a way, they were right. It occupied his every waking thought; he spent his free time thinking about and planning the next conquest; every hour spent not engaged in the hunt felt like wasted time.

At first the killing sprang from the rage simmering within him—harming other people seemed to calm the fiery torment in his heart. But after a while, it became an end in itself, as he grew to enjoy it more and more. It became his secret, his avocation, his raison d'être, the chief focus of his life. Everything else was subservient to his drive to kill, his need for more victims. He worked, ate and drank, conversed with people, even attended the many "entertainments" the city offered. But it was like treading water. Nothing compared to the thrill of the hunt, the intoxication of knowing he held the power of life and death in his hands. When he was killing, every fiber of his being pulsated with the thrill of it, and he felt alive in a way he never had before. He was Osiris, Lord of the Underworld, Judge of the Dead, and he alone had the power to decide who lived or died.

Cleo purred and rubbed against his shin; it was nearly time for her dinner. He picked up the cat and stroked her soft, sleek fur, feeling the delicate rumble in her throat as the purring grew louder. He buried his face in the thick ruff of her neck, feeling a bit morose about strangling the old lady. He had not enjoyed that. It had made him feel small, dirty, as if he were killing his own mother. That was simply a matter of survival, an unpleasant but necessary task. She had seen too much and, with her tongue loosened by drink, could not be trusted. He'd considered paying her off, but he knew better than to trust a drunk.

Pushing the window curtain aside, the cat in his arms, he gazed out at the gathering twilight. Once night fell over the city, he could ply his dark trade. He sighed and let the curtain fall. It wouldn't be long.

"Come along, Cleo," he said. "Let's get you something nice to eat."

CHAPTER THIRTY-SIX

After arriving home, Elizabeth put on her dressing gown and ate a slice of bread and cheese while standing at the kitchen counter. Then she sat down at her writing desk in the front parlor to finish her article. *Ancient Egypt: Myths, Gods, and Goddesses* lay next to her elbow. She opened it to the section on Osiris.

> *Though it is arguably the most important myth in ancient Egypt, it is difficult to find a direct description of the death of Osiris. The Egyptians believed that written words had great power and could even affect reality, so they avoided writing directly about the god's murder.*

Chewing on her cuticle—a habit her mother deplored—Elizabeth pondered this information. She had always believed in the written word, but the Egyptians, it seemed, had taken it a step further. She continued reading.

> *In the most popular version of the myth, Seth murders Osiris, cuts the body into pieces, and scatters it throughout Egypt. Osiris' wife, Isis, finds all the pieces and puts him back*

> *together, carefully wrapping him in fine linen, making him the first mummy.*

The first mummy. Yawning, Elizabeth turned to the pages on mummification.

> *The Egyptians preserved a body by first removing its internal organs . . .*

The sound of the grandfather clock striking ten awoke her; it was only when she lifted her head that she realized she had fallen asleep at her desk. Rubbing the sleep from her eyes, she read through what she had written. It wasn't bad, but it needed some rewriting, and she resolved to wake early and finish in the morning. She shuffled to the bedroom, feeling as if someone had attached lead weights to her ankles.

But something was different. The blanket of dread that had draped her consciousness since her attack had lifted. Running a bath, she felt oddly euphoric. She had still been violated, and the shame of it was still with her, along with the anger. But she felt lighter, more buoyant, and less afraid. Perhaps her stroll through Five Points had accomplished its intended goal, she thought as she slid into the steaming water, watching it engulf her limbs. She had walked the city's most dangerous streets and survived unscathed. And now she was safe in her own apartment. She no longer felt invulnerable, but perhaps she had become something more important—aware.

After her bath, she pulled herself from the tub and wrapped herself in her thickest, fluffiest towel and went to the kitchen to make herself a cup of chamomile tea—her mother's secret for a good night's sleep. Afterward, she slipped between the crisp white sheets on her bed, with its walnut headboard and cotton-stuffed mattress. She had barely pulled the bedclothes up to her shoulders before sleep enveloped her in its welcoming embrace.

Elizabeth awoke the next morning with the feeling that someone was in her apartment. She suddenly realized she had forgotten to slide the cane bolt into place the night before. Instantly alert, she sprang from bed and grabbed a heavy umbrella from the stand in the hallway. Hearing noises in the kitchen, she crept down the hall, holding the umbrella tightly in both hands. Brandishing the umbrella, she entered the kitchen ready to attack the intruder. She was confronted with the smell of coffee.

Carlotta was sitting at the kitchen table, Toby at her feet. "Ah, you're awake at last!" she said, jumping to her feet. Toby responded to this by hopping in place, wagging his stubby tail. "Whatever are you doing with that umbrella?"

"What are you doing in my kitchen?"

"You did not respond to my knocking, so I let myself in."

"What on earth—"

"I did pound on the door for quite a while, but apparently you were dead to the world. I thought perhaps you were unwell, so I took the liberty—"

"Of breaking in?"

Carlotta frowned. "Well, when you put it like that . . ."

"What would you call it?"

"When I saw you were not *dead*, but merely asleep, I made you coffee. And I brought pastries," Carlotta said, picking up a paper bakery bag. "I thought you might enjoy waking to the smell of coffee and pastries. Apparently I was wrong," she added tartly.

Elizabeth bit her lip. She knew she was being manipulated but believed Carlotta meant well. And the coffee and pastries smelled like the essence of heaven itself. She sank into one of the kitchen chairs. "How did you manage to get in?"

"I told the concierge I was your cousin and that I had forgotten my keys."

"And she believed you?"

"I can be very persuasive," Carlotta said, pouring a steaming cup of coffee and setting it in front of Elizabeth before arranging her baked goods on a blue-and-white china plate. "Besides, she knows I have a studio upstairs, so I am hardly a stranger."

Elizabeth reached for a pastry—small, cigar-shaped dough with a filling of jam and nuts. "What are these?" She had seen them in Orchard Street bakeries but couldn't remember what they were called.

"Rugelach. It's a Polish/Jewish specialty."

Elizabeth took a bite, the flavors exploding in her mouth—sweet and nutty and crispy. "Oh," she said. "Oh, oh, oh."

"May I conclude that you like them?"

"I only regret all the years I have spent not eating them." She sipped the coffee, strong and dark, the way she liked it.

"It's my mother's recipe."

"How is she feeling, by the way?"

"Much improved, thank you. And you? You look tired."

"I am writing a second article about the murder. I fell asleep before I finished it last night."

"I read your first one—it was very good."

"That is kind of you," Elizabeth replied, reaching for a second rugelach.

"How goes the case? Have the police made any progress?"

"I am not convinced they are interested in solving this."

"That would not surprise my brother one bit. He has no faith at all in the Metropolitan Police."

"I am beginning to feel the same." She told Carlotta of Detective Byrnes' odd visit to the *Herald* the previous day.

Carlotta listened carefully. "What is his angle, I wonder?" she said, pouring them both more coffee.

"I do not know, but I do not like him."

"Perhaps he feels it is an important case, and that solving it will show him in a favorable light."

"But why command us to withhold information from the public?"

"His justification sounds reasonable enough."

"That man has an unsavory aura. I don't trust anything he says."

Carlotta tossed a small piece of rugelach to Toby, who caught it midair, swallowing it in one gulp. "I shan't stay long. You have an article to write, and I have a painting in progress, so—"

"I thought you were a sculptor."

"Lately I have been drawn back to the canvas, for some reason. Which reminds me . . . I wonder if you would let me paint you someday."

"Why on earth would you want to do that?" Elizabeth asked, pouring more coffee. It was like the elixir of life; she felt consciousness returning to her sleepy brain.

"Well, you are rather . . . colorful."

"I don't know if that would be a good idea."

"Why not?"

"I would make a terrible model. I am not good at sitting still."

"Then I shall just have to paint quickly. What do you say? Otherwise I shall have to pay someone to model for me, and I don't suppose she would be nearly as interesting as you."

"So long as you bring more rugelach."

"Agreed," Carlotta said, gathering up her cloak. "Shall we say Sunday morning?"

"But not too early. It is my day to sleep in."

"Ten o'clock, then."

"Very well."

"Does Byrnes have a theory as to why Sally was wrapped as a mummy?"

"I'm afraid it is incomplete at the moment. I have been doing research."

Carlotta sipped her coffee. "What did you discover?"

"The Egyptians removed all the internal organs."

"Yet that was not the case with poor Sally. What do you think it signifies?"

"That our killer has only a glancing understanding of the process."

"Or else he did not care to be authentic," Carlotta said, helping herself to another pastry.

"He also may have had limited time."

"How long does it take to drain someone's blood?"

"I do not know, but I should imagine not too long."

Carlotta shivered. "I do not know how you can bear to dwell on such gruesome details all day long."

"Speaking of gruesome details, I believe there is a second victim."

"*What?* Why did you not mention this earlier?"

"I may be wrong," Elizabeth said, "but hear me out." She related the story of the burned corpse found in Madison Square Park, including her visit to the morgue.

"That is truly terrible," Carlotta said when she had finished. "Why do you believe there is a connection?"

Elizabeth explained her theory about the red dress and the lion teeth. "And I think Sally was meant to be an earth goddess. That would explain why she was laid in a hole in the ground. But I cannot find any Egyptian earth goddesses."

"Maybe you are looking for a link where there is none," Carlotta replied, tossing another bit of pastry to Toby, who wolfed it down and wagged his tail expectantly for more.

"My mother would say you spoil that dog," Elizabeth remarked.

"If it were not for him, we might not have spotted the mummy."

"True enough. I only wish I could figure out the connection to Sally . . ."

"I remember reading about the Egyptian god of the underworld in school. What was his name?"

"Osiris. He was widely considered to be the first mum—that's it!" Elizabeth cried out, nearly spilling her coffee. "Of course! Sally was meant to represent Osiris himself—she is the symbol of his resurrection!"

"Resurrection?" said Carlotta.

"I don't have time to explain! I must get back to work."

"It's time for me to leave, anyway," Carlotta said, brushing crumbs from her lap.

"Thank you for the pastries."

"My pleasure. I'll see myself out. Come along, Toby." The little dog followed obediently, and moments later, Elizabeth heard the front door close. Setting down her coffee, she went down the hall and double-locked the door, sliding the dead bolt and chain into place. She vowed not to forget the extra security measures again, no matter how tired she was.

She decided to finish writing the article at the kitchen table; being in the back of the apartment, it was quieter than the parlor. More important, it was within reach of hot coffee and rugelach. Energized by her discovery, she completed it in less than an hour. By eight thirty she was on the downtown El as it charged south along Third Avenue.

CHAPTER THIRTY-SEVEN

The hazy skies had dissolved into brilliant sunshine, and she alighted from the train to find people basking in the warm morning light as they strolled the avenues or sampled food from the many street vendors in Lower Manhattan. The unsettling atmosphere of the previous day was gone—until she reached the *Herald*. The moment she entered the building, her pulse raced and she began to sweat. The way the light cascaded through the tall windows, the diffuse echo of footsteps through the marble lobby, even the smell of printer's ink and paper, all combined to set off the unwelcome emotional reaction.

"Miss Van den Broek!"

Panicked, she spun around to see Karl Schuster walking toward her, a leather rucksack slung over his shoulder. Slightly out of breath, his broad face flushed, he looked as if he had stepped off an Alpine trail. He never looked entirely groomed—his hair was shaggy, his cuffs uneven, his shoes scuffed.

"I hope I did not startle you."

"Not at all," she replied as they ascended the staircase to the editorial floors.

"I just wanted to offer my congratulations," he said, shifting his rucksack to the other shoulder. "I know you yearned to be on the crime desk, and I am happy you got what you wanted."

Had she really gotten what she wanted? Elizabeth wondered. As they reached the second-floor landing, she saw Simon Sneed up ahead of them, leaning against the railing, talking with a copyboy. Inadvertently, Elizabeth clutched Schuster's arm.

He looked at her, surprised. "Are you quite all right? *Was ist los?*"

"I—I beg your pardon. I just . . . remembered something important." She hurried away from the stairs and down the hall, a puzzled Karl Schuster lumbering after her. "I must stop in here for a moment," she said, stopping at the door to the ladies' lavatory.

Schuster slid the rucksack from his shoulder and stood awkwardly, holding it in both hands. "You sure you are all right? *Ist alles—*"

"*Alles ist in Ordnung.* And thank you for your kind remarks," she said, and slipped through the door.

Once inside, she forced herself to take deep breaths. "This will not do," she muttered, pacing back and forth in front of the row of sturdy porcelain sinks.

"What will not do?"

She turned to see a zaftig young woman from the secretarial staff, a tart blonde with suspiciously red lips whose clothes always seemed a size too small. Elizabeth had seen Simon Sneed loitering around her desk on more than one occasion, and was under the impression the girl was not averse to his attentions.

"I beg your pardon?" Elizabeth said, affecting a haughty manner.

The girl pursed her crimson lips in a smirk. "You said 'This will not do,' and I wondered what you meant by that."

"I was referring to the trim on my skirt," Elizabeth replied calmly. "It is entirely too ornate. Since you made bold to ask, Miss . . ."

"Greta Volcarré. My family is Dutch, like yours."

Elizabeth wondered what else Greta Volcarré knew about her family, but she simply gave her a frosty smile. "Well, Miss Volcarré, in the future, you might consider the propriety of eavesdropping on strangers."

"Oh, you are no stranger. In fact, I should think you are quite well-known to most everyone in the building by now. Some of the girls are of the opinion that you consider yourself superior to all of us, but I disagree." She took a step forward, her face so close that Elizabeth could see the red coralline salve on her lips. "I believe," she said sweetly, "that you are no better than a common whore."

Elizabeth fought to keep her face expressionless as a cold trickle of fear slid through her stomach. "If I were you," she said slowly, "I would turn around and go back where you came from. Otherwise, I cannot vouch for your safety."

Greta Volcarré's eyes widened, and she made ready to reply but apparently thought better of it. Giving a little snort, she turned and left, letting the door slam behind her.

Elizabeth leaned on the nearest sink and wiped the moisture from her brow. What exactly did Greta Volcarré know? And who told her? More important, what did anyone else know? If the information of her assault were to get out, and twisted in the manner Greta was suggesting, it would most certainly be the end of her fledgling career as a reporter. The implication of her words was clear: Elizabeth had been a willing participant in what had happened. Whether or not Greta Volcarré believed that was immaterial: she was prepared to advance it as the truth.

Elizabeth brought her fist down on the marble vanity counter next to the sink. The sound reverberated off the room's tiled walls. The blow was painful yet oddly comforting; the physical discomfort provided a distraction from her emotional distress. Gritting her teeth, she resolved that whoever was out to derail her, she would make sure they did not succeed.

Kenneth Ferguson was conferring with two other reporters in his office when Elizabeth arrived. Seeing her, he shooed them out.

"Come in, please," he told her. "Have you finished the article?"

"Here it is," she said, handing him the pages.

"Good, good," he said, putting it on his desk. "Are there any new leads?"

"As a matter of fact, there is something." She told him of Grammy's death, as relayed to her the previous day.

Ferguson perched on the front of his desk, arms crossed. "Why do you believe her death is connected to this story?"

"I believe she knew things she was not telling me. She seemed afraid to reveal too much."

"Could it not be an unrelated murder? Your description of her suggests that her acquaintances are not the most savory of characters."

"That is not all. I now believe that Sally's death was meant to be—"

There was a knock on the office door. Ferguson sprang up and opened it to a copyboy holding a letter. As the editor reached for it, the boy pulled back and looked at Elizabeth.

"It's fer you, miss." The boy was short and chubby, with a protruding lower lip. The bit of fuzz on his chin seemed to be an attempt at a beard.

"For me?"

"Yer Miss Van den Broek, ain't ya?"

"Indeed I am."

He handed her the envelope.

"Where did you get this?"

"From a fella on the street."

"What sort of fellow?" asked Ferguson.

"Didn' get much of a look at 'im, t'be honest. On the tawl side, mebbe. Hat pulled down over 'is eyes."

"Hair color?" Elizabeth asked. "Beard or clean shaven?"

"Dark hair, I think. No beard."

"So what happened?"

"He comes up t'me, see, and gives me five cents t'deliver this to you."

"Thank you," she said.

"Sorry I couldn' be more helpful, like."

"I appreciate your assistance," she said, pressing a coin into his hand.

"Thank ya kindly, miss." Tipping his hat, he slipped back out the door.

Ferguson frowned. "There's no need to tip the copyboys."

"Surely that is my choice."

"They will come to expect it. And they are already being paid."

"Not much, I should think."

Ferguson glared at the envelope. "Do you intend to open that or not?"

She waved it in the air languidly. "I thought perhaps I might wait."

"For God's sake, woman, open it!"

She crossed her arms. "Not if I am spoken to like that."

"I . . . apologize," he said, releasing the words with difficulty, as if the act were extraordinarily painful.

She opened the envelope, which contained a single page of paper. It took her a moment to make sense of what she was seeing, but when she realized its significance, the hand holding the page began to tremble as she stared at what was written there.

"What? What is it?" Ferguson said.

She handed it to him without a word.

"Oh," he said. "Oh, dear. If this is real . . ."

"Do you believe it to be a hoax?"

"There is no way to tell."

She nodded as he gave it back to her, and fixed her eyes on the single page. Upon it, carefully drawn in blue ink, was what she recognized as the ancient Egyptian symbol for water. Underneath it, in block letters, she read: THIS IS THE NEXT ONE. —OSIRIS

CHAPTER THIRTY-EIGHT

Mary Mullins was bored. Her line of work was often tedious, but tonight was especially dreary. Sitting in the rear room of an oyster house at Gansevoort Street, one arm flung across the back of a bent cane chair, she gazed across the scarred oak table at the old man sitting opposite her.

"So he calls me over to the barn, see," he said, sucking on a cheap rolled cigarette. His fingers were stained brown from tobacco; his teeth looked like coal fragments. Mary shuddered. She abhorred smoking and avoided it whenever possible.

He was one of those clients who did not want sex—if indeed he was even capable of it anymore. He engaged her services merely to have someone to talk to. She had a number of johns like this, as she had a reputation as a good listener. When someone wanted a sympathetic ear, they were sent to Madhouse Mary (a nickname she had received after spending time on Blackwell's Island some years back).

"More oysters?" he said, slurping one down, the juice running down his gray beard stubble and onto his already stained shirt.

"Not right now, thanks," she said, finishing her beer. She didn't really care for oysters—they reminded her too much of sex. Disgusting gray things, all slimy and salty, like a man's ejaculation.

At first it was a reprieve to not have filthy, sweaty hands pawing her, but relief quickly turned to ennui as she entertained bowlegged sailors, retired cart vendors, and broken-down carriage drivers, each more decrepit than the last. Her companion tonight was a half-addled drover by the name of Walter. He was sunburned and fat, with oily, thinning hair, and his discourse consisted mostly of repetitions of stories from his youth, his romantic and professional exploits, some of which no doubt were true—he certainly repeated them often without varying their narrative. Right now he was in middle of a story involving a pig farmer and a pitchfork.

"So I sez to him, 'No, sir, I never did see a pig quite like that one.' And *he* sez . . ."

Mary's mind wandered. She continued to nod and smile, but her thoughts were a million miles away. She was dreaming of meeting a wealthy banker, who, captivated by her charms, would whisk her away to a life of luxury and leisure.

" . . . now, the thing about a pig like that is . . ."

She could hear the soft tick of the wall clock above them, painfully aware of the seconds slipping by. She hoped that she would not be like him at his age. There must be a way to escape such tedious behavior—surely it was not the inevitable by-product of growing older. He took a drag of his cigarette and coughed—a deep, hacking sound; she could hear the phlegm rattling in his chest. He leaned in toward her, and she got a whiff of his rancid breath. It smelled like a compost pile.

He chuckled as he stubbed out his cigarette. "So then he looks at me kinda funny, like, and . . ."

She sat patiently through the end of the story, thinking their session must be almost over.

"'Scuse me fer a moment," she said just as he was launching into another anecdote involving a goat and a mudslide. She had heard it before half a dozen times, and wished to step outside just for a moment for some fresh air. With each word from his lips, she felt her own breath constrict, as if he were sucking up all the air in the room. "I'll be right back," she said, hurrying past the handful of patrons in the front room and out to the street. She just needed a few moments of silence, free of his endless prattle.

The Gansevoort farmers market a block away was in full swing. The clatter of cart wheels competed with the shouts of merchants, the whinnying of horses, and the laughter of children. She inhaled deeply, soot from the nearby Ninth Avenue El gritty on her tongue. Still, it was a sight better than the smoke-choked atmosphere of the oyster house.

She desperately longed for another drink. Wrapped in a soft haze of alcohol, she might be able to better face the boredom. As she turned to go back inside, she was aware of someone approaching from behind. She spun around and saw a well-dressed man in a top hat and nicely turned-out frock coat. He carried a pearl-tipped cane and a pair of kid gloves.

He tipped his hat and smiled. "Good evening. Fancy a drink?"

She gazed inside the smoke-filled oyster house, then back at him.

"Yes," she said, flashing her most alluring smile. "I would like that very much."

CHAPTER THIRTY-NINE

Kenneth Ferguson stood at his desk, staring at the piece of paper in his hand. He looked at Elizabeth, his face serious. "Osiris? What kind of nonsense is that?"

"He was the Egyptian god of the underworld."

"How do you know that?"

She told him about the book Dr. Abernathy had lent her, and her theory about Sally's death.

"So if the mummy was meant to symbolize Osiris, why didn't he kill a man?"

"This person is not interested in killing men."

He held up the piece of paper. "Are you certain this is the Egyptian symbol for water?"

Reaching into her embroidered chatelaine purse, she withdrew a sketch she had made of ancient Egyptian symbols she had found in the book, including the one on Sally's neck.

Ferguson studied the drawing for a moment before handing it back to her. "How can we know the note is from the person or persons who killed Sally? What if it is from an impostor? Perhaps someone looking to cause trouble, or merely seeking attention?"

"Only a handful of people saw the symbol on her neck. Freddy, myself, the coroner and his staff, Viktor Novak."

Ferguson frowned. "This Viktor Novak—he is the morgue attendant at Bellevue?"

"Yes."

"Is he of reputable character?"

"He seemed so, but I cannot say for certain. Detective Sergeant O'Grady knows of it, of course. And Detective Inspector Thomas Byrnes."

Ferguson grabbed the cigar stub from his desk and plunged it into his mouth. "Corrupt bastard! Tammany Hall owns him, as they own every policeman in this city."

"You do not intend to inform him of this development?"

"Why should I? He insists on telling us what we are allowed to print. I see no reason to share information with him."

"Would it not help the police find the perpetrator?"

"The note was addressed to you; you are free to do as you wish with it. What do you make of it?"

"It suggests that the next victim will be found in or near a body of water."

"That is hardly useful information. Manhattan is an island. We are surrounded by water."

"I do not think it is intended to be helpful. I believe it is more of a taunt."

The editor rubbed his eyes and sank into his desk chair. "It concerns me greatly that the letter was sent to you. I fear you are in danger."

Elizabeth remained silent. The threat she feared lurked closer to home, but she knew better than to speak of it. "Do not concern yourself."

Ferguson sighed. "Perhaps it would be best if you were removed from this story."

"No! Please—I beg of you."

"I will not be responsible for putting you in harm's way."

"Then send someone out with me on assignment—Freddy, perhaps."

Ferguson chewed on the cigar stub thoughtfully. "Freddy, eh? He's a well-built lad, I suppose. Looks strong enough. But can he handle himself in a tight situation?"

"He is from London's East End. It's dreadfully dangerous there."

"I doubt London has anything to match Five Points."

"Ask Freddy—he loves telling of his exploits on the streets of Whitechapel."

Ferguson stroked his beard, a sign he was about to give in. "Very well," he said. "I will speak with him."

"I promise you'll not regret it."

"I'm regretting it already. What if something should happen to you? How would I explain it to your father?"

"Simply tell him his headstrong daughter acted without your permission."

"Cold comfort indeed, if you are found strangled in an alley somewhere."

"I believe you are exaggerating the threat to my person."

"I hope you are right. Otherwise, you are a very foolish young woman, and I am a poor excuse for an editor."

He looked genuinely pained, and Elizabeth felt sorry for him. She resolved to be extra careful, if not for her own sake, then for his.

She held up the note. "What would you do in my place? Would you inform Inspector Byrnes of this?"

"Inform him of what?"

They turned to see the paper's publisher, James Gordon Bennett Jr., standing in the doorway. Head cocked to one side, clad in a sable brushed frock coat of fashionable Parisian style, he was the picture of poise and elegance.

Kenneth Ferguson let out a short gasp. "Mr. Bennett! I—I thought you were in Paris."

"And so I was," the publisher said, folding his yellow kid gloves neatly before laying them on the nearest chair along with his top hat. "But I am here now, and I am given to believe there are interesting things afoot." He turned to Elizabeth. "Good afternoon, Miss . . ."

"Allow me to introduce Miss Elizabeth van den Broek, my star reporter."

"Ah, yes—I remember promising your father we would find a place for you here. And it seems we have exceeded his expectations," he said with a look at Ferguson.

"Sir, she is doing excellent work—"

Bennett dismissed him with a wave of his hand. "It is already the talk of the town that the *Herald* is the first to employ a female crime reporter. More important, your story is selling papers." He folded himself gracefully in one of the vacant chairs, looking very much in charge.

Elizabeth had seen pictures of Mr. Bennett, and always thought him rather handsome, but in the flesh he was even more impressive, with a long face, clean, firm jawline, high forehead, and well-defined cheekbones. His nose was long and straight, the lips thin beneath a somewhat bushy mustache. But his most striking features were his eyes. Though his father's eyes were famously crossed, the elder Bennett had not passed that trait on to his son. James Gordon Bennett Jr.'s eyes, large and luminous, were an unusual shade of pale coral. Deep set under heavy lids, they seemed to bore into whomever he was talking to.

He smoothed the tops of his trousers and plucked an invisible piece of lint from the crisply ironed crease. "So, Miss Van den Broek, I have read every word of your story. Now then, tell me what else you have learned. Kindly omit nothing."

Elizabeth glanced at Ferguson, who nodded.

"Very well, sir," she said. "I shall do my best."

Bennett listened carefully, chin in his hand, nodding occasionally as she talked. "You're a brave lass," he said when she had finished. "Do you not agree?" he asked the editor.

"Certainly," Ferguson snapped, as if irritated by the question.

"So what do you make of this?" Bennett asked Elizabeth, pointing to the letter.

"I believe he is taunting us."

"And perhaps testing us as well," Ferguson added.

"How so?"

"He hopes we will print this."

Bennett turned to Elizabeth. "Do you agree?"

"I do. He wants credit for his crimes."

"But would that not increase the chances of being apprehended?"

"He does not believe he will be caught," she ventured. "He is willing to take the risk, because—"

"He feels invincible?"

"Yes."

"Then we must ask why he is so certain he will not be captured," Ferguson remarked.

"Aye," said Bennett. "That is the rub. Why, indeed?"

Then, and only then, did Elizabeth consider the very real possibility that he might never be caught.

CHAPTER FORTY

James Gordon Bennett Jr. shared Ferguson's concern for Elizabeth's safety, so it was agreed that Freddy would accompany her home after work. Bennett was no fan of Thomas Byrnes or Tammany Hall—his father had been assaulted in broad daylight years ago by Tammany thugs. In the end, it was decided the paper would publish the tantalizing letter, without mentioning that it had been addressed to Elizabeth.

"I have no obligation to Thomas Byrnes—let him learn of it with the rest of our citizens," Bennett muttered before leaving Ferguson's office to dine at Delmonico's, his favorite restaurant (though he was known to pen critical editorials when a meal was not to his liking).

"What's he like, then?" Freddy Evans asked as he and Elizabeth left the Herald Building to board a northbound streetcar. "Is he as odd as they say?"

"Mr. Bennett is much like any other man," Elizabeth told Freddy as they took their seats on the streetcar. "Though somewhat better dressed."

"Does he 'ave a French accent from livin' in Paris all these years?"

"No. In fact, he sounds strangely British."

Freddy chuckled. "Posh-like, I'll wager, not an East Ender like m'self."

"I like the way you speak better." Though perhaps not entirely true, it was not exactly a lie, either.

"Why, thank y'kindly, miss."

"You are to call me Elizabeth, remember?"

"Right y'are, Miss Elizabeth."

She smiled at him and gazed out the window at the city passing by. The sun had taken on the lemony color of late summer; there was a slight crispness in the air that presaged the arrival of fall. Buildings glowed in the golden light, their windows opaque, the panes reflecting the sun's low western rays. People strolled the avenues, perusing shop displays or stopping at food carts. In the gentle early-evening light, the city looked so benign and harmless that it was hard to believe it harbored a murderous fiend hell-bent on killing innocent women.

"I believe I'll pay a visit to DS O'Grady," Elizabeth said as they advanced steadily northward. "I should like to hear his opinion of Detective Inspector Thomas Byrnes."

"But I thought you were goin' home," Freddy replied, frowning.

"I shall go there immediately afterward. Do you have somewhere to be?"

"Naw," he said, twisting his cap between his fingers. "I jes don' like th'idea of you gallivantin' 'round town."

"I promise to keep my gallivanting to a minimum."

Freddy sighed. "Yeah. Awright." He appeared woefully unconvinced.

The trip uptown concluded uneventfully enough. Freddy studied everyone who boarded the tram, glaring at them self-importantly, obviously reveling in his new role as bodyguard. Several men stared back at him; one well-dressed gentleman muttered, "Impudent fool." Elizabeth feared Freddy might goad someone into a fight, and finally managed to convince him that his task did not include antagonizing complete strangers.

They found DS O'Grady at his desk, engaged in a conversation with a tall, rangy patrolman. When he saw Elizabeth and Freddy, he dismissed the policeman and walked over to greet them. He looked glad to see them but also jittery, looking around apprehensively as he approached.

Elizabeth's inquiries about DI Byrnes seemed to unnerve him further.

"Not here," O'Grady said. "Follow me."

He led them to the same supply closet where they had conversed earlier, closing the door behind them. The room smelled of old dust and manila folders; the same broken truncheon lay in one corner.

"Why are you taking such extreme security precautions?" Elizabeth asked.

"Look here now," said O'Grady. "I shouldn't be saying anything a'tall, understand?"

"So why are you, then?"

The sergeant pulled at his earlobe and bit his lip. "It's like this, see? I don't like to be part of a police force that relies on kickbacks, bribes, and extortion."

Elizabeth smiled. "You have just done a very good job of describing the Metropolitan Police."

"So mebbe that's the price of being a copper in New York," Freddy suggested. "It weren't much better in London, I kin tell ya."

"I've looked the other way long enough to know all that," the sergeant replied. "But this latest business . . . I want no part of it."

"What exactly do you mean?" Elizabeth asked.

There was a knock on the door. O'Grady hesitated, and the knock came again, more urgently. When he opened the door, the same tall, thin patrolman he'd been talking to earlier was standing there, a worried look on his face.

"What is it, Sullivan?"

The patrolman whispered something in his ear.

"All right," the sergeant said, frowning. "I'm sorry, but I must go," he told Elizabeth and Freddy.

"Perhaps we can continue this another time?" she asked.

"I don't know," O'Grady said. "I'm not sure that would be wise. Officer Sullivan will see you out. But before you go, a word of advice. Take care, and mind how you go."

Before she could reply, he exited the room, leaving them alone with Sullivan.

"This way, please," he said politely, his tone leaving no room for discussion.

Out in the street, Freddy looked at Elizabeth. "Wha' jes happened? Why'd we suddenly get the bum's rush?"

She shook her head. "I am not convinced we will ever find out."

They hailed a cab, and a hack pulled up immediately, drawn by a sleek chestnut gelding. The driver was young and lanky, with a purple scar across his cheek, like a jagged bolt of lightning. It reminded her of the dueling scars so prized by Germanic aristocrats as symbols of their courage and elite status.

They spoke little during the ride to her building. When they reached the Stuyvesant, Freddy declined Elizabeth's offer of a cup of tea, to her relief. Tipping his cap, he strolled away, whistling. Watching him go, Elizabeth envied the carefree life of a young man in the city. He could come and go as he pleased, see whom he wished whenever he wanted, dine or drink wherever he felt like it, and lay his head down at night with little fear of nightmares shaking him, sweating and shivering, from the depths of uneasy sleep.

As she slipped her key into the lock, she heard a man's voice call her name. "Miss Van den Broek!"

Turning, she saw a man approaching from the other direction.

"I didn't mean to startle you," he said, seeing her face. "Jonah Ackerman, remember? Carlotta's brother."

Relief washed over her. "Of course, Mr. Ackerman—how pleasant to see you again. You are here to see your sister, I suppose?"

"Yes, indeed," he said, following her into the building. "We are meeting at her studio. Running into you is an added bonus." Gone was the conservative clothing he had worn last time they met. Clad in knee-high, soft leather boots, a Russian-style peasant shirt, and a square, short-brimmed cap, he looked as if he'd dressed to play an anarchist onstage.

As they stood in the lobby, the sound of quick footsteps on the stairs was followed by the appearance of Carlotta, clad in a ruffled white skirt and flowered blouse, with her usual assortment of bangles. Elizabeth wondered how much of her attire was fancy and how much form, but had to admit the look suited her. With her dark curly hair and olive skin, she looked the perfect bohemian gypsy.

She ran across the lobby and threw herself into her brother's arms. "I'm so glad you came to meet me! And you have invited dear Elizabeth to join us!"

Elizabeth looked at Jonah. "Join you where?"

"You are mistaken," he told Carlotta. "I ran into her by happy accident."

She turned to Elizabeth. "Then it's settled. You see, the Fates intend it. You must join us!"

"We are going to Justus Schwab's saloon," Jonah explained.

"The political radical?"

"Of course—who else?" Carlotta replied.

Justus Schwab, a German immigrant, had gained fame during the Tompkins Square riots when he charged through the throng during the height of police violence, waving a red flag. It was widely reported he sang "La Marseillaise" during his subsequent arrest.

"He has a saloon on East First Street," Jonah explained. "It is a meeting place for radicals and freethinkers."

"Do come with us!" Carlotta pleaded. "You can write an article about it."

"Thank you, but I am going to visit my sister this evening."

"Bring her along," said Jonah.

"I'm afraid that will not be possible. She is in Bellevue."

"She is ill, then?"

"She is . . . not well."

"Perhaps we could accompany you, then," Carlotta suggested. "Since you were so kind to introduce us to Dr. Jamison, who was so good to our mother."

"What of your plans for the evening?"

Carlotta shrugged. "We can go tomorrow. Justus will probably sing for us, and Ambrose Bierce may be there."

"The writer?"

"Yes—he is a regular. What do you think, Jonah?" said Carlotta.

"I suppose it would be all right—that is, if Miss Van den Broek would enjoy our company."

"What do you say?" Carlotta asked Elizabeth. "May we tag along?"

"It would be churlish of me to say no, when you so freely invited me to join you. But I must warn you, a visit to Bellevue Hospital is a far cry from a jolly night at a saloon." She hoped the comment would be sufficient deterrence but had not counted on Carlotta's persistent nature.

"Never fear," Carlotta said cheerfully. "Our sole purpose is to keep you company. That is, if you'll have us."

Elizabeth hesitated. "My sister's condition is . . . rather tricky, I'm afraid."

"Perhaps our presence might lighten the burden of visiting a sick relative. Is she very ill?"

"I'm afraid so."

Jonah frowned. "Is she contagious?"

Elizabeth had an impulse to dissemble, to discourage them from coming, but could not bring herself to lie to Carlotta.

"No. It is not that sort of illness."

"What, then?" said Carlotta.

"It is more of a mental disorder."

"Have the doctors made a diagnosis?" asked Jonah.

"I suppose so, but I find it extremely vague and unhelpful. They do not seem to know what to do with her."

"Well then," Carlotta declared, "let us repair to the hospital and see what cheer we can bring."

Elizabeth looked at her friend's eager face, shining with optimism and good intention. Strong as her own will was, she was tired, her nerves thin and frazzled. She felt a sense of relief at capitulating to Carlotta's energy and determination.

"Very well," she said. "Though I cannot say how she will react to your presence."

"If she is the least upset, we shall withdraw immediately," Carlotta assured her, slipping her arm into Elizabeth's.

"I'm afraid she is rather unpredictable on that account," Elizabeth replied as they left the building, the heavy iron door closing behind them with a metallic thud.

CHAPTER FORTY-ONE

As it was a fine evening, they decided to walk. The long summer days were growing shorter, and Elizabeth already missed the languorous evenings when the light lasted well past eight. The sun was low in the sky, casting long shadows in front of them as they walked east. As they drew nearer the water, they could hear the caw of seagulls and the occasional blast of a ship's horn, as a thin fog crept in from the East River. The smell of grilled meat wafted out of restaurants on Second Avenue, and Elizabeth's stomach contracted from hunger. Luckily, there was a booming street-cart trade in front of the hospital, and she bought a sausage and black bread from a loquacious German vendor.

"That smells heavenly," Carlotta said.

"*Ganz ausgezeichnet*," the seller said, winking at her. He reminded Elizabeth a bit of Karl Schuster, with his blond hair and pale eyes.

"Well, if it is that good, I must have one," she replied.

"*Sprechen Sie denn Deutsch?*" he said, spreading it liberally with grainy brown mustard.

"*Ein bisschen,*" she said, handing him some coins. "*Vielen Dank.*"

Jonah opted for a Viennese waffle; his sister explained that he was a vegetarian.

"Is that usual among anarchists?" Elizabeth asked as they ate their food next to the wrought-iron fence in front of the hospital grounds.

"I was a vegetarian before I became interested in politics," he said, wiping his mouth with his handkerchief. "But my beliefs have deepened my resolve. Many of the great philosophers were vegetarians, or nearly so. Thoreau thought it was valuable for self-improvement."

"Do you believe it to be healthier?"

"I simply do not like the idea of killing and eating animals."

"He is quite the pussycat," his sister said, brushing crumbs from his jacket sleeve in a motherly gesture. "For an anarchist, he is the mildest of men—aren't you, Jojo?"

Jonah frowned and reddened. "I am actually more of a Marxist," he said seriously.

Elizabeth suppressed a smile at his attempt to maintain his dignity. Carlotta did have a way of trying to corral people—she reminded Elizabeth of her childhood border collie. The dog often tried to herd her and Laura as if they were sheep. Carlotta seemed to have the same instincts.

"What is the difference between a Marxist and an anarchist?" asked Elizabeth. "I am woefully ill educated in the nuances of political philosophies."

"Please do not encourage him," said Carlotta. "Given half a chance, he will talk your ear off."

The lobby was quiet when they entered the hospital. Fortunately, there was no sign of the monolithic Nurse Stark. Elizabeth recognized the matron on duty, a middle-aged Irish woman with a kind face. Though it was past normal visiting hours, when she saw Elizabeth, she smiled and pointed the way to the common room. "Your sister is reading the book you brought her."

Carlotta and her brother followed Elizabeth down the hall, their shoes squeaking on the wide red-and-black tiles. They found Laura reclining on her favorite wicker settee in the common room, immersed in the book on her lap. Dressed in a loose-fitting flowered blouse and long black skirt, hair piled high atop her head, she looked elegant and—Elizabeth thought with a pang of guilt—utterly normal.

"Why, hello, Elizabeth," she said as they entered. "How lovely to see you."

"How are you, Lolo?"

"As well as can be expected, considering that I can hardly tear myself away from this book you gave me."

"What are you reading?" asked Carlotta.

"*Little Women*. Of course I have read it before, but it is one of those books that rewards a second visit. I am Elizabeth's sister, Laura," she said, extending her hand. She appeared unsurprised to have visitors—indeed, she seemed to be expecting them.

"Please forgive me—may I introduce Carlotta Ackerman and her brother, Jonah," Elizabeth said hastily.

Carlotta shook Laura's hand warmly. "I am pleased to know you, though I almost feel as if I do already. Elizabeth has spoken of you so often."

Elizabeth found this remark puzzling; she was aware of having mentioned her sister only once to Carlotta during their brief acquaintance. She wondered if Carlotta was trying to insinuate herself into her life. The thought was unsettling; not wishing to dwell on it, she concluded that her friend was just making polite conversation.

Laura held her hand out to Jonah. As it was only proper to shake a young lady's hand if she initiated the gesture, he responded immediately by removing his gloves and kissing her hand with a gallant flourish.

"Dear me, such chivalry!" she responded with a laugh.

"It is the only fitting response upon meeting a lady of such evident breeding and charm," he replied. Carlotta gave him a wry smile, but Elizabeth thought he appeared quite sincere; his cheeks were flushed, and his manner animated. He seemed rather taken with her sister.

"Will you take tea?" Laura asked, rising smoothly from the settee.

Elizabeth wondered if she should have elaborated on her sister's condition. Laura was behaving so appropriately, she feared they would be shocked at the signs of madness that, sadly, had become all too common. But Laura crossed the room to the tea service with such grace and poise that Elizabeth's heart leapt at the thought that, despite her darkest fears, her sister really was on her way to being cured.

"I hope you do not mind that the tea has gone slightly cold," Laura said. "The staff brought it shortly before you arrived, thinking the patients might enjoy it. But as you can see, I am the room's only occupant at present, so I'm sure they won't mind if I share it with you."

"I would love some, thank you," said Carlotta.

"Cream and sugar?"

"Yes, thank you. The walk over here has left me quite parched."

"Where did you come from?" Laura asked, handing her a cup.

"The Stuyvesant."

"Oh, you live there as well?"

"I have a studio there."

"Ah, so you are an artist?"

"A very gifted one," Jonah said as Laura handed him a cup of tea.

"I should like to see your work sometime. Tea cake?"

"Thank you," Carlotta said, helping herself to a slice of raisin cake.

"I so admire artists," Laura said wistfully. "I used to dabble a bit myself, years ago, but I have no talent."

"That is not true," said Elizabeth. "You just stopped—" She fell abruptly silent, realizing that her sister's painting had been interrupted by her illness.

"My sister is my greatest supporter, as you can see," Laura said with a little laugh, like the tinkling of wind chimes in a gentle breeze.

"I'll wager you are more gifted than you let on," said Jonah.

"Enough about me," Laura said. "What is your passion in life?"

"I am a theater director by training, but of late I have become interested in politics, so I am endeavoring to combine them."

"He is working on a political theater piece," said Carlotta.

"How delightful," Laura said. "You must tell me more."

"The audience enters the theater believing they are spectators but, before they realize it, become part of the action of the play. The idea is to demonstrate the shallowness and impermanence of identity, and how we become entrenched in our social roles."

Laura clapped her hands in delight. "How fascinating!"

"Theater should be more than frivolous entertainment," Jonah said somewhat pompously. "I see it as a tool for social change."

Carlotta pursed her lips and sighed at his grandiosity, but Elizabeth could see the affection and pride in her eyes.

And so the evening went. Laura was alternately charming, inquisitive, thoughtful, and witty. Apart from some finger twitching, there was no overt sign of her malady; she was the epitome of a gracious hostess. As Elizabeth watched Laura bask in the company of others, hope blossomed in her breast. More than once Laura turned an especially bright smile in Jonah's direction; at one point she touched his arm lightly, grazing her fingers over his sleeve, causing him to blush.

The time seemed to pass so quickly that it was only when everyone began stifling yawns that Elizabeth realized it was getting late.

"You must be tired," she told Laura. "It is nearly ten."

"Is it indeed? I had not noticed," she added with a flirtatious toss of her head, a gesture Elizabeth had not seen for a long time.

"Oh, yes," Carlotta said, rising. "Please forgive us for outstaying our welcome."

"You have done nothing of the kind," Laura replied with a dismissive wave. "This was the pleasantest several hours I have spent in a long time. I do hope you will return soon."

"You may count upon it," Jonah said, bestowing another kiss upon her hand.

She blushed becomingly, and it was only when Carlotta gently pulled at her brother's elbow that he disengaged himself from staring at her.

"Come along," Carlotta said. "Miss Van den Broek needs her rest."

"Oh, I do hope you will call me Laura. After all, we are friends now, are we not?"

"Indeed we are," said Jonah. "Until next time, then . . . Laura."

"Until next time," she echoed, and if it were not for Carlotta's firm grip on his arm, Elizabeth thought Jonah might have stayed gazing into her sister's eyes all night long.

The three of them made their way to the lobby and were about to leave when Elizabeth saw Dr. Hiram Jamison hurrying toward them. She had been so focused on seeing Laura that she had barely thought of him, but as he approached, she realized there was no one else in the world she would rather see.

CHAPTER FORTY-TWO

"Miss Van den Broek!" he exclaimed, a bit breathless. "Nurse Beckley told me you were here."

"Hello, Dr. Jamison," she replied. So much had transpired since they'd last met; the city now seemed a more dangerous and unpredictable place. But the sight of him was reassuring; she felt nothing bad could happen while he was around.

"I am very glad to see you," he said. "I have thought of you often since our last meeting."

Elizabeth lowered her eyes to avoid showing just how much his words pleased her. "How kind of you to say so."

"Hello, Mr. Ackerman," Jamison said. "It is good to see you again."

"And you, Dr. Jamison," Jonah said warmly, shaking his hand. "We cannot thank you enough for your care of our mother."

"How is she?"

"She is well, thanks to you."

"I am delighted to hear it."

"Good evening, Miss Ackerman," Jamison said with a little bow.

Carlotta was somewhat less enthusiastic. She did not offer her hand, and managed only a weak smile. "Hello, Doctor. Jonah has been singing your praises ever since you treated our mother."

"With good reason," her brother replied.

"How is your sister faring today?" Dr. Jamison asked Elizabeth.

"She seemed . . . quite well."

"Yet you do not seem pleased."

"On the contrary. It's just that I did not expect to see her so improved."

"What is the exact nature of her condition?" Jonah asked him. "Elizabeth said only that—"

"That is none of our concern," Carlotta chided him. "Do not be so indelicate."

"Not at all," Jamison replied. "In my opinion, we have not yet arrived at a satisfactory diagnosis. It is a difficult case."

"You must forgive us for detaining you," Elizabeth remarked. "No doubt you are very busy."

"On the contrary—I am rather at loose ends, as most of our patients are asleep at this hour."

"Speaking of which, it is late, and we must be going," said Carlotta.

"It was a pleasure seeing you again," Jamison said.

"Thank you again for everything," Jonah replied as Carlotta wrapped her arm around his, tugging him toward the exit.

Elizabeth followed after them, but Jamison stepped forward. "Pardon me, Miss Van den Broek, but I wonder if I might have a word?"

"You go on ahead," she told the others. "I will catch up."

"If it's all the same to you," said Carlotta, "we must be getting home. Please do not hurry on our account."

"Will you be able to make your own way home safely?" Jonah asked.

"I will see that she arrives home safe and sound," Jamison replied.

"Thank you," Jonah said. "Good night, then."

When they had gone, Dr. Jamison turned to Elizabeth. "I meant what I said before. I am indeed very glad to see you."

"I hardly know how to respond," she said, feeling a flush creep up her cheeks.

"You are not required to respond at all. The mystery of not knowing what you are thinking is in itself very alluring."

"I have no desire to be alluring."

"Then you have failed, for you cannot help it."

"Are you making love to me, Dr. Jamison?"

"What if I were? Would it be such a crime?"

"Not a crime, but perhaps a breach of etiquette."

"Oh, dear—a breach of etiquette. That is serious indeed."

"Are you mocking me?"

"I would not dream of it. I am, however, somewhat scornful of what polite society calls 'etiquette.'"

"Without it, society might quickly disintegrate into disorder and violence."

"True enough, I suppose—up to a point."

"What would you have instead?"

"A more sensible set of rules that took into account the endless fluctuations and variations in human nature."

"These 'variations,' as you call them—do you truly believe they are endless?"

"The more I see, the more I believe so."

"And my sister? Does she represent one of these 'fluctuations'?"

"A most unfortunate one, to be sure. Yet you said she seemed well earlier?"

"Yes, but I hardly dare hope . . . has she received any new medication?"

"No. In fact, I agree with you that sedatives are used too freely with the mentally ill. Of course, I am not the only doctor administering to your sister, but I have shared my views with my colleagues."

"Can you account for her improvement in any other way?"

"In my experience, people suffering from mental ailments can have periods of remission, often followed by a return of their original symptoms."

"So what I saw does not represent a cure?"

"I am sorry to say that it is unlikely. Not impossible, but unlikely."

Elizabeth was silent.

Dr. Jamison cleared his throat in the way people do when they are about to say something unpleasant. "I hear a bed is available at the Bloomingdale Insane Asylum. You said that your parents would like to move her there."

"But I do not!"

"Do your parents—"

"My mother would be very glad to see her go. I believe she has all but given up on Laura."

"And you?"

"I shall never give up on her."

"They seem to feel she would be more content in a bucolic setting."

"What do you think?"

"Having worked there, I can attest it is far more commodious than Bellevue."

"I would not be able to see her as often. And I very much doubt she would encounter forward-thinking medical men such as yourself."

"That is true. Dr. Smith encourages innovation and freethinking. He believes strongly in Bellevue's mission of medical advancement."

"What would you do if she were your sister?"

"That is a complicated question. My shift ends at ten o'clock. Would you permit me to escort you home?"

"That is very kind of you, but—"

"I promised Mr. Ackerman I would see you safely home."

"In that case, I cannot allow you to break your promise."

"I am so glad you are amenable to reason."

In truth, she wanted very much to spend more time with him. But she could hear her mother's voice in the back of her head: *Men do not value what is too easily won. Make them strive to win your favor.* Elizabeth did not generally respect her mother's views on such things, but her attraction to Dr. Jamison also made her wary of entering too eagerly into a situation she could not control. Before her assault, she had loved being in the presence of men, yet now she felt a disturbing skittishness that was new to her.

"If you like, you may hail me a cab."

"I will do so, but I insist on seeing you to your door. To do less would be to break my promise to Mr. Ackerman. His sister does not seem especially well disposed toward me as it is."

"Do not take it personally—she seems unusually subject to her moods."

"Have you known her long?"

"Only a few days. Yet she is quite the keen companion."

"I hope you do not think *I* am too keen."

"No, but it is early yet."

"So I could still ruin everything."

Elizabeth smiled. "From what I have seen, you do not strike me as someone who ruins things."

"I may surprise you yet."

"I am counting on it," she said as they exited onto the street. "For now, however, I would be much obliged if you would find me a cab."

Jamison flung out his hand, and immediately a cab pulled up in front of the building.

"There, you see—he was waiting for us," the doctor said as he opened the door for her. "The Stuyvesant, if you please," he told the driver.

Elizabeth recognized the same gangly young cabbie with the scar from earlier, driving the same high-stepping chestnut gelding. As she climbed in, she thought she heard the soft hoot of an owl nearby. The sound made her shiver, and she drew her cloak closer as Jamison settled next to her. A rap on the roof of the cab, a flick of the whip, the clatter of hooves upon cobblestone, and they were whisked away into the deep and inscrutable night.

CHAPTER FORTY-THREE

Standing on Water Street, inhaling the smell of brine and seaweed, he gazed at the three-story structure that once had housed the city's most notorious animal-fighting ring, Kit Burns' Rat Pit. He recalled watching the rascals, scallywags, and politicians coming and going at all hours. The unimposing brick building looked much the same, though Burns himself was now ten years dead. The sign over the door had proclaimed it as Sportsman's Hall, but that attempt to gussy it up was both laughable and repulsive. There was nothing "sporting" about what had gone on within those grimy walls—it was slaughter, pure and simple. None of the regulars called it "Sportsman's Hall"; it was known either as Kit Burns' or simply as what it was: the Rat Pit.

When he was small, he was one of the boys Burns hired to catch rats, paying them twelve cents for each one—a princely sum for a young lad. He had heard what went on in there, of course, but it is one thing to hear of something and quite another to experience it. When he wandered in one afternoon, he was horrified and disgusted by the sight of a terrier perched in the center of the stinking pit, rapidly disposing of vermin as fast as possible. Seizing a rat by the neck, the dog killed it with one or two quick shakes of its head, breaking the creature's spine before tossing its limp body into the bloody pile of carcasses lining the side of the enclosure. Tiers of wooden benches lined the pit on all sides; shouting spectators hung over the animals below, cheering on the terrier energetically killing rats. The smell of sweat and carnage mixed with alcoholic fumes so thick they turned the air yellow.

The sight so repelled him that he turned and fled the premises. He never again helped to furnish Kit Burns with rats for his unholy "sport." Terriers might have been bred to snap a rat's neck, but he wanted no part of it.

A woman's neck, however, was a delicate affair. Soft, white, tremulous as a small bird, it was equally vulnerable to being recklessly crushed. Of course, there was nothing thoughtless about his handling of them—he treated each one with great care and appreciation, mindful of the responsibility inherent in taking a life. Killing should not be a bloodthirsty, maniacal sport—it was a personal, intensely private experience, to be savored and revered.

And now he had set his sights on a new victim, someone who mattered. With her, he would take his time. He would play with her, as a cat plays with a mouse, before finally closing in. She was in pursuit of him, but he would turn the tables—and in death, he would honor her by making her a goddess. At first, his victims had been merely convenient—they were easy, would not soon be missed, and were difficult to identify. But he had honed his skills and could afford to be choosier. After all, being a goddess was a great honor.

He turned toward the river, where a steamer slowly puffed its way north, past sailboats and skiffs, barges and paddleboats. A couple of schooners had recently docked at the pier, and sailors spilled out of them like rats, tumbling over each other in their eagerness to spend their hard-earned wages on whores, gambling, and rotgut.

To the south, the New York and Brooklyn Bridge, or East River Bridge, as it was also called, still under construction, stretched gracefully across the water, connecting Manhattan to the City of Brooklyn. He gazed at its flying buttresses, the intricate ironwork delicate as lace. From a distance, they hardly looked strong enough to support the massive weight of the bridge. He had once dreamed of working on such structures, but fate had sent him in another direction.

He slid his watch from his vest pocket and opened it. It was nearly time.

CHAPTER FORTY-FOUR

"Must you fidget so?" said Carlotta.

Elizabeth sighed. "Sorry."

It was just past ten o'clock Sunday morning, and they were in Carlotta's fifth-floor studio in the Stuyvesant. Elizabeth was draped across a bolt of green-and-yellow fabric stretched across a somewhat wobbly antique armchair. Carlotta had dressed her in a black velvet gown that was too large and kept sliding off her shoulders. Standing at her easel, Carlotta wore an expression of intense concentration. Her brow furrowed as she shifted her gaze from Elizabeth to her easel and back again, her right hand sweeping with confident strokes across the canvas.

A beam of sunlight was creeping dangerously close to Elizabeth's face, and she feared she would sneeze if it reached her eyes. Her neck ached, and she was aware of a stray lock of hair tickling her forehead. Her back was sweating, and she thought her left foot had fallen asleep.

"I had no idea sitting still would be so difficult," she muttered, trying to move her lips as little as possible.

"Some people have no difficulty with it at all," Carlotta replied, dipping her brush into the palette in her left hand.

Elizabeth wrinkled her nose in an attempt to avoid sneezing and flicked at the stray hair with her index finger.

"Stay still!" Carlotta commanded. "Unless you want a nose the size of a cabbage."

"Sorry." Had she known how tedious modeling was, she never would have agreed to sit for a portrait. A fly buzzed feebly on the windowsill, then flopped onto its back and lay still. "Will it be much longer?"

"The more you fidget, the longer it will take. Do try to be still, won't you?"

Elizabeth suppressed a sigh and stiffened her muscles, resolving never to submit to this again once the painting was finished. "I'm allowed to talk, though?"

"Yes, but try to keep your head still."

Time passed with excruciating slowness. The fly wiggled its legs weakly, then stopped moving altogether.

"Oh," Carlotta said, "I meant to ask if you have heard of this new craze in London—it's called slumming."

"Isn't that when well-to-do people go down to where the poor people live just to gape at them?"

"That's right. Jonah told me about it, and I think it's horrid."

"I agree. If they are so interested in the poor, they ought to do something about their living conditions."

"Jonah hates rich people."

Elizabeth did not reply. Technically, her family was wealthy, though she did not care to think of herself that way. She tried to ignore the numbness creeping up her leg. "Who am I portraying again?"

"You are meant to be a siren. Try to look seductive."

Elizabeth considered that an impossible command. She raised one eyebrow, hoping that would suffice.

"Speaking of rich people, I finally read your article about the Astors' garden party. I found it very unenlightening."

"You may blame my editor for that. He insisted that readers were only interested in what people were wearing or eating and drinking, and how much it cost."

"Rather the opposite of slumming, then."

"Indeed. Just another form of voyeurism."

"So what are they like—really?"

"Mrs. Astor definitely has a sense of noblesse oblige. It made me a bit uncomfortable, but I liked her. And she seemed to take to me as well. Her son was rather strange."

"You met him?"

"Yes. He rather fancied me. He actually showed up at the *Herald* one day to see me." Though she spoke in a dismissive tone, Elizabeth was aware that she was bragging. Jack Astor might be an annoying boy, but he was the heir of the city's most renowned family.

"Is he good-looking?"

"Some would consider him handsome."

"And you?"

"I did not find him so. Besides, he is a child of sixteen."

"Old enough to know what he likes. Don't move! I'm trying to get the curve of your eyebrow just right."

"A young man of his age may like a great many things one minute and something completely different the next."

"He stands to inherit an estate of untold worth."

"Many years from now, perhaps."

Carlotta sighed. "Men are so . . . pointless."

"Surely not *all* men," she replied, thinking of Dr. Jamison, which made her cheeks hot.

"Very well," Carlotta said, laying down her brush. "That is quite enough for today."

"You mean you are not finished?" Elizabeth said, deflated. She could not imagine sitting through another session.

"Art takes time," Carlotta replied, dipping her brushes in kerosene to clean them. "Patience, dear girl."

"I am afraid I do not number it among my virtues," Elizabeth said, getting up from the chair and rubbing her limbs to restore circulation. "May I see it?"

"Not until I am finished. I'm parched. Is there any chance of tea?" Carlotta said, wrapping her brushes in an oily rag as Elizabeth stepped behind a Chinese screen to change.

"I can make some if you like."

"Would you like some help back there?"

"No, thank you—I shall just slip into my dressing gown."

"No corsets for you today—I approve. Nasty things."

"They have their place. But one day a week I like to go without, and today is that day."

Back down in her apartment, Elizabeth brewed tea and put out a plate of fruit and cheese.

Carlotta's face fell. "No pastries?"

"May I refer you to the aforementioned corset?"

"I do not see the harm in one small croissant. The Italians make a wonderful creation called a cannoli."

"You shall have to make do with this today," Elizabeth replied, slicing a pear.

"Your diet is entirely too virtuous," Carlotta said, cutting a piece of Camembert. "Where did you get those pretty flowers?" she asked, gazing at a sumptuous bouquet on the windowsill.

"From Jack Astor," Elizabeth said, pouring them both tea. "They arrived this morning."

"Maybe he is serious about you, after all. Those cost a pretty penny. On the other hand, someone like him has a great many pennies to spare."

"Do you wish to be a great artist?" Elizabeth asked, changing the subject. She had greeted the arrival of the flowers with mixed emotions.

She supposed young Jack meant well, but she had no interest in encouraging his advances. It was like being courted by a puppy.

"I suppose I do, yes. And you? Do you dream of fame and fortune?"

"More than that, I long to write something that stands the test of time . . . something *important*."

"But what makes a work important, as opposed to just popular? They aren't the same thing, you know."

"Sometimes they are exactly the opposite." Elizabeth took a plum from the plate and bit into it, savoring the deep purple taste, juice dripping down her chin. "I don't know why I'm so ambitious, but . . . I want people to *know* me."

"That is not necessarily a character flaw. Ambition is like anything else. It can be turned to the service of good or evil."

"I want to write about important things—I truly do care about social justice. But I also want to make a name for myself. Is that wrong, do you think?"

"I don't see why it would be. Bear with me a moment." Finishing her tea, Carlotta reached for the plate of fruit. "I want to paint this."

"Now?"

"My brushes are still damp, and the light upstairs should be perfect now. Bring the teapot, if you would. It won't take long. Come along—bring your tea."

They climbed the two flights to the studio, and Elizabeth sat on a stool behind her while Carlotta arranged the teapot next to the fruit and cheese. Chewing on her plum, Elizabeth watched her friend work. She admired the clean, practiced movements as Carlotta filled in the canvas with bold brushstrokes and color. "What are you going to call it?"

"I think I'll call it *Still Life with Plum*."

"Is that meant to be the plum?" Elizabeth asked, pointing to a rounded swirl of purple in the center.

Carlotta crossed her arms over her paint-splattered apron and cocked her head to the side. "I haven't decided yet. That's the beauty of impressionism." Dipping her paintbrush into the swirl of color on the palette, she mixed paint until it matched the rosy-red interior of the fruit. She swiped at the painting with her brush, a few drops falling from the bright slash across the center of the canvas.

Finished with her plum, Elizabeth tossed the pit into the trash bin. "I envy you. I am far too devoted to narrative. That's the curse of being a writer."

"What do you mean?"

"I am forever looking for meaning. I want everything to coalesce into a story of some kind."

"Why is that a curse?" Carlotta asked as they gathered up their things to return to Elizabeth's flat.

"I so admire the way your mind works. You don't require a narrative to organize the world around you."

"I like a good story."

"Yes, but you don't *require* it. Your mind doesn't automatically search for narrative in order to find meaning."

"But would it not be tedious if everyone thought the same way?"

"Perhaps you are right," Elizabeth said, fumbling for her front-door keys.

"Sometimes things are neither *this* nor *that*, neither good nor bad. Sometimes they just are what they are."

"That is precisely what I mean," she said as they entered the flat. "Your mind is so much more far-reaching than my own. I fear my thought process is too narrow, with its tiresome search for meaning."

As they made their way down the hallway toward the kitchen, there was an urgent knock at the door.

"Are you expecting someone?" asked Carlotta.

"No," Elizabeth said, a queer feeling in her stomach.

Carlotta stared at her. "Aren't you going to answer it?"

"Of course," she said, feigning nonchalance. She walked slowly down the corridor and peered through the peephole. A young boy dressed in a Western Union uniform stood in the hallway. She opened the door. "Yes?"

"Telegram for Miss Elizabeth van den Broek," he said, producing a yellow envelope.

"Thank you," she said, taking it. "Does it require a reply?"

"No, miss."

"Just a moment," she said, handing him some coins from a small porcelain dish on the hallway table.

"Thank *you,* miss," he said, tipping his cap.

Closing the door, she tore open the envelope.

NEW VICTIM FOUND SOUTH STREET PIER 17. COME AT ONCE.
—K. FERGUSON

"What is it?" Carlotta said, coming up behind her.

"I must go," Elizabeth said, handing her the telegram.

"When?"

"Immediately."

CHAPTER FORTY-FIVE

Elizabeth fired off a quick telegram to her parents expressing her regret that she would be absent from dinner. According to Catharina, her family's tradition of Sunday dinner dated back to when they still lived in Holland in the seventeenth century. Elizabeth knew she would not like the last-minute cancellation, but it could not be helped.

By the time she arrived at South Street, the day had grown humid and oppressive. The air hung heavily over the wooden wharves, soggy and sodden in the salty breeze blowing in from the East River. Though South Street was losing trade to the piers along the North River, it still lived up to its old nickname as the "Street of Ships." Vessels of all kinds were anchored along its crowded shoreline: clipper ships, steamers, and other smaller boats. The ebbing tide was low, exposing the rotting pillars beneath the piers. Boats rocked and creaked and strained at their moorings as the outgoing currents tugged at them, sucking them back toward the sea.

Sailors swaggered and shouted from the decks of arriving steamers and ferries, swarming in packs from the riggings of schooners and sloops, eager to get to the business at hand: whoring, drinking, and gambling. If they were lucky, they would not be robbed or drugged and shanghaied by river pirates, or murdered in their sleep in one of the many dives that passed for lodging along Water Street, which the social reformer Oliver Dryer labeled "the wickedest block in the wickedest ward in the wickedest city in America."

Hugging the water's edge of the boardwalk, Elizabeth passed a rusting clipper. Its metal sail rigging clanging against the mast made a mournful, hollow sound. Her throat tightened when she saw a coterie of policemen gathered around something lying on one of the jetties—the victim's body, no doubt. She approached the group of men, and as she neared them, one of the officers turned around. It was Detective Inspector Thomas Byrnes. Seeing her, his broad face assumed an expression of distaste; his left lip lifted in a sneer. The force of his animosity hit her like a strong wind, but she made herself keep walking without breaking stride.

Byrnes leaned over to say a few words to a young policeman, who approached her.

"Sorry, miss, but the public's not allowed any closer." He was very young and very pale, and she could see droplets of sweat above his downy upper lip.

"I am not the public," she replied somewhat haughtily. "I am the press."

"That includes you, too, I'm 'fraid."

"Can you reveal anything at all, Officer—"

"Harrison."

"So, Officer Harrison, is there anything you can tell me?"

"Well . . . ," he said uncertainly, glancing back at his commander, but Byrnes was busy talking to a man in civilian clothes.

"I already know the victim is a woman," she said.

"How d'you know that?"

"I'll tell you if you're willing to give me some information."

He stroked his smooth chin. She wondered if he was old enough to grow a beard. "I dunno . . . we're not s'posed to—"

"Tell you what," she said. "I'll tell you how she died, and then you tell me something."

He frowned. "How would you know—"

"She was strangled."

His eyes widened. He looked at where the body lay, then back at Elizabeth. "Say, you ain't a witch or somethin', are ya?"

"It's your turn."

"She's, uh, dressed in a funny costume, like."

"How so?"

"She's got strange jewelry wrapped around her arms—looks sorta like snakes. And a big tall, uh, not a hat, but—"

"A headdress?"

"Yeah, that's right. Made outta feathers."

"Harrison!" Byrnes started toward them, his face stormy.

"Comin', sir!" Harrison said, rushing back toward him. Byrnes looked as if he was about to continue over to Elizabeth, but thought better of it and turned back around to his men.

She was thinking about what to do next when she heard her name.

"Miss Van den Broek!"

She turned to see Kenneth Ferguson striding in her direction from the direction of the fish market.

"When did you arrive?" he asked.

"About ten minutes ago."

"Bloody cab broke down and I couldn't find another. Everyone's out on their Sunday promenade." He removed his hat and fanned himself with it. With the sun beating down on the exposed docks, it felt like a hundred degrees.

"Would you mind if we seek shelter from the sun, sir?"

"Good idea—bloody unbearable, this heat. Don't have this kind of weather in Glasgow. It's evil, is what it is," he said as they retreated toward the shade of a hotel awning. "I saw you talking with that young copper. Learn anything of interest?"

"I managed to pry a few details out of him before Byrnes shut him down."

"Bloody Tom Byrnes. Thinks he's such a big shot now that he's chief of detectives. So what did the young fellow tell you?"

She related what Officer Harrison had said.

"A headdress, eh? What do you make of it?"

"It's just a guess, sir, but it sounds to me like he dressed her up as Anuket, an Egyptian water goddess."

Ferguson scratched his bare head. "But why? To what end? And how the hell do you know about Ana-Ano—"

"Anuket, sir. I've been reading up on ancient Egypt. She was the goddess of the Nile River. It's obviously no coincidence that he left the body in the river."

"Hmm. But what does it *mean*?" Ferguson resumed fanning himself with his hat. "Bloody Byrnes. There's no end to the trouble he can cause us now. Well, might as well have a crack at 'im." Putting his hat back on, he strode across the steamy boardwalk toward the group gathering around the body.

Elizabeth watched as he and Byrnes conversed—she could tell from the detective's posture he wasn't giving an inch. He stood in a defensive stance, arms folded, feet wide apart. His chin was tilted upward, as if daring the editor to take a swing at him. While no doubt Ferguson would have loved nothing better, he conversed politely enough, a serious expression on his face, nodding a few times, until finally the detective dismissed him by turning away. Murderous rage flickered across Ferguson's face as he stalked off.

"Well," he said when he reached Elizabeth, "I got bloody nothin' out of the bastard. Beg your pardon."

"I shall have to accustom myself to such language if I am to work in a man's profession."

"You're a plucky lass, I'll say that fer ye." His Glaswegian accent seemed to deepen in emotional situations, as if he hadn't spare energy to control it.

"What did Byrnes say?"

"Oh, some nonsense about a press conference—the usual claptrap when they're tryin' to keep us away from a story."

"I wonder why he is so intent on deflecting us."

They looked up to see Freddy Evans running along the docks toward them, camera in tow. The instrument clacked against his legs as he loped across the uneven wooden planks, and Elizabeth feared he might trip and fall.

"Glad you could make it, Evans," said Ferguson as he approached.

"Sir," he replied, panting heavily. "Miss Elizabeth."

"Hello, Freddy—I see you brought your camera."

"Good luck getting a shot, though," said Ferguson. He pointed to a compact young man in a tweed cap loitering next to a building a dozen yards away. "See that fella over there? That's the *Sun*'s crime photographer. And over there's the page editor, Ned Strohman, and his star reporter," he added, indicating two other men not far away. Smoking and chatting, they didn't appear to be especially interested in the group of policemen a few yards from them. "Wonder who tipped them off."

The *Sun* reporters might have been feigning indifference to the grim scene on the docks, but locals and passersby displayed no such pretense. A throng had gathered around Byrnes and his men, and they were straining their necks to see past the phalanx of blue uniforms guarding the body. A few officers were dispatched to push the crowd back, but the onlookers pressed forward, straining the ability of the police to keep them at bay.

"It's gettin' t'be quite a mob," Freddy remarked.

"I just hope Byrnes' lads don't start shooting into the crowd," Ferguson muttered.

"I'm surprised the *Times* and the *World* 'aven't shown up, sir," Freddy said, shifting his camera to the other shoulder.

"Or the *Tribune*," Elizabeth added.

"I'll wager they'll be here soon enough," said Ferguson.

"Oh, look, there's Harold Sykes from the *Daily News*," Freddy said, pointing to a tall, sharp-faced man in a loose-fitting sack suit leaning against the side of the Wharf Hotel. He appeared to be idly smoking a cigarette, but Elizabeth could tell he was keeping a watchful eye over the proceedings on Pier 17.

"Racist rag," the editor muttered. The *Daily News* was known for its pro-Confederate stance during and after the war. "Do you know if the coroner's arrived yet?"

"I thought that was someone from his office," she said, pointing to the man in civilian clothing. "But now I'm not sure."

"Look," said Freddy as an ambulance pulled up, "Bellevue Hospital" stenciled in bold letters across its side.

"That's probably the coroner now," Elizabeth said as two men in white coats climbed from the vehicle. "I know them. It's Viktor Novak and his assistant, Benjamin Higgins."

"Oh, yeah, so it is," said Freddy.

"Why don't you converse with him while I have a wee chat with our rivals?" Ferguson suggested. "I want to see how much they know. Freddy, why don't you see if you can get a decent shot without incurring the wrath of Twinkle Toes Byrnes over there? If you slink around the side of the Wharf Hotel and keep in the shadows, you might get closer."

"Yes, sir—I'll do me best."

As the men went off, Elizabeth hurried toward the ambulance. "Mr. Novak!"

Seeing her, he broke into a smile. "Ah! Hello, Miss Van . . ."

"Elizabeth van den Broek."

"Of course. Good to see you again. And of course you know Mr. Higgins, Bellevue's best ambulance driver."

Higgins tipped his hat. "How do'y do, miss?"

"Hello, Mr. Higgins." She turned to Novak. "Who is tending the morgue?"

"My colleague, Mr. Branson. They were short on ambulance staff, so I volunteered. I thought it might be exciting to go on an ambulance ride for a change."

"Are you here to collect the body?"

"The hospital received a request to come to the docks, but we weren't told why," he said as he and Higgins pulled a stretcher from the back of the vehicle.

"You might be in for more excitement than you bargained on."

"Why is that?"

"There's been a murder."

Novak's eyes widened. "A murder, you say?"

"Yes, indeed. That's why there are so many policemen guarding the body."

Novak stared at the wall of blue uniforms across the boardwalk. "What happened?"

"I would be very much obliged if you could tell me. The police are rather too busy to answer questions."

"I'll see what I can find out. Are you good with horses?"

"I learned to ride at the age of ten."

"Would you mind holding Jeremy here?" he said, indicating the buckskin dray harnessed to the ambulance. "He has a tendency to wander off."

"I would be delighted," she said, taking the reins. Jeremy tossed his head a couple of times and snorted loudly before nibbling at her shoulder with his silken lips.

Higgins grinned. "He likes you. Jeremy don' act that way 'round everyone."

"Well then, Higgins," Novak said, picking up the stretcher, "shall we go collect that body?"

"Yep," he replied, taking up his end of the stretcher.

Watching them go, Elizabeth wondered what the police actually did know, what they were hiding . . . and why.

CHAPTER FORTY-SIX

"That Detective Byrnes is a piece of work all right," Viktor Novak said when he and Higgins returned to the ambulance carrying the victim's body. She was just a slip of a girl, really, and Elizabeth hated the thought of her spread out on the hard wooden dock, being gawked at by all those policemen. Now, lying on the stretcher, her dark hair matted and plastered across her forehead, damp clothes clinging to her body, though the day was sweltering, she looked cold. Elizabeth wanted to tuck a blanket around her and whisk her away from the greedy eyes of the throng of reporters and photographers who had gathered around the ambulance.

But her eye was caught by something clinging to the girl's hair—it appeared to be feathers, not from seagulls, but something much softer and fluffier. Though discolored, it appeared to have been white once. An ornament on a leather thong dangled from her neck—Elizabeth recognized it as the ankh, an important ancient Egyptian symbol.

She studied the crowd of reporters. Most of the major dailies were represented: the *Times*, the *World*, the *Sun*, the *Tribune*, as well as the "racist rag," the *Daily News*. Reporters from a few of the lesser papers had also turned up, including the *Staats-Zeitung* and the *New York Star*.

Elizabeth stood with Kenneth Ferguson and Freddy as reporters fired questions at Novak.

"What can you tell us?" shouted a *Tribune* reporter, a tall man with a scraggly beard and mustache.

"There was no form of identification on the body," Novak replied. "But apparently one of the policemen recognized her as a well-known prostitute—"

"I'll *bet* he did," Harold Sykes said. His remark was greeted by general snickering from the crowd.

"Does she have a name?" shouted another reporter.

"She is known as Madhouse Mary, but"—Novak paused to wait for a second wave of mocking laughter—"she goes by Mary Mullins."

"What's that around her neck?"

"It appears to be a piece of jewelry."

"Do you believe it has any significance?"

"That's a question better asked of the police. I understand there will be a press conference shortly."

After a few more questions, the photographers crowded around the poor girl's body, all vying to get the best picture. Novak and Higgins stood patiently watching—apparently they believed in freedom of the press more than the Metropolitan Police did.

"This isn't right," Kenneth Ferguson muttered. "We shouldn't be hearing this from an ambulance driver—it should be coming from the bloody coppers."

"Byrnes is giving a press conference in front of City Hall in an hour," said the *Tribune* reporter.

"Is he, then?" Ferguson muttered. "That'll be a treat."

Elizabeth thought his antipathy toward the chief of detectives seemed to be more than just ordinary animosity. It had the feel of a vendetta.

"How did she die?" shouted Harold Sykes.

"There is clear evidence of strangulation," Novak said. "But the cause of death has yet to be determined." He seemed to be enjoying his moment in the spotlight. Elizabeth couldn't hold it against him—soon enough he would be stuck indoors amid cold, moldering corpses, so why not savor this brief bit of attention?

After a while, the journalists disbanded, retiring to their desks to write their stories. Others headed off to City Hall to catch Detective Byrnes' press conference. Elizabeth and her colleagues lingered while Novak and Higgins secured Mary Mullins' body in the back of the ambulance. Elizabeth was gratified to see them treat the poor girl with care and respect, laying her down gently before closing and latching the rear doors.

"May I come by and speak with you later about the coroner's findings?" she asked Novak.

"If you like. We may know something as soon as tomorrow afternoon."

"Well," Ferguson said as the ambulance rattled off up the cobblestones of South Street, "he likes you, doesn't he?"

She was about to respond when, suddenly, charging toward them like a bull on the loose, she saw Detective Thomas Byrnes, waving a copy of the *Herald* in his clenched fist.

"Ferguson!" he bellowed. "What the devil were you thinking, man?"

"You'll have to be more specific, I'm afraid," the editor replied calmly.

"I'm talking about *this*!" he said, brandishing the newspaper as if it were a sword. "Publishing that damned letter instead of bringing it to me. That is police business, not for the general public!"

Ferguson shrugged. "I had no way of knowing if it was related to the killing of Sally."

"That's for me to decide, not you!" His face was the color of raw eggplant; spittle flew from his lips on each word.

Ferguson appeared unmoved. "Is it, now?"

"I've jes about had it with you, ya bloody vazey gombeen," Byrnes muttered, his Irish accent broadening.

Elizabeth had heard enough Irish slang to know a gombeen was a shady operator looking to make a quick profit. Though unsure what "vazey" meant, she was certain it was not a compliment.

"Och aye, have ye now, ya mutton shunter?" Ferguson's body tensed, his hands balled into fists. "Mutton shunter" was a derogatory term for a policeman, referring to the part of his job that included telling prostitutes to move along. It also managed to insult women as well, as mutton comes from an old sheep. Elizabeth was a little shocked to hear it come from Ferguson's lips.

"You're the one obsessed with dead whores," Byrnes taunted. "Is it because your mother was—"

Before he could finish, Ferguson's fists were flying at his face. The first blow, an uppercut, caught the detective squarely in the jaw, sending him off balance; the second drove into his soft stomach, doubling him over, and the third was a roundhouse to the side of his face, knocking him off his feet. Emitting a throaty grunt, he fell to the ground with a thud.

Elizabeth knew it was bad even before the half dozen policemen seemed to appear from nowhere, truncheons flying. She watched in horror as they pummeled Ferguson to the ground, curled into a ball beneath their blows. Freddy lunged forward to defend him, but she grabbed the photographer by the sleeve.

"Don't! They'll just beat you as well."

The whole thing was over in a couple of minutes, though it felt much longer. Detective Byrnes pulled himself to his feet with some effort, blood trickling from the corner of his mouth. Wiping it off with the back of his sleeve, he gazed down at the editor's prostrate form. Whether Ferguson was conscious—or even alive—Elizabeth could not tell.

"Take him to the Tombs," he growled. Without another word, he turned and stalked away.

Elizabeth held her breath as Byrnes' men pulled Ferguson roughly to his feet. She nearly cried with relief when she saw that he was indeed conscious, though bleeding from cuts on his face. She took a step forward.

Freddy did the same. "Sir—"

He waved them away. "Leave off, the both of you," he said, his voice hoarse. "Tell Mr. Bennett what happened, and ask him how to proceed."

"Yes, sir," said Freddy.

Elizabeth fought to keep her voice steady. "Is there anything we can—"

"Don't worry about me," he said as the policemen dragged him away. "The story is the important thing."

"I'm goin' t'follow behind, make sure they don't kill 'im," Freddy whispered to Elizabeth.

"What about your camera?"

"Oh, it's no bother. It's sorta like a part a' me, y'know?"

"I'm coming with you!"

"The Tombs ain't no place fer a lady, Miss Elizabeth."

"But—"

"Y'should do what Mr. Ferguson said—follow the story."

"Please be careful, Freddy."

"You too, miss—we all need t'be careful," he said, scurrying off.

Elizabeth stood in stunned silence for a few moments. Slowly, she became aware of the sounds around them—the clatter of wooden wheels, the caw of seagulls, the voices of people calling to each other across crowded streets, conversing, laughing, arguing, gossiping. They all sounded so carefree, so unaware of the killer among them, slipping unnoticed through alleyways, sliding between buildings, in and out of doorways, creeping down silent hallways—looking, always looking, for his next opportunity to strike.

CHAPTER FORTY-SEVEN

"He drug her 'ere in th'dead o' night."

It was a whiskey-soaked, tobacco-hardened growl, more phlegm than voice.

Elizabeth turned to see the speaker. His tattered, double-breasted blue jacket and weathered face proclaimed his profession: he was, or had been in the past, a sailor. The stained bell-bottomed trousers covered scrawny legs that once had scrambled up a rigging; the ragged jacket encased thin arms that had trimmed sails, scrubbed decks, and hauled cargo from ports around the world. The sunburned skin of his face was a maze of creases and crevices, carved by years of sun and sea air. His age was impossible to tell—he could be forty or eighty. A dirty black patch covered one eye.

She took a step toward him. "What did you say?"

"Kin ya give a poor fella some money fer a drink?"

Elizabeth fumbled in her purse for some coins. "Please repeat what you just said."

He shoved the coins into one jacket pocket and withdrew a flask from the other. Drinking deeply, he coughed and sputtered before wiping his mouth with a stained red-and-white kerchief. "What aye said were that he brung 'er here in the dead o'night." Each consonant was so congested it made her want to clear her throat. His accent had the torturous vowels and curled *r*'s often associated with pirates from Cornwall, on England's west coast.

"You mean the girl they found in the water?"

"Aye."

"You saw it?"

"I did, aye."

"Why didn't you tell the police?"

He laughed, then coughed so violently she feared he would hack out his insides. She imagined them spilling onto the boardwalk, rubbery and pink and soft, like whale blubber. When the fit subsided, he spat on the boardwalk—a fat, tobacco-stained blob of mucus. "Them coppers are crooked as a purser's books! Wouldn't give 'em the time a'day."

"Can you tell me what you saw?"

"I know what yer thinkin'. It's true I got one bum eye, but t'other one's still sharp as a shark's tooth, I tell ya."

"So what did you see?"

"I'd jes been out a-seein' a lady," he said proudly, with a cocky smile.

Elizabeth tried to imagine those wizened arms wrapped around whatever unlucky prostitute he had managed to hire. No wonder so many of them drank heavily.

"What time was this?"

"It woulda been around three—the moon had jes come out from behind the clouds, big an' bright as day. I'm at my usual spot, y'know—over yonder," he said, pointing to a sturdy pair of wharf posts wrapped in thick rope. "I were fixin' t' string up my hammock, see? An' I heard a noise behind me. Somethin' made me turn around, and I sees this fella haulin' somethin' over his shoulder."

"Could you see what it was?"

"I thought it were a sack a' grain or sommit like 'at."

"What did he do with it?"

"He lugged it to th'edge of Pier Seventeen and slid it into th'water. Struck me as odd at the time, but I had a bottle an' didn' think much more on it." Removing his battered wool cap, he scratched his head. White flakes floated from his greasy gray hair and settled onto his shoulders.

Elizabeth looked away and coughed. "Can you describe him?"

"Didn' git a close look, but th'bloke reminded me of a big bird."

"How so?"

"He 'ad feathers on 'is head—or that's wha' it seemed t'me, anyways."

"Feathers?"

"Yeah. Looked like a headdress—kinda like wha' them Injuns wear."

"Anything else?"

"He wore a cape—old-fashioned, with flaps, like."

"How tall was he?"

"Fair tall, I s'pose."

"Did you notice anything else about him?"

"A bit bulky, mebbeh, though under the cape it were hard t'say."

She fished some more coins from her bag and pressed them into his hand. His skin was rough and coarse, with the consistency of frayed rope.

He tipped his cap. "Very kind a' ye, miss. Very kind, indeed."

"I don't suppose I can persuade you to spend it on food instead of drink."

He grinned, and she wished he hadn't. His teeth (or what was left of them) were like rotting wharf timbers—pitted and worn, stained gray with age.

"Thank you for your help, Mr. . . ."

"Call me Seadog. Everyone does."

"Thank you, uh, Seadog."

He tipped his hat again and sauntered back to his spot on the pier, though his legs were so bowed that it was more of a hop and a hobble.

Watching him go, Elizabeth wondered how much of his decrepitude was from age and hard labor, and how much from drink and dissipation. He was an example of how much a human body could be whittled away by time and hardship and still endure. It was a lesson in survival, albeit not a pretty one. New York was full of people like him, whom life had beaten down, clinging tenaciously to whatever level of existence they had sunk to. The same city that contributed to their decline, in a strange way, also nurtured them. Its vast canvas had room for a wide variety of creatures great and small, from the pampered poodles of Fifth Avenue's palatial town houses to the lowliest vermin scuttling through filthy tenement basements in search of rotting scraps. Life in all its extremes was a feature of New York in the Gilded Age—and so, unfortunately, was murder.

CHAPTER FORTY-EIGHT

He stood at the top of Bayard Street, listening to the drunken singing coming from the cheerless saloon on the corner.

They had a dreadful fight, upon Saturday night
The papers gave the news accordin';
Guns, pistols, clubs and sticks, hot water and old bricks,
Which drove them on the other side of Jordan.

He knew the song well. It commemorated the last great fight between rival street gangs the Bowery Boys and the Dead Rabbits on July 4, 1857. The riot had lasted two days, with skirmishes continuing for a week after, and marked the beginning of the decline of the city's street gangs.

Then pull off the old coat and roll up the sleeve,
Bayard is a hard street to travel;
Pull off the coat and roll up the sleeve,
The Bloody Sixth is a hard ward to travel, I believe.

Like every other New Yorker, he knew the story well. The city was only slightly less turbulent than it had been in those tempestuous days—gangs might not roam the streets in quite the same way, but crime had not abated, and the poor still lived in desperate squalor.

A mangy yellow dog crept past him, head low, resignation in its weary gait. He once had felt like that dog, but no longer. Surveying the street as darkness fell, he inhaled deeply. He stood on the precipice of greatness; a vast and mighty city lay at his feet. His deeds were on everyone's mind, on their lips. Even now, he could feel it; tongues wagged in drawing rooms and hallways, in doorways and storefronts. He breathed in the night air, sweet with the promise of fall, but just beneath it lurked the fetid stench of corruption and despair.

He strolled up Mulberry, and as he approached the Bend, a rat scurried across the street, emitting a squeak before disappearing into a gutter. Five Points, it was said, was where souls went to die. Hope itself seemed to fear its crooked streets. He knew justice to be an entirely human concept, in spite of what the fortunate few would have you believe.

But now he held the reins of justice in his own hands. No captain of industry, no steel or railroad magnate, wielded more power than he did at this moment. He would be known—his influence would soon be felt far and wide. He was Osiris, Lord of the Underworld, Judge of the Dead.

And he was just getting started.

CHAPTER FORTY-NINE

After speaking with "Seadog," Elizabeth longed to join Freddy at the Tombs. But she knew those imposing granite gates, and reluctantly heeded his warning. Wending her way northward as the early-evening light enveloped the city in its hazy glow, she arrived at the *Herald* to find James Gordon Bennett Jr. nowhere in sight. This was hardly surprising, as it was Sunday night, and there was but a skeleton crew manning the editorial offices. The press in the basement was rumbling along, the Monday-morning edition already in progress, but all inquiries as to exactly where Bennett was were met with blank stares. Finally an editorial assistant told her that the publisher stayed at the Windsor Hotel when he was in New York. Elizabeth promptly sent a telegram, with the Stuyvesant as the return address for replies.

> FERGUSON BEATEN BY BYRNES, TAKEN TO TOMBS—CONTACT ME FOR DETAILS—E. VAN DEN BROEK

She did not know when Bennett would receive the message, but at least any reply would come straight to her. Impulsively, she decided to pay a visit to Justus Schwab's saloon. With any luck, she hoped to find Carlotta and Jonah there.

The saloon occupied the first floor of a five-story, redbrick tenement at 50 East First Street. Elizabeth had walked by the building once or twice, but always thought it a quiet, unremarkable block. First Street was hardly a thoroughfare—it was short, even for downtown, occupying only the three blocks stretching from Avenue A to the Bowery. Just to the south was Houston Street, a thoroughfare heavily traversed by trams, carriages, and cabs, where the steady clip-clop of horses' hooves resounded night and day.

Standing on the sidewalk outside the building, Elizabeth could hear voices—laughing, talking, shouting. The tinny tones of an upright piano floated out from deep within the saloon. The sign over the door proclaimed it to be Justus Schwab's Lager Beer Halle; letters stenciled on the front picture window advertised the sale of "Wine, Beer & Liquors." She pushed hesitantly on the door, which was whisked open from within by a smiling young man with a jet-black beard and eyebrows to match. He wore square spectacles and a cloth cap; his short jacket was cut close over somewhat baggy trousers.

"Come in!" he bellowed, clamping a hand upon her shoulder and pulling her into a crowded, smoke-filled room. "Welcome, welcome—what are you drinking, Comrade?"

"Well, I—"

"A beer, then! Only the finest lager for young lady such as yourself!" His accent was Russian, and his manner so energetic that his body seemed to be one large exclamation mark.

"I don't—"

"Is no problem—be right back!"

He disappeared through the crowd, leaving Elizabeth alone in the saloon's long, narrow front room. It could not have been more than ten feet across, with a low tin ceiling and smoke-stained walls illuminated by gas sconces. A bar at the far end of the room was manned by a scruffy-looking young man in a short jacket and a striped scarf. A dusty mirror behind him reflected the scene back on itself, making the cramped space appear larger.

A doorway to one side led to a back room, from which she could make out scattered strains of the piano, though the bar was too noisy to identify the tune. The few tables scattered along the sides of the room were occupied by all manner of men and women, in all manner of clothing. No one appeared to have dressed with an eye to what might be deemed "fashionable." Some seemed to have flung open their closets and thrown on whatever suited them, without regard to the opinion of "respectable" society. Some looked distinctly bohemian; others wore what she recognized as radical socialist garb. Still others sported a scholarly look, all in black; some of the women affected a severe hairstyle and a mannish style of dress.

Fully a third of those present were women; she also noticed several Negroes, as well as one man whose face had an Oriental cast. Old and young alike were engaged in deep conversation, peppered with bursts of laughter and long drinks from tall metal beer steins. A few people looked up when Elizabeth entered; some seemed mildly interested in her presence but soon returned to the business of talking and drinking with their companions. She felt neither overlooked nor scrutinized—her presence seemed accepted with a matter-of-fact equanimity. She had never felt so relaxed in a room full of strangers.

Straining her neck to see over the crowd of people standing, Elizabeth searched for Carlotta and her brother as the young black-haired fellow returned with two steins of beer.

"Here you go," he said, handing her one.

"Very kind of you," she said.

"Let us drink to Karl Marx!" he said, raising his glass. Seeing her hesitation, he clapped her on the back so heartily that she wondered if it was some form of a secret radical handshake. "Do not fear—you are safe here. Drink, Comrade!"

Suddenly very thirsty, she gulped down a large quantity of the ice-cold lager. The bubbles tickled her throat, sharp and refreshing.

After drinking deeply himself, her companion launched into a song; several others quickly joined in.

Stand up, damned of the earth!
Stand up, prisoners of starvation
Reason thunders in its volcano
This is the eruption of the end!

The song went on for several more verses, ending in applause and cheers from the assembled company.

"You are new to this place, then?" Elizabeth's companion asked.

"What makes you think that?"

"I see you studying crowd. You don't seem to know anyone here."

"She does, indeed!" came a voice from behind Elizabeth, and she turned to see Carlotta and Jonah. "I am so glad you came!" Carlotta said, flinging her arms around Elizabeth, nearly knocking her off her feet.

"As I am," Jonah said, shaking her hand warmly as she regained her balance.

The black-haired man smiled. "You know these two scallywags, then?"

"I shouldn't be the pot calling the kettle black if I were you," Jonah replied. "You're quite the miscreant yourself."

"Oh, leave off, you two," Carlotta said, turning to Elizabeth. "I see you have met Grigory."

Elizabeth shook her head. "We have not yet been formally introduced."

Jonah hit his forehead with the palm of his hand. "Ah! Where are my manners?"

"At bottom of that beer stein, I should think," Grigory remarked. Jonah responded with a soft punch to his shoulder.

Carlotta stepped in. "Grigory, allow me to present my friend Miss Elizabeth van den Broek."

"Very pleased to make your acquaintance," he said, kissing her hand.

"And may I introduce Mr. Grigory Kalyenkov, scoundrel, revolutionary, and man of letters," said Jonah.

"Indeed," Elizabeth replied, "I have known many scoundrels, but few men of letters, and even fewer true revolutionaries. I have yet to see all three in one individual."

Grigory grinned. "You forget to say I am also socialist."

Jonah snorted. "Psh! Everyone in this room is a socialist."

"I don't believe I am one," Elizabeth remarked.

Carlotta pointed to her beer stein. "A few more of these and you will be." She hugged Elizabeth impulsively again. "Truly, I did not think you would come."

"I am glad you join our struggle," Grigory said, throwing an arm around her other shoulder. "*Dobro pozhalovat'*—welcome!"

"What exactly is the nature of the struggle?" Elizabeth asked.

"The struggle for people's minds," Jonah answered. "We aim to overthrow the repressions and injustices of modern society—to close the gap between rich and poor."

"Elizabeth has been a guest of Mrs. Astor," said Carlotta.

"I was there as a journalist," Elizabeth corrected her.

"But apparently you made quite an impression. Mrs. Astor liked her," Carlotta told the men.

"Do not make the mistake of thinking she was interested in you," Jonah told Elizabeth. "Once she realized you wrote for the *Herald*, her job was to be certain you gave a glowing account of her soiree."

"Eto glupo!" said Grigory, throwing his arm around Elizabeth's shoulders. "Mrs. Astor simply has good taste—*I* like her, too!"

Jonah lit a cigarette. "Besides, what does it matter if one is accepted in high society? Is it an indication of true worthiness?" He waved the cigarette over his head, dispelling the smoke into the air. "Of course not! It simply means you have a pedigree."

Grigory nodded. "The privileged always strive to maintain status quo."

Jonah waved his cigarette in Elizabeth's direction. "Is that not what your ancestors left the Old Country to escape? And look at them, replicating their egotistical follies."

Elizabeth was about to reply when a tall, scraggly fellow who was the human embodiment of a scarecrow entered from the back room. Waving his hands about, he soon got the attention of the assembled company.

"Justus is about to sing 'La Marseillaise'!" he proclaimed portentously, as if he were a royal page announcing the imminent arrival of the queen.

A current of excitement rippled through the crowd, and everyone headed toward the back room.

"Come!" Grigory told Elizabeth. "You must not miss this!"

The four of them filed into the tiny back room with the rest of the crowd.

The object of everyone's attention stood next to a battered upright piano in the corner, next to a small bar with an assortment of liquor bottles on built-in shelves behind it. Tall and broad-shouldered, with a bristling mustache and a mane of bushy red hair, here was the famed Justus Schwab in the flesh. He did not disappoint, living up to all she had heard about him. A giant of a man, he really did resemble a Viking, as all the newspapers had reported after his heroics at the Tompkins Square riots.

"Come in, Comrades!" he said in a booming baritone revealing his Germanic origin. "*Es ist Platz für alle*—zer is room fer everyvone!"

The crowd surged forward eagerly, cramming even more closely into the packed room. Sliding her foot from beneath the boot of the bearded man in front of her, Elizabeth tried to move her arms, which were pinned to her sides. The lager had gone to her head—she felt giddy and light, as if the beer's bubbles were expanding in her brain. She could smell the perfume of the woman behind her, a heavy floral aroma that might have been pleasant in less close quarters. Crushed in between a socialist Russian revolutionary and a homegrown anarchist, Elizabeth felt an unexpected sense of belonging. She had never felt it in her parents' elegant Fifth Avenue town house, nor even among her friends at Vassar. These people had a buoyancy combined with a seriousness of purpose that was altogether new to her.

When the crowd had quieted down, Justus Schwab took his seat at the piano. Banging enthusiastically on the keys, he sang the words to the French national anthem in a strong, sweet baritone.

Allons enfants de la Patrie,
Le jour de gloire est arrivé!

At first the crowd listened reverently, but they soon joined in, their voices ringing off the narrow walls of the little room.

Contre nous de la tyrannie
L'étendard sanglant est levé!
L'étendard sanglant est levé!

Caught up in the spirit of the moment, Elizabeth joined in, lustily bellowing out the lyrics, a little surprised she remembered the words from French class.

Entendez-vous dans les campagnes
Mugir ces féroces soldats?

Tears spurted from her eyes as she stood amid this motley collection of people singing the French national anthem, led by a German immigrant. She felt a patriotic pride, not so much for America as for the great and beleaguered city she called home. Somehow, in this dank, densely packed back room, Elizabeth thought maybe she had found her people.

And then, without warning, the front room exploded.

CHAPTER FIFTY

There was a great banging in the front room, followed by shouts and the stamping of thick-soled boots.

"Police! This is a raid!"

Everyone froze for a moment. What followed was utter chaos. There was a mass exodus toward the back exit, as dozens of people tried to squeeze through the small door facing an alley leading to Houston Street. People panicked, pushing and shoving as they fled the barrage of policemen invading the saloon.

Elizabeth staggered backward as the cops barged their way into the room, billy clubs drawn. No one offered any resistance as they grabbed people one by one, handcuffing them and dragging them to the front room. Elizabeth was imagining the ignominy of her father bailing her out of jail when a hand grasped her firmly by the wrist. Turning, she saw Carlotta, her face flushed.

"Come along—this way!" she cried, pulling Elizabeth behind the bar just as Jonah and Grigory pulled open a trapdoor on the floor. Elizabeth glanced at the marauding police force, but they were too busy arresting people to pay attention to the four people behind the bar. "Quickly—hurry!" Carlotta said, practically shoving Elizabeth down the narrow steps leading to an underground room.

Scampering down the stairs, Elizabeth found herself in the building's basement. It seemed to be used principally for storage. Crates of beer were stacked next to cases of wine on the stone floor, which also held bits of discarded lumber and a broken chair, among other odds and ends. A small grime-caked window near the ceiling was the only source of light; cobwebs danced in the thin breeze seeping through its frame.

She had barely reached the bottom when Carlotta and the two men followed. Grigory brought up the rear, closing the trapdoor behind him.

"What about the others?" Elizabeth asked as he wiped dirt from his hands.

"They were all in big hurry to escape out back door."

"How did you know about this place?" Carlotta asked.

"I work for Justus once as bartender," he said, lighting a gas wall sconce. The flame flared abruptly to life, flickering as he turned it down. "We come down here to fetch supplies."

"What do we do now?" Carlotta asked, listening to the heavy thump of footsteps on the floor above them.

Grigory removed his cap and brushed the dust from it. "We wait."

"What if they find us down here?"

He shrugged. "Then we will be arrested."

"I shouldn't think it will be long," Jonah said. "Once they shove everyone into the paddy wagon, they'll be off."

"Might as well make ourselves comfortable," said Grigory, sitting on one of the liquor crates.

Elizabeth dusted off the top of a beer barrel and leaned against it. "Do you not find it ironic that the term 'paddy wagon' was originally an insult to the Irish people it used to transport, yet now—"

"They are the ones rounding people up," Carlotta finished for her.

"Yes," she said, a bit irritated at being interrupted.

"So goes the circle of history," Jonah remarked. "The oppressed soon become the oppressors."

"This is true," said Grigory, "but as the great Turgenev said, 'Nature creates while destroying.'"

"What is that supposed to mean?" asked Carlotta.

"It means we might as well enjoy ourselves," Grigory said, plucking a bottle of wine from one of the cases.

"You do not intend to steal that, I hope?" said Elizabeth.

"Do not worry—I pay Justus next time I am here."

"I'll ensure that he keeps his promise," Carlotta added.

Elizabeth shivered—the cellar was damp and cold, the kind of chill that seeped into your bones. Inhaling the stale, musty air, she thought about the deep, hot bath she would take when she finally got home. Standing, she wrapped her arms around her body and walked around the room.

"Are you cold?" said Carlotta.

"Would you like my jacket?" Grigory asked.

"I am quite all right, thank you." Elizabeth felt accepting his offer would imply a closer relationship than she intended to cultivate. While she admired his activism, she was not entirely prepared to associate so closely with such extreme political zeal.

A small desk in the far corner caught her eye; it appeared to be less dusty than the other objects in the room. It was not particularly elegant, but sturdy enough, and seemed to have been recently polished. Curious, she approached, and a piece of paper floated from the top of the desk to the floor. Bending over, she picked it up. It appeared to be a page from a ledger of some kind. At the top a heading was boldly etched: *LDA*. Below were columns of dates on one side, and what seemed to be payment amounts on the other, neatly penned in blue ink.

January—90
February—90
March 9—100
April 11—100
May 10—100

June 8—100
June 11—100
July 10—110

There seemed to have been an increase in March and again in July. There was no entry for August. She looked to see if the others had noticed, but they were too busy passing around the wine Grigory had opened. Elizabeth slipped the paper into her skirt pocket and rejoined her companions. Carlotta offered her the bottle, but she shook her head.

"Thank you, but I have an article to write."

Jonah grinned. "No rest for the wicked, eh?"

"Speaking of wicked," Carlotta said, "did you notice Tom Byrnes' ugly mug up there?"

Fear trickled through Elizabeth's stomach. "Detective Byrnes was here?"

"Did you not see him?"

"Why would Byrnes himself participate in such an operation?"

"I don't know," Jonah said. "But I should not care to be at the receiving end of his 'third degree.'"

"Third degree?"

"It's his term for beating the stuffing out of a suspect."

Elizabeth thought about Kenneth Ferguson, huddled in a dank, cold cell in the Tombs. She could only hope that Byrnes had been too busy raiding the saloon to subject her editor to such torment. But there was no telling what other catastrophes this horrendous, seemingly endless day might hold.

In the end, Jonah was right—it was not long before the police retreated, in a clatter of nail-toed boots and door slamming. The four companions huddled in the basement for a few minutes after the last rattle of horses' hooves and wagon wheels disappeared into the night. Creeping up the stairs, the two men unlocked the cellar door and slowly pushed it open, dislodging a haze of dust.

"The coast is clear," Jonah said, reaching a hand down to help the women up the narrow staircase.

They emerged to a scene of overturned tables, broken chairs—it looked like the aftermath of a brawl. Remarkably, no liquor bottles were broken, though more than a few appeared to be missing. Elizabeth imagined greedy officers hastily stuffing them into their pockets as they left the room.

"What now?" she asked. "Should we try to free the others?"

Grigory shrugged. "They will be released by morning. Police just want to scare them."

Jonah nodded. "He's right. I have seen these tactics before."

"Will they be charged with anything?"

"They might try for drunk and disorderly, but that would be more trouble than it's worth, and would only work if they managed to get a corrupt judge."

"Why go through all this, then?"

"Intimidation," said Grigory.

"They want us to know they can come for us anytime they wish," Jonah added.

Elizabeth looked at Carlotta, whose eyes were hard in a way she had not yet seen. "They're right. But isn't this the first time they targeted Justus?"

Jonah looked at Grigory. "They haven't come for him before?"

Grigory shook his head. "I know Justus since he first open. I hear of no raid before this."

"Why now, I wonder?" Carlotta mused.

Elizabeth was silent. Perhaps the slip of paper in her pocket held a clue, but she intended to show it to her editor. Given the confusing series of events, she was not entirely sure whom she could trust.

Her friends insisted on putting Elizabeth in a cab—Jonah and Carlotta offered to see her home, but it had been a long day, and she longed to crawl into bed. Now that the excitement had passed, fatigue turned her limbs to butter, and she could barely hold her head up.

"Good night," Carlotta said, hugging her close. Her hair smelled of vanilla and oil paint. "Please forgive me."

"For what?"

"For subjecting you to such danger."

"You are not responsible. I made the choice freely to join you."

"Still, I hope you are not cross with me."

"Of course not," Elizabeth said, closing the cab door. "Good night."

The others waved as the hansom drove away. Lulled by the rocking motion as the horse trotted uptown, Elizabeth leaned her head against the cab's leather padding and closed her eyes. By the time they arrived at the Stuyvesant, she had drifted off. Shaking herself back to consciousness, she alighted from the vehicle and paid the fare.

For a moment after the cab left, she had the feeling she was being watched. She looked up and down the nearly empty street; the only other person on it was a man walking his dog half a block away. A light rain had begun to fall; the damp cobblestones glittered in the gaslight as the man with the dog approached. A spray of droplets was scattered across the shoulders of his dark coat, white as snow in the yellow light. The dog, a black-and-white spaniel, strained on its leash as they neared, but the man pulled it back with an apologetic smile. His eyes were shaded beneath his hat, which he tipped politely as he passed. She had never seen him before on her street, which seemed odd; people with dogs were obliged to walk them at all hours. Watching him retreat into the night, Elizabeth was convinced she was just being fanciful; turning, she entered her building and climbed the two flights to her flat.

Relieved to be home at last, she double-locked the apartment door, slid the security rod in place, and slipped into her nightgown. The bath would have to wait until tomorrow. She set her alarm clock for dawn, which gave her plenty of time to finish her article. When she finally laid her head upon the pillow, the patter of raindrops upon her window was the last thing she heard before sinking gratefully into sleep.

CHAPTER FIFTY-ONE

He hauled himself up the four flights of creaky stairs to the two small rooms on the top floor of the stinking tenement. The stairwell was thick with the smell of mildew and despair. His knock drew no response, so he inserted his key and pushed the door open and stepped inside the pathetic hovel she called home. He was greeted by the stench of feces—she had soiled herself again. Drawing aside the curtain to her bedchamber, he beheld her withered, shrunken body, curled up on a dirty pile of linen on the worn mattress.

He regarded the old woman with contempt. How dare she live so long? Her liver, eaten away from years of drinking, had ceased doing its job; her yellowed skin was cracked and coarse as parchment. Suppurating sores punctuated her swollen legs like polka dots; her hair had thinned to a matted mass of rusty gray. Her nails had thickened and split; spidery veins on her face twisted in a maze of red and blue, like exploded firecrackers.

"You've lived long enough already, haven't you?" he murmured. "No one will miss you much, with your yellowing teeth, drooling mouth, and wasted limbs. You're no good to anyone—you can't lift or carry things, or stroke another's skin, smooth their hair, or wrap your arms around them when they hurt. You can't even wipe your own scraggly ass. You're useless, an unpleasant appendage, like a pimple on a cheek or a canker on a lip. You can't produce anything of value or use; you can only take, consuming precious resources meant for younger, stronger people. The most gracious and useful thing you can do now is simply to die—release yourself and me from the burden of a pitiful existence that hardly deserves to be called a life."

It pained him to think of all the men who had gladly taken advantage of that body when it was young and supple and smooth, and yet none of them were now to look after it in her decline.

He remembered the first time he had seen his father. He had always wondered who he was, but had no great hope of finding out. So many men had plowed their loins into his mother that the possibilities seemed too numerous. And yet that day, not even a year ago, when he saw the man, he knew instantly. They had the same build, the same-shaped head and pasty skin, the same unremarkable face with its doughy cheeks and rounded chin. But what sealed it was the walk, the way they both had of rolling their shoulders forward with each step, in a kind of haughty strut, as if daring anyone to take them on. His mother always told him it was silly for someone of his station to affect such a gait, but it was no affectation—it was simply the way he had always moved.

That day, on a warm spring afternoon, he had followed his father for some blocks down Broadway, lagging behind just enough so that he wasn't spotted. He did not yet know what to do with the information—that would come later.

His mother stirred and groaned, then burped loudly. A thin trail of spittle dribbled from her mouth onto the stained pillowcase. With a sigh, he went to the kitchen sink, found a not-too-disgusting washcloth and towel, and returned to the bed to clean the excrement from his mother's body.

CHAPTER FIFTY-TWO

Monday dawned bright and warm. Awaking before the alarm went off, Elizabeth got up and peeked out the window. The ground was still damp from the previous night's rain, steam rising from the sidewalks in the morning air. She was anxious to get to the *Herald*, so she decided to arrive early and finish the article there. She was worried about Kenneth Ferguson. Having not yet heard back from James Gordon Bennett, she had no idea whether he had received her telegram.

She arrived at the *Herald* just as the sun was high enough in the sky to tell that it was going to be a hot day, yet it was early enough that the editorial offices were nearly empty, save for a couple of copyboys and a few sleepy-looking reporters dozing over half-finished articles or sipping coffee from the all-night café on Williams Street. Settling in at her desk, Elizabeth had trouble concentrating, worried as she was about Ferguson. Whenever she heard footsteps in the hall, she looked up, hoping to see him striding along in his brisk way. Finally finished with her article, she rose from her desk just as the clock struck nine. She dragged her feet a bit as she walked it down to her editor's office, imagining him, beaten and bruised, languishing within the glowering walls of the Tombs.

But when she reached his office, she was beyond delighted to see his familiar form, albeit somewhat worse for wear, standing in front of his desk. His right hand was bandaged, injured when his fist collided with Thomas Byrnes' jaw; cuts and bruises were apparent on his face, and he held himself stiffly. But she had expected much worse and was overjoyed to see him alive.

"Good morning, Miss Van den Broek," he said with a rueful smile when she entered.

She had an impulse to hug him, which she suppressed, but she could not conceal the wide grin on her face. "I confess I am very glad to see you."

"I have you to thank for my relatively speedy release," he remarked, lowering himself carefully into his chair.

"Mr. Bennett received my telegram, then?"

"He did indeed, and was able to secure my freedom. Apparently some men in this town carry even more weight than Thomas Byrnes."

"Why do you hate Detective Byrnes so much?"

"He's a bully. And a crooked cop—I'm certain he is on the Tammany Hall payroll."

"That reminds me," she said, taking the folded ledger page from her purse and showing it to him. "Do you know what 'LDA' stands for?"

He studied it for a moment. "These are payoffs for police 'protection.' LDA is the Liquor Dealer's Association. It's a front for police extortion. Where did you get this?"

She told him of the raid on Schwab's saloon on the previous night, and of Jonah's conclusion that the police were sending Schwab a message.

"I believe your friend is correct. By the looks of it, Byrnes was squeezing Schwab for money, and Justus took exception to the latest rate hike. He probably refused to pay, so Byrnes decided to teach him a lesson. He is fortunate they did not do worse."

It all added up, she thought—the raid, the stolen bottles. It was a message: *Do not cross me or you will regret it.* She was beginning to understand Ferguson's hatred of Thomas Byrnes. And yet she sensed there was something else, something more personal.

"Do you think Byrnes knew you were there?" Ferguson asked.

"I don't see how he could have. It was a spur-of-the-moment decision on my part."

"You'd be surprised what he knows. He has spies everywhere."

Grigory's prediction about his radical friends being released turned out to be entirely accurate; they had been set free that morning, with no charges being filed, according to Ferguson.

"They left about the time Mr. Bennett showed up," he added. "A fine lot of misfits they were, too. Some of the women looked more like men than the men did."

Elizabeth let the remark pass. She wanted to defend them but didn't see the point—there were more important matters at hand. When she asked Ferguson what had happened while he was in police custody, he refused to elaborate, as if it were a point of shame that he had fared badly at their hands. Elizabeth was actually relieved that his injuries were not worse, though she did not say so. He did not seem anxious to revisit the issue, apparently considering it closed.

"Did Freddy's appearance last night help you at all?" she asked.

"Freddy? He never turned up. Or if he did, no one told me. Where is he, by the way?"

"I have not seen him since yesterday. When we parted, he was headed to the Tombs to find you."

Ferguson pulled at his whiskers. "I wonder what . . . Hey there, Bannister!" he called as Freddy's friend Tom Bannister passed by the office.

"Yes, sir?" he said, poking his head in the door.

"Have you seen Freddy Evans today?"

"No, sir—stood me up last night, 'e did. We were s'posed t'meet at the White Horse, but the blighter never showed."

"And you've not seen him all day?"

"No, sir, but if you see 'im, you can tell 'im that he owes me a coupla rounds."

"If you do hear from him, tell him to contact me immediately, please."

"Will do, sir," Bannister said, turning to leave.

"Wait," Elizabeth said. "I'll go with you."

"I should have this edited soon, so stick around," Ferguson said.

"I'll just be at my desk, sir," she said as she followed Tom into the corridor.

"Do you know why Ferguson hates Detective Byrnes so much?" she asked as they headed for the reporters' pool.

"You didn't know?"

"Know what?"

"He holds Byrnes responsible fer the death of 'is wife."

"I did not know he was ever married."

"Apparently she were carryin' their first child." Bannister shook his long, shaggy head. "Poor bloke."

"What happened?"

"Not sure exactly. I were still in London at the time. Somethin' t'do wi' a stray bullet, I think."

"How tragic."

"Yeah. Ever since then Ferguson's had it in fer Byrnes," he said as they entered the reporters' room. It was bustling with Monday-morning energy.

"You haven't heard from Freddy at all since last night, then?" Elizabeth asked Tom as they sat at their respective desks.

"Nix. Never showed up, an' I waited a long time." He bit his lip and frowned. "Don' like this one little bit, I don't."

Elizabeth had to agree. She feared something had happened to Freddy, something very bad indeed.

CHAPTER FIFTY-THREE

Thomas F. Byrnes, chief of detectives of the city of New York, sat in his office staring at the letter in his hand. Though the room was cool, pearls of sweat clung to his forehead, and his palms were clammy. As if doing penance, he read the words he had already perused a dozen times, till he nearly had them memorized.

> *I knew you were out there, and I have finally confirmed it. I know who you are, and by now you will know me. You should have been more careful, but since you consorted with whores, you get what you deserve. No doubt you do not wish for your wife and lovely daughters to know—let alone the general public. I warn you not to allow my capture, or you will regret it deeply.*
>
> *Yours in eternity,*
> *Osiris*

Hands trembling, Byrnes opened his bottom desk drawer and took out the metal flask of whiskey he had stashed there. Putting it to his lips, tasting the bitter metal, he sucked in the sharp brown liquid, welcoming the burn as it slid down his throat. He stared out the window at the city's never-ending stream of people. He felt personally responsible for all of them—he believed it was his job to protect every one of his fellow citizens, and he saw to his duty with a zeal seldom matched among his colleagues. It had resulted in his rapid rise through the ranks, culminating in his recent promotion to chief of detectives. It was, he thought, the most important job in the city, more important than the mayor or any politician in Tammany Hall. And he was willing to use most any means to accomplish what he saw as his duty.

Byrnes took another swig of whiskey. Closing his eyes, he leaned back in his chair, letting the sounds of the city outside wash over him. He accepted New York's rampant corruption with equanimity. If his position required certain concessions to those politicians, such as turning a blind eye to ballot-box stuffing or accepting bribes, then so be it. He regarded extortion of money from saloons, liquor dealers, and whorehouses as a "vice tax," convincing himself that it helped curtail criminal activity. This nimble bit of blame-shifting allowed Byrnes to maintain his self-image as a stalwart servant of law and order, in spite of his own considerable straying outside legal boundaries in order to enrich himself.

His fingers closed over the note, the third of its kind. Sighing deeply, he withdrew a box of matches from his vest pocket. Lighting one, he held the letter over the rising flame, which fed on it greedily until it was nothing but charred ashes scattered in his dustbin.

CHAPTER FIFTY-FOUR

Ferguson had minimal suggestions for changes to her article, so Elizabeth was able to finish her rewrites by two o'clock, leaving her plenty of time to get to her parents' house on Fifth Avenue. As her father had no cases to preside over that afternoon, her mother had rescheduled the family's Sunday dinner for Monday. Elizabeth suspected Catharina had an agenda of some kind, but she was glad she had apparently been forgiven for her absence the previous day. No one had heard from Freddy by the time she left the *Herald*, so she asked Ferguson to telegram her as soon as there was news.

As it was still early, she dropped by her apartment to change, donning a powder-blue frock with dark-blue trim and a matching short jacket. Her hair was a fright, springing in all directions in the humid weather, but she managed to tame it with a liberal application of bandoline mixed with rose water.

When she arrived at the Fifth Avenue town house, the aroma of roast lamb and parsnips greeted her in the foyer. Her mother met her at the door—it was Nora's day off, much to Elizabeth's relief. She knew Catharina longed to have more than the four servants her father allowed, but he considered four to be quite adequate for what was now a small household, with just the two of them. In addition to Nora and the cook, there was a scullery maid and Finn, a young Swedish man Catharina liked to call the valet, but who was really more of a "useful man," as they were called, who fetched wood, fixed things, and helped with other menial or physically demanding tasks. Catharina sometimes made him play butler and answer the door when Nora was not available, but as it was just Elizabeth today, she condescended to open her own front door.

"How good to see you," Catharina said, taking her hat and parasol. "Your father is in his study," she added as they went through to the front parlor. "He will join us presently." They sat by the french windows looking out onto a formal garden. A gold-trimmed china plate of canapés sat on the marble-topped coffee table, a stack of embroidered linen cocktail napkins next to them. Her mother picked up the plate and offered Elizabeth a canapé. "Shrimp and caviar—your favorite. Please have one. You look thin."

"I am very well nourished, thank you," Elizabeth said as her father entered the room.

The sight of him always cheered her up. He crossed the room in three strides of his long legs, his face breaking into the same sweet, ungainly smile she had known all her life. His awkwardness was as endearing as her mother's poise could be intimidating.

"Hello, darling Lizzie," he said, kissing her on the cheek, his beard prickly against her face. His breath was minty; a faint aroma of pipe tobacco emanated from his whiskers. She glanced at her mother, knowing she would not approve—Catharina was adamantly against smoking of any kind.

"Now then, how about a White Lion?" he said, rubbing his hands together, a gesture meant to draw others into something he was excited about.

"Why not?" Elizabeth said. The drink was one of his specialties, made with white rum, raspberry syrup, lime, and curaçao. She liked rum drinks, and cocktails were another family tradition. Formal meals were always preceded by drinks and hors d'oeuvres. Her father was proud of his carved mahogany bar, which he kept well stocked with elegant liqueurs, ports, and brandies.

While he busied himself mixing drinks, her mother sank gracefully into a gold-satin Louis XIV armchair opposite her. Elizabeth could tell from her posture she was bursting with information.

"So," Catharina said. "Guess who called on me yesterday?"

"Who?"

"Oh, have a guess!"

"The pope?"

Her mother frowned. "Be serious."

"Buffalo Bill."

Catharina snorted impatiently. "If you refuse to be serious, I shall just have to tell you." Her moods did not last long; they came and went as suddenly as a summer storm. She leaned forward, eager as a child. *"Mrs. Astor."* She spoke the name with reverence, a devout prayer offered to the gods of social prominence.

"That's nice," Elizabeth said. "You must be pleased."

"Do you know what this *means*?"

"Not exactly, but I'm sure you'll enjoy telling me."

"We would join the ranks of the *Four Hundred*."

Elizabeth wanted to blurt out that she didn't give a tinker's damn about the Astors, the Four Hundred, or anything having to do with high society, but not wanting to spoil her mother's girlish delight, she held her tongue.

"I got the impression Mrs. Astor was rather taken with you," her father told Elizabeth, handing her the cocktail in a tumbler garnished with fresh raspberries and a lime wedge.

"Thank you," Elizabeth said, taking a hearty swallow. She would need it to put up with her mother's prattle when she had more pressing matters on her mind.

"Isn't that what she said to you?" Hendrik asked his wife, settling next to her in a sturdy Dutch walnut armchair, a seventeenth-century family heirloom. "That she was quite taken with our daughter?"

Her mother fiddled with her cocktail napkin, folding and refolding it. "She didn't exactly come out and *say* it, but she *implied* it."

"Well, there you are, then," he said, raising his drink. "Here's to the success of the Van den Broeks' entry into high society."

"Don't make fun of me," Catharina said, pursing her lips in a pout, which only made her more alluring.

"My dear, I wouldn't dream of it," Hendrik said, patting her hand. "But I do think you can give Lizzie some credit for the great lady's coming around."

"Of course I do! It's just a pity that she works at the *Herald*."

"What's wrong with it?" Elizabeth asked.

"It's just so . . . well, *common*."

"You mean sensationalist."

"Well, yes. Couldn't you work for—

"The *Sun*?" Elizabeth said, knowing full well that the paper was popular with the working classes. Her father read it from time to time, but it did not appeal to her mother's innate snobbery.

"No, I meant—"

"The *Daily News*?"

Her mother snorted. "Don't be supercilious! If there's one thing I cannot abide, it's—"

"Sarcasm?"

Catharina glared at her. "I was going to say a cavalier attitude."

"Where would you *like* Lizzie to be working, then?" her father asked.

"Well, maybe the *Times* . . . or the *Tribune*."

Elizabeth sighed. "Oh, Mother. Is anything ever enough for you?"

"What on earth do you mean?"

Elizabeth rubbed her forehead. A splinter of pain stabbed her left temple. "Never mind."

Finn appeared in the doorway at that moment, his long Nordic face pale and stern, as if sculpted from ice. "Begging pardon, madame, but dinner is served." Elizabeth liked the peaks and valleys of his accent; listening to him was like skiing down a Scandinavian fjord.

They had just finished the soup course when the front-door chime sounded.

"Who could that be? Are you expecting someone?" Catharina asked her husband.

He smiled at her warmly. "No, dear—my attention is entirely yours."

"Perhaps someone has an urgent need for a warrant," Elizabeth suggested.

"See who it is, will you, Finn?" said Catharina with a rather imperious wave of her hand. Elizabeth had never seen her make that gesture, and wondered if she was practicing for her role as a member of the Four Hundred.

"Certainly, madame," said the Swede, who had been waiting patiently at attention after serving the soup course. Catharina seemed to enjoy having servants standing around during meals, whereas Elizabeth always found it unsettling.

Finn disappeared into the foyer, returning with a familiar yellow envelope. "Telegram for Miss Van den Broek."

Elizabeth's hand trembled as she took it from him.

"Why would someone send you a telegram here?" her mother asked, her voice alarmed. Elizabeth wondered the same thing as she tore it open. She read it, her heart thumping wildly.

Sorry to interrupt your dinner. The next will be The Hidden One.
And closer to home. Try to find the unfinished link. Time to fly!
—Osiris

Elizabeth looked up at her parents. “I'm sorry, but I must leave.”

Her mother stared at her in alarm. “But why?”

“I'll explain later. I will be in touch as soon I can.”

Without giving them time to protest, she grabbed her hat and parasol from the foyer and left the town house.

CHAPTER FIFTY-FIVE

Kenneth Ferguson paced his office on the second floor of the *Herald*.

"He sent this to your *parents'* house?" he asked, holding the telegram in his bandaged right hand.

"Yes."

Ferguson dropped the telegram on his desk. "Good God. How did he know where to find you?"

"I don't know, sir," she replied, trying to suppress her gathering panic.

"I do not like this development," he said, rubbing his forehead. "I fear he is targeting you."

"He seems to be giving us a riddle to solve."

"He's also threatening you."

"Not necessarily."

"'Closer to home'? If that isn't a threat . . ."

"Perhaps, but 'the unfinished link' seems like a clue to me. It's unfortunate the handwriting is of no use." The writing, of course, belonged to the telegraph operator who had translated the Morse code from the original telegram.

"We might send someone to interview the telegram operator who sent the message. He may remember who gave it to him."

Elizabeth shook her head. "He is too smart for that. He would have paid someone to deliver it for him—a young boy, perhaps."

"What does he mean by 'the Hidden One'?"

"That may be a reference to Amunet, an ancient Egyptian goddess of air or wind. Her name means 'She Who is Hidden.' That would also explain the reference to flying."

Ferguson chewed heavily on his cigar stub. "I'm going to bring this to Mr. Bennett's attention."

"What should we do about the telegram, sir?"

"Obviously we run it in tomorrow's issue," he said, glancing at the wall clock; it was half past four. "There is time to include a brief article before we put the issue to bed—can you write it?"

Elizabeth cleared her throat and swallowed hard. "Yes, sir."

"It is wrong to ask that of you. Perhaps I should write it."

"No, sir. I'll do it," she said quickly.

"Importune our readers to come forward with any information they may possess about this individual. Do not include the fact that it was sent to you—be vague about how we came to be in possession of it. And of course we will not print the address portion, to avoid giving any information that might identify you."

"But should we not—"

"Under no circumstances are you to mention that this was addressed to you. I see no reason to place you in any more danger than you are already in."

"And the police, sir?"

"Let them read about it in the paper," he snapped. "Now that Freddy has disappeared, I must find another way to protect you."

"Any news of him?"

"No, and it's not like him to go on a bender, especially at a time like this."

As if on cue, Tom Bannister appeared at the door. One look at his face told the story all too well.

"What happened, man?" asked Ferguson.

"It's Freddy, isn't it?" said Elizabeth.

"They found 'im in Five Points," Tom said, the words tumbling from him like sobs. "Beaten to a pulp."

Elizabeth's head swam, and she had to grab the back of a chair to steady herself. "Is he alive?"

"Only just. They took 'im t'Bellevue. I'm goin' over there now."

Ferguson's face darkened. "I'll wager Byrnes is behind this," he said, his jaw tight.

Elizabeth stared at him. "Surely you don't think—"

"He's capable of anything."

"But why—"

"Because Freddy was one of ours. Because we're getting too close and he's trying to warn us off."

"You mean because he doesn't want us solving the case first?"

"Or he doesn't want it solved at all."

"Why not?"

"That is something I would dearly like to know."

They looked at Tom Bannister, clutching the doorframe as if he would fall to the floor if he let go.

"Why don't you take tomorrow off, Tom?" Ferguson said gently. "Go see Freddy and then get some rest."

"If it's all the same ta you, I'd rather not. I'd like t'fine out what happened ta Freddy."

"Why don't we leave that for now?" said Ferguson. "Five Points is a dangerous place, and things can happen—"

"So yer jes gonna let the coppers 'solve' it, then?" he answered bitterly.

"I didn't say that, but we're not in the business of crime solving."

"Why don' ya tell *her* that?" Tom said, glaring at Elizabeth.

Ferguson stepped forward. "Now, Tom—"

"She's the reason they went after Freddy! Pokin' her nose in where it don' belong. It's not right fer a woman t'be doin' such things!"

"That's enough!" came a voice from behind him, and James Gordon Bennett appeared in the doorway. Elegant as always, he wore a red-carnation boutonniere in the breast pocket of his dove-gray frock coat.

"Beg pardon, Mr. Bennett—didn' see ya there," Bannister said.

The publisher waved his hand. "Never mind, Tom. Why don't you get over to Bellevue? We're all concerned about Freddy. Send a telegram about his condition, if you would," he added, pressing some money into Bannister's hand.

"Yessir," the photographer said, and skulked away down the hall.

"Well," Bennett said, turning to Elizabeth, "this is what comes of a woman trying to do a man's job."

Ferguson's face reddened. "Are you saying she isn't fit, sir?"

"Not at all. I am merely pointing out that this will not be the last such accusation she will face. The obstacles are many," he told Elizabeth. "And you may find them coming from friend and foe alike. The question you must now ask yourself is whether you are prepared to face them."

A week ago, Elizabeth would have answered in the affirmative without hesitating. But now, under the gaze of the two men, she felt smaller and sadder. She remembered something her father used to say: "When in doubt, ride it out."

Lifting her chin, she returned Bennett's gaze. "If I am not now prepared, then no one ever will be."

CHAPTER FIFTY-SIX

In the library, he was invisible. Quiet and unobtrusive, he faded into the stacks like a shadow. Women brushed past him, with little idea of what danger they might be in. The smell of their hair, the rustle of their skirts, the feathery whiff of air as they passed—it all gave him an indescribable thrill.

He gazed at the popular dime novels on the library shelves, with titles such as *Red as a Rose Is She*, *Wife in Name Only; or, A Broken Heart*, and *Good-bye, Sweetheart!*. Just looking at them made him sick. He turned away in disgust. Love was a construct, a fantasy concocted by people who led bland, sheltered lives, and believed the lies fed to them in these execrable books.

Murder, though, was something else entirely. Murder was real. It was an observable fact: a person once was living, and then they weren't. It made him feel alive—like an actual corporeal being. Killing people gave him a sense of agency: he could have an impact on the world. He could, in fact, change the course of history. The effects of murder radiated outward, like ripples on a pond when a pebble is tossed into it.

He slipped to the familiar section of the stacks where he had spent many a happy hour perusing the volumes on ancient Egypt. Running his fingers lightly over the bindings, he selected a favorite, which he had practically memorized: *Gods and Goddesses of Ancient Egypt.* He had chosen his next goddess. This time he would proceed with great care. She must be prepared, groomed, educated. The gift of this book would be the first initiation into the ritual. He sighed as he pressed the book to his bosom, imagining her face, by now so familiar, as she saw the book.

Later, at home, he smiled as he combed his hair in the mirror, parting it with care, adding a splash of lime pomade. He lived in the biggest pond in North America. All that remained was to find more pebbles to toss into it, then watch as the ripples spread throughout society. That was power, the only true power he or anyone possessed, the ability to control life and death. And it was a power he was wielding with increasing skill.

CHAPTER FIFTY-SEVEN

By the time Elizabeth finished her article, it was nearly seven, and after a protracted argument with Ferguson about her safety, she left for Bellevue to see Freddy. No word had yet come from Tom Bannister, and everyone feared the worst. After assuring her editor that she would let him know Freddy's condition immediately, she stepped out into the balmy evening air.

The streets were quiet when she hopped on an uptown tram, and she had most of the car to herself. A drowsy chimney sweep huddled in one corner, his face black with soot, his long-bristled brushes at his side. The boy could not have been more than twelve, and yet here he was, out at work on a Monday night. At his age, Elizabeth would have been climbing out of a hot bath just about now, ready for milk and cookies before being tucked into bed by her doting father. He loved tucking his daughters in, and would read them a bedtime story. Sometimes he made up his own. Looking at the dozing boy, she wondered whether he had a father or mother waiting for him. Or had hardship and poverty already worn down his overworked mother? Had his father already taken up with another woman, and did he beat the boy on the rare occasion they met?

The boy stirred and leaned his head on one grimy hand, closing his eyes again. What was he going home to? she wondered. If he was lucky, a cold-water flat, perhaps, and maybe even a bowl of soup. And he would consider himself fortunate if there was a bit of meat to go with it, or a slice of day-old bread and a piece of cheese.

She stared out the window at the darkened streets. August would soon slip into September, and daylight seemed to be shrinking more rapidly with each sunset. The boy got off at Houston Street, and the tram continued uptown as a pregnant moon rose over the East River. Heavy in the humid summer air, it seemed to hang over the water for a moment as if it were about to plunge into the dark, swirling depths.

As they approached Kips Bay in the gathering twilight, Bellevue loomed ahead, moonlight glinting on the letters carved into the wrought-iron entrance gate. With its round turrets and towers, it looked like a castle out of a fairy tale rather than a hospital.

The receptionist had trouble at first finding Freddy's whereabouts but finally directed Elizabeth to the third floor, after informing her with gratuitous solemnity that it was the ward "for the grievously injured."

When she arrived at his room, Freddy was conscious, though heavily bandaged. His head was swathed in gauze, his nose was swollen, his face bruised and cut. Both eyes were blackened. Elizabeth nearly cried when she saw him. Tom Bannister sat at his bedside. When he saw Elizabeth, Freddy tried to sit up in bed, moaning as he attempted to change position.

"Miss Elizabeth," he said in a weak voice, "thanks fer comin' t'see me."

"Oiy, mate, don' try an' move," Tom said. "Gotta save yer strength, yeah?"

Elizabeth remained in the doorway, unsure of her reception. "Hello, Freddy. How is he?" she asked Tom stiffly.

"Doctor reckons he'll live, if he don' do noffin' stupid," Tom said, with a glance at Freddy, who gave a wan smile.

"How bad are his injuries?"

"Broke a few ribs, an' his nose, which jes might improve his looks. Busted collarbone. Lotta bruises and bashes, and prob'ly a concussion. Lost a bit a blood, didn' ya?" he asked Freddy, who seemed to have fallen asleep. His eyes were closed, and his breathing appeared regular, which Elizabeth found reassuring. Tom rose from his chair and tiptoed over to her. "They were worried 'bout internal bleedin', but so far he's holdin' his own," he whispered.

"Thank you," she said. "I promised I would report on his condition."

"Oh, I was s'posed to do that. I forgot."

"Never mind—I'll take care of it. Did he say who did this to him?"

"Coupla thugs, he says. Didn' get a good look at 'em."

"Not in uniform, I assume?"

"No."

"It figures. Byrnes would be too smart for that," she said, turning to go.

"Uh, miss?" Tom said hesitantly.

"Yes?"

"Look, I shouldna' said wha' I did. It weren't yer fault—I was jes angry, an' took it out on you. It was wrong, an' I apologize."

"Thank you, Tom—I appreciate that. We're all worried. I'll go send that telegram now."

"Yes, miss. Thank you, miss." Going back into the room, he resumed his bedside vigil.

The hospital had its own telegraph office on the first floor, and after reporting on Freddy's condition to the *Herald*, Elizabeth went back to the lobby and followed the signs to the Pavilion for the Insane. As she trod the by-now-familiar route, she heard quickening footsteps behind her. Panic gripped her, and she spun around to see Dr. Jamison loping toward her. Relief flooded over her at the sight of him, and something more than relief as well.

"I'm sorry if I startled you," he said, catching up to her.

"Good evening, Doctor," she said without breaking stride. Every cell in her body rejoiced at his presence, which was precisely why she did not want to reveal to him how glad she was to see him.

"You are here to see your sister?"

"Do you have any news of her?"

"As a matter of fact, I was on my way to check on her now."

"Why? Is something wrong?"

He did not reply immediately, which was in itself an answer.

"What is it?" she asked. "Please tell me."

"I would rather you see for yourself," he said as they rounded the corner leading to the patients' common room.

They found Laura seated in her usual place, the wicker settee by the window, clad in a pale-yellow dress, nearly the same shade as her fine, silky hair. As they entered the room, she was staring out the window, golden moonlight filtering in through the sheer curtains. For a moment Elizabeth imagined it was her mother in the chair, the resemblance between them was so close. Laura turned as they entered, and the blank expression on her face was like the thrust of a dagger.

"Hello, Lolo," Elizabeth said softly.

Her sister cocked her head to one side without smiling. "You are a vision."

Elizabeth waited for her to say something else, but she remained silent, shifting her gaze to Dr. Jamison.

"Good evening, Miss Van den Broek," he said. "How are you feeling this evening?"

"I am flying," she said in a curiously flat voice. It was as if their presence meant no more to her than the chair she was sitting on, or the cold cup of tea on the table next to her.

"What have you been reading?" Elizabeth asked, indicating the book on her lap.

Her sister picked up the book and studied it curiously, as if she had never seen it before. "*Gods and Goddesses of Ancient Egypt.*"

"Where did you get that?" Elizabeth asked tightly.

"From a ghost," Laura said vaguely.

"What makes you think it was a ghost?" Jamison asked.

"All in white, dark as the night," Laura replied in a singsong voice.

"You mean it was someone wearing white?" Elizabeth asked.

Her sister nodded. "Dressed in white, black as the night."

"Was it a Negro?" asked Jamison.

Laura shrugged and bit her lip. The change in her affect since Elizabeth had last seen her was heartbreaking.

"The orderlies wear white," Jamison said. "And so do most of the staff."

"It's summer," Elizabeth pointed out. "A lot of people wear white." She turned to Laura. "Can you remember who gave you the book?"

Her sister frowned and shook her head violently.

"This seems to be upsetting her," Jamison said gently. "Might we change the subject?"

"Well, I—"

"It's not important, is it?"

"It may prove to be very important indeed. Will you excuse us for a moment?" she asked Laura.

"Of course," her sister replied with a gracious wave of her hand. To Elizabeth's relief, she seemed to have calmed down.

Elizabeth beckoned to Jamison, then led him into the hallway. Lowering her voice, she told him of the recent killings and their links to Egyptian mythology. He listened thoughtfully.

"I see why you are concerned. I shall conduct an inquiry first thing tomorrow to get to the bottom of this."

"I cannot thank you enough."

"Of course you are aware there is a great interest in all things Egyptian these days. It may prove to be merely a coincidence."

"It may indeed," she agreed, though the more strange turns of events piled up, the less she believed in coincidences.

CHAPTER FIFTY-EIGHT

Laura was no more forthcoming during the rest of her visit, until finally Elizabeth's patience wore out. She had never seen her sister so unresponsive; her expressionless face and flat affect were puzzling and exhausting. She seemed only vaguely connected to reality. After about half an hour, Elizabeth agreed with Jamison that it was time to leave.

"I see why you were vague about her condition earlier," she said as they retraced their steps down the long corridor leading to the lobby. "You did not want to upset me."

"I also did not want to plant preconceived notions of her behavior that might lead you to treat her differently." As they reached the front door, he turned to her. "I am quite ravenous. Would you care to dine with me?"

Elizabeth, too, was starving, having given little thought to food most of the day.

"There is a small café around the corner I am very fond of. The owner treats me well, and I would be honored if you would join me."

"That is very kind of you," she replied. "But first I must attend to something."

"May I ask what it is?"

She told him of Madhouse Mary's murder and the subsequent events. "I want to go down to the morgue. If Viktor Novak is there, he may let me see Mary."

"A gruesome task, I should think."

"No more so than what you do every day."

"Touché," he said with a rueful smile.

"No doubt you think it is more difficult for me because I am a woman, but I can assure you I am no more fragile than any man."

"Truly, I do not doubt it," he said earnestly, and she believed him.

They agreed to meet in the lobby in half an hour. He went to look in on some patients, while Elizabeth left the Pavilion for the hospital wing housing the city morgue. She arrived to find Viktor Novak seated at his desk in the small front room, absorbed in paperwork.

"Ah," he said when he saw her, "I wondered when you would be paying me a visit. Several of your colleagues—or perhaps I should say rivals—have been here already."

"What did you tell them?"

"The same thing I told the police. The coroner's autopsy revealed the cause of death to be drowning—though, as in the other case, there were marks indicating strangulation."

"But no exsanguination?"

"No."

"So he strangles them, but not to the point of death."

"So it would seem."

"And the Madison Square Park victim?"

"The body was too damaged to determine whether or not strangulation was involved. And no, we have not yet identified her," he said, anticipating her next question.

"Why strangle them at all, then?" she mused, as Benjamin Higgins strolled into the room, sucking on a piece of licorice.

"Maybe he likes the feeling of power it gives 'im," he suggested. "Evenin', miss."

"Good evening, Mr. Higgins."

"I'm surprised you have so much time on your hands," Novak remarked.

The ambulance driver shrugged as he wiped a smudge of licorice from his white jacket, which was snug across his bulky shoulders and muscular chest. "Slow night. What brings you down here, miss?" he asked Elizabeth.

"She is investigating Mary's murder," Novak replied.

"Oh, yeah?" He shook his head ruefully. "Terrible thing. Hard t'imagine what goes through the head of a fiend like that."

"I feel certain these are lust murders," Elizabeth replied.

The suggestion seemed to mortify Higgins. "What? No—surely not. He didn't, uh, molest them, did he?"

"No," Novak replied. "Though in my experience, that does not preclude a sexual motive. No doubt you would like to see the body," he said to Elizabeth.

"Yes, indeed, if you don't mind."

"Right this way," Novak said, with a glance at Higgins, who plunked himself down in a chair, chewing contentedly on his licorice, which had stained his lips and tongue black.

Elizabeth followed Novak into the room where bodies were stored in refrigerated metal drawers. He approached the one labeled "Mary Mullins" in a tidy, handwritten script.

"Here we are," Novak said as the drawer slid forward smoothly on its oiled rollers.

Mary looked much the same as she had the previous day, except for the Y-shaped incision on her torso. Someone had taken great care with the suturing—the stitches were small and closely spaced, as if they had tried to mar her milky skin as little as possible. Elizabeth wondered whether it was a sign of respect, or merely a surgical resident practicing his technique on a compliant corpse.

She studied the deathly white skin of Mary's shoulders and chest, the strangulation marks still visible around her neck.

"Were there any other markings on her body?" she asked Novak.

"There were some cuts and bruises. Are you looking for anything in particular?"

Elizabeth pulled a slip of paper from her purse and showed it to him.

"What's that?" he said after studying it for a moment.

"It's an ancient Egyptian symbol for water."

"H-how did you know?" He looked genuinely spooked.

"Can you show it to me?"

Without a word, Novak lowered the sheet to expose the rest of her torso. There, neatly carved into her abdomen, was the symbol Elizabeth had shown him. She looked up to see Benjamin Higgins standing in the doorway, his mouth agape.

"Heaven and saints preserve us. It's the work of the devil."

"Actually," Elizabeth replied, "I believe it is the work of Osiris."

CHAPTER FIFTY-NINE

Elizabeth's visit to the morgue lasted just over half an hour, and when she arrived back in the hospital's main lobby, Hiram Jamison was already there.

"I'm sorry if I've kept you waiting," she said, hurrying across the tile floor to where he stood.

"Not at all," he said, smiling. "But I am quite famished—I do hope you like French cuisine."

"I can think of nothing better," she replied, and they stepped out into the night.

The air was still balmy, even though the sun had set some hours ago, and as they walked down First Avenue, she reflected on how, even on a gentle night such as this, terrible crimes were taking place within the shores of this strange, unpredictable island.

Café des Gamins was even more charming than she had imagined, its Continental flavor aided by the French accents of the owners. Hiram Jamison explained that the couple was from Montreal, not Paris, which accounted for the thickness of their consonants and twisting diphthongs. They seemed to regard him as their special pet, and insisted on treating him to a bottle of fine Burgundy.

When the food arrived, he insisted she try a bite of his coq au vin, which was good, but her *truite aux fines herbes* was even better. Drenched in a buttery lemon sauce topped with parsley, chives, chervil, and tarragon, with roast potatoes and asparagus, it was the closest thing to heaven Elizabeth could imagine.

Her initial hunger satiated, she leaned back in her chair and looked around the café's cozy interior. Wall gas sconces flickered merrily, aided by the light of a dozen or so candles on the fireplace mantel, window-sills, and tables. The room was decorated in a French farmhouse style, with white lace curtains and bouquets of dried lavender tied up with ribbons in flowered vases. Gleaming copper pans hung on the walls, alongside a few reproductions of Old World masters—Elizabeth recognized a Vermeer, a Rembrandt, and one of Monet's *Haystacks*.

Her gaze fell on Jamison just as he looked up from his plate. Their eyes met, and to her surprise, he laughed.

"I was about to apologize for being so absorbed in my food, but I see your appetite matched my own."

He was right—she had eaten half of her meal in just a few minutes. She felt a blush creep onto her cheeks. "If my mother were here, she would be mortified."

"Your secret is safe with me."

"She so wishes I were more like her."

"The saddest moment in some people's lives is the realization they will never really change another person."

"My mother has not yet reached that level of enlightenment."

"I have never understood why some parents feel they must mold their child in their own image."

"It sounds as if your parents avoided that temptation."

Jamison smiled. "More wine?" he asked, reaching for the bottle.

"Yes, please." She looked around the room, which had emptied considerably since they arrived. The waiter was serving dessert to the one other couple by the fireplace. "I was wondering if we might talk about my sister for a moment. Of course, if you'd rather not, I entirely understand."

"I don't mind at all," he said, taking a sip of wine. His jade eyes were darker in the candlelight, his skin dusky, and his hair appeared jet black. His complexion was entirely unlike her own, which was probably one of the reasons she was attracted to him.

"Perhaps you would rather take your mind away from your work—"

"I must confess I find my work so absorbing that I am never far from it."

"Very well," she said, wrapping her napkin around her fingers, the way her father did when he was preoccupied with a problem. "Do you have any idea why my sister has taken this turn for the worse?"

"Not specifically, but I have been arguing for a different course of treatment."

"How so?"

"First, there is the overreliance on sedatives that I mentioned before."

"I entirely agree. But what then?"

"I think we need to make more of an effort as clinicians to communicate with the patient, to get inside their head, as it were."

"Do you believe you will convince others to try this approach?"

"If I can get the ear of Dr. Smith, I believe he will listen to me. He is the reason I came to Bellevue. I have also long suspected that some madness may have a biological origin. I am not alone in this, of course, though so little is currently known that I fear new treatments may do more harm than good."

"Do you . . ." She hesitated, realizing she dreaded the answer.

"Yes?"

"Do you believe she can be cured?"

"I have not yet enough experience in the field. But I do think it is possible, one day, to find a more effective treatment for people like her."

His words offered enough hope that Elizabeth felt a renewal of her own commitment to Laura's health. "I cannot thank you enough for your care and interest in my sister's condition," she said, impulsively laying her hand upon his. His skin was warm, and softer than she had expected. The current of electricity she felt made her withdraw her hand rather quickly.

She regretted her gesture, and there was now an awkwardness between them; he gave a little cough and picked up the menu. "What do you say to some dessert?"

In truth, she was exceedingly full, but did not want the evening to end. "That would be lovely," she said.

"Does anything strike your fancy?"

"You choose."

He ordered a raspberry tart, something called a Lafayette Gingerbread, and two coffees.

As they waited for dessert to arrive, her mind strayed to the recent murders.

"A penny for your thoughts," he said when she lapsed into silence.

"I did not mean to be rude. I just cannot help wondering how he manages to transport the bodies so readily."

"You are speaking about this strange series of killings."

"Yes. He does it at night, of course, but still . . ."

"He might use cabs."

"But then the drivers would be witnesses."

"He could pay them to keep quiet."

She wrapped her napkin absently around her fingers. "Perhaps he has his own carriage."

"Which would indicate he is a man of means."

"I can't help thinking such a man would eventually attract attention. And yet this one seems to move about like a ghost. I know of only one person who has seen him."

"Who might that be?"

"An old drunk down on Pier 17, by Fulton Street. And that was in the dead of night."

Their desserts arrived, and proved to be just as good as the rest of the meal. They agreed to share both, and Elizabeth was very glad. The tart pastry was flaky and light, with a Chantilly cream filling topped with fresh berries, and the gingerbread was served warm, topped with vanilla ice cream. Redolent of fresh spices, butter, and eggs, it was so delicious that Elizabeth quite forgot her feeling of fullness and ate with relish.

"Well," Jamison said when they had finished, "I see we were both equally famished."

"That was truly excellent—thank you."

"It was my pleasure."

Elizabeth accepted his offer to see her home. When he hailed a cab, one pulled up immediately in front of the hospital. The driver looked familiar—then she saw the long scar on his cheek. She recognized the same spindly young man from before, driving the handsome chestnut gelding, tossing his head in the harness, eager to trot onward.

"You certainly get around," she remarked to the driver.

"Yes, miss," he said, tipping his hat politely as she took her seat in the cab's snug interior.

After a short ride, they arrived at the Stuyvesant. After telling the cabbie to wait, Dr. Jamison escorted her to the front door, and as she fumbled for her key, she heard a door slam on the first floor. Startled, she dropped the key.

He leaned over to pick it up. "Are you all right?" he asked, handing it to her.

"I am just tired," she lied. "Thank you for a lovely evening."

"It was my pleasure," he said, the gaslight soft on his dark, curly hair. She could smell his lime cologne, and her fingers turned to stone as panic rose in her throat. The keys slipped from her grasp again, and again he fetched them.

"Are you quite sure you are well?" he asked, handing her the keys.

"How clumsy of me!" she said, hoping her voice did not shake. "Thank you again," she said. This time the key slid into the lock, and she stepped into her lobby. She watched through the window for him to get back into the cab, and stood still until the sounds of hooves on cobblestone receded into the night.

She did not really believe Hiram Jamison was her attacker, but the smell of lime cologne made her nauseous, and as she walked up to her apartment, she felt dizzy. After locking herself securely inside, she ran a hot bath. Lying back in the deep tub, steam fogging the mirror over the sink, she finally allowed her body to relax. Drawing in a long, slow breath, she was unprepared when her exhale took the form of a ragged sob. It was followed by another, and another, her hot tears mixing with the bathwater, until her stomach ached from the rhythmic heaving.

Afterward, she crawled into bed and stared out her window at the pregnant gibbous moon high in the sky. For the first time, it occurred to her that some injuries might never heal.

CHAPTER SIXTY

Kenneth Ferguson looked up from his desk when Elizabeth rushed into his office on Tuesday morning.

"He drives a cab!" she exclaimed breathlessly.

"What? Who drives a cab?"

"The killer! That's how he transports the bodies without being noticed."

"How do you know this?"

"Does it not make perfect sense? He drives around in the middle of the night with impunity, answers to no one, and attracts little attention."

Ferguson stroked his whiskers. "I take your point. Everyone is used to seeing cabbies out at all hours."

"And that would explain how he knows where my parents live."

"He would have taken you there at some point, you mean?"

"Exactly." She told him of her repeated sightings of the lanky cabbie with the scar on his cheek. "I am not certain it is he, but that is what gave me the idea."

"But how did he know you were there yesterday evening?"

She frowned. "I can only conclude he has been watching me."

Ferguson frowned. "There are hundreds of hacks in the city. It's a pity no one has witnessed his placement of the bodies."

"There was one witness."

"*What?* Who?"

She told him of her exchange with the ancient sailor at the docks. "Of course I should have told you earlier. With everything else going on, I quite forgot."

"I did not see mention of it in your article."

"No, because I feared if I wrote about him, he would come to harm."

"Yet he did not see the vehicle, you say?"

"No."

"So the killer is a nighthawk," Ferguson mused. "Nighthawks" were cabbies who prowled the city streets at night, notorious for cheating their customers and servicing New York's widespread vice market.

"There's something else," she said, and told him about the strange book her sister had received.

"And you don't know as yet who gave it to her?"

"Dr. Jamison is attempting to find out."

"You mean perhaps it is someone within the hospital?"

"The possibilities are numerous. It could have been given to any staff member to deliver to Laura; it could have come directly from a visitor. It could even have been given to her by a fellow patient. Her recollection is quite foggy, I'm afraid."

"Does the hospital keep a visitor log?"

"Unfortunately, no. They are understaffed as it is."

"I don't like this," Ferguson said, chewing on his cigar stub. "I don't like it one little bit."

"I'm going to my desk to work on a follow-up piece," she said.

"When Bannister returns from the hospital, I want him to accompany you home."

"I don't see—"

"There will be no further discussion on the matter."

Though she would not admit it, in truth Elizabeth was relieved. Her bravado was little more than a pose. She was surprised that it convinced anyone, when she hardly believed it herself.

As she passed the main staircase on the way to her desk, Elizabeth saw Simon Sneed and Greta Volcarré engaged in conversation at the top of the stairs. Heads close, bodies nearly touching, they presented a picture of intimacy. When they saw her approaching, they stepped away from each other, but it was clear they knew she had caught them.

Simon Sneed approached her, his customary sneer plastered on his face. "Well, well, if it isn't Ken Fergie's star reporter. I hear you're very talented—even Mr. Bennett seems impressed. How many other men have you 'impressed'?"

Standing feet away from him, Elizabeth could see his eyes were bloodshot and his hands exhibited a slight tremor. The implication was clear: Simon Sneed was an addict.

"Well?" he said, blocking her way. "What's a fellow got to do to sample your 'talent'?"

"Get out of my way," Elizabeth said in a low voice. "And if you ever lay hands on me again, *I will kill you.*"

His eyes widened in surprise, and he stumbled backward as if he had been pushed. She took advantage of the moment and continued on her way without looking back. Though the building was cool, she was perspiring. Her response to Sneed's threatening presence had taken her as much by surprise as it had him. She was simply fed up—tired of the criticism, innuendos, comments, and threats. Tired of having to play the games society demanded of women—of being good and nice and kind and respectful to people she neither liked nor respected. As she walked, the weight of anxiety slid from her shoulders like an ill-fitting cloak, replaced by a kind of gleeful nihilism. People might try to control her destiny—they might even succeed—but she would not allow them to make her miserable.

Elizabeth returned to her desk, feeling unaccountably calm. Something inside her had shifted. Faced with so many people who wished her ill or sought to stand between her and her job, she could suffer for only so long. The surfeit of emotion from the past week seemed to have reached a shut-off point. Even her anguish over Freddy's beating was replaced with a hard, cold anger, as though all the softness had drained from her body. She also believed, rightly or wrongly, that there was most likely no link between her assault and the murders. The behaviors were so completely different that she did not think there was a connection.

Concentrating on her story, she worked uninterrupted for several hours, finishing just before the clock struck five. Marching into Ferguson's empty office, she dropped the article on his desk along with a note, and left the Herald Building with Tom at her side.

She had no way of knowing that her relative peace of mind was about to be shattered.

CHAPTER SIXTY-ONE

Elizabeth arrived at the Stuyvesant to find the concierge waiting for her in the lobby. A French-style concierge was one of the building's allures—her mother was very impressed by it—but once she moved in, Elizabeth found she had little use for the amenity. But now, as she entered the lobby, she was greeted by Mme. Vernier. (Hiring a concierge who was actually French was another effort to make the building more like "French flats.") Clad in a pink chenille house robe, the good lady scurried across the lobby, shaking her hands up and down as if they were wet and she was attempting to dry them. Middle aged and fleshy, with a plump, florid face, she had what Elizabeth's mother called avoirdupois—a genteel way of calling someone fat. Her hair was twisted around rags, a popular method for producing curls, especially if one lacked a lady's maid.

"*Mademoiselle, quelque chose le dérangeait vraiment!*"

Elizabeth had enough French to know that she was saying not that the person in question was deranged but that he was very upset. "*Pardon, madame?* Who was concerned?"

"*Le jeune médecin!*" Her imploring brown eyes searched Elizabeth's face.

"*Quel médecin?*" Elizabeth asked. Mme. Vernier spoke English, but when she was excited, it could be a challenge for her to find the right words.

"*Très beau, avec des cheveux noirs.*"

Handsome, with black hair. The description removed any doubt—it was Hiram Jamison.

"What did he want?"

"*Votre sœur*—your sister—there is a problem."

"*Quelle sorte de problème?*"

"*Elle a disparu*—disappeared."

It took Elizabeth a moment to realize what Madame had said, and another to actually believe it.

"He told you that? What else did he say?"

"He said you must to come *à l'hôpital*—to the hospital."

"When was this? *A quelle heure?*"

"It was not twenty minutes ago."

"Thank you, Mme. Vernier—your assistance is invaluable. *Votre aide est précieuse.*"

"*Mais quelle catastrophe, Mademoiselle! Je suis vraiment désolée.*"

Dashing up the stairs to her apartment, Elizabeth took her grandfather's Stormdolk from her dresser drawer and slipped it into her purse. Hurrying from the building, she left the concierge wringing her hands and muttering to herself in French.

The fastest way to get to Bellevue was of course by cab, but Elizabeth was not willing to risk it, given her belief that the killer was likely a hack driver. Hurrying east toward Third Avenue, she saw a man driving a cart with commercial lettering stenciled on the side: RUFUS STORY, DEALER IN COFFEE. Waving her arms, she flagged him down. A tall Negro with refined features, he gazed at her with a puzzled expression as she approached.

"I beg your pardon for stopping you, but I will give you a dollar to take me to Bellevue Hospital." It was, she knew, twice the price of a cabbie's fee.

He stared at her; then his eyes narrowed. "Say, miss, is this some kind of a joke?"

"I assure you it is not. In fact, it is very urgent."

"Well then, hop on and make yourself comfortable."

She took his offered hand, and he pulled her up to sit next to him. With a flick of the whip, they were off, the strawberry roan gelding stepping smartly as they crossed Eighteenth Street. The seat had but a thin cushion, and as they rattled eastward, she had to hold on to her hat to keep it from being jostled off.

"How do you get used to such a bumpy ride?" she asked.

"You don't, miss."

"It must be very bad for your health."

"Oh, yes, miss. Every driver I know gets piles."

She coughed delicately, not entirely convinced such specifics were necessary. She turned to him as they turned north on First Avenue.

"My name is Elizabeth van den Broek, by the way. I am a journalist."

"Pleased to meet you, Miss Van den Broek. I'm Rufus Story."

"Oh. So you're—"

"Rufus Story, coffee merchant."

"Ah. How nice to meet you, Mr. Story."

"You thought I was his employee."

"Well, I—"

"It's all right. There's not many like me yet, but there will be more, mark my words. Come to think of it, there's not many like you, either."

"But as you say, there will be more. I hope you don't think me impertinent, but you have an unusual accent."

"Boston, born and bred, miss," he said as they approached the hospital. Elizabeth dug a dollar from her purse as they pulled up to the front entrance.

"Thank you kindly, miss," he said, tucking it into his pocket. He wore a very smart frock coat, a dark-mustard color, elegant but sturdy. Hopping from his perch, he offered her a hand.

“Thank you,” she said, climbing down. “If you were willing to wait for me, I would reward you handsomely. That is, if you’ve no pressing engagements.”

“My shop is closed for the day, and I was just heading home for the evening. A good businessman does not turn his nose up at income.”

“Well then, Mr. Rufus Story, here is a down payment,” she said, fishing out another dollar.

“Much obliged,” he said, with a tip of his hat.

“Hopefully, I shall not be long.”

“I will be here,” he said, fetching a feed bucket from the back of his wagon. The roan gelding bobbed his head enthusiastically at the sight of it, snorting softly.

“I am most grateful,” she said. Picking up her skirts, she jumped over a puddle and beckoned to the attendant to open the tall iron gate leading to the hospital grounds.

Outside Laura’s room, she found Hiram Jamison interrogating a young, round-faced nurse. Approaching the doctor from behind, Elizabeth kept very quiet so as not to disturb them.

“Are you telling me *no one* saw her leave?”

“I saw her with an orderly earlier this afternoon, but that’s the last time I saw her,” the girl said, trembling. She looked as if she were about to cry.

“Never mind—it’s all right,” he said. “You aren’t to blame.”

“I’m ever so sorry,” she said, hiccoughing.

“Did you get a look at the orderly?”

“Only from the back.”

“Did you notice anything about him?”

“He was tall, strong-looking. Light-brown hair, maybe?”

“Very well, Nurse Holman. Thank you for your time.”

“Yes, Doctor.” Wiping her eyes, she turned and retreated down the hall as the slanted beams of the late-evening sun crept through the long windows lining the corridor.

Turning, Jamison saw Elizabeth. "Miss Van den Broek! I am so very sorry—"

"I am sure you are not to blame," she replied, though she knew no such thing. "Please tell me everything."

"I fear there is not much to tell. Your sister was last seen just after the midday meal, at approximately two o'clock. When I made my rounds, I was told of her absence. I went immediately to your apartment building."

"My concierge alerted me as soon as I came home."

"Have you any idea where she might be?"

Reaching into her purse, she showed him the telegram she had received at her parents' house.

"What is this?"

She explained its relevance to the murders and her theories about the perpetrator.

"You believe there is a connection to your sister's disappearance?"

"It may be what he meant by 'closer to home.'"

His face darkened. "Oh, no. It cannot be."

"I fear the worst," she said, as the sun shot its last shuddering beams through the tall casement windows.

"The hospital has already filed a missing-persons report with the police, of course," Jamison said. "It does not hurt that she is the daughter of a prominent judge."

"Have my parents been notified?"

"That is the job of the police."

"I doubt they will be of much assistance."

Making the excuse that she was going to her parents' house to deliver the news about Laura, Elizabeth left Dr. Jamison to his rounds. She had already come to a conclusion about the curious wording in the telegram, convinced that it was a clue—and she had an idea of what it might mean.

She found Rufus Story where she had left him, brushing down his gelding with a currycomb while the horse chewed contentedly on his bucket of oats. Elizabeth inhaled the aroma of the sweet-smelling grain, transported momentarily to the Kinderhook barn where she and Laura had spent many happy summers feeding and grooming their ponies before riding them into the woods. Mr. Story's horse was obviously well cared for, and Elizabeth thought that a man who looked after his animals was someone you could trust.

"Hello, Miss Van den Broek," he said as she approached.

"Thank you for waiting for me. I hope it wasn't too long."

"Joey always enjoys a bit of fussing and a bucket of grain."

"Well, Mr. Story, are you game for another ride?"

"I don't see why not."

She handed him two dollars. "I would be most appreciative if you would take me to the New York and Brooklyn Bridge."

CHAPTER SIXTY-TWO

Traffic was light, and fortified with oats, Joey trotted steadily until they reached Houston Street, where First Avenue turned into Allen Street. Mr. Story slowed the horse to a walk. The streets were narrower downtown, and people could lurch out in front of vehicles without warning. Elizabeth had seen more than one accident involving drunk or careless pedestrians who ended up under the wheels of a carriage, horse cart, or streetcar.

Her hand tightened on the handle of her grandfather's Stormdolk as the New York and Brooklyn Bridge came into view. Its steel towers gleamed in the moonlight. The first bridge to connect Manhattan to the City of Brooklyn, it had been under construction since 1869, yet it remained unfinished. Suspension cables stretched across the river, connecting the towers, but engineers were still far from constructing the roadway. A wooden catwalk led from the land to the first tower, crisscrossed by platforms for the workers to stand on. A lone figure, silhouetted in the moonlight, made his way along the catwalk, carrying a woman in his arms.

"Here, miss?" Mr. Story said, pulling his wagon alongside the entrance to the catwalk.

"This will do, thank you," she said. Her teeth were clattering, not from cold, as it was a temperate night, but from dread. She dearly wished she had asked Hiram Jamison to accompany her, but he would never have agreed to what she had in mind.

"Would you like some assistance?" Mr. Story asked as he helped her down.

"No, thank you," she said, looking up at the catwalk, which looked fearfully steep. She did not like heights and could hardly imagine herself climbing it. She turned to see Rufus Story gazing up at the bridge.

"Are you sure, miss?"

"Quite sure, thank you."

"I'll just wait here for you, then," he said, his face impassive.

"It's not necessary."

"No charge. As I said, I have nowhere else to be."

"Thank you," she said, very glad of having met Rufus Story.

"I don't know what you have in mind, miss, but please be careful."

"Thank you, Mr. Story."

As she approached the entrance to the catwalk, she noticed an ambulance parked on a side street, with its familiar logo: "Bellevue Hospital." This was not surprising, as Bellevue was the only hospital in the city using ambulances. There was no sign of its driver, or indeed of anyone, which struck her as curious.

A light rain had begun to fall, the kind of steady drizzle that drowned out starlight and cast a halo over the gas lamps. The catwalk was slippery as she grabbed the hand railings, pulling herself forward with each step. The figure ahead had stopped and seemed to be watching her slow progress. He appeared to have lit a torch; a light flickered and then flared to life. Dread and relief warred in her breast; she was glad she did not have to climb much farther, but seeing him waiting for her nearly made her knees buckle. He looked gigantic, far taller than a normal human being. For a moment she fancied he really might be an Egyptian god come to life.

As she got closer, she realized that he looked taller because he wore an elaborate headdress made of feathers. Stopping to catch her breath, she called out, "Osiris!" He did not reply, so she called out again. "I have come for you!"

There was a pause, and his voice floated across the distance between them. "I have been waiting for you."

Wiping the rain from her eyes, she forged ahead. A wind had whipped up over the water, and the catwalk swayed beneath her feet. Clinging to the handrail, she trudged onward. When she was but a few yards away, she could finally make out his features in the light of his torch, which he had fastened to one of the cables. This was followed by a sickening realization of the significance of the abandoned ambulance.

She had been mistaken—the killer was not a cabdriver. The man wearing the exotic headdress, the one who had kidnapped her sister from her bed at Bellevue, was none other than the friendly ambulance driver, Benjamin Higgins.

He clasped Laura to his side with one strong arm. She was clad in a long white gown, a thick gold necklace around her neck. Upon her head was a strangely shaped red headdress, which Elizabeth recognized as the deshret, the crown worn by the ancient Egyptian goddess Amunet.

"Behold She Who is Hidden!" Higgins cried, holding her upright. She appeared to be semiconscious, only vaguely aware of what was happening. "Amunet, goddess of the air!"

"I have a proposition for you, Mr. Higgins!" Elizabeth called to him. She was only about twenty feet away, but the wind whistled in her ears, and sound was carried away by the rushing air.

"Call me by my name!" he yelled back. "I am Osiris, Lord of the Underworld and Judge of the Dead!"

She took a few steps closer. "Osiris, I have a proposition for you."

"You may speak."

"Take me instead!"

"Why?"

"I am the *true* Amunet, goddess of the air—she is an impostor!" Elizabeth said, pointing to her sister, limp in his arms.

He looked at Laura, then back at Elizabeth. "Prove it!"

She pointed to a flock of pigeons above their heads. "Behold my subjects!"

"Command them!" he ordered.

She watched as they approached the near tower, knowing they would have to turn or else fly around it. Raising her arm, she swept it in a circle, pointing it back in the direction they had come. "I command you to turn!" she cried. To her relief, the birds obeyed. Spooked by some unseen obstacle—the multitude of cables, perhaps—the birds swirled in a circle and flew back toward the shore.

Watching them, Higgins gestured to her. "Come forward! I will grant your request, O Hidden One!"

Her heart thumping wildly in her throat, Elizabeth advanced toward him, one hand on the guardrail, the other clutching the dagger. When she was but a few feet away, she stopped. "Release her!" When he hesitated, she ordered him again, making her voice as commanding as possible: "I said release her!"

This time he obeyed, letting go of Laura, who swayed uncertainly, looking around as if only just realizing where she was.

"Run, Laura!" Elizabeth cried. "Go back to the shore!"

Her sister looked puzzled, then took a few halting steps toward her. Seizing her by the shoulders, Elizabeth whispered fiercely in her ear, "Listen to me! You must go—hold on to the guardrail! There is a man with a wagon waiting for you. His name is Rufus Story. He is a tall, handsome Negro with a strawberry roan horse."

"Like the one we used to ride," Laura replied with a vague smile.

"Yes, just like that. Now go—do not look back!" Pushing her gently back toward the shore, Elizabeth watched as her sister's steps, hesitant at first, quickened to a flat-footed scurrying. For a moment, Elizabeth considered fleeing as well but knew that, if she tried, Higgins would soon overtake her.

When Laura had covered half the distance to the shore, Elizabeth turned to face him. "I am ready, Osiris."

CHAPTER SIXTY-THREE

The wind whipped at her face as Elizabeth marched slowly toward the tall man in the long robe and ostrich-feather headdress, the fingers of her right hand wrapped tightly around the handle of her grandfather's Stormdolk.

"Are you prepared to meet your fate?" he asked, the feathers on his head swirling as the wind changed direction. Once again, it occurred to her that he reminded her of someone, but she could not think who.

"I am."

"Come then, Hidden One, and fulfill your destiny!"

She took one final step toward him, her dagger at the ready. But quick as a cat, he grabbed her around the neck, his fingers tightening around her throat. Startled, she let go of her weapon, which clattered to the catwalk floor. Terror gripped her as he tightened his grasp, cutting off her air. Summoning her strength, she kicked him hard in the shin. With a yelp, he loosened his grasp and doubled over. She dove for the dagger—on her hands and knees, her frock wet now, she gripped the handle just as he reached down for her. With all her strength, she plunged the blade deep into his thigh.

He emitted an unearthly scream and fell to his knees, holding his wounded leg. Without letting go of the weapon, she scrambled away, half crawling, until she could stagger to her feet, still gasping for air. Slipping the dagger back into her purse, she pulled herself forward on the handrail as she scrambled down the catwalk, afraid to look over her shoulder.

The sharp report of a gun brought her up short. Lifting her head, she saw, ahead of her, Thomas F. Byrnes, a revolver in his hand, a thin stream of smoke trailing from its muzzle.

"What have you done?" she cried, but he seemed oblivious to her presence.

Marching deliberately forward, he approached the prostrate figure on the catwalk, aimed the pistol carefully, and calmly fired three more shots. Then, to her horror, with the toe of his boot, he rolled Higgins off the walkway and into the roiling waters of the East River. He watched impassively as the body hit the water. Even over the whistling wind, she imagined she heard the splash. It was a sickening sound.

Turning, Byrnes walked back toward her, his face expressionless. Terrified that he was about to dispatch her in the same way, Elizabeth stumbled toward the shore as fast as she could go, until she felt a strong hand grasp her arm. Flailing, she struggled to free herself, digging for the dagger in her purse with her free hand.

"Calm yourself," he said. "I'm not going to hurt you."

"How did you know to come here?"

He laughed softly. "Sure now, I thought you'd have realized I've been watching you for some time."

Elizabeth thought for a moment. The significance of certain encounters became clear: the man with the dog, the bootblack in Five Points . . . and of course, the cabbie with the scarred face. He was no killer—he was a police spy. She realized with a chill that Byrnes had eyes everywhere.

"Why d-did you s-shoot him instead of arresting him?" she asked, her breath coming hard and tight through her bruised windpipe.

"Some people just need to be dead, now, don't they?" he said, his voice hard. Looking at his implacable face, she realized why Higgins had looked familiar. The resemblance was unmistakable; she was surprised she hadn't seen it earlier.

"He was your son," she said with a gasp.

The smile that crawled across his face was even more disturbing than his lack of expression had been. "So what if he was, then? Who could ever prove it?"

"He was blackmailing you, wasn't he?"

"You know," Byrnes said, his face so close she could smell his fetid whiskey breath, "sometimes a little knowledge can be dangerous. If I were you, I'd take the credit for defeating a deranged criminal single-handedly. It would be safer for everyone concerned," he added, emphasizing "everyone." The implication was clear.

As Elizabeth looked at his smug face, with its drooping mustache and cruel little eyes, it occurred to her that any choice she might have in the matter was no choice at all.

CHAPTER SIXTY-FOUR

"I don't understand," Carlotta said, dabbing her brush in a circle of gold paint on her palette. "Why would Byrnes shoot his own son?"

"To avoid scandal," Elizabeth replied. "He has a wife and daughters, and a reputation to uphold. Once Higgins realized Byrnes was his father, Byrnes was never going to be safe. That's why he tried to hinder our investigation—to stop us from identifying Higgins. Byrnes didn't want Higgins arrested. He wanted him dead."

It was Wednesday afternoon. Carlotta and Jonah had joined Elizabeth in a visit to her sister, Carlotta having the bright idea to paint her, while her brother tagged along for his own reasons, obviously smitten with Laura.

"But how could Higgins *prove* he was Byrnes' son?" asked Carlotta.

"You would only have to see them together to be convinced," Elizabeth replied. "Higgins is a nearly perfect younger version of his father."

"And just as nasty, by the look of it," Jonah remarked. "The apple didn't fall far from the family tree."

"Would you tilt your head slightly, please?" Carlotta asked Laura. "Just like that—perfect."

Elizabeth gazed at the peaceful scene in front of her. The previous night's events felt strangely like a dim and distant dream. After getting Laura safely back to Bellevue, with the help of Rufus Story and the trusty Joey, she had collapsed into bed, waking nearly twelve hours later from a deep sleep to find her editor banging on her door. Kenneth Ferguson had not been pleased to hear of Byrnes' murdering his own son in cold blood, but neither was he surprised.

"Ach, I always said he was a crooked copper, and now he's gone and proved it."

After Elizabeth told him of Byrnes' not-very-veiled threat to her and her family, he insisted on keeping the detective's role out of the story. Ferguson suggested she write a first-person account as a special supplement in the *Herald*, and was awaiting Mr. Bennett's approval. In a typically impulsive move, the publisher had suddenly set sail back to Paris without telling his editors, and Ferguson was obliged to cable him.

Meanwhile, Elizabeth paid a quick visit to her parents to assure them she and Laura were safe, no matter what they read in the papers. Her father seemed very relieved, though her mother seemed more interested in talking about the party she intended to throw for Mrs. Astor.

"Hold still," Carlotta commanded Laura, who stretched her arms languidly from her position on the chaise in Bellevue's common room. She had been unusually placid since her ordeal, agreeing to let Carlotta paint her. Dr. Jamison had heartily approved, believing that an outside stimulus was an essential element of treatment. Elizabeth had revealed only bits and pieces of her adventures the previous night, knowing he would find the actual details horrifying. She was waiting for the right time to tell him, maybe over a bottle of Bordeaux at Les Gamins. Like everyone else at Bellevue, he was shocked and dismayed to hear that the friendly ambulance driver was the nefarious criminal who had set the city on its ear.

Jonah plucked a grape from a wooden bowl on the windowsill. "And how did you solve the riddle of the telegram?"

"I knew 'the Hidden One' referred to Amunet, the Egyptian goddess of the air. There was a reference to 'the unfinished link.' Since he has always left his victims at places with symbolic and historical importance, I thought the unfinished bridge was the most likely location."

"Very clever," Jonah said, peeling a grape. "But you could have been wrong."

"True. I was lucky—but I never yet knew of a victory that did not involve some measure of luck."

Carlotta stared at her brother. "Why on earth are you *peeling* that grape?"

"For her majesty, goddess of the air," he said, offering it to Laura. She examined it as if it were a precious gem, then popped it into her mouth, bestowing upon him one of the sweet smiles Elizabeth remembered so well from childhood. Her heart leapt a little, and hope nestled inside her breast like a cat curling up for a nap. It was a thin promise, but it was something.

She understood fully for the first time that her mother's actions had come from a place of pain so deep it was beyond reach. Catharina's despair over her brother's death must have been nearly unendurable. What Elizabeth had seen as silliness—such as her obsession with approval from people like Mrs. Astor—she now believed was an attempt to alleviate her guilt, to take her mind off what must be a constant reminder of her family's frailty. Catharina no doubt felt responsible for her daughter's condition. It was a family flaw; her bloodline was tainted. But if she could enter the august society of the Astors and their ilk, she could somehow feel whole again. For the first time in her life, Elizabeth felt very sorry for her mother.

"No one ever peeled *me* a grape," Carlotta muttered, peering at her canvas.

"Perhaps if you were a goddess, they might," Jonah replied with a little smile.

Carlotta dabbed at a smudge of paint on her face with a clean cloth. "So no one will ever know of Byrnes' actions in this?" she asked Elizabeth.

"Not unless you tell them," Elizabeth replied, gobbling down a few grapes from the bowl. Ever since her ordeal, she had been ravenous, eating anything in sight. "Even Mr. Ferguson thought there was nothing to be gained from revealing that the chief of detectives is a murderer."

"I'd wager it's not the first death he's responsible for," Jonah remarked. "The police in this town are all thugs."

"Not all of them," Elizabeth said, thinking of Sergeant O'Grady.

"Most of them, then," he said, peeling another grape.

"So you will be given credit for defeating Higgins single-handedly?" said Carlotta.

Elizabeth shrugged. "Mr. Ferguson is writing the story. No doubt he will make up something convincing."

"Very pretty," Carlotta told Laura, who seemed to have less trouble sitting still than Elizabeth. She appeared to enjoy being painted, for which Elizabeth was extremely relieved, hoping Laura would replace her as Carlotta's model.

"Making progress, I see," Dr. Jamison said, strolling into the room. "That's very good," he added, studying Carlotta's painting. He looked crisp and fresh in his white lab coat.

"If you don't mind, I don't care to have anyone look at my work until I'm finished."

"It's true," Elizabeth said. "She won't let me see the portrait of me because she's still working on it."

"Ah, the prerogatives of genius," he said, sitting across from Elizabeth.

Carlotta pursed her lips and rolled her eyes without interrupting her brushstrokes.

"Say it often enough and she'll start to believe it," Jonah remarked, feeding Laura another peeled grape.

Sunlight spilled into the room, turning her sister's hair into spun gold, and Elizabeth felt the events of the night before recede by the moment.

"You look much more rested," the doctor commented, studying her face, his gaze causing a pleasant sensation of warmth on her skin.

"I am much improved."

"Laura seems calmer as well. Did he really believe he was the incarnation of Osiris?" he asked.

"He seemed to. I never had the sense that he was just pretending."

Jamison shook his head. "I wish I could have spoken with him. What a case history that would have made. I have a special interest in delusional disorders, but I have not yet come across that one."

"I hope to never see anything like it again," Elizabeth replied, though she didn't entirely believe herself. The whole thing was terrible and tragic and sad, but even now she missed the sensation she'd had on that dark and rainy bridge—in the face of death, she had felt totally and thrillingly alive.

"Perhaps we could discuss it over dinner tomorrow?" he asked.

"That would be lovely," she said.

"On one condition."

"Name it."

"That you will never, *ever* do anything so foolish again."

"I do not think it is a fair thing to ask."

"You do realize that it was hopelessly reckless, do you not?"

"I suppose I do, in retrospect."

"If you ever face a situation like that again, you must call on me. Otherwise, I shall never forgive you."

"You are full of ultimatums tonight, Dr. Jamison."

"If one didn't know better, one would think you are an old married couple," Carlotta remarked.

"Marriage is an archaic institution," Jonah muttered.

"You must forgive my brother," said Carlotta. "He has the sadly mistaken impression that every time a thought pops into his head, no matter how absurd, he is obliged to share it with the world."

Everyone laughed, even Laura. Jonah pretended to be cross, but Elizabeth could see him biting his lip to avoid smiling.

"Why *did* you go alone?" Carlotta asked. "At the very least, it was foolhardy."

"I thought that as a lone female I would be less threatening, and Higgins would be more likely to listen to my proposal. I feared a man's presence might cause him to harm Laura."

Jamison shook his head. "That is not a good reason to endanger yourself."

"Well, it is over now," said Carlotta. "And I'm certain she'll never do anything like that again."

The afternoon wore on lazily, as Carlotta worked on her painting, Jonah attended to Laura, and Dr. Jamison returned to his duties. As evening approached, Elizabeth was suffused with an unaccountable longing. Even the prospect of dinner with Hiram Jamison the next evening did not dispel the yearning in her breast. Sitting over a pot of steaming tea with her friends and sister as the afternoon wound to a peaceful close, Elizabeth thought maybe she was the crazy one, to have such thoughts.

Later, walking home through the falling twilight, she felt the city gather around her in an embrace. The thread that bound all life was woven through every street, every alley and doorway; every abode, no matter how humble, thrummed with the invisible force common to all living things. Whether fighting or lovemaking, looking out for one's neighbor or at each other's throats, the citizens of this great city were inextricably linked. New York was like an organism, a great throbbing hive that held its inhabitants close.

At home in her apartment, she threw open her curtains and raised the window, inhaling the lingering smell of late-summer rain. She listened to the sounds of a thousand voices all around, people going about their daily business, laughing, crying, singing, and sighing. This was her city, her home, in joy and grief, in sorrow, despair and celebration. She watched as all the pink bled from the sky, a lingering wash of pale blue trailing in its wake as the rain returned. As the streetlamps flickered to life one by one, she gazed at the raindrops cascading down her windowpanes, falling on rich and poor alike, ferrying pinpricks of ghostly yellow light through the gently gathering dusk.

Acknowledgments

Thanks to my awesome agent, Paige Wheeler, as always. Deepest gratitude to Jessica Tribble for her unflagging good humor and sage editorial advice, and also to Dennelle Catlett, Adrienne Krogh, Erin Calligan Mooney, Sarah Shaw, Lauren Grange, Nicole Burns-Ascue, and Kellie Osborne for their invaluable work. And thanks to everyone at Thomas & Mercer for their unwavering support.

Thanks to Anthony Moore for his tireless research and passion for all things historical. Much gratitude to my dear and accomplished cousin Jacques Houis—scholar, teacher, writer, translator—for his help and advice on French words and phrases. Thanks to my brilliant assistant, Frank Goad, for his intelligence and expertise. Thanks, too, to my good friend Ahmad Ali, whose support and good energy have always lifted my spirits, and to the Stone Ridge Library, my upstate writing home away from home. Special thanks to my parents—raconteurs, performers, and musicians who taught me the importance of art and the power of a good story.

Last but not least, eternal gratitude to the heroic health care professionals and other essential workers of this great city who kept us going through the worst pandemic of our lifetimes. You are an inspiration. I only wish Stephen Smith himself were alive to appreciate your sacrifice.

About the Author

Photo © 2017 Patricia Rubinelli

Carole Lawrence is an award-winning novelist, poet, composer, and playwright. In addition to *Edinburgh Twilight*, *Edinburgh Dusk*, and *Edinburgh Midnight* in the Ian Hamilton Mysteries series, she has authored novellas, short stories, and poems—many of them translated internationally. She is a two-time Pushcart Prize nominee for poetry and has won the Euphoria Poetry Prize, the Eve of St. Agnes Poetry Award, the Maxim Mazumdar playwriting prize, the Jerry Jazz Musician award for short fiction, and the Chronogram Literary Fiction Award. Her plays and musicals have been produced in several countries, as well as on NPR; her physics play, *Strings*, nominated for an Innovative Theatre Award, was produced at the Kennedy Center.

A Hawthornden Fellow, she is on the faculty of NYU and Gotham Writers Workshop, as well as the Cape Cod Writers Center and San Miguel Writers' Conference. She enjoys hiking, biking, horseback riding, and hunting for wild mushrooms. For more information, visit www.celawrence.com.